A
DISHONORABLE
FEW

Also by Robert N. Macomber

The Honor Series

At the Edge of Honor
Point of Honor
Honorable Mention
A Dishonorable Few
An Affair of Honor
A Different Kind of Honor
The Honored Dead
The Darkest Shade of Honor
Honor Bound

A
DISHONORABLE
FEW

the continuing exploits of
Lt. Peter Wake
United States Navy

Robert N. Macomber

Pineapple Press, Inc.
Sarasota, Florida

Inquiries should be addressed to:

Pineapple Press, Inc.
P.O. Box 3889
Sarasota, Florida 34230

www.pineapplepress.com

Library of Congress Cataloging-in-Publication Data

Macomber, Robert N., 1953-
 A dishonorable few / by Robert N. Macomber.— 1st ed.
  p. cm.
 Sequel to: Honorable mention.
 ISBN 1-56164-339-4 (alk. paper)
 1. Wake, Peter (Fictitious character)—Fiction. 2. United States—History,
Naval—19th century—Fiction. 3. United States. Navy—Officers—Fiction.
4. Americans—Caribbean Area—Fiction. 5. Mercenary troops—Fiction.
6. Caribbean Area—Fiction. I. Title.
 PS3613.A28D57 2005
 813'.6—dc22

                                                        2005011424

Hb 13-digit ISBN 978-1-56164-339-4
Pb 13-digit ISBN 978-156164-518-3

First Paperback Edition
10 9 8 7 6 5 4 3 2 1

Design by Shé Hicks
Printed in the United States of America

This novel is very respectfully dedicated
to the outstanding seamen of the M/V *Hamburgo*,
with whom I voyaged through perils and paradise
for 10,000 miles:

Captain Ullrich Nuber
Chief Mate Sergiy Yudyentsev
Chief Engineer Wolfgang Winter
2nd Officer Jens Graf
2nd Engineer Herbert Sander
3rd Officer Eljohn Cervantes
3rd Engineer Allan Rico
Bosun Ole Klingmueller
Electrician Valery Mosiyenko
Able Seaman Jerry Quintilitisca
Oiler Margarito De Guzman
Able Seaman John Manzan
Oiler Jade Tupaz
Ordinary Seaman Andrew Arimas
Engine Appr. Bernardo Arco
Ordinary Seaman Ernesto Del Rosario
Cook Edmundo Medenilla
Ordinary Seaman Lito Alcala
Steward Richard Cagwing

and to merchant seamen around the globe,
who brave the oceans to bring us the world's bounty.

Central America 1869

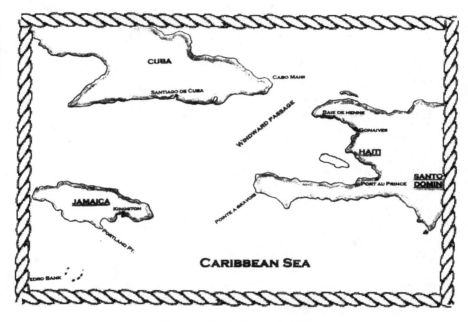

Upper Caribbean 1869

Preface

The year is 1869. Lieutenant Peter Wake, veteran of six years in the United States Navy, is stationed in a backwater of that service, Pensacola, Florida, the first shore assignment of his career. Pensacola Navy Yard is a shadow of its former importance, but Wake still does his best, learning how a navy is supported and maintained. The U.S. Navy has declined considerably since the end of the Civil War, when it became the second largest naval force in the world and intimidated several powers from attempting to push the United States around. It is now twenty-sixth largest in the world, many ships are obsolete, funding is a fraction of what is needed, and morale is low. However, the navy still has serious commitments around the world and somehow struggles to fullfill them.

In the devastated South, military occupation is still in full force in many areas. Pensacola is luckier than many places, seeing economic growth in the fishing and lumber industries and the end of the U.S. Army's martial government. Bitterness continues among some, but most are trying to look ahead, desperately hoping the South will recover.

The world in 1869 is very dangerous. In the Caribbean and Central America there are widespread economic depression, political turmoil, and intercultural hatred—all of which feed the incessant wars that plague the region. It's an area ripe for mercenaries, many of whom come from the ranks of the warriors in the recent North American bloodbath. It is also an area the Europeans are again eyeing closely.

Wake is excited to be back at sea, heading for the Caribbean, where he learned during the war that nothing is quite as it first appears. And in addition to all his other problems during this unique mission, Lieutenant Peter Wake is about to learn more than he ever wanted to about the dark side of human nature—the hard way.

1

Innocent Passage

February 1869

Central Caribbean Sea
Latitude 14 degrees, 32 minutes, North
Longitude 80 degrees, 11 minutes, West

The seas built up by the easterly trade winds were just large enough to make walking on the steamer's deck difficult. Venezuelan Naval Cadet Mendez was thankful that they were heading downwind—if they were going the other way it would be even more dangerous to be on deck. He struggled to keep his hat on in the wind and at the same time steady his telescope on a far-off ship, whose bow plunged down into the waves and then launched up into clear air as she charged against the wind toward them.

As he focused the scope, Mendez thought the steamer a magnificent sight, the black hull and rigging forging ahead against the deep blue of the waves and the powdered blue of the sky, gray smoke billowing up a few feet before being swept away into nothingness. The power of it all was a symbol of the triumph of man over nature—a scene you couldn't even imagine back in the musty confines of Commander Depaz's drowsy seamanship class at the academy in La Guaira.

He studied the ship a few moments longer, finally arriving at the conclusion that he disagreed with the second mate about the ship's possible intent. As its image bounced around in the lens, he carefully formulated his answer to the second mate's earlier comment.

Though Mendez was only seventeen, his Spanish was better than the mate's, as expected of someone attending the prestigious Academia Nacional Naval de los Estados Unidos de la República de Venezuela, but he was always careful not to sound arrogant when speaking to his superiors here. This was a training cruise aboard a merchant ship and he was only here to learn. Still, he was expected to have an opinion and tried to sound experienced in his response.

"We're too far out off the coast for a problem like that, aren't we, sir? And that's a large steamer, an ocean steamer—too expensive and complicated for them to have, isn't she? I think she's probably only a merchant ship outbound from Bluefields in Nicaragua to Santo Domingo or Puerto Rico."

The second mate smiled at the youngster's attempt at a serious assessment. This one from the academy was different. The boy had obvious potential and someday, the mate hoped, he would make a good officer for the navy.

"Maybe you are right, Mr. Mendez. And maybe . . . just maybe . . . I am right, in which case we will have trouble. I truly hope you are the one who is correct, son. But occasionally a sailor's eye can see things that his brain can't explain with logic. An odd feeling he cannot define—he just knows when things are not right. You will learn that as time goes on. And Mr. Mendez, always remember . . ." The older man paused, his eyes on the other vessel.

"Sir?"

"Never ignore that feeling."

Further forward on the main deck stood a gentleman and lady dressed in city clothing looking out over the heaving seas at the approaching ship. The second mate pondered for an instant whether he should convey his concerns to the gentleman, then decided there was no reason to worry them yet. Especially not these particular passengers. It wasn't his place; let the captain do it. Besides, from what he had seen of them so far on this voyage, he figured they probably wouldn't understand and just think him an alarmist.

Unaware of the mate's deliberations behind them, Doña Esmeralda, wife of Don Jorge Monteblanco, the recently appointed Venezuelan ambassador to Mexico, put a hand out to steady herself on her husband's arm. These first five days steaming from La Guaira, the port of Caracas, the voyage to their new assignment had been far more than rough, but now was getting slightly better.

For the first three days, the seas off the coast of New Granada had frightened her with their ominous size as they advanced on the steamer from what seemed to be all directions, lifting the vessel and sliding the hull sideways in a sickening contortion. The captain had pleasantly explained to her how the countercurrents and prevailing winds in this corner of the Caribbean, along with the Río Magdelena's huge outpouring of fresh water from the continent, frequently made waves that were abnormally large and unpredictable. Doña Esmeralda had replied that she thought it was all just horrible, secretly hating the captain's condescending attitude and idiotic grin.

She never got used to the seas and the deck's motion. Doña Esmeralda's sense of balance was lost at the beginning, forcing her to grab anything, or anyone, close by for support. Several times she had ended up in a clump on the deck, embarrassed, bruised and angry with herself, but far more angry with her naïve husband for taking this assignment.

He had the seniority to obtain a comfortable position within the foreign ministry in Caracas, close to their family and friends, but had not insisted on it. Instead, when the foreign minister had convinced him that now was the time when Venezuela needed a strong relationship with Mexico, recently liberated from French occupation, he had accepted the post out of a sense of duty. The minister had been very flattering to her husband, telling him that in their current turbulent times a veteran was needed to keep the republic out of war and moving forward in a position of leadership in the region. He had further promised that Monteblanco could return home two years hence, in 1871, to the position of deputy foreign minister. One last assignment, the minister had said. Doña Esmeralda remembered her husband's recital of his superior's enticement with cold resentment, but what could she, a mere wife, do? Her husband had fallen into the trap of pride.

Each time she grimly held on for dear life when a wave came, Doña Esmeralda thought of their lovely home in Caracas, filled with beautiful mementos and gifts from their assignments abroad. She missed her children and the new grandson, born just this year. This was just so unfair.

Now they were off the coast of Central America and the seas had diminished, but were still large enough to make her stomach uneasy and catch her off guard. The young cadet officer told her this morning the depressing news that they were only near the shoals of Serrana Bank, still three full days from their first port in British Honduras, and they had at least six days after that to Vera Cruz in Mexico.

Other than the high winds and seas, the trip was uneventful, but Doña Esmeralda saw that the reaction of the ship's officers to the vessel now approaching them was anything but nonchalant. She watched the other vessel get closer and listened to the second mate yell to a seaman.

"Go to the captain and present my respects. Tell him I request him on deck. There is a strange ship that has altered course and is bearing down on us fast. She doesn't appear to be a warship, but I don't like the looks of this."

Don Jorge Monteblanco was not a man to panic easily and he wondered what it was about that other ship that could concern the experienced officer. It looked like the few other vessels they had seen while steaming along the coasts of Venezuela and New Granada. Then he realized that the ship was heading directly for them very fast, smoke pouring out of her stack. She was smashing headlong into the seas with huge fans of spray exploding from her bow with each wave. The violence of her progress against the seas toward them seemed an ominous warning, he realized with a cold shudder. The uneasy feeling within him grew as the distance from the other ship diminished.

Don Jorge had worked almost half a century as a diplomat and a man dedicated to making peace. He and his wife were proud that one son had felt the call to become a priest in the Jesuit order, another a doctor, and the third a diplomat—all were respected men who, like their father, had never worn a military uniform. Don Jorge had developed a lifelong distrust of men in the military and knew that frequently they made difficult situations worse, many times ruining the efforts of the diplomats to resolve issues without bloodshed.

His wife held his arm tighter as she looked up at him, seeing his mien change from curious to grim. "I do not understand what the concern is about that ship over there, Jorge. It looks like any other. Why are the sailors upset? Is it connected with the war in Nicaragua?"

Don Jorge was trying to listen to what the second mate told the captain when he came on deck in response to the sighting but he turned to his wife.

"It is probably a normal concern, dear. We are safe out here in international waters, and neither the Nicaraguans nor the rebel forces have any steamers. In fact, I do not believe they even have a navy of any sort. Perhaps that ship needs some assistance of some kind."

All the ship's officers gathered around Captain Rivera, the senior ones using the ship's three telescopes. The first mate snapped his shut and asked the captain what to do when the other ship arrived alongside in a few minutes.

"If they fire a gun we will stop. If not, we continue. Send up our ensign."

Doña Esmeralda turned to her husband and pulled on his sleeve. "Oh, Jorge, did you hear that? He said if that ship shoots at us we will have to stop. This must be some type of mistake. Let that other ship know that there is an *ambassador* on this boat. They won't bother us then. We have immunity under international law, don't we?"

"If we were in Europe with civilized people, yes. But here it is another matter, dear."

Don Jorge heard the flapping of the red, blue, and gold Venezuelan ensign as it ascended the halyard above them. Though not a man of the sea, he did know this meant that the other ship should now raise her national flag, and he waited. A small speck of color suddenly flashed from its rigging. It was black and white.

The officers and Captain Rivera made a collective gasp. The other ship was flying the flag of the rebel republic. Don Jorge tried to hear what the officers were saying but became aware his wife was asking something.

"Well, Jorge? Are you listening? I said to tell Captain Rivera to tell them you are an ambassador."

"Esmeralda, that is the flag of the Indian rebel province that has declared itself independent of Nicaragua. I am not at all certain that they will be impressed that I am a Venezuelan ambassador. In fact, they may resent it. Venezuela is supporting the central government against them."

The look on his face earlier had worried her earlier. Now it terrified her. "What does that mean, Jorge?"

Don Jorge held his wife of four decades by the shoulders and tried to find the words. They had served at the embassies in London, Madrid, and Rio de Janeiro, but never in an area at war. Never at a place where they were hated.

"It means, my dear, that they may treat us as an enemy, and that they may not care about international law and immunity.

They are not recognized as a sovereign country and therefore may not behave like one."

"But we are traveling from Venezuela to Mexico. We are not at war with Nicaragua or the rebel province. We are not at war with Venezuela. Why would they treat us as an enemy? We are out in the sea innocently traveling along."

"Because they have fought for the last three years to be independent of Nicaragua, and because Venezuela has sold munitions to the central government, they may view us as part of the people who are killing them." He did not finish the thought that was in his mind.

"But that is not correct at all, Jorge. They must be able to see that—this is all so ridiculous. We are *peaceful*, for the sake of God."

"War has a way of altering perceptions of enemy and friend, dear. Ah, here is our captain."

Captain Rivera put a hand on Don Jorge's arm and turned him away from his wife. "Don Jorge, you and your wife go below with Cadet Mendez right now. I am sorry, but Mendez will have to come back up here and you will have to wait down there alone. Hide there and do not come out until I personally tell you it is safe." The captain spoke deliberately, almost sadly, his eyes locked into the ambassador's. "Do you understand *exactly* what I mean, sir?"

"Yes, Captain. We understand. We will wait out of sight."

"Precisely, sir. I do not want them to know you are aboard."

Don Jorge led his wife after the young cadet but stopped for a moment, holding up a hand. "Captain, one thing though. The rebels have a steamer? Where did they get a steamer? I thought even the central government didn't have a steamer."

The captain's eyebrows raised and he nodded. "You are right, sir, the government *did not* have a steamer, only a few schooners to patrol the coast. And the rebels certainly did not have a steamer either, only a few small sailing vessels manned by their piratical mercenary scum. We were always able to steam away from

7

them easily if they ever came this far off the coast, which was very rare. But it appears that all that has changed now, Don Jorge. We can't outrun that ship over there. They will be here in a few minutes and your presence here may . . . aggravate them."

"I understand that, Captain. We will stay out of sight. What will you do when they get here, Captain?"

Captain Rivera shook his head. "I do not know exactly, Don Jorge. I wish to God that I did."

2

A Demented Heart

The rhythmic pounding of the propeller slowed and then stopped. The engine itself gave a hissing scream, then a gasp as the steam was bled off the boilers. Soon the reassuring sound of the engine was gone and they knew that Captain Rivera had lost control of the ship.

It was absolutely dark in the steerage hold. The air was rancid from the bilge water that sloshed around their feet and cloying coal dust that was everywhere. Now that the machinery noise had ended, the groaning of timbers and frames overwhelmed all other senses. Don Jorge and his wife held each other desperately as they sat on a massive frame, their legs cramping with the effort not to fall completely into the filthy bilge water as the stopped ship careened wildly in the seas. Huddled there in the black hell of the hold, they wondered what was happening above them.

Suddenly Don Jorge heard men's voices approaching, garbled at first, then clearer. Occasional words could be barely discerned but not understood. He thought it might be the native dialect of the Moskito coast—the rebel coast. From the bantering tone of the voices it sounded as if the men were searching the holds, seemingly in a general way, as if to see what items of value they might find.

The shine of a lantern grew closer, increasing from a flicker to a glow, shadows darting around the hold with the sway of the light. Don Jorge counted three separate voices. The tone was no longer friendly. The men were in a hurry and sounded annoyed. The lantern was coming nearer now. The ship abruptly lurched and one of the men yelled out in rage as he hit his head on a beam. The others laughed, a cruel and mirthless laugh of sarcasm. Don Jorge gently moved his wife lower down to get below the cast of the lantern's light, and felt her shudder as she immersed in the slime of the bilge water. He then sat down next to her and kissed her forehead and cheek, tasting the tears running down her face, his heart broken that he had gotten her into this situation.

A loud shout, victorious and excited, erupted from the closest man. The other two replied, then called up to someone on the deck above. The lantern rapidly began to advance until it was almost to them, the man holding it coming into focus from the glow. As Don Jorge stared in mute terror at the sneering face of the man holding the lantern over him, he felt another man come up from behind and pull him roughly away from his whimpering wife, running his head into the roughhewn side of the hull. His wife screamed as they jerked her up out of the bilge water by her dress, but the grip of the man behind him kept Don Jorge off balance and he couldn't get to her. The men pushed the ambassador and his wife forward to the crude ladder, punching and kicking them to ascend the steps.

The Monteblancos emerged into the sun's blinding glare and were dragged along the main deck until they got to the smokestack, collapsing in each other's arms on the searing deck, where the men motioned them to stay. Captain Rivera and the crew of the packet steamer were nowhere in sight as Don Jorge tried to calm himself and take stock of the situation.

He examined the men around him. They were dark, rough-looking men with expressionless eyes, wearing filthy rags and armed with cutlasses and pistols. All appeared to be either *mestizo*, Indian-Hispanic, or full-blooded Indians. Some were exchanging comments in their language about the disheveled couple on the deck. Don Jorge knew the only hope left was his ability to speak with reason and understanding. It was what he did in life—try to bring a positive light to difficult situations and resolve problems with words. He had done it for many years with some of the toughest minds in the world. He attempted to appear nonthreatening and un-frightened as he stood, hoping that one among them understood Spanish

"I am Jorge Monteblanco. May I speak to the man in charge here?"

Sudden words from the afterdeck silenced the men and they parted to allow two men, slightly better dressed than the others in that they wore trousers and shirts, to come up to Don Jorge. The older one, a *mestizo*, spoke in the broken Spanish of the isthmus.

"They don't speak your language . . . Your Excellency Don Jorge Monteblanco. But I do. I am *Mister* Cadena, first officer aboard the warship *Venganza*." He saw the reaction at his use of Monteblanco's title and leered. "And yes, I know who you are and what you represent. That little boy cadet told us all about you as he begged to live."

Don Jorge could hear his wife weeping behind him. Mendez had been one of her favorites, reminding her of their son the doctor. "Then you know that my wife and I are no threat to you, and that our country is not involved in your conflict. I see that you are sailing under the flag of your new country. Now is the time to demonstrate the civility of your cause, sir. We are traveling to Mexico and need to be on our way."

Cadena laughed and said something in the native language to the man beside him, which caused the crowd to cackle with laughter. Cadena shook his head and went back into Spanish, his partner translating it for the other men. "Then you have no luck, Don Jorge Monteblanco, Ambassador to the Republic of Mexico from the United States of Venezuela. No sir, you have no luck at all, because according to your country, we have no cause and no civility. In fact, we do not even *exist!* So therefore, I think we do not have to demonstrate anything to you, except what we demonstrated to the fools who sailed this ship so close to our coast without our permission."

The men grumbled as they heard the translation, then grunted louder at the ending. Several moved closer and Don Jorge could see blood on the cutlass of one of them. He tried to placate the leader.

"We thought we were at least thirty to forty leagues off your coastline, sir. The ship's officers told me that."

"Ha! How arrogant of them. They know we claim fifty sea leagues for our new nation. Everyone knows that—"

"Cadena!"

The shout stopped them all. Don Jorge saw that Cadena instantly lost his haughty demeanor. The shout came again, followed by oddly accented Spanish that Don Jorge could not place.

"Cadena! There is nothing more back here. Let's return to the ship. Burn this bitch."

A tall, muscular, blond-haired man stepped out from the after cabin and halted, looking at the scene on the deck. His gaze settled on the ambassador and his wife. "Cadena, who are these two? I thought they were all dead."

"These two were hiding in the bottom of the ship, *Jefe*. That boy officer told us they were there. The man is the Venezuelan ambassador to Mexico. That is his wife."

The tall man gazed at Don Jorge, studying him. Then he smiled. "Really? So does he have any money on him?"

"No, we looked. People like him do not carry it on their person. They have it in their baggage. We got it all out of that."

Don Jorge finally recognized the accent of the stranger's Spanish. It was from North America, from the United States. His heart lightened. There was a chance. He took a step forward and spoke in English.

"Excuse me, sir. Please allow me to introduce myself in

English since I think I recognize your accent as that of the United States. I am Don Jorge Monteblanco and this is my wife, Esmeralda. We are from Venezuela and traveling peaceably to my new assignment as ambassador to Mexico. We respectfully request permission to continue on with our journey. May I have the pleasure of knowing your name, sir?"

"You think I'm from the United States?" came the reply in English, the tone low and menacing.

"Why yes, sir. And now that I hear you speak English I am certain that you are from the great United States of America. From the northern states, I believe, sir. One of my sons is the assistant to the deputy ambassador at the Venezuelan Embassy in Washington. Perhaps you know him? Pablo Monteblanco."

"Yeah? Well you're wrong, mister high-falutin' ambassador. *Dead* wrong. I'm from nowhere. I don't have a country." He pointed over at the tattered flag flying from the rigging on the other ship. "Hell, I don't even claim that little pissant excuse for a country. I just use the flag 'cause it's fun to see the look in people eyes when they see it. And I don't care one whit about you, that fat cow of a wife, or your little brat in Washington."

"Please sir, we are no threat—"

"Shut up, you old man. You mean nothing to me."

Cadena interrupted in his fractured Spanish. "So, *Jefe*, what do we do with them?" He eyed the woman. "Kill them now or maybe have a little bit of entertainment?"

Don Jorge's momentary sense of hope was extinguished when he heard Cadena. He stepped backward to where his wife knelt on the deck, their hands instinctively reaching for each other. The tall *norteamericano* pursed his lips pensively and squinted up at the blazing sky, then gazed leisurely around at the horizons, his arms akimbo and legs planted far apart in an intimidating stance as he swayed on the heaving deck. His face, burned dark red by the sun, swiveled further around and stopped to regard the couple before him. The gray, lifeless eyes communicated their own reply to Cadena, making Don Jorge shudder as his bowels involuntarily voided, staining his trousers to the laughter of the mob around him.

The man turned to descend the ship's side to the longboat floating alongside and spoke, his words coming out in a soft sigh. "Cadena, I do not truly care what the hell you do. We will be gone from here in ten minutes, so until then you can do whatever your demented little heart desires, as long as they are dead at the end of it."

3

Backwaters

March, 1869

"Oh, Peter, just look at that. She's becoming quite the big sister, isn't she? See the way she's watching over him."

Peter Wake and his wife Linda stood just above their two children on the gently sloping hillside by Fort Barrancas. Wake smiled as he watched his four-year-old daughter, Useppa, playing mother to her little eighteen-month-old brother, who stumbled and rolled a little way down the hill, laughing at it all.

It was a beautiful day. The sea breeze from the south brought warm Gulf air and cottony clouds, bright white against the faded blue sky, over Pensacola Bay. The change in sky and temperature broke the cold spell they had been having. The winters in Pensacola really could be very cold, Wake admitted to himself, then chuckled out loud as he remembered the winters of his youth in New England. Good Lord, he thought, even I am becoming a transformed Southerner.

"What dear?" His wife swung her gaze around to him, her long auburn hair so soft on her shoulder where his hand rested.

"Oh nothing, Linda. I was just thinking how cold it's been lately. Then I remembered winters in New England and what truly cold air felt like. This place isn't even cool compared to there."

His wife, who Wake thought was becoming more beautiful with the years, pulled him close, a mischievous twinkle in her dark green eyes. Her hair smelled of jasmine, a scent he always associated with her—with love and gentleness. She pulled his head down to hers, whispering as she kissed him.

"Well, I try my *very* best to keep you warm."

"And a job well done. *Very* well done."

It was a long kiss, until a tiny hand tugged at his trousers.

"Daddy! I said look at Sean. He's pointing at the boat," said Useppa.

Wake looked over at Sean and found that he was indeed pointing at a ship steaming out Pensacola Bay channel. She was the *Nygaard*, the last of her class of gunboats from the war still in commission. She had just gone through minor repairs and maintenance at the naval yard and was returning to her patrol duty. From their vantage point Wake could see over a large expanse of the bay, from Warrenton in the east to Fort Pickens in the south. *Nygaard* had almost made it out the channel to sea. She was almost free, he ruminated.

"See, Daddy. Sean wants to be a sailor, like you! Will he be a sailor, Daddy?"

"Well I don't know, sweetheart. He can be anything he wants to be. But I think he has a little while before deciding about all of that."

Useppa reached up and traced the gold cuff lace of his uniform with a finger, then looked up at him. "Do you want him to be a sailor like you, Daddy?"

Wake was aware of Linda listening to his replies while trying to suppress a laugh. Could she have somehow gotten Useppa to ask that question, he wondered? No, she wasn't the type to have children ask her questions for her. But he did have the feeling this particular answer would be remembered for a long time, possibly to be entered into family lore in the years to come. Wake was the son of a son of a sailor and knew about the influence of family lore.

"Only if he wants to be a sailor, honey. To be a sailor can be a good life, but it's not easy. You have to *want* to be a sailor for it to be a good life." He looked at Linda and shrugged his shoulders. "So how was that for an answer, dear? Pass inspection?"

She made a show of deliberation, chin on hand. "Not bad, Lieutenant Wake. Predictably positive . . ."

He suddenly felt the need to press further. "Do you disagree?"

"No, Peter. You're right, of course. If it's in his heart, then he'll have to go to sea or he'll be miserable. I don't completely understand this mystical bond with the sea, the yearning sailors have for it when they're ashore, but I do recognize it." She hesitated, looking into his eyes. "I've seen it in you lately."

As usual, Wake told himself, Linda got right to the point. He appreciated her candor and her independence. Linda was strong enough not to be one of those clinging wives, but gentle enough to be there with a soft word or gesture. He wondered how in the world he had been lucky enough to find her and keep her during the war. He also wondered if his demeanor lately had given away his secret longing for watery horizons, for which he felt a twinge of guilt flush through him.

"Yes . . . I suppose you have. How does that make you feel?"

"The perfect answer would be that I'm happy that the man I'm married to now is the same kind of man I first married five years ago. Right?" She sighed. "You're a sailor, born and bred, Peter Wake. I knew all that when I said yes, years ago in Key West. I just wish you didn't want to leave me and the children and go to sea so much. We've been a real family here and I just want that to continue. I guess I'm a fool for that."

"Linda, you're no fool, and I am absolutely the luckiest sailor on earth to have you for a wife."

Wake held her tight again and they stood watching the children playing in the grass, the bay beyond a mass of green water flecked with white wave tops. Useppa rolled Sean over, causing more giggles. He glanced at Linda's face as she smiled at the antics of her children.

Wake himself didn't understand a sailor's bond with the ocean. How could a man who had a wife and family like this still want to go to sea and leave them behind? Sometimes he thought it might be a type of sickness, a self-centered destructive defect in his character.

Growing up as the son of a Massachusetts merchant schooner captain, he had not seen his father for as much as a year at a time. By the time his father had finally come ashore in older age to run the office of the family shipping business, Wake had gone off on his own to sea. That had been the way of his family for generations.

Wake's brothers were sailors too. One was killed in the war aboard a navy monitor gunboat near Charleston. Another had returned after the war to sailing schooners on the North Atlantic in the old tradition. It was a hard and strange life for both the seaman and his family, either making eve ryone stronger or destroying relationships. He had known families who were examples of both.

But Linda had never really complained before this, sharing vicariously his sense of awe about the sea and displaying sincere pride in his accomplishments in the navy. She, more than most, knew what he had overcome during the war and how far he had come in the last six years.

For the past two and a half years, Wake had been on his career's first shore duty assignment, at the Pensacola Naval Yard as the assistant to the assistant commandant of the yard. It had been an education in the seemingly mundane and desperately crucial support side of the United States Navy, made even more difficult by the drastic funding cuts instituted since 1867. Since then the navy had gone from over six hundred ships during the war down to fifty, and competition for sea billets had been fierce. Wake, a relatively junior lieutenant, had been stationed at the yard since his last command assignment aboard the armed steam tug *Hunt* had ended. He had learned quite a lot about how the navy functioned, and frequently dysfunctioned, in that time. And he had worked hard to make the yard as efficient as he could in his position.

Still, every time he saw a ship put to sea he dreamed of standing on her deck as she made her way out there beyond the horizon. Of being her captain and having a crew like the one he had on the *Hunt*. There was no feeling like that ashore, where so many officers were now assigned.

The navy had changed not only in ship numbers, it had changed in attitude and atmosphere too. The budget decline and slow promotions and politics had taken their toll, with many officers simply putting in their time, spending much of their energy in petty intrigue during shore duty to further their careers. It depressed Wake when he thought of it.

Action—real action where things *got accomplished*, had become rare in the navy, but it was still around, he knew. You just had to be the type of officer to create your own luck out there and make things happen.

He watched the *Nygaard* pick up speed as she rounded the point of Santa Rosa Island. She was heading to the Mississippi River for a port call at New Orleans. He visualized her captain on the quarterdeck, checking the officer of the deck's calculation of course and speed, and glancing back at the receding shoreline as the restrictions of the channel ended and the freedom of the sea opened ahead of them. It was something Wake had done many times on the three ships he had commanded during and after the war. His mind could see it with absolute clarity.

At eight o'clock the next morning he was to see the commandant of the yard. Wake's present tour of duty was ending and he would get his next assignment. Many officers were going on the half-pay assignment termed "awaiting orders," an indefinite suspension of their careers made necessary because of the lack of positions at sea or ashore. But Wake had heard rumors about his orders and could barely wait, anticipating the meeting with an excitement he hadn't felt in years. He took in a deep draught of the sweet, thick sea air and gazed at the line of the far-off horizon.

Wake thought of his celestial observation the previous night when he was doing his weekly practice of navigation skills. Sweeping the naval telescope forty-five degrees above the southwest seaward horizon, he had spotted Sirius, the bright star of the constellation Canis Major, the "faithful dog" who always followed Orion the Hunter's red star across the sky. He remembered first seeing Sirius as a new naval officer sailing out of Key West during the war and had always associated it with the excitement of beginning his career. Seeing it again was like an omen to Wake and a chill of the old anticipation had flooded through him in the darkness.

Standing there holding Linda and gazing out to sea in the bright sunlight, he knew he was going to return to where he belonged. He was going to sea again.

4

Fortune's Hand

The next morning the sun was just rising but already warming the breeze as Wake strode down the narrow bricked footpath beside Central Avenue in the center of the old section of the naval station. Under the shade of magnolia trees he passed the octagonal white frame chapel, where sailors serving out a disciplinary sentence were trimming the gardenia bushes under the scrutiny of a scowling master-at-arms. Returning the petty officer's salute, Wake continued on to the end of the street and crossed to the other side of North Avenue, where the senior officers of the station lived.

Instead of turning left, where the captain and commanders lived, he followed another brick walk straight ahead, to where the largest of the houses stood apart from the others. It was an imposing framed structure with a huge verandah that wrapped around the front and sides. A signboard in front proclaimed it as Quarters Number One. It was the home of the commandant of the Pensacola Naval Yard, Commodore Samuel Micah Redthorn, hero of the 1862 battle of Fort Quincy on the Kentucky River. Wake proceeded up the walkway bordered with just-budding red and yellow roses, their scent lightly perfuming the air. The rose beds were famous among the officers' wives and had been faithfully tended for years by Mrs. Redthorn.

As Wake mounted the steps he heard a screaming steam whistle over at the boiler repair shop two blocks to the south. The shriek rose above the constant percussion of hammers at the boat shed he had just left. It all made the morning feel alive to him and, senses keyed with anticipation, he almost shouted to relieve his tension.

A servant, his white hair stark against the leathered ebony of his face, stood in the doorway like a statue. In dark blue waistcoat, tie, and jacket, he looked ancient and frail but greeted Wake in a pleasant slow bass drawl that belied his appearance.

"Good morning, Lieutenant Wake. The commandant is expecting you and presents his compliments. Would you be so kind as to wait in the library, sir? The commandant will be down shortly."

"Thank you, Nelson. I trust that all is well?"

Nelson had been the servant to the commandants of the Pensacola Naval Yard for the last fifteen years, which included the Confederate commandant in 1861. The man knew everything that went on in Pensacola and in the navy, but his discretion was legendary, his furrowed face never showing the secrets his mind held. Nelson gave his standard reply.

"All appears well, sir."

Wake, as a member of the commandant's staff, had been to the house many times. Frequently the commandant liked to have private meetings at his home in the morning before he went to his office. Wake nodded his assent to Nelson's offer of tea and sat in a cane chair in the musty library, reading the titles in the commandant's historical and theological collection. Redthorn was an avid reader of the Bible and history and often would ask his staff their opinion of some ancient strategy of the Romans or Phoenicians. At the naval yard's wardroom, officers circulated history books among themselves to try to be ready for any sudden queries from Redthorn.

Wake reviewed his situation while waiting. He had the impression that the commandant liked and respected him, but wasn't certain. With a man like Redthorn it was hard to know for sure. His career was very unlike Wake's.

After three and a half decades in the U.S. Navy, Redthorn had been set to retire with the rank of commander when the Confederate rebellion broke out and one third of the officers resigned to fight for their states, but he stayed in the service out of a sense of duty. He was immediately assigned to assist Flag Officer Foote in the western theater of the war, where he commanded two makeshift gunboats converted from river steamers.

His only combat of the war was a minor but successful engagement where his command dislodged a small rebel artillery fortification on a tributary off the Kentucky River, a small success during a time of constant Federal failures. Immediately afterward, he was ordered to return to Washington and spent the rest of the war at the Navy Department headquarters, in charge of ship design and procurement in the Bureau of Construction.

Wake thought that odd—successful officers were seldom taken from combat commands—but had never heard an explanation. Redthorn was promoted to full captain in 1864 and after the war was assigned as a commodore to relieve Admiral Thatcher at the downsized establishment at Pensacola, so Wake reasoned that he must have had some success in Washington during the remainder of the war. The commandant was due to retire in a few months, and speculation about a replacement was rampant among the staff.

The lumbering clump of descending footsteps heralded the arrival of Redthorn on the first floor, by which time Wake was standing at attention. It was joked among the officers at the yard that the main reason Redthorn had not been given command of a ship since 1862 was the fear she might go over from excessive top-heaviness. Wake had to agree that the commandant's bulk would definitely be a problem in any ship's boat.

Redthorn moved ponderously into the room and squeezed

down into a large upholstered wing chair, waving a hand toward the one opposite as he breathlessly greeted Wake.

"Ah yes, Lieutenant Wake. I trust you have had a good and productive day so far?"

After more than two years serving under him, Wake knew that the commandant did not ask rhetorical questions—he wanted to ascertain what Wake had accomplished so far that day.

"Yes, sir. I checked on the boat shed's progress and those cutters are still on schedule. They should be done by the end of the month. The hauling dock is cleaning up after the *Nygaard's* departure and should be ready for the next ship tomorrow. That will be the *Powhatan*, of course, sir. Minor repairs. She's due to arrive later today and will be done next week. Oh, and the foundry shop is still waiting for that blacksmith coal. It's supposed to come in by rail soon. Maybe today."

"I see. Very good. All as I expected."

That was as much of a compliment as Wake had ever heard from Redthorn. He waited for the commandant's next words.

"So, Lieutenant Wake, tell me what you have learned here."

Wake hesitated, caught off guard. "During the last two years' assignment here, sir?"

"Yes. That's what I said. I'm not accustomed to having to repeat myself, Mr. Wake."

"Well, yes, sir. Ah, probably the most important thing I have learned here is the value of routine maintenance done regularly aboard ship. It most definitely decreases the time a ship loses to a yard refit, diminishes the cost for repairs and replacement for the yard, and increases the ship's efficiency. Most of that is an engineering officer function, but I think the deck officers bear much responsibility for it also."

"And what about the ship's captain, Mr. Wake? How much of it falls to him?"

"Well, of course, the responsibility and authority is ultimately his, sir. But he needs to delegate it to his officers to accomplish."

"And when you commanded the *Hunt* during the late war, how did you view the necessity of ongoing routine maintenance?"

Wake raised his eyebrows and smiled. "Not nearly as critically as I do now, sir."

Redthorn stretched his neck and regarded Wake. "I just asked a simple question that had an obvious answer, Mr. Wake. I was not wondering what you would say—that much was predictable—but far more I was wondering how you would say it. I was looking for *conviction*, Lieutenant.

"It is my assessment that you have learned a great deal while with us here, and that you do understand and value the role of maintenance, especially when done preventively in a continued fashion."

Redthorn paused as if to collect his thoughts, then went on.

"We entered a new age of industrial innovations and progress during the war, Mr. Wake. Even though Congress doesn't see fit to equip us appropriately now so that we are the equal to the Europeans, we have changed considerably in the last twenty years from the days of sail only. But all the machines in the world won't do us any good unless they are kept in working order. If not, they are merely hunks of iron.

"Unfortunately, our Congressional stewards have not seen fit to fund the maintenance of machinery as it should be done. That means innovative ways must be created and used to keep our ships at sea, where they belong. And *that*, Lieutenant Wake, is where bright young officers such as yourself will stand out in times such as these. . . ."

Wake filled the pause with the only comment permitted. "Yes, sir."

A trace of smile started to appear on Redthorn's face. "So I would imagine that you are wondering where your next assignment will be, are you not?"

"Yes, sir. I am."

"And I would further imagine that you have asked around to see what the chances are of going back to sea, am I correct?"

Wake tried not to show embarrassment, knowing that Redthorn had him dead to rights. I wonder if the yeoman told him I was asking, Wake pondered. It had been the yeoman that let slip a hint Wake might be getting a command.

"Well, sir, I . . . actually, ah . . ."

Redthorn held up an arm and laughed. "It's all right, Mr. Wake. It's quite all right. I used to pester the clerks to find out where I was going, too. I seriously wonder about those who blithely wander along in their career without the slightest gumption or care about their assignments. If they're uncaring about themselves, how do they feel about their ships, I wonder?"

"Yes, sir."

"Well, I won't continue the suspense any longer. You're going to sea on the *Canton*."

"*Canton?* I'm not familiar with her, sir. Oh wait. She's the one that's been up at Portsmouth Yard in Maine, isn't she?"

"Yes. She's the only new construction out of Portsmouth in quite a while. Laid down in sixty-three, then stopped in sixty-five as they were nearing the end. Restarted construction two years later and launched last year. Politics kept getting in the way, as usual. It's a wonder she was ever finished, really."

"A gunboat, if I recall correctly, right, sir?"

"Yes. A smaller version of the Brits' *Cormorant* class. The designers copied the plans to give it a quicker turnout time. Took ten months off the startup—just used their plans. Bought them off the British builder, Wigram, then modified them down to fit our shallower coasts and rivers."

That information surprised Wake. He had never heard of the United States Navy using another country's ship design. "Really, sir? I didn't know we did that. Very unusual."

Then he remembered who was a senior officer in 1863 in the Bureau of Construction at Washington. Redthorn cocked his head, an eyebrow raised.

"Yes, it was unusual, but I thought it was a good idea at the time, and still do. If the politicos had continued the funding, we would have had her out in time to help in the war. But," he sighed, "they wanted to spend money on other projects in other Congressmen's districts, so it got diverted."

Wake hoped that Redthorn didn't think he had been critical. The political battles of Washington were still foreign to him, although he had learned a bit about them on this shore duty. "I see, sir. It sounds like it was a very good idea. Logical actually. At least we have her now."

"Yes, well, one more thing, Mr. Wake. This won't be a command for you. I know you wanted one, but you don't have enough seniority yet. She would've rated a lieutenant during the war, but now with fewer ships and too many officers, she gets a lieutenant commander. You'll be the executive officer. I can't remember the captain's name. Didn't recognize it. Just so many officers these days I don't know. Can't keep up with them all."

Wake tried not to let the disappointment show. Command had been too much to hope for in reality. He knew he had been very lucky to get even the number two billet aboard her.

"Yes, sir. Executive officer will be fine. Do you know where and when I join her?"

"Your orders are at the office, but I think it's Key West in several weeks. The initial paperwork came down from Washington a few days ago."

A hundred questions about his new ship and her captain suddenly flooded Wake's mind. There was so much to do. He struggled to stay focused on the commanding officer sitting in front of him.

"Well, thank you for the word, sir. It'll feel good to get back out to sea."

Redthorn leaned back, making the chair creak with strain. He regarded Wake carefully. "You deserve it, Lieutenant Wake. You've done well here. I hope you retain what you've learned here."

"Yes, sir. I will."

The commandant braced his arms on the chair and heaved

himself up with a grunt. Wake leaped up as Redthorn continued with paternal softness replacing his usual grumpy tone.

"Very well, Lieutenant. I see that it is now eight. You may return to your quarters and have a nice breakfast with your family, then get under way for the office afterward. I'll see you over there about nine—not before that, mind you. Your orders are being sent to your home now, so that you can read them in privacy."

That was an extraordinary gesture of kindness on the commandant's part, Wake knew. He was touched. "Thank you very much, sir."

Redthorn resumed his command presence. "Yes, well . . . once you get to the office, I want to see the detailed request list on *Powhatan's* repairs. She's due to be flagship of the Home Squadron when she leaves here for New York, and I want everything squared away. You will be in personal charge of those repairs. I advise you to make acquaintances with her officers, since *Canton* will be in their squadron. This is a good opportunity for you."

"Aye, aye, sir."

Redthorn called back over his shoulder as he trudged down the hallway from the parlor. "Oh, and Lieutenant Wake. One more thing . . ."

"Yes, sir?"

In the shadow of the hallway the massive bulk of Samuel Micah Redthorn stopped and turned around to face Wake. The voice came out from the old man's distant past. It was a quarterdeck voice, thunderous in the confines of an old house.

"You take *damn* good care of *my* ship when you become her exec, young man. I went through hell to get her built for us and I want her to be kept in excellent shape. And I've gotten you aboard her to do precisely that. Understood?"

Wake couldn't help smiling. "*Absolutely*, sir."

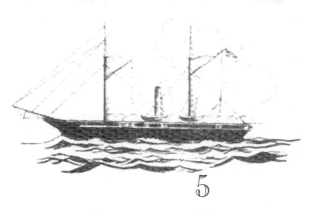

5

La Langue Diplomatique

Don Pablo Monteblanco, special assistant to the United States of Venezuela's deputy ambassador to the United States, thought about what he had just done. Men would die because of it. He did not care.

Monteblanco knew that the details of his conversation a moment earlier with the officer commanding the Bureau of Navigation of the United States Navy would immediately go to Admiral David Porter, the senior admiral and a war hero of the navy, who was looking bored while standing against the wall over in the corner, and from him to Adolph Borie, the brand new secretary of the navy holding court on the other side of the French embassy's ballroom. Borie, fifth glass of champagne in his hand, was conversing with the French ambassador and trying to be impressive, but Monteblanco had heard that his own naval officers despised him as an incompetent political appointee. It made no difference, as long as the decision was made and carried out.

Monteblanco's own ambassador, who would certainly not approve of his conversation, was standing close by the young diplomat, engrossed in an evaluation of Caribbean sipping rums with the Portuguese charge d'affaires and the Dutch trade attaché. Curiously enough, no one at the French embassy soiree was talking about the worsening relations between France and Germany. It was as if an unpleasant subject such as a possible war mustn't hamper a nice evening among friends.

Accepting another glass of champagne offered by a passing steward, Monteblanco watched across the room as Borie, pulled away from his French host, frowned while being advised of something by Admiral Porter. The admiral was making his point by pounding his fist down into his other hand, then nodding toward the Spanish ambassador by the large doorway.

Monteblanco had not expected Porter to be at the French embassy's gathering but was pleased that it was the great admiral himself who was obviously passing along the information. It would lend tremendous credibility to a message that had a strong element of threat in it.

A veteran of ten years in the foreign ministry and two years in Washington, and a man so devoted to his work that he had had no time for a wife or family, Monteblanco had learned early in his career how to get an idea to another nation's leaders without the signature of his own country. One only had to understand who had influence with whom and what their particular fears were, then tailor the message to the person and the fears. It was a technique characterized by some people as underhanded, but within the profession it was known with a shrug as *la langue diplomatique*—the diplomatic language of civilized countries used around the world for hundreds of years.

His father would disapprove of his action as less than honorable, of course, but his father and mother were dead, killed by a merciless pirate just a month and a half earlier. Though he inherited his title, Don Pablo Monteblanco decided that his father's quaint ways of honor were useless in the modern world and that a little deception was in order in this situation. After all, he reasoned, this was about removing a disease that was consuming his country's part of the world. No, he admitted as his jaw tightened, in reality it was about more than that. It was personal vengeance for his father and mother. As he glanced over again at the American admiral, Monteblanco decided that his action was not only effective, it was appropriate, since the man who had killed his parents and spread the disease of terror was none other than a former United States naval officer.

"Congratulations. You have made them very angry, no?"

Monteblanco was startled by the sultry whisper in his ear from behind. He turned to find the demure young wife of the elderly Spanish ambassador smiling at him. Her husband was old enough to be Monteblanco's grandfather, but the woman he was standing in front of was young enough to be his sister.

"Who is angry, Señora Palma?"

"Now, Pablo, you know who. The one you wanted to make angry. I have been observing you observe the *norteamericanos* tonight. I believe that you are pleased that they are angry. It is very intriguing."

"I do not know what you are speaking of, madam. The United States of Venezuela does not indulge in such things, and we have the greatest of friendship with our hemispheric brethren in the United States of America."

She studied his eyes as he spoke, then shook her head slowly. "And what of your brethren in your mother country of Spain? How does your little Machiavellian deception tonight affect them, Pablo?"

He realized she had overheard him and understood the import of his words earlier. Her present coy manner belied her intellectual grasp of his idea. Somehow she had gotten close enough to hear him tell the American naval officer that the piracy committed by a renegade former American naval officer along the Caribbean coasts of Central and South America had enraged the governments there. He advised the officer that the American mercenary pirate had disrupted the commercial trade in the area to the point where the Europeans, particularly Spain, were considering military action since the United States was evidently unable to take care of the problem created by one of their countrymen. And it had become obvious that the United States was equally unable to enforce the much-touted Monroe Doctrine.

The countries in that region depended on the Europeans for financial and commercial support—without it their economies would fall apart—and he told the naval officer they would endorse such an action by the Europeans, although no ambassador would publicly or even privately venture to say so. After the French flaunted the Monroe Doctrine without American resistance in a blatant invasion of Mexico six years earlier, and the Spanish in Santo Domingo from 1861 to 1865, Monteblanco had continued, confidence in the hemispheric leadership of the United States had rapidly diminished. The doctrine was seen as a charmingly idealistic historical dream that was, in reality, quite useless.

He had ended his conversation with the naval officer by suggesting that an immediate decisive action by the United States Navy would accomplish several things. It would remove the piracy problem; remove the stain upon the honor of the U.S. and her navy; remove the opportunity for the Europeans to once again engage in military operations in the Caribbean; and it would bolster the confidence of the Latin American republics in the word of the United States, weaning them away from their European partners, particularly Spain.

But, of course, if the United States did not feel itself strong enough to do that, well then . . .

The naval officer had listened intently, nodding in agreement and promising to pass the information along to his superiors—quietly, and with the source remaining anonymous, of course.

Now Monteblanco examined the woman in front of him as he spoke. "Well, what does your husband say to that information, Señora Palma?"

"He does not know, Pablo."

"You seem to continually surprise me, Señora. Why is it that you have not passed it along to him?"

Her smile was more of a leer. It was unnerving. "Because I

like secrets, Pablo. And I especially like having a secret with you."

From Monteblanco's mind emerged the memory that the Spanish ambassador's wife was from Santander in Cantabria, in the far north of Spain, an area well known to be independent minded, if not rebellious, from the central government in Madrid. That she could be duplicitous to her husband and her country did not surprise him. Her eyes were saying far more than her words, however. He knew he was on dangerous ground.

"Then, Señora Palma, I think we should have a toast to our secret. The problem will be solved, but I assure you that Spain will not be hurt."

"What a pity, Pablo. Spain should receive what it is due. Overdue . . ." She put her hand on his arm, and lowered her voice even further. "Do you always get your way, Don Pablo Monteblanco?"

"Well, Señora—"

Her hand slid inside the cuff of his sleeve, caressing his forearm and instantly arousing him.

"Call me Carmena. After all, Pablo, since we are close enough already to be sharing a deep secret, I think we are close enough to use first names. I wonder what else we may share?"

He knew he shouldn't succumb to such an obvious invitation by a married woman. Especially *this* married woman, who, rumor had it, had used a similar ploy of pleasure to gain herself a rich husband. He knew he shouldn't expose his country to potential embarrassment.

But Don Pablo Monteblanco, man of the world, also knew that sometimes men were weaker than women.

6

Requested and Expected

After Wake returned home from the commandant's talk, he read the newspaper while having breakfast with his children, enjoying the morning with almost an hour still to relax before going to his office. A mischievous giggle caused him to look up.

"Useppa, put your little brother down. Now."

"Down on the *deck*, Daddy?"

Wake laughed and said, "Yes, dear. Right down on the *deck*. He's still very little and we don't want to drop him, do we?"

"Oh Daddy, I know that. I need a . . . a . . . bock . . . an' a tackwul, don't I, Daddy?"

"Very good, sweetheart! A block and tackle, yes. Then you could sway him right on up to the weather deck of the table there."

Linda came into the room, a concerned look on her face. "Peter, don't do that. Now she'll try to make a block and tackle to lift him up."

Wake's face brightened. "Do you think so, really?"

"It's not funny, Peter. Sean could get hurt."

"Yes, well, of course you're right, dear." He leaned down to his daughter. "Honey, you aren't big enough to do that just yet. But someday you will be and you can lift up your brother and help Mommy even more." He glanced over at his wife with a grin as a knock came at the front door.

It was a messenger from the office with an envelope for him. A moment later he was sitting in a chair in their tiny parlor, his wife looking over his shoulder, as he broke the red seal and opened the deep blue envelope. Inside was a standard cover letter explaining that the enclosed orders were for Lieutenant Peter Wake, U.S.N., Pensacola Naval Yard. He pulled out the next sheet and read it through.

Lt. Peter Wake,
Dockage & Cordage Officer
Naval Yard, Pensacola, Florida

Lt. P. Wake is hereby requested and expected, pursuant to this order, to join U.S.S. Canton, for duty assignment. You are to proceed by ship to Key West Naval Station and arrive there by no later than the 20th day of April, 1869. At that Station you will join said U.S.S. Canton in the capacity of Executive Officer with a tour of duty of two years, commencing as of the 20th day of April, 1869. At the end of said tour you will await further orders from the office of the Secretary of the Navy.

Should no naval vessel be available for transport to Key West within the expected time, allowance for commercial travel will be made, with voucher for expenses to be submitted via Pensacola N.Y. to Naval Headquarters, Office of the Fourth Controller, Washington.

Separation, on leave status, from immediate duties at Pensacola, until departure for Key West is authorized with pay at the leave rate, subject to concurrence by present commanding officer.

Acknowledgement of these orders is expected by tele-graph or letter as soon as practical, with concurrence of pres-ent commanding officer.
    Sent this 27th day of March, 1869
    J.S. Crowley, As't to Chief
    Bureau of Navigation
    U.S. Navy
    Washington

The third sheet was the concurrence of Commodore Redthorn, Commandant of Pensacola Naval Yard, with the orders and leave authorization, effective one week hence. It was-n't a command assignment, but it was obvious that Redthorn had done all he could to help Wake, and that made him just as proud.

Linda leaned down and put her arms around his chest, touch-ing him but not holding him. There was an edge to her voice. "Well, that's it then, Peter, isn't it?"

He tried not to sound excited. "Yes, dear. I go on leave in a week, then we have a week together. No work. Just us."

"And then you go to sea for two years."

"Two years in the Home Squadron—with every chance that I'll be able to visit Pensacola several times by ship or on tempo-rary leave by rail, Linda. If I was assigned to the Pacific or Mediterranean, it would be very different. This will be sea duty close by."

Linda came around the chair and sat on his lap, her lips pursed as she said, "Sea duty close by? What area does that squadron work?"

Wake knew that she wasn't fooled by his sugarcoated descrip-tion. She probably already knew the squadron's area of opera-tions, from the other wives if no one else.

"The east coast, Gulf of Mexico and Caribbean, and South America down to the Equator. But most of the time is on the east coast, Gulf, and Caribbean. Easy duty. No war, just patrolling."

Linda breathed sharply. "That's right, isn't it. The war is over and you'll just be sailing around. How is it they say it? *Showing the flag?*"

"Exactly. No danger. Just routine peacetime patrolling."

Linda took his head in both hands, kissed his cheek, and whispered, "I think we should put the children to bed early tonight, don't you?"

7

Den of Power

April, 1869

Even before the meeting started, Adolph E. Borie, Secretary of the Navy of the United States, was not in a good mood. Porter had ruined his evening at the French party that night and President Grant had ruined his morning an hour ago. Grant had not been impressed with the urgency of the problem in the Caribbean. He told Borie that he had too many other important things to worry about. The president then told him to *handle it*, since "it was a pirate boat problem" and he was "in charge of the damn navy boats."

And so, for the first time since he had come to Washington seven weeks earlier from Philadelphia and taken this political appointment, Borie was faced with a serious decision. His special naval aide was no help and Porter, the admiral in charge of the fleet, was no help. In fact, he was nowhere to be found today. Borie had asked for advice from staff after his return from the White House and was told there were not enough ships in the Caribbean area to immediately eliminate the piracy problem caused by a former American naval officer running amok. It would take a squadron, a real squadron of ten ships or so, to efficiently wipe out the problem quickly and permanently. He was told that the best they could do was to send a couple of vessels down there to patrol and hope they came across some of the renegades—but for now there was only one ship available for rapid response.

And then there was the added burden that had arrived that very morning. The Venezuelan embassy had requested passage for one of their diplomats to go south to his homeland. He was the son of an important Venezuelan killed by the renegade American, and Secretary of State Seward had already assured him that the United States would be honored to offer passage aboard a warship—without even asking Borie!

All of which was the reason for this quick meeting. And it had to be quick, because Borie had a political gathering of the party faithful, and some unfaithful, at four o'clock and wanted to get this mess assigned to someone before then.

Lieutenant Commander Parker Terrington, newly appointed commanding officer of the USS *Canton*, waited in the outer office on the Navy Department's fourth floor nervously tapping his shoe on the wood flooring. Rear Admiral Carter, chief of Admiral Porter's staff, had ordered Terrington to meet him at the office of the secretary at three p.m. sharp. Terrington, whose ship was moored at the Washington Navy Yard, got there at two-thirty out of anxiety.

Anxiety had filled Terrington's life recently. The nervous days of waiting for a command had given over to the frustrating time of trying to fit out a new ship with ridiculously meager funds for equipment, training, provisions, and ammunition. *Canton* had enough men, but she did not have enough of nearly everything else. Terrington had graduated from Annapolis in 1861, commanded a monitor with the North Atlantic Blockading Squadron later in the war, and been the executive officer of a ship in the Mediterranean Squadron in 1868. He got his latest promotion and this command through the political influence of his home congressman and knew exactly what was needed to get a ship ready for service. He knew all the procedures by heart—if only he had been given the things he needed.

But his ship wasn't ready for service, and Lt. Commander Terrington had not been able to overcome the bureaucracy's inability to support his ship. He knew that other captains had somehow gotten their ships ready, but they had done it in a manner that wasn't in the regulation books, and therefore was completely foreign to Terrington. He consequently feared that the ship's shortcomings would become known, and she would be taken away from him. And now he had been summoned to the highest authority in the navy. His head was aching with every pounding beat of his heart and he wished he had some of his medicine to take, just to calm down a little.

The secretary's civilian clerk, another political appointee from Philadelphia, had no information for him and didn't even deign to meet his eyes. The naval aide, a commander, just gave him a shrug and said "good luck" while passing through the room on his way out somewhere.

Finally, at two fifty-five, Admiral Carter came in, nodded grimly to Terrington, and told the clerk to announce their presence. A moment later they were both standing in front of the civilian head of the navy.

Borie did not invite either man to take a chair, but the admiral sat in one anyway, leaving Terrington standing in a position of semi-attention. When Carter spoke first it did nothing to quiet Terrington's nerves.

"Mr. Secretary, this is Commander Terrington, captain of the *Canton*. She is here in the District, was headed down to the West Indies anyway, and is ready to get under way. Correct, Commander?"

Terrington tried not to wince as he said, "Yes, sir."

Borie glanced at the naval officer standing three feet in front of him, nodded and asked, "Has he been briefed?"

The smugness was barely perceptible as Carter replied, "No, sir. He has not. I knew you would want to do that personally, given the delicate nature of this assignment."

Borie leaned back in his chair. Over his years as a businessman, and later as a prominent member of the Republican Party, he had learned that leaning back and appearing pensive gave a distinguished impression and could gain a delay of fifteen to twenty seconds. That was particularly handy when a delay was needed to size up the man across from you. It did nothing to alleviate his concern—the man standing there looked like a scared rabbit.

Borie turned his attention back to Carter. "Admiral, are you sure this ship—*Canton* was it?—can do the job?"

"No, I'm not sure, Mr. Secretary. Several larger ships would be much better, but she is it—all that is available. Of course, she is new and in good shape, and Commander Terrington here is an experienced man."

Borie did not seem convinced to Terrington, who was now starting to get angry at the conversation referring to him as if he weren't there, and that his ship was incapable of handling whatever they had in mind. He was about to speak when Borie addressed him directly.

"All right, Terrington. Here is the situation. One or several of your former brother navy officers are down in the Caribbean playing pirate or something and stirring up the people down there. Those people are causing problems for the U.S. and saying we can't handle our own renegades in our own backyard. So *you* are going to go down there and end this problem one way or another, without antagonizing our Latin American neighbors any more than they are already."

Carter held up a hand. "Are you familiar with the situation the secretary is speaking about, Commander Terrington?"

Terrington had read something during the last few months about the revolutions in Central America but had thought nothing of it. They were always doing that down there. But he also remembered hearing the talk among other officers that some of the volunteer naval officers had gone mercenary down there following the war, after being dismissed from the navy. Actually, those men were all over the world, doing what they had been paid to do for four years for the federal government—fighting enemies. Had some really gone even further and become pirates? Complete outlaws? To Terrington's orderly mind it seemed a bit too much. There must be some misunderstanding down there among the Spanish-speaking countries. No *American* would do such a thing. Not in this day and age.

"Vaguely aware from the newspapers, sir."

"Yes, well, you'll get some more detailed information sent to your ship before you depart, which will be tomorrow with the Potomac ebb, by the way."

The next day! Terrington's mind started reeling with the enormity of that casual statement, but he said, "Aye, aye, sir."

Borie added, "And another thing. You'll have a passenger on the trip down to that area. A Venezuelan diplomat that the secretary of state offered a ride on your boat. Evidently, his father was an important man down there and was killed by the pirates, or whatever they are. My staff aide will notify the State Department people to tell this diplomat to go to your boat tomorrow."

Terrington felt weak in the knees—this wasn't getting any better—but managed to reply, "Yes, sir."

Carter shook his head slightly, then stood. "Mr. Secretary, I know you have a very pressing matter to attend to soon. Is there anything else for the commander, sir?"

Borie thought of those renegades of his own that he would have to bring under control at the party meeting. "Yes, Admiral, you're quite right. I do have to be off to the Willard and no, I don't have anything else at this time. You and Terrington will have this matter under control, then?"

"Well, Mr. Secretary, it won't be *me* that will take care of it. It'll be the man at the scene." Carter smiled and gestured to Terrington. "But I have every confidence in Commander Terrington."

8

Faint of Heart

Cadena watched intently as they approached the remote island of Old Providence, haunt of the early English buccaneers, three miles distant. If any vessel larger than their own was sighted, they would turn and run. Those were *El Jefe's* orders, though many aboard did not understand. Had they not been victorious over all they had come upon? But Cadena understood. *El Jefe* was a veteran of the great war to the north and knew much about the life of a raider, for he had been one of those in the *yanqui* navy who had searched for them.

Cadena did not know much about the man he called *Jefe*, not even his real name, but he did know that the chief had experience in this way of life and was most certainly not a man to suffer fools. One look into those gray *gringo* eyes was a warning of that.

A sailor coughed behind him, the subtle signal that *Jefe* had come on deck. He wasted no time in pleasantries upon his entrance. It was hot and he did not like to stand in the sun any longer than necessary.

"Cadena, nothing in sight except Old Providence?"

"Correct, *Jefe*. No sighting of the schooner or any other vessel."

"Very well. Remain on the west side of the island, south of the bay, one mile off shore. Tell me when any ship is sighted."

"*Sí, Señor*. Remain one mile off the island, south of the bay on the west side, and tell you when any ship is sighted. It will be done as you wish, *Jefe*."

Cadena knew the second he uttered that word it was a mistake. The gray eyes bored into him. "I did not *wish* it to happen, Cadena—I commanded that it happen. I do not wish for anything. Only children and idiots wish for things."

Cadena knew there was only one response when *El Jefe* got this way. "I meant no offense, *Jefe*. It will be done as you *commanded*."

He breathed a silent gasp of relief as the giant *gringo* walked away. *El Jefe* always carried two pistols and a stiletto, and there was good reason why he was also known as *el gringo loco*. Cadena had seen him shoot a man for a perceived insubordination six months earlier, when they had started this voyage. The man had merely said good morning cheerfully, but *Jefe* thought he was mocking him and the man was shot without warning in the stomach. Others were forbidden to help the seaman, who stayed where he dropped, writhing while clutching his abdomen. It took him two hours to bleed out and die, moaning and crying right there on deck, while *Jefe* had calmly eaten his breakfast ten meters away at the stern.

The schooner came into sight three days later and the two vessels were soon drifting close by each other. The schooner's captain, who only went by Rosas, had had an agreement for several months with the *gringo loco*. The schooner would take items from him to Cartagena and sell them, then meet the raider at certain islands on certain dates to give the money earned and get more items for sale. The schooner captain got a percentage of the profits, but Rosas wished it were more, for this *norteamericano* scared him.

And now, because of the notoriety of his actions, even the governments of the area were starting to talk about searching for the *gringo* pirate. In the *tavernas* of the ports it was common talk among the seamen. Everyone had heard about the pirate without a heart. It was said that he had taken forty, even fifty, ships since October. That he had killed hundreds of men, women and children. Only a few survivors had been found, people who had hidden from the pirates by swimming away to a nearby shore, and they told horrific tales.

Many ships were now carrying more weapons, captains vowing to die by fighting rather than by torture. The earlier bragging in barrooms by some of the men who sailed with the pirate had stopped. No one was bragging now. The stories had become too gruesome. In February, one of the braggarts had had his throat slit in Porto Belo and was found the next sunrise hanging from a lamppost with a sign jammed down into the gash—"One of *El Gringo Loco's* animals."

Rosas wanted to be done with this business. Stealing was one thing, but the grisly murders were too much, even for the Caribbean. Routine smuggling was safer. The *guardia costas* patrolling the coasts could be paid not to work so hard—no one got hurt, everyone made money. This would be his last rendezvous with the *gringo*, Rosas decided.

Besides, sailing all over creation, to God-forsaken places like Old Providence Island off Nicaragua, took too much time and made him an easier target for a navy ship. No. This is the last time and I will tell him after I give him his money, Rosas told himself. Gently, of course, but I will tell him.

The cabin was dark. *Jefe* liked it that way, for he believed it was cooler. The little light that came in through the stern ports and the overhead scuttle also let in a little air, but did nothing to diminish the ominous feeling inside the cabin. Cadena sat on the bench in the corner and quietly watched the schooner captain enter. Rosas was acting odd today. Cadena could see that *Jefe* had observed that too.

The *norteamericano* sat bare-chested at the small table, his reddened arms, face and neck contrasting with the brightness of his white skin usually covered by clothing. He spoke to the visitor with no warmth. "Come here, Rosas. How much do you have?"

Rosas was used to the *gringo*'s lack of even the basic courtesies used by everyone in Latin America and dropped a burlap bag heavily down on the table. "A good amount this time, *señor*. One thousand four hundred and fifty silver Mexican dollars, one thousand one hundred gold Granadan dollars, and two thousand American in paper. Our joint efforts were very productive."

The reddened arms reached across a thin shaft of sunlight for the bag and spilled the contents onto the table, spreading the money around and counting as he replied. "What joint efforts? You just sell the stuff I give you to those greedy little bastards in Cartagena, and you take a quarter of the profits. I take most of the risk out here. They all are looking for me, not you."

"It was good they do not know about me, *señor*, otherwise we could not make so much money. But now, now I wonder if they are becoming suspicious of me. I do not know, but think it would be best to alter our plans. To keep the authorities from discerning our methods."

The American had already counted out the silver and was working on the gold as he said, "How do you want to change the plans?"

Rosas had gone over this presentation many times in his head as he had sailed west from Cartagena the four hundred miles to Old Providence Island. It was the critical moment. The *gringo* must not be aroused, only convinced the change in plan would help him make more money. And in the meantime, Rosas could hope some warship, or one of *El Gringo Loco*'s own men, would kill him.

"By changing our dates and locations of rendezvous, *señor*. Make them less frequent for the next four months or so. Instead of every three weeks, make them every two months. And make them nearer the Moskito coast, instead of out here in the middle of the Caribbean."

Cadena saw a smile spread on *Jefe*'s face. It was danger sign.

"Why Rosas, is it getting too . . . hot . . . for you, *mi buen amigo?* I would think you would be used to heat, since you are a piece of stinking vermin scum that's lived in this cesspool of the world your whole life. I would think you'd like the heat. Do you agree, Cadena?"

Cadena leaned forward. It was time to show support to *El Jefe*. "Yes, of course, *Jefe*. Rosas is used to being on the wrong side of the law." Cadena could see the man swallow hard. "Rosas, why the Moskito coast? The rich targets for us are all out here in the shipping lanes. We have taken all the good targets inshore along the coast. There is also freedom of movement for us out here."

Rosas had anticipated this question, if not the hostility in his brother Hispanic, but before he could answer, the *gringo* growled out sinisterly, "Because the bastard wants us boxed into that coast, with nowhere to run, Cadena. That's why. He knows that if we are holed up there, we can't go west or south. He also knows that there aren't as many steamers for us to get coal from there. It would make it so much easier for the 'authorities,' as he so grandly calls those pompous frilly asses, to find us and kill us. And that, Cadena, would make this piece of dung's life so much easier too. Hell, he'd probably even get a reward."

Rosas stood and attempted to cover his terror with outward

rage, knowing that he would be dead in seconds if he did not convince this man that he was totally committed to their enterprise.

"*Señor!* You have the *cojones* to call me, Rosas, a turncoat! The man who delivers your money to you for the last six months in spite of the many men looking to kill us both. You think I have not been in great danger all of the time because of our business efforts? Facing danger in the center of the searching forces in Cartagena! No, you are too intelligent for that—you know the danger I have been in. You know they would kill me in an instant if they found out about me. This is a business decision, not anything else. You are smart enough to absolutely know that."

Rosas stood there, waiting. It was silent except for the sound of wood grating on wood, as the gringo slid his chair back into the shadows. Cadena could hear Rosas breathing hard, could imagine the man's blood pounding inside his ears. He knew there was nothing more Rosas could say or do now.

A laugh, cynical and short, came from the shadows. Rosas no longer appeared enraged. His face was sweating profusely. He looked like he was about to cry as the *gringo* spoke.

"You are entirely correct, Rosas. I do not think you have made contact with the government. I do not think you have become a turncoat. And I do not think you have cheated me out of the money due me. You are far too smart to have done that in the past, for you know that I would find and kill you if you did."

Rosas visibly relaxed, his shoulders lowering, his chest deflating. He smiled as he said, "*Gracias, señor.* I knew you would understand. Business is business. And we can continue our business."

The *gringo* moved the chair forward into the light again, gray eyes examining the man standing by the table with curiosity. "Yes, Rosas. You are right, business is business. But no, you are also wrong. We cannot continue our business. Our business is done, my friend. For while I know you have not done me wrong in the past, I am no longer certain of your behavior in the future. You see, I think you have a heart problem. I think it is growing faint."

Rosas did not understand the reference to the old saying in

English, but he comprehended the meaning of the sounds he heard. He held up his hands. "No, *señor. Por favor,* no . . ."

The *gringo* shook his head. "No to you, *amigo.* You are now out of business."

The noise was deafening in the confines of the cabin—the two shots fired so close together that they sounded as one—as Rosas's head snapped back when the .45 caliber Navy Colt rounds hit his face and took out the back of his head, chunks of skull ricocheting off the far bulkhead. He was dead even before he fell sprawled on the deck.

Because of the concussion in the small space, Cadena could barely hear his leader say, "Get someone in here to clean this mess up. *Before* it starts to stink."

"Yes, sir. *Jefe.*"

"And explain to Rosas's crew that they have a new business leader. Me."

"Of course, *Jefe.*"

The *gringo* stood and pulled on a faded blue shirt, started to leave, then stopped. "Also, tell Romero that he will be the new skipper of the schooner. I want him to take her to the San Blas Islands at Panama. Cayos Holandes. Don't take any ships until we get there. I want that schooner to stay clean. He leaves immediately. We will meet him there in two weeks.

"I think we need to expand our business horizons, Cadena. Our friend Rosas gave me a good idea just before we parted company. His schooner will come in handy."

"As you command, *Jefe.*"

"Oh, and Cadena, I'll be on deck under the awning now that the sun is low. Send up some fruit and rum for dinner. All this work has made me hungry."

9
Vivid Memories

The *Powhatan* had only minor repairs for the yard at Pensacola. The yard's boiler shop was able to rerivet the plates that had warped, seal the main expansion tank, and replace two of her condenser tubes. The boat shed furnished a brand new gig and recaulked her second cutter, while the rope-walk took in the old main hawser and gave the famous ship a newly spliced twelve-hundred-foot-long towing hawser. Other equipment requests were granted and she was ready for sea even before scheduled.

Commodore Redthorn was pleased but did not show it, acting in front of the squadron commander and the ship captain as if his backwater yard did this sort of thing every day. The evening before *Powhatan* departed, a dinner was held aboard for the yard's officers. Wake attended and got to increase his familiarity with the ship's officers he had already met. They wished him good fortune in his new assignment, the junior ones looking envious, and told him they looked forward to when he would join the squadron in his new ship.

The captain of the *Powhatan* overheard some of that conversation among the junior officers, came up to Wake and quietly said, "Lieutenant Wake, you are going to the new gunboat, the *Canton*, if I understand rightly?"

The captain's manner made Wake feel uneasy as he replied that he was joining the new ship as the executive officer.

"Hhmm . . . well, here's some information that may be of interest to you. I just got a telegram from headquarters in Washington with our orders. Included was the individual vessel disposition report for the squadron. *Canton* is not joining the squadron rendezvous in May at Norfolk. She is on immediate detachment and left Washington Navy Yard a few days ago, heading southbound. It didn't say what the detached assignment was about. I presumed something in the West Indies."

Wake was confused. The Home Squadron met each year in May for squadron evolutions and gunnery training. *Canton*, as a new ship, would most certainly be wanted there. But if she had left Washington a few days ago and was headed south, she could be in Key West any day now.

Wake thanked the captain for the information and pondered its meaning for the rest of the evening. The next day he would go on leave until departing to join his new ship in Key West in a little over a week. What was going on, he wondered.

Two years had gone by since Wake had last been in Key West. Signs of the great fire of 1866 could still be seen around the town, but there was also evidence of new growth, mainly from fishing. With the railroads spanning the nation in the previous few years, providing cheap and fast transport westward, Key West's crucial location on the New York to New Orleans or Galveston shipping lanes was losing its importance. But the little island was still a port of some significance for ships coming in and out of the Caribbean, particularly from Cuba. And it still had the old naval wharf and depot, though very much diminished since the war and in the charge of an old bosun and a civilian caretaker.

Key West still smelled the same to Wake—an earthy combination of fruit trees, rum parlors, sponge docks, and sail lofts. He couldn't help smiling as he stepped onto the dock at the foot of Duval Street from the Mallory Steamship Lines packet. There were so many memories here.

Some of the memories were wonderful—the tender moments he and Linda stole away from the chaos of the war, the hilarious gatherings of the junior officers in the bars, his old bosun friend Rork's antics at the Anchor Inn, his wedding at the old African graveyard on the south beach during a beautiful tropical sunset.

Other memories brought past anguish back to him—Linda's zealot pro-Confederate father and uncle, the death of her beloved mother from yellow fever, the cynical innuendoes by other naval officers about Wake's affair with an "enemy" girl, the way that many island women treated Linda for consorting with a Yankee occupier while their men were fighting and dying with Lee in Virginia.

But Wake could see his future here, for lying alongside the old naval wharf was the United States Steamer *Canton*, newest ship in the Navy. She had pulled in the night before to bunker coal and secure provisions. As Wake lugged his sea bag and valise along the waterfront, he smiled. She was a good-looking ship, easy on the eyes. He stopped to get a good look at her. She was the first warship he had seen painted dark gray with a continual black sheer line stripe. It accentuated her one-hundred-eighty-foot length and hid her considerable armament, since her gun ports were not painted a different color. Wake knew that when required, she could deal with any ship her size by utilizing the potent one-hundred-ten-pound breech loading rifled gun forward, or the four sixty-four-pound smooth bores mounted in broadside.

The one thing he worried about was her speed. It was only ten knots, since they had not installed one of the larger types of engines that had been put on merchant ships since the war, but instead retained the original reciprocating six-hundred-ninety horse power version from her initial building in 1863. Commodore Redthorn had told him that was because of budgetary constraints, but that at least she had large coal bunkers and could make a transit of almost a thousand miles under steam—if the Navy Department would part with enough money to top off those bunkers. Wake, the old schooner man, saw that *Canton* had gaff and square sails on the fore and main masts. Good, he thought, at least we can get her moving a little bit if the mechanical steam monster decides to quit.

Wake started toward her again and was stepping around a coil of hawser on the wharf when he felt a tap on his shoulder and heard a voice from the past.

"Now Peter Wake, afore ye step on that gangway an' naval tradition takes over our reunion, preventin' a proper hello between ol' sailors, let me jes' say that it's been many a dreary day since I last laid eyes on you, my friend. I am sorely glad we're shipmates once again."

It was the one and only Sean Rork, Boatswain, United States Navy—and Wake's best friend, whom he hadn't seen in a year, since Rork's last ship had put into Pensacola.

"Good God above, man! I didn't know you were aboard *Canton!*" Wake ignored naval regulations against fraternizing with enlisted personnel and hugged his old friend.

"This is excellent, Sean. Really excellent news."

"An' just how is me namesake and his lovely sainted mother? An' pretty wee Useppa? Must be about four years now, an' cute as an Irish lily, I'm a-thinkin'."

Wake was beaming. He and Rork had served together during the war on several ships, and gotten through many scrapes by relying on each other. One of those times Rork had saved his life. It was not by chance that his only son was named after this Irish immigrant seaman who had made a home in the U.S. Navy.

"All hands at home are doing well, very well. I thought you

were still on *Wyoming*, bound for the Med squadron?"

"Aye, I was. Then I heard from a yeoman—it was old DeTar, if ya remember him—that a new ship was needin' some bosuns an' he had a notion I might like to request her. When I found out who the executive officer would be, why it 'twas like an order from Saint Patrick himself. I had to get aboard."

"Are you joining her here?"

"Aye. Been waitin' for a week at ol' Mrs. Boltz's on Duval Street." A statuesque dark-haired lady, Martha Boltz was much loved by the sailors who had stayed at her boarding house over the years. Wake was glad she had escaped the fire. Rork added with a mischievous smile. "An' jes' guess who is assistin' Mrs. Boltz there?"

"No idea," laughed Wake.

"Why that cute wee lass Mary Alice we met back in sixty-five. She's been helpin' the freedmen for the government, teachin' writin' an' such, an' staying at the boardin' house. But she's no girl anymore. Grown to a very pretty lady, she is, sir. Fancy an' fetchin' as a spring day in Waterford. Her sister Cynda is in Puerto Rico now."

Wake did indeed remember both ladies. He really liked Mary Alice. "Good to hear that, and good to serve together again, Sean. Just like the old days."

"Aye, like days past, it is, sir. Why, I even saw those ol' troubadours, the Yard Dogs, playin' their tunes at the Green Parrot Tavern. Remember them?"

Wake smiled as he remembered the carefree musicians, former Union soldiers who settled in Key West after the war. "That I do. They were in the pub riot in sixty-four."

Lost in memories, they were quietly walking to the gangway, Rork carrying Wake's sea bag on his shoulder, when the bosun stopped, a grin on his face. "An' sir, you won't be believing who is the father of the main deck gun on this ship. 'Tis fate, I tell ya."

Wake looked at him and started grinning too.

"No! It couldn't be. Not old gunner Durlon! Mark Durlon's aboard?"

"In the rum-soaked and wrinkled flesh, as I live an' breathe."
Rork slapped his thigh. "DeTar got him aboard afore he got me.
Ya know, that ol' dog DeTar always was a sly one. Me thinks the
three of us owe him a bit o' Nelson's nectar the next time we're
near naval headquarters."

"Good Lord, Sean. This really *is* like the old days in the
war—the three of us in Key West, the Yard Dogs, the little Rosey,
St. James, and the *Hunt* . . ."

"Ah, but here's new gam for ya. The ol' gunner's got a new
twist. Seems he'd been a holdin' out on us about his past. A shady
thing, that. But 'tis worked out well an' he's still on course."

"What in the world are you talking about, Sean?"

"Why the gunner isn't named Durlon! Nay, sir. Had his name
legally changed up in New York after he killed a man over—you
guessed it—a lass in Connecticut, way back when. Been on the
run since then. It happened years an' years ago, back in the early
forties, afore he shipped in the navy for the first time. Now he's
found out they ruled it not murder an' he didn't have to change
his name an' run all those years ago. So the silly sod's changed it
back to his real name, an' there's the joke. The whole lot of the
petty officers aboard are havin' a laugh at it."

"So what's his real name?"

"Durling! Mark Durling changed his alias to Durlon to
escape the noose. Can ye imagine it? He used an alias that sounded like his true name, the silly damn bugger. Good bloody thing
he can shoot a cannon, 'cause he's worthless as a fraud."

Both of them stood there and roared with laughter,
bystanders wondering what could be so funny. Finally, they made
their way through the debris of the dock toward the ship. When
they neared *Canton*, Wake mentioned the names of the ships they
served on. Rork nodded and sighed as he remembered some of
their shipmates that didn't make it. "Wish ol' gunner McDougall
were here. An' Mr. Emerson an' Mr. Rhodes. We could have quite
the fancy time then. But, alas me friend, no's the worry—those
boyos slipped anchor an' went home to Saint Michael, God bless

their souls, leaving us to do the sailor's work o' the country a wee bit longer."

The two men walked around some sailors carrying boxes of provisions from a cart on the wharf. Nearby, two women on the wharf were arguing with an officer up on the main deck of the *Canton*, explaining in lewd terms how one of the ship's sailors had cheated them of money he owed for services rendered, which they described as laundering, and had run off.

Rork laughed. "Aye, 'tis the same in every navy port—no matter the year, no matter the navy. Now, I'll be the Bishop o' Wexford if either o' them doxies have even laid a hand on soap in a month. Launderin' me ass. I feel for the poor lad who woke up next to her. 'Tis he that needs a coin for his fright!"

They reached the gangway and started up, Rork's demeanor changing from friend to senior petty officer as he took the valise from Wake and announced up to the quarter deck, "Lieutenant Peter Wake, the new executive officer, arriving, sir."

The officer of the deck, who had been distracted by the women, spun around at Rork's warning and raced to the gangway, to stand at attention. Just before he stepped officially aboard, Wake saluted the ensign floating from the stern staff, then repeated the gesture of respect to the quarterdeck. Rork came up behind Wake, paid the same respects, laid the baggage down on the deck, then disappeared without further word—they were back in the world of naval discipline, where their friendship could not be displayed.

"Lieutenant Peter Wake reporting aboard as ship's company as ordered."

The young ensign was flustered at not having noticed Wake's approach until the last minute. "Yes, sir. Welcome aboard. I'm Ensign Kennard Moe, officer of the deck. The seaman will take your gear to your stateroom and the captain is being notified of your arrival right now, sir. Very sorry I didn't see you coming, sir, or we would have had men down on the wharf to get your things for you."

Moe looked very young. Probably right out of this year's class at Annapolis, Wake thought. He had heard they were graduating them two months earlier this year, in April, as a budget constraint. The young man looked worried that he had given a bad first impression to the executive officer.

"Very good, Ensign Moe. No problem on not seeing me. I could tell your attention was temporarily distracted by those, ahmm . . . ladies. Just be more careful in the future—it might be the captain or an admiral, you never know."

A messenger boy arrived almost out of breath, stretched to full height in front of Moe and stammered out that the captain presented his compliments and would see Lt. Wake when it was convenient for the lieutenant.

Wake nodded his acknowledgment and followed the messenger to the captain's stateroom. As they walked aft, Wake took in the activity around him, but mainly concentrated on the men themselves. There was no shouting, no cursing, no threatening. That was the sign of a confident and motivated crew and it cheered Wake. He caught the glances his way—the whole ship by now was aware of his arrival and, courtesy of Rork and Durling, they knew of his record. He knew they were also gauging their new executive officer by the way he walked, the way he interacted with the men, the expression on his face.

So far Wake was impressed with the ship and men. His spirits were building as he emerged from the companionway into the captain's stateroom, after the messenger had announced him and opened the door. He walked in, heard the door close behind him, and stood at attention in front of the desk, but the captain wasn't there. The lamps were not lit; only the skylight was providing a little illumination.

"Lieutenant Peter Wake, reporting aboard as ordered, sir." He called out, peering around the gloom of the cabin for the captain, but seeing no one.

"Yes, Lieutenant. Come over here and sit down."

In the corner he could make out a figure relaxed with legs

crossed, sitting back in a comfortable chair. The man was in his early thirties, Wake's own age, with wavy black hair combed straight back. He was wearing the tropical working uniform of white cotton duck shirt and trousers. The shirt was open at the collar and the sleeves rolled up past the elbows. The blue coat was thrown on the berth. The man waved an arm to the other chair.

"Sit there. I'm Captain Terrington."

This is different, Wake thought. He didn't know much of anything about Lt. Commander Terrington, but he instantly understood that the man who had authority over them all on this ship was not the usual naval officer. This is very different, he repeated to himself as he lowered himself into the proffered chair and faced his new captain. For some reason he couldn't fathom, Wake became very wary.

10

Welcome Aboard

"Tell me about yourself, Lieutenant Wake."

"Yes, sir. I have six years in. Served in sailing gunboats with the East Gulf Blockading Squadron in sixty-three and sixty-four, then had the tug *Hunt* until sixty-seven. Since then I've been stationed at Pensacola."

"Very succinct, Lieutenant. So you have been a small ship man?"

"Yes, sir."

"And before the war?"

"Schooners in New England, Captain."

Terrington leaned closer, examining Wake. "And you managed to get a regular commission from a volunteer brevet at the end of the war?"

"Yes, sir."

"How? There were six thousand volunteer officers in the navy and only a hundred and thirty-three were given regular commissions. How did you get yours, Lieutenant?"

It hit Wake suddenly and everything became clearer. Terrington was drunk. Not falling down drunk, but under the influence enough for his speech to be slurred and slow. There was the faint odor of rum in the cabin. The grog issue had been prohibited since 1862, but was still found among senior officers. And now Terrington, an Annapolis graduate, was thinly veiling his question about Wake's background.

"The old-fashioned way, Captain. I earned it by my actions." Wake set his jaw and said no more. He was right on the edge of anger.

Terrington acted as if nothing was strained and continued. "So this is your first real ship?"

It was a blatant insult, one that would have resulted in bloodshed ashore in a bar among equals, but here he had to take it. That he was being baited was obvious, but why?

"Captain, this is the largest ship I have served on, but not the first."

Terrington nodded, pursed his lips pensively, and took a drink from a glass beside him. Wake could see him swilling the liquid around in his mouth.

"Very well, Lieutenant Wake. You have been assigned to me as the executive officer." Terrington paused with a sigh, then took an exaggerated breath and resumed. "So you need to find the gunnery officer, Lieutenant Connery, and he will fill you in on our mission, our diplomatic guest aboard, and our ship and crew. Dinner will be at seven in the wardroom, full dress, with guests from shore. The mayor, a judge, and somebody else. As executive officer, you will be in charge of the dinner to make sure it goes off without a hitch. Tomorrow we get under way, at sunrise." Terrington waved toward the door and said, "Dismissed."

Wake was stunned at his captain's demeanor and for a second sat there, then got to his feet, stood at attention, said, "Aye, aye, sir," and walked out.

He stopped in the companionway and thought about what had just transpired, but it was too much to digest. Besides, he didn't have time to ponder rude behavior on the part of his captain. He had to find this Connery quickly and find out what was really going on aboard the USS *Canton*.

Lieutenant John Connery was a short man, but had a voice that could stop a bull in his tracks. He greeted his new superior with good-natured hospitality, took him to the wardroom for a glass of juice, then asked Wake to step into his tiny cabin so they could speak privately. While Wake sat on the berth, Connery sat down on a stool and began in a low tone.

"All right, sir, a briefing on our situation. Yes, sir. Guess I'll start with our mission. Here it is. We are to take Mr. Monteblanco, the Venezuelan diplomat, back to his country as a favor. Then we are to search the lower Caribbean for a pirate named *El Gringo Loco* and kill or capture him. Then we get to come home. That's the short of it, but not all of it by a long shot."

Wake could see it was far more complicated than that—this would take awhile.

"Mr. Connery, please start at the beginning and tell me the whole thing, but try to be concise."

"Yes, sir. Well, here it is in the full version. There is a renegade American naval officer who has turned pirate down off Central America. Apparently a former Union volunteer officer, who I presume was dismissed like the rest in sixty-five and, like so many, found employment in the navies down there. But this one evidently alienated even those people, which I think is quite a feat, and was kicked out. Then he turned to piracy. They call him *El Gringo Loco* because he is said to be without any civilized norms. The man has become a lunatic. He tortures people, steals everything, kills without remorse. Monteblanco's parents were two of his victims back in February. The whole region is enraged that a Yankee navy man is doing this, and Washington wants it taken care of immediately."

"Where in the lower Caribbean?"

Connery shook his head. "That's the thing, sir. We don't exactly know. He has struck from British Honduras to Venezuela, from Jamaica to Panama. That's a huge area."

"They usually send a squadron for this kind of thing. Who else did they send and where are the patrol areas?"

"We are it, sir. There are no other ships. They didn't tell us anything except go to the area and take care of the problem. I read the orders myself."

That reminded Wake that Connery had been acting executive officer. "All right, what about the ship and crew? Start with the ship."

"The ship is in very good condition, sir, as you would expect. Our supplies are not topped up due to funding problems, and the locals ashore won't take departmental credit chits anymore, say they're worthless and they don't want to deal with the bureaucracy up in Washington. I can't get anyone ashore to help us, really, and this is our last American port."

"What are you short of?"

"Everything on the provisions list, sir."

Wake had an idea on how to handle that. "What about coal?"

Connery shook his head. "I thought we'd try to bluff some Spanish port into taking our credit chits. No one here will and the navy coal pile here has dwindled to almost nothing. We got the last of that yesterday. We have enough to make a Cuban port."

Wake was sure he had a remedy for that. That left ammunition. "Our guns and magazines?"

Connery cheered a bit. That was his division. "Yes, sir. We are in good shape. Powder was new and most of the shells as well. I got to take our gunner with me to pick the good stuff at the yard in Washington. The gunner was an old shipmate of the yard's gunner."

"Our gunner is Mark Durling?"

"Yes, sir. You know him? A crotchety old salt, but looks like he knows his weaponry."

Wake laughed for the first time since coming aboard. "Oh yes, I know Durling. A very good man with a 12-pounder. I can't imagine the damage he could do with our one-ten. We're lucky to have him." He held up a hand to the gunnery officer. "Which brings up the subject of the crew. Are we full to rated compliment?"

"Yes, sir. In all divisions. Mostly veterans, too. The officers are all experienced, except for the new ensigns, of course. Lt. David Custen has deck division, with Ensign Kennard Moe assisting. My assistant in gunnery is Ensign Robert Noble. The chief engineer is Manfred Winter and his assistant engineer is Josie Cardle. I wrote out a list for you, sir. The petty officers, there's a dozen of them, are listed by division as well."

Wake took the list and studied it. All in all, the ship seemed to be almost ready. Connery got his attention. "One more thing, sir. I got word this afternoon that we are having guests aboard for dinner, a formal dinner. The captain said that you would be in charge of getting it done, sir. His words, sir."

Wake nodded. "Yes, I was informed of that. No problem, we'll handle it." He pulled out his watch and saw the time. "Very good, Mr. Connery. I see we don't have much time to get everything done we need to do, or even to have an officers' call right now for me to get acquainted, so listen carefully. You will have to pass these orders along."

"Yes, sir."

"First, regarding provisions. Have Bosun Rork take Ensign Noble ashore to Sally Walthrop's store. Rork has known her for some time, probably better than he should," Wake flashed a rueful grin, "and she'll hopefully trust him still. She will be able to fill our provision list."

Connery, like the rest of the ship, knew that Wake had served in Key West during the war, but didn't know he still had ties. "Aye, aye, sir."

"As for the coal, we'll get some at Fort Jefferson. The army has a supply there. It's not the best, but they do have to take a credit chit, so we'll top off bunkers there. Let Mr. Winter know that."

Connery had never been in Key West or the fort at the Dry Tortugas. "I'm amazed, sir. I thought the fort wasn't being used anymore."

Wake smiled and raised an eyebrow. "It's not, really. There's only a caretaker there—and the old pile of coal by the dock."

Connery was entering into the spirit. "Very good news, sir. I was really worried about that."

"And of course, the dinner tonight is at seven, in four hours." Wake paused as he studied the list. "Have Rork take O'Malley the cook with him to Sally's and get the makings of the dinner. Who is the treasurer of the officers' mess?"

"Ensign Moe is, sir."

Wake checked his watch again. "Very well, then he just got elected to lead the dinner effort. Once he is off watch he can make sure all is ready, clean, and squared away. I presume we have wine for the dinner?"

"Yes, sir."

"Very well, Mr. Connery. I will now take a turn about the ship and see what's what."

"Yes, sir. Do you wish me to show you around the ship?"

"No, you have enough to accomplish, but there is one other thing, Mr. Connery."

"Sir?"

"There will be a brief officers' call tonight at six-thirty, in my cabin."

Wake left Connery to his work. He walked back into the wardroom, then stopped and contemplated what had been bothering him about the conversation with Connery. It was Parker Terrington. Wake realized that other than Connery's brief aside about the dinner, neither of them had mentioned the man.

It was as if the captain didn't even exist aboard the *Canton*.

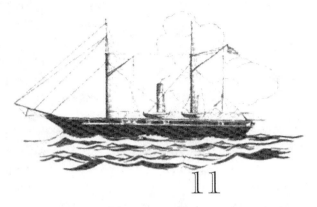

11

Good Impression

Wake's uneasy feeling about Captain Terrington was reinforced when he knocked on the captain's door an hour later. He wanted to update Terrington on how they were going to overcome the fuel and provisioning problems. But Terrington refused to allow him to enter and muttered through the closed door, "Wake, I told you to take care of things. Now just do it."

Wake had never heard of such a thing. The normal relationship between a captain and his first officer was such that they could and would talk frequently—they would have to for the sake of the ship and crew. And Terrington's rudeness in omitting the traditional title "Mister" before Wake's name did more than anger the executive officer. It worried him.

Perhaps I am just nervous and imagining all this, Wake thought as he made his way to his own cabin for the officers' call scheduled a few minutes hence. I hope I am imagining it, he brooded. Two years could be an eternity under the wrong man's command.

The cabin was hot and humid with the five men crammed inside. It was unusual to hold meetings there, but Wake wanted to see them all before the formal dinner.

"Gentlemen," he started as he looked into each man's eyes, "I want to compliment you on what you have accomplished with this crew in such a short time since commissioning. As I took a turn about this afternoon I could see that they are experienced and morale is good. Their efficiency is a reflection on all of you, particularly Lieutenant Connery, who has done a fine job as acting executive officer prior to my arrival. Congratulations."

This had his desired effect upon them and they loosened up a bit. Wake continued. "I understand that each of you has been told of our mission. It will require initiative and decisiveness, for we will be alone in a hostile part of the world. We must know and trust each other—for there will be no one else to call for help. Remember that when times get difficult."

He let that sink in. Several of the officers nodded in agreement.

"Over the next few days, I will be spending time with each of you, discussing your division and your men. I look forward to it and to serving aboard this great lady."

Wake allowed a smile. "But for now, this evening we will dine with our guests and impress our local civilian leaders with how their tax money is being spent." He paused while they laughed. "So let's all have a nice dinner, for tomorrow morning the mission starts in earnest. Any questions?"

Wake got the impression that several did want to ask something, their eyes shifting from him downward, but no one spoke up. "No? Well, if you do, you can ask me at any time. Let's go spend a nice evening together."

With that Wake led them into the wardroom. The steward

and Ensign Moe had arranged things in a neat and orderly naval fashion, complete with names at the place settings. Wake looked around, but didn't see the captain. Probably will come in last, for effect, he surmised, then turned his attention to the arriving guests from shore. Mayor Mahoney and his wife, Judge Whitehurst and his wife, and the Episcopal rector were shown to their seats by very nervous ensigns Moe and Noble, and afterward the officers began to sit down. Finally the door opened, but instead of the captain, it was their distinguished passenger, Don Pablo Monteblanco. Monteblanco walked straight up to Wake.

"You are the new assistant captain, no?"

Wake bowed slightly. He didn't really know exactly what to say or do around diplomats, and replied, "Yes, sir. I am Lieutenant Peter Wake, the executive officer, the position just below the captain of the ship. It is a honor and pleasure to meet you, Don Pablo. I hope you will be comfortable while aboard."

Monteblanco shrugged. "We shall see, Mr. Wake. Is the captain attending tonight?"

"Why yes, sir. From our conversation about the dinner this afternoon, I believe he is looking forward to seeing everyone tonight."

Monteblanco seemed surprised. "Have you known the captain long, Mr. Wake?"

"Not at all before I reported aboard this afternoon, sir. I am looking forward to serving under him."

The Venezuelan eyed Wake closely. "Yes, well, the mission from your government is very important. I wish you success."

Wake wondered if he should offer condolences, and further wondered how much the foreign diplomat knew of the *Canton's* orders. He decided to stay on a safer subject.

"Thank you, sir. May I introduce to you our guests from the island?"

Wake saw the diplomat spread a courteous smile as he turned to the others, obviously experienced in social matters with politicians. "But of course, Lieutenant. I am looking forward to making the acquaintance of these respected leaders of your civil society. And so very lovely, too," said Monteblanco as he gazed into the eyes of Mrs. Mahoney, who was old enough to be his grandmother, causing her to become flustered and whisper to her husband, "Oh Danny, these Latins are *charmers*, aren't they?"

The captain never appeared, even after Wake sent Moe to remind him he was late. Moe returned, clearly frightened to tell Wake the reply. "The captain said he was sick, sir, and wouldn't make dinner."

Wake tried not to react, burying the anger, and turned to the others explaining that the captain was unfortunately ill and sent his regrets. And so the evening went on in the way those affairs always did for Wake. By the end his facial muscles were tired of smiling and his ears thought they would burst if he heard Mrs. Mahoney compliment Monteblanco on his manners another time. He missed Linda. The two of them could have had a good time together, enduring the excruciating event with humor and flirting.

Later, as the guests were leaving, Monteblanco told Wake he wanted to have a word with him about the situation into which they were steaming. When Wake suggested they go to his cabin and talk, the Venezuelan said no, the next day would be fine and that he was tired from the evening. Wake got the impression that Monteblanco also was exhausted by playing the role expected of him. In fact, Wake decided, the only person who looked like they were having an enjoyable time that evening was Mrs. Mahoney, who was probably still talking Mayor Mahoney's head off about "that Latin charmer."

Wake fell down onto his berth feeling totally drained of energy. It had been quite a day, and tomorrow would be the first day of this strange mission.

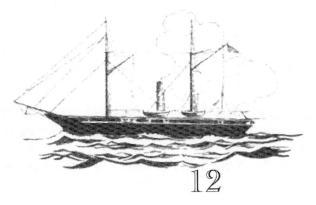

12

Distant Horizons

The captain was in his berth when Wake entered. Knocking on the door had gotten no response, the captain's steward reported that he had been told repeatedly to stay out, and Wake finally decided to just go in. By the light of a lantern turned low, Terrington could be seen sprawled half on and half off the berth, a bottle of British White Duster rum empty by his side. Wake touched the man's shoulder.

"Captain, it's Lieutenant Wake. Eight bells in the fore watch, sir. Sun will rise in about two hours. We're fully provisioned and need to get under way for Fort Jefferson in the Tortugas. We can fill the bunkers up there, then head out, sir."

"What the hell are you babbling about, Wake?"

Wake gritted his teeth and looked around. No one was close by in the companionway. Even so, he closed the door. The officers and men shouldn't see Terrington like this, he knew, and wondered if they had already on other occasions.

"Getting under way, Captain."

"So get under way, Wake. Do you need me to steer the damn thing too?"

Wake ignored the sarcasm, deciding to try being positive one last time. He put his hand under Terrington's shoulder and began to lift him up. "Captain, how about I give you a hand in getting up this morning, sir. You look like you're recovering from your illness last night. Splash of cold water on your face, a mug of hot coffee, and some fresh air out on deck will make you feel even better. I'll have the steward set up some breakfast, sir."

"Get the hell away from me, you damn fool!" Terrington came up off the bed and looked at Wake with crazed, reddened eyes. "I said to get her under way!" Then he slumped back down and grunted, "Now, get the hell out of here."

"Aye, aye, sir."

As he was leaving the cabin he saw the captain's steward, Morely, come up out of the dark. Morely looked startled to see Wake. "Good morning, sir. Just coming to see if the captain would like an early breakfast, seeing's how we're getting under way this morn."

"No, Morely, he doesn't. He won't be needing you for a while. He's still feeling poorly and will stay in bed until later."

Wake watched Morely's face for any type of reaction, as he must have heard the captain's ranting, but the veteran steward showed none, his eyes carefully neutral. "I see, sir. Then I won't disturb the captain and let him get his rest."

The sun was climbing up as they steamed south out the channel that was so familiar to Wake. At Sand Key they turned to starboard and ran westbound with the wind for Fort Jefferson, setting the mizzenmast spanker sail to assist the engine. As the sun rose, its illumination penetrated the waters and Wake could see the reefs sliding by below, the water so crystal clear that it looked like they were in a balloon sailing through the air over the colorful landscape below. It was shaping up to be a beautiful day and he let the glory of it all fill him and wash away the disgust he felt for his commander.

An hour later Monteblanco arrived on the gently rolling deck and laboriously made his way aft to where Wake was breathing in deep draughts of the heavy sea air, enjoying the moment.

"Mr. Wake, good morning. Would it be appropriate at this time to have our background talk about the area to which you are going? I am thinking that you should know as much as possible before you go there. I will not be with you then to help you understand these matters."

The morning's fresh exhilaration evaporated for Wake as he said, "Yes, Don Pablo, now would be fine."

Wake listened as Monteblanco explained the current situation in Venezuela, New Granada—also known recently as Colombia—and the Central American countries. It was not simple. There were many shades of nuances and meanings, and many relationships among the major figures, but Wake's orderly mind distilled it all into a pattern that he understood and could use as a foundation for the mission.

Monteblanco's country, the Estados Unidos del Gran República de Venezuela, was in the midst of a civil war between the conservative sitting president, General José Tadeo Monagas, and the liberals under General Antonio Gúzman Blanco. Monteblanco thought the liberal reformers would probably win eventually. His father had been a personal supporter of their cause, even as he carried out his duties as a professional diplomat for whatever government was in power. Monagas was not in favor of having European navies come in and clean the pirates out of the area; the liberals were in favor of much closer ties with the Europeans as a way to thwart North American hegemony.

The United States of New Granada was now going by the name Colombia, but many people still used the former. The central government was very weak, and the Caribbean coast, where many outlaws and pirates were based, was currently under the power of a liberal local government that was anti-American, but that could change at any time. The government had no control outside the main cities anyway, and sometimes not even there. Cartagena was a center of lawlessness, where everyone was paying someone to allow them to do almost anything.

The American Transit Company unofficially controlled some of the Caribbean coast of the Isthmus close to Aspinwall and Porto Bello by way of a concession to operate the railroad between the Caribbean and the Pacific that it obtained from the Colombian government in 1855. Monteblanco thought perhaps the American company was paying off the local bandits to allow it to operate its lucrative inter-oceanic transshipping relatively unmolested. The French were appearing in that area with surveying parties, looking for a canal route.

Costa Rican president Jesús Jiménez was in a power struggle with revolutionary reformer Colonel Tomas Guardia, and no one was in real control of that Caribbean coast. Monteblanco expected to read in the papers any day now that Guardia had won the day, which would increase that country's interaction with the British, who had some trading settlements on the Moskito coast. Every few years the Royal Navy would patrol there, during which time the piracy would cease, so Monteblanco thought an increased British presence would be a good thing.

In Nicaragua they were not in favor of Americans, for their memories of the Walker filibusterers were too vivid and recent. Conservative president General Tomás Martinez was in disagreement with the British about their settlements along the Nicaraguan part of the Moskito coast, and he was attempting to entice the French into a potential canal building concession, so perhaps the French Navy might be starting to show up in the area.

The Moskito coast was in a continual state of insurrection from the governments in Costa Rica and Nicaragua. The British alternately supported and abandoned claims of independence by the English-speaking settlers and Indian people of the coast, depending on their impressions of the likelihood of a trans-isthmus canal through that area. Currently, he explained, it looked like the canal might be in the Panama province of Colombia, and be constructed by the French.

Monteblanco laughed and said that whole area made Venezuela look tranquil in comparison, but Wake was still bewildered a bit by it all. He thanked the young diplomat for the instruction in the area's political situation and said he hoped to solve the problem without antagonizing the countries there.

Monteblanco held up a finger for emphasis and said, "That is the point I am trying to make here, Lieutenant Wake. *El Gringo Loco* is now hated by everyone. He started out working for the revolutionaries on the Moskito coast, but now is on his own. They all want him dead. Decisive action by the U.S. Navy now will gain the respect and amity of all the legitimate parties in the area. Kill him, Lieutenant Wake."

Wake thought that this was probably the time to bring up a painful subject. "You haven't told me about your parents, Don Pablo. I was sorry to learn of their death. Do you have any information regarding that . . . horrible event . . . that would assist me? I regret having to ask, but I need as much information as you can give."

Monteblanco lowered his head. "Yes, but it is only a little bit of information. Some of my mother's jewelry, a necklace with a large emerald, was sold in Cartagena. Our Venezuelan consul in the city heard of it and arranged to obtain it. He sent it to my brother the priest in Caracas. The man who sold it in Cartagena goes by the name Rosas and has a trading schooner he sails in the area. He has disappeared, according to a letter I received just before I left Washington."

"Any other jewelry recovered, Don Pablo? Do you have a list of her jewelry?"

Monteblanco looked intensely at Wake, "Nothing else was recovered, and yes, I do have a list. Do you want to make a copy of it?"

"Yes, sir. It might lead us to someone who knows where this pirate is located."

Monteblanco stared at Wake, his eyes beginning to fill. "You are the first *norteamericano* that has asked, *señor*. I do believe that you truly care. I tried to tell Captain Terrington all of these things I've explained to you this morning, but he said it would make no difference. That I should go home and live life. I found his attitude offensive, Lieutenant."

Wake didn't know what to say. Terrington's attitude didn't surprise him. "Don Pablo, I can only say this. I will do my best to get justice for you and the many other victims. That this pirate is apparently a former American is a stain upon my country's honor. That he has hurt your decent and honorable family is a wound on my heart. I will do my best, sir. I can promise no more."

"And I can ask for no more, *señor*. I am grateful to you for your efforts. I have no doubt at all that they will be successful, and I will ask my brother to have a special mass to ask for God's protection for you and your men in this quest."

Monteblanco turned away suddenly and descended the hatchway to his cabin below, leaving Wake gazing out at the distant horizon to the south, toward his future rendezvous with an American renegade that had turned into an animal. Wake wondered how he was going to fulfill the promise just made to a victim of that animal.

Especially, he realized, with a man like Captain Parker Terrington in command.

13
The Old Fashioned Way

May 1869

The voyage from Fort Jefferson in the Dry Tortugas to Punta Maisi at the eastern end of Cuba was a long hard slog to windward against the trades. *Canton* smashed into the waves at seven or eight knots on the good days; on the others she was reduced to three or four knots. They still had to round Cuba, double the southwestern cape of Haiti, and steam into the trades along the southern coast of Hispaniola Island before they could ease off and head south toward Venezuela, hopefully with the wind far enough aft on their port beam that they could set some sail to assist the engine and make some better speed.

Chief Engineer Winter had expressed concern to Wake about the fuel consumption so far. They had filled the bunkers at Jefferson, but were using it very quickly. He didn't think they could make Venezuela before exhausting their supply of coal at this rate. Wake knew the U.S. Navy had a coal contract at Santo Domingo, on the southern coast of Hispaniola, so decided it would be better to get some more there before heading south. But that meant advising the captain.

Captain Terrington had been surprisingly pleasant for the first few days outbound from the Tortugas, complimenting Wake on his resourcefulness in obtaining supplies and fuel and handling the social obligations of the ship. The man never mentioned the episodes in his cabin or his drinking. Wake did not see another hint of alcoholism or animosity in Terrington's behavior and was beginning to doubt his own sanity of recollection. Was this the same man? What had brought about the change? Or was it Wake who had overreacted to a sailor's temporarily excessive indulgence in rum?

Then, one morning at sunrise off the northeast coast of Cuba by Puerto Padre, Terrington had stormed up on deck and without warning accused Wake, in front of the change of watch, of stealing his navigation instruments.

"Those were given to me by Admiral Goldsborough himself, and you damn well better have them on my chart table in five minutes, Wake. And next time you're in port *buy* your own set." Then he marched back below, with a stunned Wake standing there.

Wake sent for the captain's steward immediately.

"Morely, have you seen the captain's navigating instruments, the parallels and dividers and such?"

Morely looked amused. "Yes, sir. They're where the captain told me to put them, in their special box in the sea trunk in the hold. Said he would use the ship's and didn't want to lose them. I think he got them from an admiral."

"When was that?"

"At Tortugas, when we was at that Fort Jefferson place coaling, sir."

"I see. Well, go below into the hold and fetch them for the captain. He needs them."

Morely's amused face turned to fear. "Sir, I'll have to ask him for the keys to the trunk."

"All right, Morely, I'll go with you to the captain's cabin while you explain to him."

The relief on Morely's face was apparent, but what worried Wake was the fact that the captain evidently had not done any position checks on his own for the last week, something that most captains did.

When Morely explained to Terrington in front of Wake what had happened, it was as if the captain were a different person than the one who had been up on the deck thirty minutes earlier. "Yes, well, quite all right then, Morely. Here are the keys. Go and bring those to me. I do like to use them for sentimental sake. Admiral Goldsborough gave them to me when he commanded the Med Squadron on Farragut's triumphal tour of Europe, you know."

Then Terrington shifted his gaze to Wake. "You see, Mr. Wake, I *do* know when things are missing from my cabin. Good thing this was not of mal intent, and merely a misplacement."

Wake's eyes met his captain's. "Yes, sir."

"Anything else, Lieutenant?"

Wake remembered the coal problem. "Yes, sir. Mr. Winter says the coal is getting low faster than expected due to our head-winds, so I suggest we put into Santo Domingo to top off before heading south across the Caribbean. We'll also get a better angle on the wind from there."

"Santo Domingo? Who do they belong to these days?"

"Themselves, sir. The Spanish left the second time in sixty-five. They've been independent since then."

"So it's a gaggle of criminals too, just like every other tin pot country down here." Terrington paused, a sneer forming on his face. "No, Wake. I don't feel like dealing with any peasants masquerading as civilized people. We won't go to this Santo Domingo. We'll do it the old-fashioned way. We'll sail down to Venezuela and drop off the fancy pants man. Then we'll find this renegade and shoot him and return to the Home Squadron. And we'll save money, which the Navy Department looks very kindly upon. Admiral Porter disapproves of using engines exclusively, says a sailor should sail. I, of course, agree with that belief, so yes, we'll sail her down. You know how to do *that*, don't you?"

"Yes, sir." Wake answered, trying to keep calm. "That will leave us with very low coal supplies for our operations in Central America, but maybe we can get some at Cartagena."

"Just follow your orders, Wake. You're not the captain of *this* ship."

Wake's hand balled into a fist. He stood silently, glaring into Terrington's eyes. The captain sighed and sat in his chair, looking out the stern ports.

"I gave you an order, Wake. But I haven't heard you acknowledge it."

"Aye, aye . . ." Wake paused until Terrington turned around to face him—" . . . sir."

"Very good, Wake. I think I might make a good executive officer out of you yet."

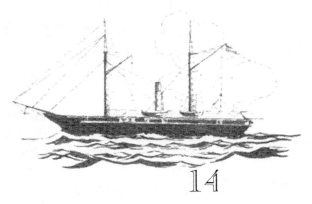

14

The Empires' Men

HMS *Plover* had been stationed in the West Indies flotilla of the North American Station for a year now, but ironically had never been to most of the West Indies, only to Jamaica. Other than port calls at New Orleans and Mobile, she had spent all of her time along the coasts of Mexico, British Honduras, Guatemala, and Honduras.

But her captain, Commander Rodney Russell, had just been ordered to Kingston for repair and refit, and both he and his men were looking forward to some different scenery and some people who spoke English for a change. His original visions of spending time with beautiful, and desperately lonely, plantation daughters in Barbados, Antigua, or Jamaica were dashed early on when the ship first checked in with his commander, Commodore Forester. The commodore explained that there were already ships patrolling the Leewards and the Windwards, and the relatively new and shallow-drafted *Plover* was needed in a more far flung part of the empire which hadn't seen the "red duster" ensign in a while.

So, for the last ten months *Plover* and her crew had steamed from Vera Cruz to Belize to sometimes Bluefields in Nicaragua, keeping the traders calm and occasionally solving local disputes. Lately, they had spent most of their time keeping things tranquil with the Guatemalans, who were upset with the encroachment near the Río Dulce by the Hondurans, who were still upset that the British acted as if Roatan Island was theirs.

Russell had met some of the former Confederates who had settled in British Honduras after the American war and thought that they might be of assistance to the colony because of their industriousness. Many had returned to their previous homes in the South, but those that remained were building large sugar cane operations. Russell had also heard about a crazed Yankee mercenary, the rumors said a former naval officer, robbing and killing on the reef-strewn Moskito coast of Nicaragua. He thought the rumors were probably the product of Latin excitement, but still, he was glad he had too much to do where he was and no orders to investigate the Yankee, for if true, the man sounded mad.

And now, finally, they were being allowed to go to a semi-civilized place. One more day and they would be there. Eight more months and Russell would be heading back home aboard a packet to Teignmouth, Devonshire, his tour of duty completed. Then he would be almost as far away from the miasmic jungles of Central America as one could get. He counted the days.

The imperial Spanish navy's gunboat *Sirena* was only seven years old, but hard service on the Cuban and Santo Dominican coasts made her look twenty. The Caribbean sun and sea aged ships before their time, Captain Fernando Toledo reflected with a sigh as he gave the helmsman the course for the main channel leading out of Santiago de Cuba. Built in Spain in 1862, *Sirena* was a good ship, once pretty, but the West Indies Squadron did not have the proper funding for her yard work, so Toledo did the best he could with what he had, and she suffered for it.

Thank God they had ended that ridiculous venture in Santo Domingo. Four years of warfare to restore Spanish rule over the islanders, whom Madrid foolishly expected to flock back to the imperial colors after decades of independence, had ended with a stalemate and eventual Spanish withdrawal. Toledo had done his part in the operations, but saw from the start that it was based on false expectations.

Of course, part of that was due to the idiots who had surrounded the despotic queen, Isabella II, back at home. The mutiny of naval ships at Cadiz the previous year had hastened the downfall of Isabella, which Toledo thought was good, but he was embarrassed that Spanish sailors had mutinied. He had heard that there was still unrest back home, but felt certain it would not last long and was probably exaggerated by the newspapers he had seen. He hoped his country would be returned to normalcy by the time he returned there the year after next, after a very long ten-year colonial duty assignment.

And now problems had started here in Cuba, Spain's "Most Faithful Isle." On the previous October 10th, revolutionaries issued *El Grito de Yara*, a call for independence from the mother country. Toledo was sure the *yanquis* were behind it, for they had coveted Cuba for years and many of the Cuban revolutionaries were supported by friends in the United States. The insurrection was spreading across the island with a rapidity that concerned Toledo, particularly since almost all of his enlisted men were Cuban. The sentiment on the island was what alarmed him the most—the Cuban people were not rising up to defend the empire against the heretics, they were either openly against the Spanish or sullenly neutral.

In fact, only months ago, in Guaimaro, the rebels had had the temerity to gather in a public assembly and adopt a so-called constitution providing for a republican government. Then they elected a man named Céspedes president—as if they were the official rulers!

Toledo was worried what side his men would be on if it came down to an order to fire on fellow Cubans. A native of his namesake city, who had been assigned to the West Indies since '61,

Toledo had come to appreciate Cuba and her people, but he was loyal to Spain. He just wished his men were too.

But for now his main problem was to get *Sirena* to Mayaguez, in Puerto Rico, where she would join the admiral's squadron as a dispatch vessel during the annual maneuvers that were supposed to impress the other powers in the Caribbean. The fact that *Sirena* only steamed at seven knots, and couldn't frighten anything bigger than a schooner, did not bother Toledo. He was just happy for the diversion away from Cuba for his men.

Swanson Singleton, known to most in the city as "Swan" because his name was hard for Spanish speakers to pronounce, shook his head ruefully. It was incredible how plans, simple logical plans, could become transformed into a completely hopeless mess with a few hours of meddling by the officials of the city of Cartagena. Of course, Singleton knew what had gone wrong and knew that it was his own fault. He had made the fundamental error of failing to include a payment up front for each person in the scheme. Singleton couldn't believe it—he had overlooked the advance money for Toro Caldez, cousin of the city's *alcalde*, or mayor, in the deal he had made for the coffee to be loaded on the Dutch ship. That was a stupid mistake, Singleton admitted to himself, for Toro controlled the cart drivers in the city.

The man was called "Toro" because that is how he reacted when angry—like a bull. And from what the *alcalde* had said when he had stopped by a few minutes earlier, Toro was angry now and coming to Singleton's office.

Singleton shouted for his assistant in his crude Spanish. "Bring out the good stuff from Venezuela. Toro is coming."

A moment later a bottle of Pampero rum, wrapped in a fancy leather bag, was put on the table in front of Singleton. He poured himself three fingers' worth, smacked the cork back into the bottle, and swallowed the rum in one gulp just before the door slammed open and Toro barged in, pointing a finger at Singleton.

"Swan, you *gringo hijo de puta*, you think you can ignore me? You think my cousin doesn't tell me? Are you stupid, or are you having a death wish?"

Singleton shrugged his shoulders and shoved the bottle across the table.

"Here, sit down, Toro, and hear my confession that I was stupid. I was in a hurry and forgot the advance facilitation fee for the transportation of cargo to the dock. Please accept this new bottle of excellent sipping rum as a token of my apology. It is virgin. Never been drunk."

Toro kicked a chair out from the table and sat down. A greasy hand ripped the cork out and tipped the bottle back into his mouth, the rum spilling down over his stubbled chin. He then wiped his face on the back of his forearm and belched.

"This is good, but ten percent is your penitence."

"Ten percent! You get five percent for the fee."

"That is when you remember to pay me at the proper time. You forget and the price goes to ten percent. Do not forget again. Nothing moves to or from the dock in this port until that money is in my hand. Within two hours."

"I won't have that much money until tomorrow when I get paid by the Dutchman. This is all planned by now, Toro, my friend. *Mañana* there will be the money, but I do not have anywhere near that much money available to me today."

The Colombian stood and leaned down into Singleton's face. "You are not my friend, Swan. I do not care for your troubles. Two hours or you are finished. I am tired of having to deal with you." Toro smiled for the first time. "Perhaps another fool could be found to be the agent for the ships."

Singleton was a veteran of a lifetime of facing down hostility, always adhering to the rule of never showing weakness, but he knew that his was a precarious position in Cartagena. It was a very unsafe town, especially for a *norteamericano*. He decided to use his trump card, one that he used very sparingly but had worked in other threatening situations.

"Toro, you know that the captains and cargo shippers trust me. And, of course," he waited a moment for effect, "you know that I am the official consul in this port of the United States of America, and represent our government. It is a diplomatic post of great importance, backed by the authority and power of my country."

Toro let out an ugly deep grunt. "This is what I know, Swan, you *gusano*. I know that you do not live in the United States of America because there is some kind of warrant for you under your real name. I know that you are a thief and a cheat, just like me and everyone else here in Cartagena. I know that you cheated somehow to get named to this position. And I know that if the money you owe me is not in this hand," he thrust his right hand to within an inch of Singleton's face, "within two hours, that the exalted and powerful United States of America will be short one consul in Cartagena, Colombia. And also, mister official representative, I know that they will not even *care* a goat's ass."

Then he brought his fist down on the table, cracking the wood, and walked out.

Singleton looked down and saw his hands shaking. This is what he had feared for three years—that the veiled threat of using his official American position would someday no longer work. He had always attempted in his dealings with the Colombians, through innuendo mostly, to equate the U.S. with the other great imperial powers and himself as the front man for that empire. It gave him value and a degree of protection, and had worked for some time, but obviously no more.

He sat there thinking, remembering that he had cheated prison or death several times before in his life when all looked bleak. Of course, Singleton had the money. Everyone in Cartagena had money hidden somewhere for times like this. He would have to use his concealed stash of contingency money to pay off Toro, but he knew that the animal smelled blood and would not back off. The demands would get worse, and then when they stopped—he would die.

Singleton analyzed his strengths and his weaknesses, and a plan began to form in his mind. Yes, he would pay Toro the money—to buy time. Time to exploit an opportunity to use the empire he represented. Time to communicate. After all, Washington only knew him as a hard-working consul ensuring that trade was not interrupted in a volatile corner of the world. A man to be trusted, and supported.

By force if necessary.

He needed Fuentes the property dealer to get hold of Rosas, wherever the hell he had gotten off to lately. Rosas still owed Singleton money for arranging the sale of some of the latest loot he had brought in, which hadn't been easy because of the unique value of the jewelry and the obvious identity of the previous owner. No, Singleton decided, he wouldn't take the money from Rosas, but he would take a favor instead.

A grin flickered on his face as he thought the plan through to the end. It would be dangerous on several levels, but it would have an especially satisfying end.

15

All Roads lead to Colón

The packet steamer *Colón American* blew off her pressure in a blast, startling Kramer and setting off a cacophony of shrieks from the howler monkeys in the jungle nearby. The dark laborers trudging up the gangway under their load of sacks never slowed during the burst of steam; they just kept moving, eyes down, shuffling one foot in front of the other. Their work went on for twelve hours, six days a week, at the same pace, rain or shine. After this steamer was filled, within an hour they would be loading another ship at the docks on Front Street, in the town of Colón, which the *gringos* called Aspinwall, in the Colombian territory of Panama.

The steamer was nearly loaded and Captain Underhill, his foot nervously tapping to an unheard beat, wanted to use the ebb and be gone. He was already two days behind schedule because the railroad from Balboa, over on the Pacific side of the Isthmus, had broken down again, for the third time in a week. It drove him mad with frustration sometimes.

Captain Underhill's packet ran a regular route from Mobile to Panama and back and was known for its reliability. Shippers and insurance companies trusted Underhill, a rare thing in the Caribbean. John Kramer particularly appreciated Underhill's reputation for efficiency, and the profits he generated for the American Transit Company of Panama, for he was the president of the company.

The warehouses at both ends of the fifty-mile-long narrow gauge railroad that connected the Pacific and the Caribbean were always full, ensuring the company always had money coming in. But the expenses were enormous. It was the most hostile working atmosphere that Kramer, who had run enterprises all over Latin America and the Far East, had ever known. In addition to the deadly diseases, exhausting climate, and constant mechanical breakdowns, Kramer had to deal with bizarre Indians, recalcitrant black laborers, incompetent Colombian bureaucrats, transient European shysters, disgruntled American mechanics and engineers, and lately in addition to everything else, pirates.

And these were not the usual thieving scum who could be bought off, but lunatics who struck terror into the employees of the company and would not negotiate. For six months they had periodically come in from out of nowhere, killed and looted at Nombre de Dios and Porto Bello and Colón, and escaped to places unknown. The word along the coast was that a crazy *gringo* was their leader, but Kramer doubted he was really an American. The stories were too grisly for that.

A few minutes later Kramer watched as the gangway to the ship was being dropped onto the dock. At least the packet had escaped so far. Her top speed, sixteen knots, was such that most ships could not catch her. In fact, she was thought to be the fastest steamer in that part of the Caribbean. Even her average speed on the route, twelve knots, was impressive. Two and a half days after leaving Colón she would be recoaling in Jamaica; four days after leaving Jamaica she would be recoaling in Key West; and three days after that she would be in Mobile, Alabama. She carried not only commercial cargo north to the United States; she was trusted enough to carry the mail from all over eastern Central

America and northern South America.

The *Colón American* was the most valuable ship in Central America, and Kramer hoped her luck would hold. He waved goodbye to Captain Underhill as a cloud of black smoke erupted from her stack and the ship slowly left the dock, gliding out into Limon Bay. She would make it, Kramer told himself. She had to make it. She was his lifeline with home.

La María Alicia was not the biggest or fanciest schooner on the coast, but she was completely owned by her captain and he loved her as he would a daughter, which was who she was named after. Captain Roberto Gomez had sailed the ship for thirteen years, paying off the amount owed until now the profits from his voyages went into his pocket, not some distant owner in Barranquilla. His current cargo was copra, coffee, and red beans. He was two days out, bound on an easy downwind run from Santa Marta in Colombia to Límon in Costa Rica. From there he would look for another cargo to take to Jamaica or Cuba or Colón, then back to Barranquilla.

It was not an easy life, and was sometimes frightening when the sea became angry, but it was the life he chose fifty years earlier and the only one he knew. And unlike so many livings men could make on land, it was clean and honest. Roberto Gomez was a man content with his place in the world.

Following *El Gringo Loco's* orders, Romero made it in Rosas' schooner, the *Abuela*, to Cayo Holandes in the San Blas Islands. The coconut palm–laden sandy island was little known and seldom visited by merchant ships. It wasn't even located on charts of the area. The island was named after Dutch sailors who had died of disease after being shipwrecked there two hundred fifty years earlier. The native Cuna Indians, short in height but tall in stature and dignity, called the area Iskardupo and shied away during the rare times when whites were in the area.

Romero and his crew spent the days lolling around on the island, eating the few bananas and the many coconuts there. They had heard that the Cuna viewed each coconut palm in the islands as almost a sacred possession and the nuts as the exclusive currency of the owner of the tree, but the renegades didn't care. Occasionally a Cuna *cayuca* canoe was seen sailing among the islets around them, but the Indians never came close. The outlaws laughed about the prospect of a confrontation. Let the little savages come out and claim their nuts—Romero and his men needed some target practice.

El Gringo Loco had said to wait there, so Romero and his men waited. The first week was not so bad, but the days of inaction started to wear. They had rum but no women, and Porto Bello was so close. Romero knew he would have to watch them carefully. They didn't know *El Jefe* like he did.

Cadena told the man on the wheel to "steer small, damn you, and stop letting the ship fall off to starboard." They were southeast bound toward the shipping lanes from Panama to Jamaica and *Jefe* had told him to be at longitude 79 degrees west and latitude 12 degrees north at sunset on the second day after leaving Old Providence Island. Cadena did not know the plan—*Jefe* seldom told him—but he did know that the clever *gringo* had something profitable brewing in his mind. The sun was going down behind them and Cadena was reasonably certain his position was where *Jefe* wanted to be, the latitude sight had been a good one at noon and the distance run corresponded.

There was a stir among the men on deck, causing Cadena to turn aft just as the *norteamericano* was emerging from the deck hatch.

"We are at the position, *Jefe*."

"Reduce the steam. I do not want any smoke to be seen. Heave her to with the mizzen and double the lookouts. Especially to the south. A gold dollar to the first man who spots a steamer coming up. We need to see her far off," he swung his gaze around the darkening horizon, "so that we can build up steam to intercept her from ahead. We'll never catch her in a chase."

Finally understanding the plan, Cadena was instantly thrilled and alarmed at the same time. This was very audacious. *Jefe* had planned out the capture of the fastest and richest ship in *el Mar Caribe*—the steam packet from Panama. But this would be different from all of their earlier ship captures: this one would be an American ship. Incurring the wrath of that country worried Cadena, but he knew he must not show it.

"*Jefe*, it is a brilliant plan. It will show everyone who is the master of the Caribbean—even those arrogant *yanquis* who own the Panama packet will be cast in fear of you from now on." Cadena watched the *gringo* intensely to see his reaction about the mention of the *yanqui* owners, but the reply was without emotion.

"A target is a target, Cadena. This one is faster but richer. That is the only difference. We should have taken the tub earlier."

"We will watch with vigilance, *Jefe*."

"You do that, Cadena. If you're lucky maybe she will have some women or girls aboard for you and your depraved little friends to have some entertainment with afterward."

Cadena felt a stir in his loins at the image of that and leered back, crooked teeth visible in the dark, his voice getting husky. "Oh yes, *Jefe*. That would be a great pleasure. It has been too long since the boys and I got to have that kind of entertainment."

"Yeah, Cadena. I thought that would get you enthused."

Captain Underhill was not known for kindness to his crew. He was behind schedule and time was money. They needed to get to Kingston as fast as possible to make up for lost time. The stokers were told to shovel faster and generate more heat to make more steam pressure.

The beam sea from the east was making the *Colón American* roll her guts out, even with everything in the schooner rig set, but Underhill saw that she was doing all of fifteen knots or more by the speed log. In smooth water she'd be making her top speed of sixteen. At this rate they would sight Jamaica the following evening. He nodded to himself and went below for dinner.

Gomez, like many captains who were shorthanded on crew, reduced his sail at night. It was just safer, and besides, what was another day to the coffee and beans?

La María Alicia was rolling her way slowly downwind to the west, her main and fore sails out wing and wing on either side of the vessel, with Gomez's fourteen-year-old nephew Ricardo at the big tiller. Gomez took a look around, checked the sand glass—he could not afford a fancy chronometer—and told Ricardo to call for him after the glass had emptied four times and to wake him if anything unusual happened.

"*Anything*, Ricardo. Never hesitate to wake a captain. The time you do not, is the one time bad things happen and it is too late to say I am sorry."

"Yes, Uncle. I will," said the boy with confidence.

It was Ricardo's first voyage, but already Gomez thought he had the makings of a good sailor. Someday he might even command a schooner.

"I see a light! Over there, down to the south. I saw it first, Cadena. The dollar is mine!" The shout came down from the foremast crosstrees, waking a dozing Cadena from his spot on the afterdeck. He saw a pale ghostlike shape come up beside him in the gloom of the starlight. It was the *gringo* without a shirt, his tone bored and disdainful.

"Eleven o'clock. Right on schedule, the fools. Get up, Cadena, and get the fires stoked. We will head directly south to her and increase the closing speed so she can't get away once she sees us. Keep the stoke even, I don't want a shower of sparks out of the stack."

Cadena gave the orders to the engine room gang and went to stand by the starboard bulwark, next to the eerie white shape of his leader.

"*Jefe*, you *knew* they would be here right now, at this spot? I am amazed. How did you know that?"

The *gringo* laughed. "Because the stupid predictable bastards never va ry. Same route, same speed, same time. They always try to leave on a Wednesday with the tide. But if they get delayed because of the train having problems, it will be on Thursday or Friday night, but always here. All roads in this part of the world lead to Colón. Even a simpleton like you could figure that out, Cadena."

16

The Richest Prize of All

There was no name on the stern of Cadena's steamer. *El Jefe* had forbidden it, saying it was too sentimental and that they didn't have that luxury. The original name, *La Creola*, had been painted out shortly after they had captured her and killed the crew. She was just referred to as "the ship" by the men aboard her.

Now they were racing through the water toward the light to the south. The closing speed of the two vessels was near twenty-seven knots, and it didn't take long for the shape of the steam packet to emerge against the stars on the horizon. They would be upon them in ten minutes, but Cadena wondered how long it would be until the packet crew saw the darkened ship ahead and raised an alarm.

As if he had read Cadena's mind, the *gringo* said, "Once we are close, we'll turn into their portside bow and grapple them, then swarm their deck before they can react. I'll take men aft. You secure the foredeck, then go below and ask them nice and polite to come up from below and parley—then kill them. Just like always."

"*Sí, Jefe*. The men have wanted a good fight. It has been a while."

"Yeah, well, they're gonna get their chance to prove their manhood in a few minutes. Going alongside her while she's moving at full speed is going to be dangerous. Put Rivera at the wheel—he's the best you've got. We'll only have one chance to do this correctly. The timing on the turn must be exact."

The only time Cadena ever saw *El Jefe* get obviously invigorated was when he discussed an upcoming confrontation. It was as if another person inside would come out, the man who had previously been a naval warrior. It never failed to fascinate Cadena to see it happen.

"I said, do you understand, Cadena? Stop dreaming about your future entertainment and pay attention to me."

"Yes, of course, *Jefe*. It will be done as you . . . *command*."

The third mate of the *Colón American* thought he saw something ahead, a black shape on the northern horizon blanking out the stars. With the speed they were going and the bow plunging up and down ten feet or more, it was hard to focus his eyes on the horizon, but yes, there was something out there. A small cloud maybe? He tried the telescope but it was dancing around too much, so he called for a seaman to go aloft in the main ratlines and see what he could tell about the shape.

The seaman called down that it wasn't a cloud. It looked too small and was probably a ship. A moment later he shouted down that it was definitely a ship, a steamer, and she was heading due south, dead ahead of them about half a mile.

The third mate immediately ordered the helmsman to turn to starboard three points, or thirty-three degrees, the usual response to this type of situation, so that the approaching ship would pass on their port side. He took a deep breath—it would be close, but they would miss each other.

He then sent word below to Captain Underhill that a ship

without lights had been seen dead ahead, they had altered course to starboard to avoid her, and that they would be back on course in three or four minutes.

The old bosun strode over next to the third mate shaking his head and stared out at the approaching dark shape. "Ya know, Mr. Morrison, it's gettin' too damn crowded out here anymore. An' what with the speed we steamers're makin' these days, by the time ya seen 'em, they're on ya. Ah my, but for the ol' days when ya could see what was what afore 'twas too late."

Morrison was still perplexed. Who was that ship? Was she heading for the company docks at Panama? He was able to see her now with the glass, but didn't recognize her. She was off the port bow a couple hundred feet away. "She's coming awfully close alongside to pass, Boats," he said to the bosun, using the sailor's slang for the title. "Something's odd here."

Morrison's mind registered the threat just before his eyes saw the steamer turn into the packet. The bow came around and within seconds crashed into the packet's portside forechains, driving the *Colón American* over on her beam ends to starboard and knocking down everyone on her deck. The noise of the collision and subsequent smashing of the wooden hulls as they plunged northward together was chaotic and deafening.

Morrison mumbled to himself, "Oh God . . . the pirate steamer from Moskito coast." Then his wits returned and he yelled to the men on his watch. "Break out the small arms!" but he saw it was too late, for a dozen evil-looking men were already coming across onto the packet's foredeck and more were following. Shots popped forward and the packet's crew were dropped where they were, gunned down immediately without chance for surrender.

Morrison grabbed a belaying pin, but only made it a few feet when he was shot by a tall pale man dressed in white who loomed up suddenly in the darkness. He fell to the deck doubled over, clutching his guts to try to stop the spasming pain. The flash of the gun had blinded him, but he could hear the pale man calmly shouting orders amidst the noise of screaming and gunfire. Then he was roughly picked up by another man and heaved over the bulwark and down into the dark sea.

Once the main deck was cleared of the packet's men that had been on watch, by shooting them and throwing the bodies overboard, Cadena took his men below through the forehatch and led them aft, telling the victims to come out and surrender, then killing any man they saw by either blade or bullet. *El Jefe* stayed on deck and made sure the grappling lines were cast off and the ships separated, afterward turning his attention to getting the packet under control. He rang the annunciator for the engine to slow down slightly, put a man at the wheel and told him to turn to port and head south, and sent a man below to check the bilges for incoming water. Within minutes both steamers were heading toward Panama at ten knots in the starlit darkness.

Cadena arrived on the main deck from the after hatch a few minutes later, laughing insanely. The *gringo* turned to see the packet steamer's captain trying to stand up, one ear missing and blood pouring from the gash.

"Cadena, you're making a mess on the deck. Just kill the son of a bitch and pitch him over."

Underhill was attempting to talk, but words wouldn't come out. When the ship lurched he fell down again and started to babble about international law. Then the cutlass in Cadena's hand sliced down into the base of Underhill's neck and the babbling stopped. The body was dumped over the stern like refuse as Cadena cackled in delight.

"*Jefe*, we did it. The Panama packet is ours! She is absolutely *loaded* with luxuries we can sell. We will all be rich, *Jefe*. Rich!" In his crazed excitement, Cadena reached out and grabbed the arm of his leader.

Instantly he was spun around, felt a stiletto pricking into his nostril, and saw that the blade poised to pierce his brain. The swaying deck caused it to begin to cut into his nose, but Cadena said nothing, frightened of the look in the man's eyes that were inches from his. The voice of Cadena's *jefe* came out as a hiss.

"I told you *never* to touch me, you filthy piece of rotting garbage. Next time I will just end my misery and kill you."

He flicked the stiletto out and down, ripping open Cadena's nose, then flung him down to the deck.

"Now, I want both ships going through the reef at Cayo Holandes at sunrise. Head south for one hour, then southeast."

Without looking back, *El Gringo Loco* descended the after hatch ladder, to see what he could find in the packet captain's cabin.

Cadena held his face, trying to stop the bleeding and avoid the eyes of the men around him. *El Jefe* had insulted him many times before, but had not gone this far. Cadena stood, attempting to regain command of his dignity, and said to the man at the wheel. "You heard *el Jefe*. Steer south."

Ricardo thought perhaps he was imagining the vision before him. To the west, in front of the schooner, he saw two ships, one from the right, which he remembered would be the north, and the other from the left, or the south. They were steamers and they appeared to be heading for each other—way out here in the middle of the sea. He called down below for his uncle to come up.

Gomez woke out of a lusty dream, rubbed his eyes, and made his way up the ladder to the deck where his nephew was yelling something about ships colliding and guns shooting. Then he saw the flashes himself, just two hundred meters directly in front of them! It took several seconds for him to register what was happening. When he realized it was a battle, he also knew there were no naval wars going on in this part of the sea, and that meant only one thing.

Pirates . . .

The two ships had turned and were heading southward rapidly, steaming next to each other and already several hundred meters away from the schooner. Gomez could hear the screams even at that distance. There was not any time to lose, they must get away from this place.

"Quickly, Ricardo, get the others on deck. Do it quietly! We must turn and sail north—it will be our faster point of sail. They have not seen us. We can escape in the dark."

The fourteen-year old dropped down through the hatch and got the others to wake up, whispering to them that pirates were out there. When he came on deck again with the other three men in *La María Alicia*'s crew, Gomez held a finger up to his mouth, signaling that they should be quiet.

The captain had already swung the tiller over, bringing the foresail across the deck so that they were on a starboard tack broad reach, sailing fast to the north and directly away from the steamers. The schooner heeled over from the increased wind and speed, her leeward deck nearly awash. Gomez watched the steamers astern, terrified, waiting for the pirates to notice them, turn, and come to kill everyone aboard *La María Alicia*.

Suddenly Ricardo pointed at something in the water just ahead of the schooner. It was the form of a man waving for help. The boy went forward on his own with the boat pole and Gomez faced a quick decision. If it was a trap to get pirates aboard—and he had heard stories of such—they might all die.

But what if it wasn't? To die alone at sea at night, with the sharks coming for you, was a sailor's worst nightmare. He turned to the men on deck who were waiting for his judgment.

"I will steer for him. All of you help get that man aboard. Maybe we can save him."

It all happened fast in the dark, their speed making it unfold in a chaotic instant. The man was snagged in the clothing by the boat hook, swung around into the arms of two of the men who heaved him halfway up out of the water, the boy and other man pulling him the rest of the way onto the deck of the schooner.

They all sat there for a moment, stunned with how close they had come to losing him, then the crewmen went over and examined him, stripping off his clothes. He was dressed like a *norteamericano* and had a bad wound in the stomach. He looked almost dead. They carried him below to the captain's crude berth and dressed his wound with a relatively clean cloth, bringing him hot coffee. The wounded man managed to utter a few words before he collapsed unconscious back into the bed.

"Morrison . . . of . . . the *Colón* . . . *Ameri* . . . *can*. . . . Pirates . . . *Gringo Loco* . . . killed them . . . all."

The words were not all understandable to the men of *La María Alicia,* but they did understand the tone. And like most of the seamen of the coast, they had heard the stories of *El Gringo Loco*.

Gomez made another quick decision. This man needed medical help quickly. Sailing south toward the pirates was no longer an option. Sailing west would take too long, and there were no real doctors on that coast. Sailing east, against the wind, back to Colombia would take far too long. The only real choice they had was to continue on their present course at this good speed. In three days, with God's grace, they might make Kingston in Jamaica, where there were good doctors.

Gomez knelt down next to the man in his bunk and said a prayer to the Virgin Mary, to please help this victim of pirates live until Jamaica.

And to keep those pirates heading south.

17

El Hermanidad de Marineros

The sun was rising off their port bow when Wake asked Lieutenant Connery, the officer of the deck, the bearing on Cap Tiburon, farthest tip of Haiti's southwestern peninsula. When Connery replied, Wake suggested that it would be a good navigational exercise for the ensigns to plot a running fix of their position, then the course to the next headland on the south coast of the island, Cap Gravois. Connery grinned and said that yes, the young gentlemen should certainly do that, with breakfast afterward as a reward only if they were accurate.

As Connery sent a messenger down to rouse Moe and Noble, the lookout called down from aloft. "Deck there! Vessel under sail by the shoreline, three points off the port bow. About four miles distant."

Connery swung his telescope toward the sighting. Wake used the ship's binoculars, newfangled things that took some getting used to. Connery reported while still focusing on the ship, "Steamer with her sails up, but they don't appear to be helping her much, sir. Look at that leeway."

Wake agreed. She was a steamer, but there was no smoke and

her sails were not giving her much headway against the eighteen-knot trades from the southeast. In fact, it looked like she might be in trouble. The angle of his vision and depth perception was such that it might be an optical illusion, but she seemed to be sliding down to leeward rapidly, toward the rocky shoreline.

"Alter course for her, Mr. Connery. She may be in trouble."

Canton was still steaming but would soon, per Captain Terrington's order, shut down her engine and turn south for Venezuela. Wake had estimated that they would be far enough east along the Hispaniola coast by midnight that they could make the turn and lay the course toward Curaçao, where he hoped to find coal with the Dutch. From there they would steam against the trades to Caracas and disembark their passenger.

Connery interrupted his thinking. "Sir, I think she is definitely in trouble. She's not able to round Cap Gravois on that course and I'm wondering if they can't get her about to tack off-shore. They're riding in toward that cliff, sir."

Wake could see that now too. "Yes, you're right. It looks like they may have a mile or so before they hit. Ring up full speed. Perhaps we can make it to them in time."

The annunciator bell rang once, then three times, and Wake resumed his mental calculations of the geometry in the problem before them. It was a triangle formed by the distant ship, the rocky shore, and *Canton*. Could her increased speed get her there in time? It would be close.

"Mr. Connery, lay out the number two hawser aft, with the floating grass messenger line, and call for the bosun."

"Aye, aye, sir. Ah, sir . . . should we notify the captain also?"

Wake sighed, angry at himself for forgetting that cardinal rule. "Yes, of course, notify the captain and tell him I have charge on deck and will handle the situation."Connery's voice revealed no opinion in his reply. "Aye, aye, sir."

A shout from aloft shifted their attention to the lookout. "Deck there! A ship coming around the far point of land. Steamer running down fast."

Lieutenant Custen joined them, all three officers trying to see the newest vessel.

"Getting a bit crowded around here, suddenly," jested Connery.

Custen put down his telescope, rested his eye, then raised it again. "That damn sun is in my eyes, but I think I see the flag of the native republic on that steamer. I wonder if she is their gunboat? I heard they have one."

"Deck there! The steamer inshore just hoisted an ensign."

It was the white and gold of Spain. Wake switched his binoculars to the other steamer. She was flying the blue and red of the Republic of Haiti. Wake ordered the ensign sent up and a moment later the Stars and Stripes streamed out from the mizzen gaff peak.

Connery recognized the Haitian vessel. "Yep, one's Spanish and the other is the gunboat the natives got from the Brits. She's bigger than us. Has two four-point-sevens for her guns. Brits trained the crew. A bad mix, Lieutenant Wake. Haiti fought Spain only a few years ago, when the Spanish tried to reoccupy Santo Domingo."

Wake put down his binoculars and saw that Monteblanco had come up beside them and was watching the ships also.

Rork arrived and reported to Wake. "Hawser's laid out an' ready to send. Grass line is bent an' ready to float to them downwind, sir."

"Very good, Rork. You are in charge of the line work on this effort."

Rork gauged the position of the Spanish steamer and the shoreline.

"Aye, aye, sir. 'Twill be a close-run thing, but by the God o' the Irish, we're the lads what can do it, Lieutenant. Have no fear."

Custen, still eyeing the Spanish steamer, spoke up. "We can dip downwind and come up their port side, sir. Stream the line right across their course, then belay it down and turn them around to the south."

"Very good. Alter course and steer as you see fit. You have the deck, Mr. Custen."

They were now smashing into the seas in a race against time to get to the Spaniard before she wrecked. The Haitian gunboat was closer, but making no obvious attempt to assist.

Wake said to Monteblanco. "*Señor*, we may need an interpreter. Would you please help in that capacity?"

"But of course, Lieutenant. Just tell me what you want to say and it will be done."

Custen shook his head. "Good Lord, sir. She's a Spanish Navy gunboat!"

Connery added, "A naval vessel in that predicament. Not a good day for that captain's career."

Wake instantly felt sympathy for the naval officer commanding the gunboat. This would be the end of his professional life, unless they could get there in time. It was only half a mile now. The Haitian gunboat was already slowing down, turning broadside to the Spanish.

The *Canton* kept surging forward, the crash of the seas against the cliff clearly seen and heard now—it was only a quarter mile away. The leadsman cried out from his position in the forechains that there was no bottom found. The water was deep right up to the rocks.

Wake could see the Spanish captain now, standing by the stern, grimly looking between the American warship and the rocks just to leeward. The *Canton* was coming up from astern and passing along the Spanish vessel's port side, between the ship and the rocks. Custen ordered a reduction in speed as Rork, amidships on the starboard side, got ready to make the heave with a line weighted with a rope-worked monkey fist.

Wake watched Custen, pleased to see that he was calm and giving the proper orders. He also observed that the name on the stern of the Spanish ship was *Sirena*, and that her sailors understood what the Americans were going to attempt. The Spanish captain was giving orders of his own and sailors were standing by to receive the line from Rork.

The bosun stood up on the caprail of the starboard bulwark, his left arm crooked around a main shroud, and swung the coil of line three times with his right hand. On the third swing he yelled out in Gaelic, "*Éireann go Brách!*" and the monkey fist, trailed by the light line, soared through the air and across the *Sirena's* foredeck, where her men quickly started heaving it in. Within seconds the heavier hawser was snaking through the water and being belayed on the *Sirena's* fore bitts.

Canton overtook the bow of the other ship and forged ahead and around to the right, turning her course away from the shore. The deck was a mass of noise and movement as Rork made sure his men were ready to take the sudden strain on the hawser. Monteblanco shouted over to the Spanish captain, and Custen gave orders to the helmsman.

Then a voice boomed out above it all. "*What in hell is going on here!*"

An enraged Captain Parker Terrington strode directly up to Wake.

Captain Fernando Toledo thought that not only his career, but very probably his life, was going to be over in a matter of minutes. The engine, reluctant at the best of times, had completely shut down, the engineer explaining that her boiler had too many leaks to build pressure and the piston crank arm that he was always predicting would fail from metal fatigue had done just that. And, he added sorrowfully, there were no replacements east of Havana.

They had sailed *Sirena* many times, but the old girl just wasn't a good sailing ship to windward, and windward was where they needed to be right now. He knew even as he ordered her sails set, that they would never get her to tack through the wind around to an offshore course. The old girl was a bitch to turn that way, too much weight aft. He tried to wear her around, turning downwind, but without sufficient speed she would not turn. So they drifted—unable to get away from the quickly approaching rocks.

Then the Americans came around Cap Tiburon and made their bold dash at full speed to try to get close enough to pass a line. Toledo knew exactly what they were trying to do, and smiled at the audacity of it. As they got closer he thought it was a magnificent gesture, alas too late.

But they made it. Incredibly they made it, and Toledo's men grabbed the line thrown and hauled away, literally as if their lives depended on it. Within seconds the hawser was aboard and secured and everyone waited for the tension to be taken up by the American gunboat. If it broke, they were gone. If it held, they were saved. It stretched like India rubber, the water squeezing out of the quivering line until Toledo was sure it would explode in a hundred pieces.

But it held.

Sirena's bow swung rapidly to starboard as she followed the American around and away from shore. Toledo joined the many men on the deck who were crossing themselves in thanks to God for saving their lives, afterward raising a cheer for the Americans.

As they passed the Haitian gunboat, the *22 Decembre*, Toledo saw that her decks were cleared for action and the guns pointed toward him. He was, after all, illegally in their waters and the Haitians had good reasons to be suspicious of Spanish motives. Another legacy of our failed venture at Santo Domingo on this island, he said under his breath. He saluted the Haitian captain, then shrugged his shoulders in a gesture of wonderment. The black man who appeared to be in charge merely stared menacingly in return as the Spanish gunboat was towed past him out to sea.

"We're towing the Spanish gunboat off the lee shore, Captain. They were about to wreck."

Terrington glanced at the *Sirena*, then back at Wake. "Who gave you permission to risk this ship, a United States warship, on a stupid trick like this?"

Rork, standing six feet away, shouted at his men to take the strain easily, to put their backs into it, then walked forward and lashed down the hawser end in a double hitched bowline around the mainmast. Custen moved to the leeward deck and Connery walked aft. Monteblanco stood by the mizzenmast, watching the scene. Wake saw the sailors also move away from the captain, averting their eyes from the confrontation between captain and executive officer.

"I had the authority and I used it. Sir," said Wake, still looking at the hawser between the ships.

Canton jolted temporarily as the strain went on the line. Wake heard a cheer from the Spanish sailors as the *Sirena*'s bow turned away from shore. A responding cheer went up from the Americans, grinning and slapping shoulders all around.

Terrington's face was crimson and he was shaking with rage. "You should have asked permission, Wake. Goddammit all to hell, Wake—*I am the captain of this ship!*"

Terrington stopped, as if stunned by his own words. His eyes looked out over the sea, but they were vacant. Monteblanco walked up to Wake, ignoring Terrington, and shook his hand.

"That was one of the bravest actions I have ever seen, Lieutenant Wake. You saved the lives of those Spaniards today, and I will make sure my government hears of this gallant action by you and *your* men."

The diplomat then addressed Terrington. "Captain, your officers and men are heroes, which will, of course, reflect greatly upon their commanding officer. You will also be mentioned in my report, as their leader."

Terrington seemed as if he had physically deflated, his tone dejected as he muttered toward Wake, "You should have asked, . . ." and walked aft to the hatch where he climbed down the ladder.

Wake suddenly felt exhausted. He gave orders to continue the tow southerly for two miles to seaward, then told Custen he still had the deck, and went below. He was heading for his cabin, but knew that after Terrington's outburst on deck he had to go aft to the captain's cabin. They had to get this solved. Now.

He knocked at the door and entered without permission. Terrington was at his small desk reading a paper, apparently a letter.

"Captain, we need to talk, sir."

Terrington's voice was oddly plaintive, almost juvenile. "No, not now, I'm busy with this correspondence. Maybe we can talk later, Wake."

Wake was caught off guard. He had expected hostility, maybe even violence. "No sir. Now. And it's *Mister* Wake, at least in front of others, Captain. You might not like it, but in the eyes of the U.S. Navy I am an officer and a gentleman and will be treated as such by everyone, below and above me . . . sir."

The captain turned and smiled, as if seeing Wake for the first time that day. "Yes, of course, Mister Wake. You are right, of course. I have been sick lately, and perhaps a bit testy. No hard feelings?" And with that Terrington shocked Wake by offering his hand.

Wake shook it and cautiously responded. "Thank you, sir. Perhaps I have not been as understanding of your illness as I should have been. Can we start from here, sir? We have a good crew and a tough assignment, but we can do it."

"Yes, of course, Mr. Wake. Start from here. Start fresh, as it were."

Something wasn't right, Wake could tell. But what? "Yes, sir."

Terrington nodded and reached into the desk drawer, pulling out a rum bottle. "A toast to new beginnings between us, Mr.

Wake. And to the good and jolly crew of the USS *Canton*."

Wake submerged his disgust and merely said, "No, thank you, sir. I'll be getting back up on deck now and leave you to your paper work. Thank you, Captain."

He closed the door behind him and tried to calm down. The captain was a drunk, but there were a lot of drunks in the navy—the life bred that. This was something more, something insidious. Wake didn't know what exactly it was, but knew he would have to figure it out—the lives of the men aboard the *Canton* were at stake.

With Monteblanco as the interpreter, Captain Toledo expressed his appreciation for the fourth time to Captain Terrington, who offered another round of rum in celebration.

Wake also sat at the table in Terrington's cabin. "But now what will you do, Captain Toledo?" he asked. "Your ship can't get to your squadron at Puerto Rico. It's more than four hundred miles upwind."

Toledo looked out the stern ports at his ship hove to a short distance away. Once the hawser had been cast off, he had been rowed to the *yanqui* ship to offer his sincere thanks. He brought his best bottle of rum, which Terrington was draining steadily.

"I do not know, my friend. *Sirena* is a good ship, but she sails poorly. The nearest replacement part for the engine is in Havana, seven hundred miles away."

"But what about Jamaica?" Wake suggested. "Kingston is less than two hundred miles from here. The Royal Navy is on good terms with the Spanish Navy. They could help with the part, perhaps."

Monteblanco spread his hands up, signaling he had an idea. "Why not continue the *tow* over to Kingston? I do not mind the slight delay, and I think it would serve all three countries very well for their navies to cooperate in such a manner."

Terrington, his words sluggish, said, "Well, I don't know about doing *that*, Monte, ol' boy."

Monteblanco continued. "Captain Terrington, you have already scored a great honor for your country by saving the lives of Captain Toledo's men. Why not cap that with a gesture of friendship, a feat that will be celebrated in Madrid, London, and Washington? Did I not tell you that I know the great Admiral Porter from my days in Washington? He would be especially impressed with your feat. And this tow would take, what, a day or two?"

Toledo did not understand the exchange in English and Monteblanco didn't translate it for him. Wake marveled at the way Monteblanco led Terrington into the idea.

"You know, Monte, maybe you're right. Porter, did you say? A great gesture of friendship, celebrated in Washington. Yes, I can see that. And it's only a day or two. What the hell. Mr. Wake, what say you?"

"It can be done, sir. *Sirena* could set some canvas and we'll set ours, helping the speed. We could be in Kingston in around," Wake spread his fingers as ad hoc navigating dividers and measured off the distance on the chart before them on the table, "approximately thirty-four hours at five to six knots average, or at about sunrise two days from now."

Terrington, sounding grandiose, waved a hand and said, "Then make it so, Mr. Wake. Make it so."

When Monteblanco translated the idea to Toledo, another burst of thank-yous came forth from the Spanish naval officer, with pledges of eternal friendship and brotherhood. Then Toledo stood and proposed a toast to the president of the United States, the great uniter of his nation, Grant, which even Wake felt compelled to join in. Terrington proposed a counter-toast, with a giggle, "to whoever the hell is in charge of Spain these days," which Monteblanco translated diplomatically for the Spanish captain. Toledo, overcome by emotion and the fact that his life and career was just saved by these strangers, made the last toast with tears in his eyes. "*A ustedes, mis compañeros, y al hermanidad de los marineros por todas partes del mundo.*"

Terrington, who was on the verge of laughing, suddenly got quiet and asked Monteblanco what the Spaniard had said.

"He made a toast 'to you, my comrades, and the brotherhood of sailors everywhere in the world,' Captain Terrington."

Terrington stared at Toledo. "By God, Mr. Wake, I think the silly old bastard actually means it . . ."

Wake slowly shook his head at a stunned Monteblanco, then looked at his captain, who was pouring another glass of rum. This will be a long voyage, Wake rued. I just hope my discipline holds.

18

Naval Goodwill

HMS *Plover* lay on her hook at the Port Royal fleet anchorage. Captain Russell was about to descend to his gig for the row to Admiralty House when he heard the officer of the deck exclaim, "Look at that! A Yankee gunboat towing a Spanish."

Russell stared like the rest of them as the *Canton* steamed by, towing the *Sirena* into the general anchorage off Kingston proper. Naval gun salutes started to echo off the hills around the bay. Further in, the German patrol gunboat *Meteor* and the French *aviso* gunboat *Bouvet* added their powder to the salutes.

I wonder what the story is behind that affair, pondered Russell as he resumed his journey ashore. Knowing that it was customary for visiting naval officers to always call on the local naval authority immediately upon arrival, Russell surmised that he might have the story pretty soon.

The guard boat for Kingston Harbour directed *Canton* to a

mooring spot in the anchorage between Plum Island and the city's docks, then departed to report to the naval headquarters. Soon the whole harbor was abuzz about the Yankee and the Spaniard nested together at anchor. The tavern keepers of Kingston sensed a good night coming, as did the chandlery owners and wherrymen. Bumboats were already closing in on the *Canton* and *Sirena*, and Wake remembered to tell Custen and Connery not to let the bumboat vendors get too close or the men would be drunk in ten minutes.

"Sir, what about the Spanish sailors? Our boys will get rum from them," said Connery.

Wake thought about that for a moment, then chuckled. "Put Rork on the first watch, stationed on the side with the Spaniards. Tell him my orders are 'no trading.'"

Terrington was passed out in his cabin again, so Wake prepared to make the official arrival call ashore, accompanied by Monteblanco and Toledo. He invited them to ride in his launch, to which they enthusiastically agreed.

As they rowed past the ships anchored in the harbor, Monteblanco pointed out the German and French vessels. "Odd seeing them anchored close together. If only their countries were that close."

Wake did not understand. "What do you mean, sir?"

"The German federation and the French republic are upset with each other. It is getting hostile between them in Europe, but here they at least appear to be friends, as it should be."

The launch took them past the anchorage for small trading vessels, including one which Toledo gestured toward and said had a very pretty name, *La María Alicia*. The schooner had her mainsail up, ready to weigh anchor and return to sea.

"A most fascinating tale, Lieutenant Wake. I am glad it turned so well for eve ryone," said Commodore Mason Forester, commanding officer of the Royal Navy's West Indies flotilla of the North American station.

"Lieutenant Wake demonstrated skill and courage, Commodore. I was there and saw it, and will make sure it is known in Washington," added Monteblanco, to Wake's embarrassment.

Forester chuckled at Wake's blush. "Eve ry naval officer could use a little help that way, Don Pablo. Now, if you will excuse me, there is an urgent matter I must attend to, but I want to once again personally invite you to a reception at seven o'clock this evening at Admiralty House that the governor is putting on for naval officers. All of the foreign vessels are invited to send three officers.

"And Don Pablo, I would very much like it if you would honor us with your attendance as well. After what you witnessed, I do believe you are, at the very least, a naval *enthusiast* now!"

Wake, Monteblanco, and Toledo accepted with thanks, then walked out of the naval headquarters past a line of British officers waiting for their time with the commodore.

Five minutes later Commodore Forester was sitting at his desk as the flotilla's flag lieutenant reported on his follow-up to a disturbing report that had come in the previous evening from the hospital.

"Commodore, it's true. I spoke with the man this morning. He is still in mortal danger from a gunshot wound in the abdomen, but was lucid enough to answer my questions."

"Very well, out with it. What happened?"

"The man, a Jeffrey Morrison of a place called Tonawanda in the state of New York, was brought in last night from the harbor guard boat. They got him from a Barranquilla schooner that picked him up in the water and sailed him here for help. The schooner's captain confirmed Morrison's story—he sailed up on the battle in the darkness." The lieutenant took out a pad of paper and went through his penciled notes.

"Morrison is the third mate aboard the Panama packet steamer, the *Colón American*. She was ten hours out from Colón several days ago, bound for this harbor on her usual route, making fifteen knots or so due north, when Morrison saw a dark shape on the horizon ahead of him. He was the officer on watch at the time . . ."

The lieutenant proceeded to relate Morrison's story, along with Captain Gomez's last view of the two steamers heading south, toward Panama. When he was done, Forester asked if there were any other known or possible survivors.

"No sir. And that fits what we've heard via rumor for the last several months—no witnesses. This man Morrison is an anomaly, sir."

Forester raised his eyebrows. "Many would call him a miracle, Lieutenant."

The laconic aide nodded and suggested, "Ironic, is it not, sir, that an American gunboat should appear at the same time as an American renegade pirate?"

"And your point, Lieutenant?"

"They haven't sent a naval vessel to these parts in a while. Now one is here. I think they are sending them south to end the problem sir."

"And?" The flag lieutenant could infuriate Forester sometimes with his slow presentations.

"And it might be a good opportunity for us to associate ourselves with the American effort and cruise the Moskito coast alongside them. We thereby lend credence to our interpretation of the parts of the Clayton-Bulwer Treaty that the Nicaraguans and Hondurans dispute—namely that we really do have a presence in that coast and therefore do have legitimate claim to the log wood settlements. And, of course, sir, it *is* a righteous cause."

Forester thought about that for a moment. It had possibilities.

"Lieutenant, you are quite the Machiavellian. You are also correct. Make sure the opportunity arises this evening for us to talk with our American cousins about a joint venture."

Wake's second call was to the American consulate. The consul was attending the party that evening as well and told Wake he would enjoy it immensely. Wake thought it prudent not to tell the man that he never enjoyed such social functions, that he thought them boring and a waste of considerable money.

After paying his respects to his countryman he met with the Venezuelan and the Spaniard. Their consuls were going to attend that evening as well.

"A gala international affair, a good *fiesta de la noche!*" said Monteblanco with obvious delight. "Peter Wake, my friend, you looked pained at the thought of a party. Really, you are allowed to relax occasionally, and the English girls, they have such a pretty accent of your language, no?"

"Yes, Don Pedro Monteblanco, you have me there. The English girls do have a pretty accent."

Monteblanco rendered that into Spanish for Toledo, who laughed and gave a good-natured punch to Wake's arm. Then Monteblanco added in English, with a mock conspiratorial air, "And Peter, I think they have *other* pretty things as well. . . ."

Toledo joined Wake in a laugh when that was translated, then made his own opinion known.

"It is all for naval good will, my friends. All for naval good-will."

19

A Myriad of Motives

Cayo Holandes was a small island. With *El Gringo's* men from the steamer all on the island, it soon got overcrowded. The celebration lasted three days, with men drinking until they dropped, then waking up and drinking again. What they did not have for a party was women, for none were on the packet when they captured her. And that made them all drink that much more and get that much more violent when the fighting started.

El Gringo Loco knew they would start fighting among themselves on the second day, but he didn't care. He had too many men anyway, too many hands in the till, too many mouths to feed, and too many chances for rebellion. He didn't mind at all if they killed off a few of their number.

Besides, he was very busy going through what he had found in the captain's cabin. It wasn't loot—the valuable commercial cargo was carried forward and since there were no lady passengers there was no jewelry—no, for him it was more intriguing than that. It was the official mail, coming from ports all around the lower Caribbean. And the really fascinating thing to the renegade American pirate was that some of the correspondence was about *him*.

There was the official mail from the Colombian authorities in Bogotá acknowledging the presence on their nation's coast of a *yanqui* pirate and warning all port captains to be on the lookout for information regarding him. There were descriptions of him from Nicaragua and from the American company in Panama. Noticeably absent was any mention of him in letters or reports from Cartagena, except one.

He smirked with humor as he read Swanson Singleton's letter to the Department of State in Washington, asking as the official consul of the United States, for the assistance of a U.S. Navy gunboat in tracking down an ex-American mercenary "gone bad, very bad." Singleton detailed how the pirate, he did not know the name, used a man in Cartagena named Toro Caldez to sell the belongings of his victims. He went on to say that Caldez periodically went to sea with the pirate and had a part in the brutal slayings of innocent women and children. Singleton said the only way the depravity would be stopped was if this Caldez was killed, then the renegade American would have no base of operations. According to Singleton, Caldez was the mastermind of the whole thing.

El Gringo realized that his original plan could be enhanced by this new information. He was very glad he had taken the time to read all of the mail. Mail, he knew from his days of tracking Confederate raiders, was a weak link to most endeavors.

Now, when he next went into Cartagena to see his friend Swan about selling some items, he would have an even more profitable time because he would be getting more of the money since old Swan wasn't going to get any. He would be dead.

And that would happen soon, for he was leaving tomorrow.

Toro knew something was wrong. Singleton wasn't acting frightened anymore. He had paid, of course, but since then hadn't acted like others who had felt Toro's wrath. Toro had planned on keeping him around for a while, but perhaps, he surmised, it was time for Swan to go away. Who would deal with the ship captains? Toro did not know, but was sure that there would be little trouble in finding another *gringo* to accept the money for the task There were many in this port who would do anything for a lot of rum and a little gold.

Toro laughed when he remembered Singleton's threat about being an important American government official. Only in his mind, Toro said aloud as he smacked a fist down on the plank bar top in the *taverna*, scaring the girl beside him. Only in his greedy little mind.

As much as Wake hated the reception at Admiralty House, Monteblanco reveled in it. As he explained it to Wake and Toledo, where they were warriors out at sea, his field of battle was in the political arena, and his weapons were his mind and his mouth. The two naval officers looked at each other and grudgingly admitted that the Venezuelan was right, and that frequently the real warriors were at the mercy of the diplomatic ones.

Terrington was there as well, playing the role of senior American naval officer present rather well, Wake thought. He handled his liquor and made no social gaffes, explaining pleasantly to Wake that he had been trained at the naval academy at Annapolis, where they bred gentlemen. At first Wake though he was joking, and almost laughed, but then realized the man was completely serious.

As they were preparing to make their departure, Commodore Forester asked the American, Spanish, French, and German naval officers to stay for a drink in his study. Monteblanco was also asked, as were the consul generals of Spain, France, Germany, and the United States. All accepted, intrigued by the offer.

The men arrived in the study, where each was given a glass of port and made his way to a chair or corner with his national colleagues, stewards gliding silently among them with chocolates, nuts, and fruit.

Finally Commodore Forester spoke, thanking them all for staying and explaining that yes, he had an ulterior motive for the invitation beyond their excellent companionship.

"It is late, we are all tired, and I will be mercifully brief, gentlemen." He got the hoped-for laugh. "We, all of us, have a problem. A deadly serious problem. Piracy is afoot in these waters, and I am not talking about the usual thieves and scoundrels we have had here for hundreds of years. I am talking about a modern, sophisticated, and absolutely ruthless pirate organization that makes anything else we've had to deal with paltry by comparison."

He paused long enough for the French consul to say, "Really, Commodore, worse than say . . . Morgan? Or Drake?"—which raised another laugh from the men, except from the Spanish, who still were angry about the notorious English depredations three hundred years earlier.

"Incredibly, Mr. Consul General, yes—even worse than the English buccaneers." Forester had their attention as he continued. "There is a former American naval officer," he glanced at the Americans and shrugged slightly in apology, "who has been using a steamer to plunder ships and kill people along the Moskito coast and the Panama isthmus. He has been getting bolder and bolder. Several days ago he attacked and captured the Panama steam packet that routinely comes to this port." Several of the men gasped at the news, others shook their heads and looked at the floor as Forester went on.

"They killed everyone aboard and threw the bodies overboard, but through a miracle of God one man has survived and is in this port as we speak, struggling to live. He has given a description of the event and the pirate—a tall, muscular man, who is very pale with splotches of sunburn. The man is without human decency of any sort.

"The reason I have asked all of you here this evening is

twofold. One, do any of you know anything further about this man or his evil endeavors? And two, will you provide naval assistance to an effort to go after him and rid our area of this scourge? Captain Terrington, as senior vessel commander present by virtue of your rank, could you be kind enough to start?"

Terrington's eyes went wide. He had been about to order another port from the steward and was caught by surprise. He began stammering something about a routine patrol cruise when the U.S. consul general held up his hand and told Terrington to just tell everyone why he was really in the area.

"All right, we are here specifically to track down this man and stop him."

The German *oberleytnant*, commander of the *Meteor*, guffawed and said, "With one gunboat? You will be chasing your tail around the Caribbean! Where is your navy?"

Commodore Forester didn't like the German's rudeness and came to Terrington's defense. "The Americans have demonstrated to us in the Royal Navy *twice* in the past hundred years just how much damage a single ship can do to the enemy, Captain. I would never underestimate them." Forester turned to Terrington, to whom he had taken a disliking, but still needed for his plan. "Captain Terrington, would you like our assistance in your efforts?"

Terrington glanced at his consul general, who nodded. "Why yes, sir. It would be greatly appreciated."

"Quite welcome, Captain Terrington. Does anyone else wish to assist in the effort?"

There was a commotion among the Hispanics—Monteblanco, Toledo, and the Spanish consul all speaking at the same to each other. Monteblanco took control and turned to the others in the room.

"The Spanish consul has asked that I relate first that their navy is profoundly grateful to the Americans for saving their ship and that second, they would be honored to assist their colleagues in the American and British navies, but the *Sirena* needs repairs to be completed before she can participate. Then she is at your disposal. The consul for Spain has given his authority and approval, sir."

The Spanish consul added, "We will not shrink from our duty, if only our ship can be repaired quickly enough here in Kingston."

Forester bowed to the Spaniards in appreciation while mentally noting that they had just gotten the British to fund a repair job for their warship. Neatly done, he thought.

"On behalf of our American friend, and the Royal Navy, I say thank you to the gallant gentlemen from Spain. I must also add that our own vessel which will be part of this effort, the *Plover*, must undergo some scheduled repairs herself before departure. Captain Terrington, do you mind waiting for a week at the most? Our ship will be ready by then, probably earlier, and we can get *Sirena* repaired in that time also."

"Ah . . . no, sir. No problem with that. We'll wait a few days," answered Terrington.

"Excellent. This is shaping up nicely. Now, do the distinguished gentlemen of the French Navy care to join? Or our friends from the German Federation of States?"

The German consul was the first to reply with a flat "no, this is not our concern." He was followed by the French consul who said that the men of his navy would love to go down to that coast and kill the vermin who prey upon innocent men of the sea, but *unfortunately* the naval ship had orders to return to Martinique and could not participate.

"Ha! At least the Germans are honest," whispered Monteblanco to Wake. "The French hope the pirates get even bolder for now because they are trying to get the Colombians to sell transit canal rights to their engineer Lesseps, who just dug the Suez Canal. They want the American company to fail in Panama." Wake nodded, amazed at the complex myriad of motives and relationships in the Caribbean. Nothing was easy, or as it first appeared.

Forester appeared unfazed by the refusals to help. "Very good, gentlemen. I think we now have an idea of the situation. I thank you all for coming and being so candid and helpful. And of course, I trust that as gentlemen you will keep our meeting and conversation confidential."

They all said that oh yes, it was confidential, it must be, that it shouldn't get out—making Forester wonder how many hours it would be until everyone in Kingston knew about the operation.

20

Senior Officer Afloat

June, 1869

It was normally two or three days' sail from Cayo Holandes to Cartagena, but it took *El Gringo* a week after he left Cadena and Romero at the island. *Abuela* was a slow, leaky, foul-bottomed pig, and he cursed Rosas several times a day as they tried to get the schooner to sail close to the wind, but fell back each time. Finally they got her up to Barbacoas Bay, around to Isla de Rosario, and into the ancient fortified harbor at the center of the city, where they anchored among a hundred other decrepit-looking schooners.

The ex-American, dressed as a common seaman in filthy ragged clothes and broad-brimmed straw hat, had himself rowed into the heart of the city, past massive fortresses built hundreds of years earlier, to the old imperial dock. There he started his walk through the crowded, winding streets with their overhanging balconies, the sounds of *puya* music and smell of cooking beans, fish, and rice everywhere. He stopped at a tavern around the corner from the Plaza de la Aduana, smiling as he thought how much the treasury police would most certainly like to get their hands on him, if they only knew he was so close.

As he ate his pork and rice, washed down with rum and beer, he listened to the music and the sailors' conversations in English, Dutch, and French, as well as Spanish. He talked with the girls, but did not buy one, just waited. Attracting no special attention, he looked like another *gringo* seaman in a town full of lost souls from around the world.

He had no doubt that Swan would come eventually, the shyster had been stopping there each week for years to spend time with the old lady in the kitchen during *siesta*. It was just a matter of waiting.

Wake had had a headache for days, but hoped this sea air would help. The frustrations of dealing with the British and Spanish were taking their toll. And Terrington wasn't helping at all. He stayed in his cabin during the day, emerging at night briefly to go ashore for social dinners with the consul. Telegraphs reporting the situation had been sent to Washington, via Havana and Key West, and finally, after six days, approval had been given for *Canton* to lead the multi-national expedition against the pirate operation.

The British and Spanish ships had taken a week to refit and repair, while Wake put his own men through their paces to make sure that all was ready for action when it came. Gunnery and small arms exercises, rowing competitions between the launch and the cutter, and emergency damage repair were practiced every day.

But it was Terrington, more than anything else, that was bothering Wake. The man was a mercurial drunk, of course, but his behavior indicated that something more than alcohol was fueling his bizarre mood changes. Wake became sure of that the day Commodore Forester invited the senior officers of the expedition, which by now included Monteblanco, *ex officio*, to meet him at the hospital so they could question Morrison.

Forester's thinking was that perhaps they could think of a question the Brits had not, and therefore reveal a piece of information that would be instrumental in the hunt for the pirate who was causing this destruction. Wake agreed and joined the group, but Terrington declined until Forester pressed him, saying as senior ship captain he should certainly know everything available.

When they got to the hospital Terrington hung back, not entering Morrison's ward until the Jamaican nursing sisters brought him in. Morrison was obviously in pain and still critically ill. It was still not known if he would live through the wound's infection, but he was answering the questions as well as he could—until Terrington walked in. Then Morrison grew quieter, looking anywhere but near the American captain. Wake noticed it and was sure that others had too. He also saw that Terrington asked no questions and stood behind the others.

Then two odd things happened, the first of which surprised Wake and the second of which disgusted him.

Captain Russell asked the final question of Morrison—could he please provide as detailed a description of this *Gringo Loco* chap as he was able to remember. Morrison gave the particulars: six feet, three or four inches; thin but muscular; short light-colored hair; very fair skin, splotched with sunburn; and a neutral northern states accent, probably from the middle of the region. Then he pointed at Terrington and said, "Just like him." The assembled officers, except for Terrington, who looked aghast, chuckled nervously. Forester thanked Morrison and then departed the room, followed by the others.

And then, as they were walking out of the hospital, Wake spotted his captain remaining behind in an office area and talking to one of the black nursing sisters, who was handing him a distinctive small blue bottle. Wake knew what was in it—they had similar bottles in the medicine chest aboard *Canton*. Terrington came down the hallway a moment later and greeted Wake cheerfully, saying that he was glad the hospital visit was over, he hated the smell of the places, and that they should return to the ship.

Wake was too disgusted to ask Terrington why he needed a bottle of laudanum. Besides, he admitted to himself with a sigh, by now he already knew—his captain was not only a drunk: he was a drug addict. And Wake didn't know what to do about it.

The first day of June, nine days after Commodore Forester had called his late night naval gathering, *Canton*, with her coal replenished, led the three ships steaming out of Kingston Harbor, past the naval station at Po rt Royal and the batteries at Fo rt Charlotte and on Henderson Hill. Wake thought of the days of Morgan as they steamed beyond Gallows Point and shook his head in wonderment of his own mission in this modern day in 1869. More pirates.

The gun salutes were still echoing off the hills as they made their way around Drunkenman's Cay and the South Cays and, with massive Portland Point on their starboard, took their departure south toward Panama. Monteblanco had agreed to the plan, even though it delayed his return to Venezuela. He told Wake that he thought perhaps he could be of service, not only for his language skills, but because he knew the politics and personalities of the region so well. Wake had been hoping that the diplomat would stay aboard—his insight had been invaluable—and also understood the personal motives of the man. Wake would need to be there too if he were in Monteblanco's place.

The plan was vague. They were to head south and search for the renegades, engage them, and kill them. Apprehension for trial was not even discussed. Exactly how and where they would search was left up to the expedition commander, Parker Terrington.

It was agreed among the parties that the Americans would lead the effort since they had the senior man among the ship captains—Terrington was a lieutenant commander, Russell was jun-

ior to him, and the Spaniard was only a lieutenant—and because
the leader of the pirates was an American, or *former* American as
Wake corrected them. What was not said, of course, was that if
things went badly, the Americans would be at fault. And a lot of
things could go badly, Wake admitted at a meeting of *Canton's*
officers in the wardroom.

They were heading into an area that was mostly uncharted,
with hostile Indians, terrifying diseases, legendary poisonous animals, swarms of biting insects, a swirl of political machinations,
and on top of all that, Wake pointed out to his officers, an enemy
that had forgone any humane tendencies. If you were captured by
this enemy, he told them as he remembered Morrison's vivid depic-
tion of the attack, you would be begging to be killed quickly.

But the preparations were in the past. They were all as ready
as they could be as they stood out to sea, and left the civilized
comforts of Jamaica and the British Empire behind them.

Wake realized that at some point a more definitive plan would
have to be decided upon and that Terrington was neither competent, nor coherent, enough to accomplish that task. So he met
with Custen, Connery, and Monteblanco the first night at sea
and went over the possibilities.

They knew that Cartagena was important as the place where
the pirates sold their booty and obtained things they could not
find aboard their victims' ships. It was the source of their money.

They knew that the Moskito coast of Costa Rica and
Nicaragua was the hidden base of operations for the pirates, and
that the area impacted by their depredations extended from
Colombia to Honduras and from Panama almost up to Jamaica.
That area included several small islands out in the Caribbean.

As they discussed the problem and their assets, it became obvious to Wake that they would have to split up and search different

areas. The Spanish would be well suited to cover the Moskito coast, the British could search along the Panamanian coast, and the Americans would go into Cartagena. They would split up after checking at Old Providence Island and St. Andrews Island for signs of the pirates, then reassemble at Porto Bello, on the Panama Isthmus, in three weeks to assess their options at that point.

Wake proposed the plan to a surly Terrington the following morning and got a half-hearted, begrudging approval. An angered Wake was tempted to confront the man about his addiction, but wondered what he would do next if the captain forced a showdown. Should he forcibly remove him from command? *Could* he forcibly remove him from command? The naval regulations allowed for relief of a captain when he was incapacitated by wound or catastrophic illness—but Wake's question was right on the dangerous edge of mutiny.

Deliberating in his cabin, Wake grimly reasoned that it was better to maintain the captain in his present position than to disrupt the efficiency of the mission and image of the U.S. Navy by a possibly violent confrontation with Terrington. There was no telling where such a confrontation would lead, and Wake knew that once he started down that road he would have to be ready to go all the way, using force if necessary to remove the captain from command.

The men of the *Canton* were going into a perilous area against dangerous men, alongside new international allies. Now was not the time to compound the uncertainty and danger of the situation. Besides, so far he had been able to contain Terrington as long as he thought he was in command. Surely this strategy would work a little longer, long enough to complete this mission and then get Terrington to a place where he could be helped—and never be in command again.

Wake sat there in the swaying gloom of his cabin. He was uneasy, wondering whether his decision not to confront the captain had more to do with personal hesitancy than professional evaluation—and if they would make it back to an American naval station before he had to employ that dreaded last resort.

Singleton expected that it would take weeks, possibly a month, before he would hear from the Office of Consular Affairs at the Department of State in Washington. In the meantime he would placate Toro and maintain his business operations, while replenishing the get-away stash he had hidden.

It bothered him that Rosas was gone so long. It had never been this long before. They had had mutually profitable dealings for some time now, and the man's absence was troubling. Had Toro gotten to Rosas? Had Rosas switched business partners? Was this another sign that Singleton's days in Cartagena were dwindling?

He put it out of his mind as he walked down *Calle Real,* past the *Catedral de San Pedro Claver,* to the waterfront to deal with the merchant ship that had just come in from Aruba. She had some Dutch ironwork and fancy goods to sell, and her captain had heard that the man known as Swan could be trusted.

Singleton laughed inwardly at the thought that someone had said he was a man to be trusted. He wasn't even really Swanson Singleton. The real Singleton had been killed in a robbery on his way to his new post in Cartagena on the long road from Bogotá. The man's identification papers and consular documents had been sold cheap by the outlaws, and since the real Singleton was unknown in Cartagena, it had been easy to *become* the man.

Singleton got into a rowboat at the docks, told the old man the name of the Dutch ship, and sat down in the stern while he was taken to where she was anchored in the outer harbor. As the old fisherman labored away at the oars, Singleton eye's swept over the anchorage to see if any new ships, and potential deals, had come in that he didn't know about. He examined the inner harbor in the *Bahía de las Ánimas,* then looked over the outer harbor. But his eyes returned to something odd in the inner harbor.

Singleton felt a chill run down his neck as he looked at one vessel among the others.

There, anchored in her usual place, was *Abuela,* the schooner of that old goat Rosas.

The ships swayed gently in the undulating swells on the leeward side of St. Andrews Island. The fishermen ashore at both Old Providence and St. Andrews had told the American landing party that they had seen no sign of any pirates, but the way they said it indicated fear of reprisal. Rork, in charge of the landing, told Wake he thought they were lying.

Meanwhile, the meeting of the ships' captains was held in Terrington's cabin. The American captain actually impressed Wake, putting on his best façade and asking each foreigner for their views of the situation and suggestions on how to accomplish their mission. He then asked his executive officer to present the proposed plan.

After it had been laid out and questions about individual responsibilities answered, Terrington stood up at the table and asked the others if they would please give him a "vote of confidence and approval."

The assembled naval officers were stunned, Monteblanco confused, and Wake was embarrassed. The cabin was silent except for the creaking of the frames. Terrington's eyes darted around, and Wake was trying to think of something to say to salvage the American Navy's reputation when Captain Russell spoke up.

"Ah, Captain Terrington . . . sir. You've been given command of us by our superiors, sir. You don't need a referendum, Captain. Your authority and responsibility for this operation is total and unquestioned. You are the senior officer afloat."

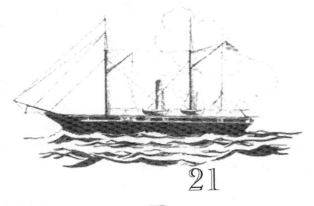

21

Patience

Cadena was initially excited that they now had three ships. The possibilities were endless with the power they now enjoyed. In fact, Cadena grandly realized, they were the most powerful force of ships in the lower Caribbean. He, Alfonso Cadena, son of a whore and an unknown father, was the second in command of a *fleet* that caused everyone to have fear.

Romero and Cadena had their hands full handling the men, who were getting restless. Porto Bello was less than five hours steaming time away from their hideout and several of the louder men were making noises that they could strike at sunrise, take loot and women, and be back by the sun's meridian. And then, they told the others, a serious party could be had on this miserable little island.

But the men did not understand that they needed discipline to use the ships in the best manner. *El Jefe* understood, and while Cadena's hatred of the man was growing, he did admit that the *gringo's* leadership had brought them this far. Many of the men had drunkenly dismissed their success as merely the good luck of a roll of dice. Cadena knew differently.

Captain Fernando Toledo was pleased because of several things. First and foremost, his ship had not wrecked at Haiti on her way to Puerto Rico, and for that he would be forever grateful to the American sailor Peter Wake and to God. Second, the British, of all people, had taken care of his repair needs and even cleaned his hull, and who would have ever thought that would happen? And third, his government had given permission for *Sirena* to participate in the operation against the pirates, which would give his crew a chance to do what they were in the navy to do—fight enemies, not their own citizens. It would also get them away from the problems in Cuba, give them pride in the glory of Spain, and respect from the Americans and the British.

For Fernando Toledo, this was an opportunity of a lifetime. A personal moment of truth. And he had made it quite clear to his officers and petty officers that the *Sirena* would be successful in their mission to search the coast of Nicaragua and Costa Rica. They would find the enemy, and they would destroy him.

However, he had no false expectations, for Toledo knew the coast was very dangerous aside from the pirates. It was full of uncharted reefs and islands, the diseases were notorious, and the Indians very dangerous.

As they closed on the Los Cayos Moskitos, a group of coral rock islets thirty miles off the coast, Toledo set his jaw and told the officer of the watch to call out the landing party. They would search every part of these islands. Then they would search the coast. The men of *Sirena* would continue without end until they found the pirates.

HMS *Plover* rolled heavily in the following sea as she headed due west from St. Andrews Island to Punta Perla, far north of the Costa Rican-Nicaraguan border and more than two hundred miles north of where the Americans had directed Captain Russell to go. Captain Terrington's orders had been to search the coast from the Costa Rican-Colombian border eastward, and Russell speculated what the Americans' reaction would be if they knew where he was actually heading, and why.

Russell watched the sun rise in the mist to the east and thought about his rather delicate position. He had been taken aside by Commodore Forester after the meeting that night at Admiralty House and given further instructions. Private instructions. At some point during the operation, preferably near the start, *Plover* was to close on the Nicaraguan coast and visit each of the English logging and fishing settlements that had sprung up there decades earlier. Russell was to document the English settlements and any complaints the inhabitants had about the Nicaraguan government's lack of protection for them, religious persecution of them, or thievery from them. He was to give out some provisions to engender goodwill and also promise the settlers that their home country would provide the protection they needed, but that his visit was to remain confidential from the Nicaraguan authorities for the time being.

A foreign office official that Russell had seen at the earlier gathering was at the private meeting also. He suavely explained that the Clayton-Bulwer Treaty of 1850 and the Anglo-Nicaraguan Treaty of 1867 had ended the quasi-official British protectorate of a theoretically independent "Moskitia" along that coast, returning the area to Nicaraguan sovereignty. But, he added with an insincere attempt at a regretful tone, recent developments had brought the validity of the assumptions in those

treaties into question. Therefore, Captain Russell's covert recon-
noitering of the situation would prove quite useful in Her
Majesty's subsequent negotiations in the region.

The foreign office man, who had been silent throughout the
evening when the guests were present, smiled and thanked the
captain in advance for his service to the Crown. Then
Commodore Forester had bid Russell good night.

It was an order and as a professional Russell would obey it, but
not with enthusiasm. He respected the American naval officers'
plan and felt more than uneasy about his duplicitous failure to follow it as they expected. Skullduggery . . . and all for what? So the
empire could be expanded? What the hell was on this Godforsaken
coast that Queen Victoria could be proud of governing?

And then it hit him like a belaying pin from above: the old
idea of an isthmian canal across Nicaragua. As part of the treaty
twenty years earlier, the Americans and British had jointly agreed
with the Nicaraguans to someday build a canal, keep it neutral
and unfortified, reimburse Nicaragua, and keep transit rates for
all three countries equal. But what if the coast didn't belong to
Nicaragua? What if the idea of the British protectorate was
revived and officially sanctioned? And what if the white people of
the coast—the Indians wouldn't count—voted in a plebiscite for
British protection? The previous treaties would be null and void,
for the Nicaraguans would not own the Caribbean entrance to
the canal, and thus the British would have control over the most
important canal in the world. Russell slowly shook his head at the
deviousness of it. He had to admit, in a way it was brilliant.

The windswept rock known as Little Coco Island was passing
to port as Russell went over in his mind the positions of the expedition's ships. The Spanish ship *Sirena* was arriving at the Central
American coast only about a hundred miles north of him, and he
knew that he would need to keep going south along the coast well
ahead of her in order for the surreptitious British plan to work.
He did not tell his officers of his private briefing or the ship's
secret mission, only that they would search for the pirates a bit

further north, then head south and east along the coast to meet the other ships at the rendezvous in Panama.

He hoped he could carry off his mission and not embarrass himself or the Royal Navy. "This could end up a right bloody mess," he muttered to the rolling sea.

Monteblanco was buttering his toast at breakfast when Wake asked him for suggestions on how to go about looking for the pirates' contacts, or the pirates themselves, in Cartagena. The *Canton* would be at the infamous city the next day and Wake still did not know what they would do there. The Venezuelan chewed his breakfast while cogitating a response, for he had been thinking about the very the same thing.

"I think we should use the proverbial carrot and the stick, my friend. Go into the town and offer money for information. But do it with a sense of quiet intrigue, so that those who have that information will not be found out when they give it to us. That would be the carrot. The *Canton*, of course, is the stick. If we do not get the information the easy way, then *Canton* stays offshore in international water and searches every vessel coming in or out. That will take more time, but definitely get results also."

"Explain further, Pablo. I understand the stick—that's usually *my* method. But the carrot. How do we offer money to people but not let people know?" said Wake.

"Ah, that is the art of the matter, Peter. You only offer the money to the people you think would know."

Wake was still confused. "How do you know who those people are?"

Monteblanco raised an eyebrow, a grin starting to form. "By the ancient military practice of reconnaissance, my friend. Only in this situation it is not done with a formation of cavalry, boldly riding throughout the countryside. No, no." He waved a finger. "It is done with the quiet but effective assistance of rum, and perhaps a female, in *tavernas*. Do you see my idea now, Peter Wake?"

Wake did indeed see the idea. "And who, by chance, would be doing this reconnaissance?"

Monteblanco laughed mischievously and shrugged his shoulders in the classic Latin style. "Why, the two men most suited for this dangerous mission. You and I. Not dressed as we are now, of course."

Wake laughed at his friend and the notion, then thought about it. Maybe it would work. It was worth a try. "How much money would we need, Pablo?"

"Not so much, I think. Maybe a hundred in gold coins. No, my friend, what we will really need is something that is everywhere in Latin America, but something you Americans find it difficult to use."

"And what is that?"

"Patience, my friend. Patience . . ."

23

Simple Solutions

"Deck there—land ho! Two points on the port bow! A flat-topped mountain."

The officer of the deck, Custen, shielded his eyes against the sun, then turned to Wake and Terrington and repeated the lookout's report. He was acknowledged and dismissed by the captain, who usually never came out in the midday tropical sun, preferring to stay in his cabin and have Wake come there. Wake realized the captain was very concerned about something, or he wouldn't have broken his habit. Terrington returned to the subject of his conversation with Wake.

"Let's see. You and the passenger are going to go gallivanting around Cartagena disguised as a couple of itinerant ne'er-do-wells, drinking rum and trying to give away one hundred gold dollars from the ship's funds in a half-baked effort to get some scummy harbor dregs tell you some probably negligible information about the pirates we are supposed to be after. Do I have that right, *Mister* Wake?"

Wake had to fight to keep from laughing. Terrington was being sarcastic, but his rendition did make the plan sound very farfetched. Maybe he is right, Wake admitted to himself, but how else will we find out anything?

"Sir, the other option is to stay offshore and search every ship, thereby disrupting the other legal trade in the port, some of which takes places with Americans. But that will take weeks or months, and what if the pirates strike in the meantime, when with a little initiative we could have obtained information on them and struck *them* first, sir."

He could see that the captain was weighing the options. Terrington looked down at the deck and shook his head. His brow was creased as if in pain, like he had a severe headache.

"Don't get that damned Venezuelan killed in some knife fight ashore, Mr. Wake. Good God, can you imagine the hell there'd be for me to pay if we got our passenger, a highfalutin diplomat to boot, killed in some bung hole of a bar in a South American shanty town?"

He was still shaking his head while he walked aft toward the hatch as Wake responded. "Don't worry, Captain. I won't get him killed. And . . . sir?"

"What, Wake?"

"I'll try hard not to get killed myself, Captain."

Terrington harrumphed and began to go down the ladder, saying, "You're not the one I'm worried about. You're expendable."

Custen came up and reported, "Sir, that mountain is Cerro La Popa, from what I can figure. That's the mountain at Cartagena. Looks like we're dead on and should sight the city soon. The counter-current here wasn't as bad as the Spanish captain told us it might be."

"Very good, Mr. Custen. Keep everyone alert. They may see a *guardia costa* craft, but probably not. I don't think they have much of a coastal patrol in these parts."

"I guess if they did we wouldn't have to come down here, sir."

"Good point, David."

The wind and seas from the east diminished as they steamed closer to the coast. By the time they had identified the large islands of Baru and Tierra Bomba, and the little islands of Las Rosarias, they were in calm water.

"The chart says to use Boca Chica to enter the main bay, sir," said Custen, one finger on a chart that was strapped down to the chart board by the binnacle. "Evidently, the Spanish built an underwater wall across the mouth of Boca Grande, right next to the city, so we have to enter the bay miles away and steam up to the city from that way, around this island called Baru."

Monteblanco stepped up beside them and explained, "Yes, the British pirate Drake sacked the town three hundred years ago, forcing the Spanish to subsequently fortify it, including building the wall that is under water. Since then, you must take a circuitous route into the city by water. There are fortresses all along the route through the bay. It is the most heavily fortified city in the Western Hemisphere, gentlemen. No fleet has taken it since then, and none can take it now."

Connery joined the group. "Those old walls were pretty good defenses until rifled artillery was placed aboard ships, Don Pablo. A modern rifled gun, even a small one like ours, would make short work of those fortresses."

Monteblanco gave him a questioning look, then glanced over at Wake. "Really, Lieutenant Wake? These are massive fortresses. The very biggest I have ever seen. You will be impressed."

Wake nodded in agreement with Connery. "During our late war, Don Pablo, the Confederates were holed up in some massive fortresses and thought themselves impregnable. The United States Navy showed them otherwise. Lieutenant Connery here was at Savannah when they reduced Fort Pulaski and it surrendered. He saw it firsthand."

"That I did, sir," said Connery. "Went ashore with some other officers afterward to examine our work. Incredible what rifled shells can do to brick or even stone."

They could see the walls surrounding the city six miles away as the *Canton* steamed past Isla Tesoro and into the narrow channel at Boca Chica, still not challenged by a coastal patrol. But then they saw the red, blue, and gold Colombian flag soar up the poles at the two forts that flanked the entrance.

Monteblanco pointed to the forts and explained, "The one on the left is Fuerte San Fernando and the one on the right is Fuerte San José. This is the bottleneck of the route. Both of these forts are covered by the large one up there," he indicated a hill on the large island of Tierra Bomba, "called Castillo San Angel. And there are many others."

Wake saw what he meant, in addition to the ones he had described—San Angel was huge—there were smaller forts everywhere.

Custen asked Monteblanco if the forts were manned, and if yes, by what type of soldiers.

"Very good question, Mr. Custen. They are impressive-looking, but the quality of the armaments and soldiers has diminished since the Spanish left. Only a few regular artillery men and some militia doing their annual duty are in the forts. Unless, of course, an alarm is sounded, then all of the area's militia will rally to their local fort."

Wake was intrigued. "Don Pablo, this is the only way in or out of the bay, and the city, by water?"

"Yes. There is only a meter of water above most of the underwater wall at the Boca Grande entrance. It is an illusion—a trap. You do not see the underwater wall. This is the only way out. You are thinking of something?"

"Well, you never know. That is an important fact to know. What kind of artillery do they have at these forts we are approaching that cover Boca Chica?"

Monteblanco shook his head. "They are old. I know not the details."

Connery looked at the forts through the telescope, then at Wake. "Can't tell for sure, sir. But I'd wager they're some old iron muzzle-loading 32-pounders, the bigger ones're maybe sixty-fours. Probably from the colonial period. Very likely unserviceable except for rendering low-charge salutes. I wonder how long since any have fired a real shot?"

"The war of independence, when the Great Liberator, Bolivar, defeated the Spanish in the city," offered Monteblanco. "Forty-eight years ago."

"And I wonder how many people know the real condition of the forts? I agree, Don Pablo, they do *look* impressive," said Wake as he ordered Custen to render honors to the forts as they passed. Soon shots boomed out across the five-hundred-foot-wide channel.

Connery said, "I was right. Sixty-fours, and old by the sound of them. Even if they can fire shot, I'd not put more than half a charge in them. Range would be a mile, if that."

Custen glanced at his friend and laughed, "So you think they could do the five hundred feet?"

"You're right on that one, David," admitted Connery. "They may not be big or modern, but they don't have to be to cover this channel. They could do it with half-charged grapeshot."

Once through the narrow entrance they continued east into the huge Bahía de Cartagena, sheltered from the Caribbean by Isla Tierra Bomba, then proceeded northward the six miles toward the city itself. Inside the bay were hundreds of small fishing sloops and coastal schooners in dozens of smaller bays and coves. From out at sea the coast by Cartagena had looked sparsely populated, now Wake could see that it was a huge sprawling city.

After they passed Isla Tierra Bomba on the port side, they saw a large gap opening the bay to the Caribbean. Monteblanco gestured toward it. "Boca Grande. That is the false entrance."

Wake could see no sign of the wall just below the surface of the water. Then the peninsula of Cartagena itself started on their left side, wrapping around into the bay as protection for the anchorage within. Dominating the city was the mountain of Cerro le Popa, topped by a monastery that was also a fortress, five hundred feet above the harbor.

No harbor guard boat escorted them, only a few bumboats as they arrived in the outer anchorage by another massive fortress, Castillo Grande. The *Canton* continued into the harbor, letting go in ten fathoms by a small fort, named Punta Pastelillo on the chart. Further up, in the inner harbor, Wake could see many schooners and brigs anchored close in to the shore, which was topped by a thirty-foot-high wall that stretched around the city. Behind the wall, spires and cupolas could be seen. Small boats were in action all over the harbor.

Monteblanco was completely right, Wake acknowledged inwardly, Cartagena was the most fortified city Wake had ever seen. But, he thought with a grim smile, a wall can keep a man inside too.

The plan called for Terrington to stay aboard and handle the official greetings with the port officials and the American consul, and to tell them that the *Canton* was on the coast on a goodwill cruise and to investigate vague rumors of piracy. Monteblanco and Wake, dressed as common seamen, would go ashore in a bumboat that evening.

The Venezuelan and Wake stayed out of sight while Terrington waited for the officials, dressed in his best uniform. Two hours later the delegation, including Singleton the consul, arrived and was entertained by Terrington, who was in a pleasantly gracious frame of mind, in his cabin.

Singleton was mystified when Terrington downplayed their search for a pirate, repeatedly saying they were just cruising the area since it had been so long since an American naval ship had been there. That fooled no one in the delegation, Singleton saw, and the Colombian officials responded by being politely indefinite about the exact nature of the piracy problem on the coast. Was the *Canton* there because of his letter to the State Department, Singleton wondered? It was a far faster response than he had hoped for.

The delegation, after consuming food and drink, departed the ship amidst much handshaking and bowing, leaving Singleton loitering behind. He asked for a private conversation with Terrington, and when they returned to the captain's cabin, Singleton asked if the warship was in Cartagena in response to the letter sent to Washington.

"What letter? I know of no letter," answered Terrington.

"Oh. I sent one to Washington because I know who is the number two man in the piracy gang. A man named Toro Caldez, right here in Cartagena. He sells the loot for them and has arranged," Singleton slowed down to make sure the captain heard the next part, "for men to be killed, ships stolen, and even for white women to be taken into bondage."

Terrington was shocked. "Right here in this city? *White* women into slavery? Good God, how barbaric!"

The captain was hooked, Singleton knew. "Oh yes, Captain. That's why I was so happy to see your ship. The Stars and Stripes. Civilization and decency. Thank God you've arrived."

Terrington wanted to know all about this man Toro and why the authorities did not arrest him themselves. Singleton explained that they were afraid of this man, that his reputation for ruthless killing intimidated many in the city. That part of his story was true, Singleton joked to himself. He just didn't tell the part about how Caldez paid off everyone and how his relatives controlled the government. Several were in the delegation that had just visited the ship.

"He should be shot down like the dog he is, Captain. No trial for the likes of him. He would only use it to make a mockery of our flag." Singleton stood up in his performance of outrage. "He is an *animal* and the sooner he is dead, the better off we will all be."

Terrington agreed but didn't see how they could accomplish that, this being a foreign country. There was international law to think about.

"There is no law here, Captain, international or otherwise. You and our American flag are the only real authority, moral or legal, in the area. It is your decision, but a small group of armed men could end this problem once and for all in Cartagena. One bullet and the problem is ended—the coast in this area is free for innocent shipping since the pirates at sea won't have anyone to sell their loot, and the Americans are seen to be strong and just.

One bullet, and your mission is completed."

Singleton knew he was over the hump, Terrington was nodding agreement with him in principal, but he just couldn't figure out how to accomplish the deed. Singleton would help. "I'll pass the word for Toro Caldez to meet me in his boat in this harbor. It is a red boat and he will be by himself at eleven o'clock tonight by Punto Mazanillo, just astern of you. Instead of me in a boat waiting for him, though, you'll have a boat of armed men waiting, they shoot him—you can come up with any story convenient—and the problem is ended. Piracy in Cartagena is done. You get to go home as a man who did his duty."

"Sold *white* women into slavery, you say?" Terrington repeated.

"A month ago, it was horrible. He's a monster."

"Then the monster will die this evening. It is a duty that must be done."

"On behalf of the decent people of this city, thank you, Captain," Singleton said with sincerity.

"Disagreeable, but necessary, Mr. Singleton. Now, do you have any further information regarding the alleged American pirate?"

Singleton gauged the tone of Terrington's question carefully, noting the lack of conviction, almost as if he didn't want to hear about the *gringo* pirate. No sense in causing problems for *El Gringo Loco*. In fact, with Toro out of the way, perhaps he could do more business with the strange *gringo* robber. Yes, to have Toro killed was one thing, but the American robber was another. Singleton could make even more money from the pirate with Toro gone.

"I think the stories that say he is an American are exaggerated. I think there is probably an Englishman or Irishman with the pirates that these locals mistake for an American. And once their money supplier Toro Caldez is out of the picture, the pirates will probably leave the area."

"Really, you believe that? You feel certain of that?"

"Without a doubt, Captain. I know these Latin people. Once

they see your ship here and know that Toro is gone, they'll fold up and go somewhere else. Don't forget, sir, I've had years of experience here, as the official consul for the United States of America."

"Yes, well I suppose you're right. Then by tomorrow we may have accomplished our mission."

It was getting dark when Terrington showed Singleton to the side of the ship for his departure. The two parted as good friends, congratulating each other on solving the problem expeditiously.

As the captain made his way across the main deck, he saw Wake walking up to him. "Did the consul have any good information for us, sir? I see that he stayed around for a while after the others left."

Terrington had thought this part out. Wake was a cocky, arrogant upstart who had gotten a lot of fame from his stunt with the Spanish ship on the Haitian coast. Well, this time, promised Terrington to himself, the fame would belong to the man who really deserved it—the *captain* of the USS *Canton*. While Wake was off playing cloak and dagger games with that fool from Venezuela, Terrington would make sure that the problem was solved by action. He was looking forward to the reaction on Wake's face tomorrow.

"No, Mr. Wake. He just wanted to spend a pleasant evening with a real live American naval officer. Someone who spoke his own language and could tell him news from home."

"Yes, sir," said Wake, noting the odd demeanor of his captain and wondering if he had been in the laudanum. "Well, we'll be leaving in a few minutes, sir. I'll report as soon as we get back."

"Take your time, Mr. Wake. Take your time. I have no doubt that this problem will have a simple solution and be ended soon."

23

Twists of Fate

They certainly looked the part, dressed in dirty pants and shirts, ripped straw hats, and with grease and dirt rubbed on their skin, Wake thought, as they shuffled along the Muelle de Pegasos, the city wall by the imperial docks. It had been years since Monteblanco had been in Cartagena, but he remembered the general layout and was in the lead.

Wake had asked his friend why they could not contact the Venezuelan consul who had found some of the Monteblanco family jewels being sold, but was told that the man had died suspiciously of a fever a month after recovering the stolen jewelry. So that option was not available. They would have to do this on their own. Monteblanco felt that more of his family's jewelry was probably in the city, and that of other victims as well.

"We go into *Getsemani*, the lower-class part of the town, Peter. That will be the area where we will find a *taverna* with the proper ambiance and clientele."

"I get the feeling you have done this before. Am I right?"

Monteblanco smiled. "Of course. It is what diplomats do. Get information for their country. But I usually do it in far more gentle surroundings—parties, receptions, balls, with champagne and fine food, and dressed as a gentleman."

Wake nodded his understanding. "But the concept is the same."

"Completely, Peter."

Passing by the *Puerto del Reloj*, the original gate in the fortress walls of the inner city, where there was a huge clock, Monteblanco led them to the right, along the *Calle de la Media Luna*, and into the notorious district of *Getsemani*.

"The name of this street means Half Moon?" asked Wake quietly.

"Yes, it stretches in a curve through *Getsemani*. And *Getsemani* is outside the walls of the inner city, just as the original is in Jerusalem. A very difficult area. Be careful, Peter."

Wake noticed that they had two men following them fifty yards back. He mentioned it to Monteblanco, who replied, "They are assessing our value for robbery."

Rounding the corner at an ancient church, the *Iglesia de San Roque*, they entered a side street full of cheap bars and taverns. It looked like any other port to Wake, except that he could hear screaming and laughing in many different languages, and the people in the street looked angry, wary. The two of them walked slowly, shuffling and blending in with the others who went about with eyes cast downward, as Wake tried to find the two men behind them. They were gone.

"We passed the first test, Peter," Monteblanco explained. "They decided we were not worth the effort to rob."

Wake was not so sure, but decided to have faith in Monteblanco's assessment.

"Ah! This is a likely-looking place," Monteblanco said as he led them inside a doorway. Overhead was a clapboard sign that proclaimed "Taverna Internacional" in big uneven red letters. Wake heard a roar of raucous noise as the door opened and they walked inside the dimly lit, crowded room, his senses immediately assaulted by the stench of ale, sweat, and urine.

El Gringo Loco was still waiting. He had consumed half a bottle of rum and several ales and was almost asleep when he heard a commotion from the kitchen. The old lady came out and hugged a man entering by the side door, her words a rattle of unintelligible Spanish to the American. She was obviously happy to see the man and quickly took him into the kitchen. Then the *gringo* got a look at the man and smiled. It was his old acquaintance, Swan Singleton. This would be enjoyable.

El Gringo moved among the tables and back into the kitchen. He found them in an embrace, the woman shedding her apron. She glanced up in fright at the odd-looking man approaching. Singleton turned around and stood there, stunned.

"Go away, woman," the pirate commanded in rude Spanish.

She scurried out the door as Singleton edged backward and carefully, using the title the man preferred, said, "Hello, *Jefe*. It is good to see you again. Do you need me to sell some items tonight?"

"No, Swan. I don't need you to do anything for me anymore, as a matter of fact," said the *gringo* as he closed and slid the bolt on the door to the main room, his eyes never leaving Singleton.

"Something is wrong. What's happened?" Singleton tried to maintain his sense of confidence. "Usually you use Rosas to come to me, and he hasn't been around here lately, though I saw his schooner in port today."

"Rosas? Nah, he is no longer important, Swan. I left him over by Nicaragua and took his ship. He won't be needing it anymore. Our business relationship was severed." He slowly stepped toward Singleton, who had backed into the corner. "In fact, I am reducing the size of my staff, as it were. Weeding out those who are counterproductive."

Singleton knew he was about to die unless he could talk the

man out of attacking him. Singleton always carried a knife, but knew *El Gringo Loco* was faster and stronger. Singleton had always relied on his wits. They had gotten him this far.

"Very good then, we can make more money with fewer people taking it out of the pot. Also reduces a chance for something to go wrong."

"Yes, precisely. By chance, I was reading a letter by someone who was advocating that very thing lately. Of course, he didn't say it in those exact words to the Department of State, Office of Consular Affairs, but the outcome would be the same. By the way is Toro Caldez around? I think he would be very interested in reading that letter. I know I was."

Singleton tried not to show the abject terror welling up inside him, but he saw that his hands were trembling as he put them up in supplication. *El Gringo Loco* had somehow gotten the letter and knew. "No, *Jefe*. You do not understand what has been going on here since your last visit. I had to write that letter. Toro is out of control. He is alienating the ship captains and the city people. He has gone crazy with power and will ruin it for us all."

The pale man raised an eyebrow. "Crazy, Singleton? Some have called *me* crazy. That is their name for me."

"But not me, *Jefe*," Singleton pled. "I see your wisdom, your vision for making money." He was trying to speak without fear, but his voice was cracking. He had to hold together. There was one more asset that he had. It was time to use it, and he summoned up all of his abilities.

"And, there is an American warship that came into the harbor this afternoon. Obviously not in response to my letter. She is here on anti-piracy patrol to investigate the rumors. Of course they contacted me and asked my opinion, as the official representative of the American government. I told them that the rumors were exaggerated about a former American running the . . ." he tried to think of an appropriate word, "enterprise, and that once Toro was out of the way, things would return to normal. I told them he was the leader, and they are going to take care of him. Tonight in the harbor, they will eliminate him. We will be free of his bungling and the Americans will leave, knowing they have solved their problem."

Singleton felt more confident as he talked. The lunatic *gringo* robber was listening intently. The shyster knew he had turned the corner and would live. "I have given you a chance to escape, *Jefe*. And to increase your profits. It has worked out well, for my official position here is very valuable for us in the future. The American navy will believe anything I say."

"I agree, Swan. Until they find out who you really are, they will believe you."

"They won't find out," replied Singleton. "I don't know your real name," he said, trying to sound sincere, "and you don't know mine. Besides, this captain, named Parker Terrington, is an idiot. He believes me completely."

That got the lunatic's attention, Singleton saw.

"What was his name did you say?"

"Terrington . . . and in a way, he sort of looks like you."

El Gringo Loco's mind was working rapidly. His finger was tapping on the table as he mulled over the situation. This latest information about the American captain was unexpected, shocking. What were the odds of that happening? But, he realized calmly, it could all work out very well. He was glad he came personally to Cartagena. Anyone else, like Cadena or Rosas or Romero, would not understand the ramifications, would not know what to do.

There was a thud at the door. The owner shouted that he wanted his kitchen back, they had people waiting for food. Then another thud on the door.

Singleton relaxed, the danger was over. This would pass. He smiled and moved toward the open back door, gesturing to the other man.

"Come on, *Jefe*, let's go have a drink and something to eat. We can think of more ways to make money. I will buy!"

"I think not, Swan. But thanks for the information," muttered the *gringo* pirate as he pulled out the Navy Colt from his waist in a smooth forward motion and put one round into Singleton's face, splattering the back of his head against the wall while the body fell back onto the floor. The thudding against the door stopped.

"Besides, as you said, Swan—only an idiot would believe *you*," said the *gringo* as he stepped over the twitching body and dropped the consular letter down in the widening pool of blood, on his way out the back door of the *cantina*.

Rork was nervous for his old friend. Wake had gone ashore without him, but instead with the foreigner diplomat. And dressed as common sailors. The whole crew was speculating about their mission, most of the conjecture gruesome. Then, after the executive officer had departed the ship, word came below decks for the gunner to send four of his best small arms men aft to Lt. Connery's cabin.

And now Rork, Connery, and the four sailors were drifting in the dark by a point of land, waiting for a pirate to appear. All of them except for Connery, who was wearing a brown shirt and not his uniform, were lying down in the bilges of the launch, so it would appear that the lieutenant was alone and a potential victim. It all sounded like folly to Rork, but the lieutenant appeared to be in favor of it and told the men that when the pirate showed up to rob him, they would suddenly stand up and shoot before he could be shot.

The sounds of revelry drifted across the harbor, punctuated by screams and threats that no one in the boat understood. After an hour, they heard the splash of oars alongside and a Spanish-accented voice calling out in English, "Swan? Is that you? You *hijo de puta*! You had better have a good reason for this. I was about to go to—"

"Now men!" yelled Connery and the sailors stood up and fired a volley into the other boat, shattering the night air, the flash blinding all of them.

"Rork, search him," ordered the lieutenant as they regained their vision and their wits. Rork climbed over into the smaller boat. The man was dead from three rounds into his chest, which the bosun noted with satisfaction were in a small shot group, but wondered where the fourth had gone. He examined all of the pockets, finding a pistol stuck down in the waist and a knife in a pocket, then looked around the boat. He found no papers, nothing else.

"Dump him over, men," said Connery. The sailors exchanged looks, then went over to the small boat and heaved the dead weight over the side, watching it sink down into the scummy harbor water. They looked to Rork, who shrugged and nodded as the lieutenant ordered them back aboard the navy launch.

"You did well, men," Connery told the sailors. "One less pirate to worry about, but there are others out there to deal with. We'll go after them too."

When they returned to the *Canton* and had gotten everything squared away, the sailors went below, ordered strictly by Connery to tell no one what had happened, for the other pirates in the area would be warned. Rork stayed up on deck and stopped Connery just as he was about to report to the captain.

"Ah, Lieutenant, sir. Could ya give me an idea o' what we just did out there? The lads an' me are a bit confused."

"We shot a pirate, Bosun Rork. Simple as that," replied Connery in a harried tone as he climbed down the after hatch.

Rork watched him go and said quietly to himself, "It didn't look that simple to the likes o' me, Lieutenant." The bosun shook his head sadly. "Aye, not that simple at all."

El Gringo Loco heard gunfire as he rowed his own boat in the darkness through the harbor back to his schooner. A volley of rifles he guessed. Somebody was shooting somebody in the harbor. Perhaps the end of Toro Caldez, as Swan Singleton had suggested? If so, then Parker was more stupid than he remembered.

The *Abuela* was just ahead, in the inner harbor, but he rowed past her. He wanted to see the American warship. Finally, he saw her anchored close to shore in the outer harbor, deck lanterns glowing. He could see men moving about on her, the anchor watch probably, and he rowed around to her stern and looked her over from a safe distance in the night. She looked new. Relatively fast. And more importantly, she had those new rifled breech loaders.

He turned his rowboat around and pulled for his schooner, thinking about what the U.S. Navy could do to his operations with a ship like that, then shook his head and laughed out loud. It didn't matter what kind of ship they sent, for as long as she was commanded by the one and only Parker Terrington, she would be no threat to him at all.

El Gringo Loco ruminated on it all, as he eased his oars going alongside the stolen schooner he now called his. What a very odd twist of fate that they should have sent Parker here . . . to get *me*.

24

La Heroica

The tavern was like a hundred others Wake had seen in at ports during his time at sea. It had the same girls sitting along the wall, with the same vacant eyes evaluating the wealth of each customer as he entered, the same tired barmen pouring rum and ignoring complaints, and same angry doorman pushing drunks without money out the door.

The false gaiety and affection of the girls, which lasted as long as the customer had coins in his pocket, gave the room a seething appearance. Behind it all, he saw the same kind of bossman, watching the action without emotion from the corner, that he had seen in so many other places. This saloon did have something unique, though. Wake saw that in the middle of the room, dimly lit by lanterns from the ceiling, was a pit, ten feet across and surrounded by a three-foot-high stone wall.

Monteblanco and Wake made their way across the crowded room, coming close to the mass of men and girls yelling in at least four languages as they watched something going on five feet below them in the pit. Wake looked down as he passed and saw a large caiman alligator chasing a tiny dog around, thrashing its tail as the terrified dog ran this way and that, trying to get away from the snapping jaws. Wake looked at the frenzied faces of the people cheering and tried hard not to show his disgust.

They got a rough plank table near a corner, along a moldy stone wall. A girl came over immediately, introduced herself as Bonita, asked what kind of rum they wanted, and went to fetch them two glasses and a bottle of Diablo. Arriving back, Bonita sat without invitation on Monteblanco's lap, took off his straw hat and stroked his hair, whispering things in his ear that made him laugh. Seconds later, another girl came over and sat in Wake's lap, caressing him while she felt his pockets for money. She said her name was Flora and squealed with delight when she quickly determined he was a *gringo*, for he would probably have more money than a local sailor. A shout went up by the gator pit, and the group of spectators returned to their tables, money exchanging hands, presumably because the dog had finally lost.

The four of them sat there and drank the dark syrupy rum, the girls drinking out of the men's glasses in order to drain the bottle quickly and get more. Two bottles into the evening, Wake was beginning to doubt the wisdom of their plan as Flora fondled him while she whispered things in Spanish in his ear. He looked to his partner for an idea of what to do, but Monteblanco was engaged in a serious conversation in Spanish with Bonita. Wake tried to figure out what to do with Flora, whose putrid breath was about to make him gag, in addition to her making him nervous with her hands.

Then he saw Bonita stand up and leave, winking at Flora, who also got up and disappeared. He turned toward Monteblanco. "What was that about?"

"She is going to get the bossman, who will know where you—the man who wants to know—can find someone who will sell certain jewelry for sale at a good price. You want to take it to the States to sell. I am your interpreter."

Wake tried to think of all the potential avenues of negotiation, the time they had to do it in, and the many dangers to which they were now wide open. He spoke in a low voice to Monteblanco just as Bonita returned. "Tell them the money is not on me tonight, or we'll never get out of here alive."

Monteblanco nodded his agreement as the girl squirmed her way back onto his lap and told him that the bossman was coming. A moment later a stocky man with a ragged scar from his nose to his left ear, and the long straight black hair of an Indian, arrived at the table. He pulled a chair out from under a man at the table beside them, gave him a menacing look, and sat in it across from Wake and Monteblanco. Bonita, staring at the bossman, quickly got up and disappeared.

He had the improbable name of Jesús and the continual habit of bringing his hair out of his eyes and sweeping it behind his head. Jesús said nothing for a moment, examining the two men, gauging them with dark narrow eyes. Then he spoke to Monteblanco in the Creole patois of the coast.

"You want jewelry? No problem. And what ship did you tell Bonita you were from?"

"The *Condor*," Monteblanco explained, "just in tonight from Maracaibo. We leave tomorrow for Kingston, then Mobile."

"I see, *señor*." Jesús scrutinized Wake. "And your friend here, he is the captain?"

"No, no. He is the mate," Monteblanco corrected. "The captain is drunk aboard and doesn't know about our little business. We need to be quiet about such things. He thinks we went ashore to get provisions only."

Jesus nodded, understanding their situation completely. The loud mouth Manuel would be the man for these two. He handled jewelry, among other things.

"You have the money?"

Monteblanco looked askance. "Yes, of course not with us. No offense, my new friend, but some of your patrons do not look trustworthy."

Jesus gave a grudging nod. "Wait here. I will return."

Monteblanco translated the conversation for Wake, then

looked up as Jesús returned, standing there with a smiling man who introduced himself as Manuel Fuentes, purveyor of all things. Fuentes was the opposite of the menacing Jesús and spoke in a breezy pretentious tone, his hands gesturing all of the time.

"My good friend Jesús tells me you are looking for some jewelry to take with you to the United States for resale. Emeralds perhaps? Colombia is famous for our emeralds placed in beautiful gold settings."

Monteblanco replied, "Yes, jewelry. But particularly we are looking for diamonds, large diamonds. One set as a pendant. Those do well these days up in the States."

Fuentes stroked his goatee, then said, "Yes, I know of one. You require this tonight, Jesús said?"

"Yes, we are under obligations to leave and must conclude the transaction tonight."

"I will return in one hour," Fuentes said pleasantly. "Stay here and kindly order another bottle of rum from my friend Jesús. He needs the business, for he has many mouths to feed, some of which are even children."

Monteblanco ordered another bottle as Fuentes left, then explained to Wake that his mother had had a large diamond set in a pendant on a necklace. There couldn't be that many in Cartagena and he would recognize it instantly if he saw it. They could conclude the deal, then take Fuentes out somewhere and get the information from him.

"I would take it as a great favor if you would allow me the pleasure of getting the information from him," requested Monteblanco. "I think you know why."

Wake did indeed, and said, "That is no problem, Pablo. No problem at all."

By Wake's pocket watch it was two o'clock in the morning—two hours and two more bottles later—when Fuentes returned to their corner table. The girls spent the time vividly describing various pleasures they could give the men, while downing rum along with them. Jesús watched the four of them the whole evening from his perch in the far corner. Even at two in the morning, the place was full and noisy, and English and Spanish and Dutch and French all could be heard in the din.

Wake felt light-headed and uneasy. He looked over at Monteblanco, who appeared untouched by the strong cane alcohol. "Are you all right?" he said, glancing at the bottle by Monteblanco's hand.

"No problem, *mi amigo*, Peter. When you are born to drink rum it does not hurt you so badly," replied the Venezuelan as Fuentes sat down with a flourish across from them.

"My wonderful new friends! I have something like what you seek. It is beautiful and very special, having been in the dowry of the daughter of the viceroy when we were still a colony of the empire of Spain. But alas, my friends, it is not cheap," reported Fuentes as another bottle arrived and the girls disappeared again.

"We do not have much money, Manuel Fuentes, but we are here in good faith and will see your offering," countered Monteblanco.

Fuentes looked furtively around them, then pulled a dirty rag out of his pocket and unfolded it in his lap. He held it under the level of the table so that the other two could see that a large diamond pendant, secured to a gold necklace, was resting in the rag. Wake glanced at Monteblanco for any sign of recognition, but saw none.

"Let me hold it and check the weight, Manuel, my friend," asked Monteblanco.

Fuentes hesitated, then allowed him to hold it. Monteblanco examined it more closely, finally asking, "It is not as heavy as I was hoping. Americans judge their diamonds by weight. How much for this piece of stone?"

"For you and your friend, *señor*, a mere one hundred and seventy dollars. In gold, of course. It is obviously worth so much more, but unfortunate complications prevent me from selling it for its true value."

Suddenly a shout went up from the crowd around the pit—another tiny dog had been dropped in and the betting on his time to live was heated. Fuentes immediately snatched the diamond pendant from Monteblanco and placed it back in his pocket.

"Yes or no, *señor*? I have other buyers waiting and must not be rude to them."

Monteblanco translated for Wake, who then shook his head and told him to negotiate on his own initiative. Wake observed Fuentes listening closely and wondered how much English the man understood. In seaports many people understood at least a little English.

"No, *Señor* Fuentes. We do not have that much, but sixty-five dollars would be feasible," said Monteblanco.

Fuentes stopped smiling. "One hundred fifty."

"Unfortunately no." Monteblanco shook his head. "But perhaps seventy-five?"

"Far too low. I have expenses I must pay, my friend—one of which is that evil-eyed Jesús. One hundred and twenty-five. No lower."

"I am sorry, but that is too much, Manuel. We are poor sailors, not rich businessmen like yourself. Eighty-five dollars is as high as we can go."

"One hundred ten. Take it or leave it."

"Ninety-five."

"One hundred ten."

"One hundred dollars American, in gold, and the deal is done right now, *Señor* Fuentes," offered Monteblanco. "That will pay your expenses and give you a nice profit. If that is not agreeable to you, we will take our leave now. We must go before the captain sobers up."

Fuentes stroked his goatee again, then made a show of resignation.

"You drive a hard bargain, but it is done. Where is your money?"

Monteblanco smiled and shrugged. "In a very safe place, *señor*. Meet us at the *Puerta del Reloj* in twenty minutes." He pulled out his watch and showed the time to Fuentes. "We can exchange there, in the open, for the safety of us both."

Fuentes nodded his assent, then listened as Monteblanco continued. "Oh, and my friend, if anyone follows us then the deal is off, and we will become angry. Very angry."

Monteblanco rose from his chair, dropped coins on the table for the rum and the girls, and walked away without waiting for a reply from Fuentes. Wake walked beside him as they shuffled their way through the crowd at the pit. Wake caught a peripheral glance, without intending to, of the alligator closing his jaws on the screaming dog as a shout went up from the onlookers. He gritted his teeth and kept moving, following Monteblanco out the door and into the street.

It was hot and humid, the wind that had kept down the heat earlier having vanished. They retraced their steps quickly, repeatedly glancing behind to check for followers but saw none. Wake asked his friend if he recognized the diamond pendant and was told yes.

When he asked if Monteblanco was absolutely sure, the Venezuelan stopped and said with barely controlled rage, "When I asked to see it more closely I saw my father's initials on the back. He gave it to my mother for their twenty-fifth anniversary. I remember it very well, Peter."

Then he started walking again. When they had gone several blocks Monteblanco stopped and quickly sidestepped into an alley, explaining that here was where they would take Fuentes.

As they waited in the darkness Wake drew his revolver from his pocket, feeling troubled that he was standing there like a common criminal, in a city of common criminals. It was as if he had become one of them.

They heard steps coming up the street. Fuentes was accompanied by another man who walked three paces ahead of him, examining the doorways and alleys, obviously some sort of bodyguard. Wake and Monteblanco pressed themselves against the wall, in the black of the night shadows, as the first man walked by. Then they leaped out behind Fuentes, grabbed him quickly by the throat from the rear, snatched him off his feet and back into the narrow alley, choking him into silence.

The bodyguard heard the sounds behind him, turned and saw nothing, his man gone. He ran back, pistol drawn, and turned into the alley to find himself staring at the muzzle of Wake's revolver, inches from his eyes. Wake took the gun from the stunned man and waved him back out into the street. The bodyguard raised his hands and retreated slowly, saying, "*Tranquilo, señor. Tranquilo, por favor,*" until he was in the street. Then he ran away toward the *Puerta del Reloj*.

Monteblanco dug the diamond out of Fuentes pocket and used the rag to gag him as he pushed him along the alley. Wake saw the Venezuelan's eyes were even and cold. Wake's unease was building. This was going to be murder, and no amount of explanation could justify it. They emerged on another street, Monteblanco still pushing Fuentes violently along, the man's eyes bulging with fear above the rag stuffed in his mouth.

At another alley, Monteblanco suddenly kicked Fuentes into the shadows and then hit him hard in the left eye, knocking him down into the gutter. Wake watched the street, trying to decide what to do. He couldn't allow his friend to kill Fuentes, but they needed the information to stop others from being victims.

The Venezuelan knelt and leaned close to Fuentes, his voice low and measured through clenched teeth. "That diamond is from my mother, Fuentes. Do you understand? From my mother who was on the ship that the *gringo* pirate took." Fuentes started to cry, whimpering into the rag.

"I want to kill you slowly, like they did to my mother and father. You will pay for dealing in the filthy trade you practice. You will pay for every single victim." Fuentes began begging unintelligibly.

Monteblanco produced a small pocket knife, flicked the blade out and put it to Fuentes' throat. "I will gut you and bleed you out like an animal. But I want to hear you beg first."

Then he took the rag out, holding it in readiness, and Fuentes choked out the words, "Please. Please. I am sorry. I was not there. I did not know."

Monteblanco rammed the rag back in and sliced the knife lightly along Fuentes' neck. Wake moved closer, about to intervene as his friend continued.

"But you *do* know. You know a lot about *El Gringo Loco* and how he works. Do you want to live, with your face intact? I have waited for this exact moment. To avenge my mother and father, and you are my target. You will pay. Now."

Fuentes nodded his head, kept nodding and whimpering until Monteblanco released the rag slightly.

"I . . . will . . . tell," he gasped. "I will tell what I know. Please let me tell," he begged.

"You are going to tell me everything you know."

"Yes, I will. Please let me live. I did not know. I swear I did not know it was from your parents."

"You have five minutes to convince me to let you live."

Fuentes could barely speak from terror, but he gradually explained that *El Gringo Loco* had several dealers in Cartagena that he worked with. One was Fuentes, who only occasionally dealt in the pirate's stolen jewelry. Another was the American consul, Singleton, who dealt in ships' cargo that was taken from the pirate's victims, and the third was a man named Rosas, who sailed a schooner called *Abuela*, and who dealt in stolen ship's equipment and sometimes jewelry.

He said Rosas' schooner was in the inner harbor, but the man was missing. Everyone assumed the *gringo* had killed him somewhere and taken the boat. There was also a rumor that earlier that ve ry evening someone had killed Toro Caldez, a man who transported much of the *gringo* pirate's loot out of the city and who made a deal to exempt Cartagena vessels from being victimized.

Caldez got away with it because of his relation to the city's leaders.

Wake was astonished as Monteblanco translated Fuentes' narration. The American consul was part of this? And the pirate's schooner was here?

In response to Wake's and Monteblanco's questions, Fuentes said he had met *El Gringo Loco* three times, many months ago. The rumor was that the man had skin that could not stand the sun, so he stayed off the deck in the day, only coming out at night or for capturing a ship. He did not know the man's name, but believed he was a former naval officer in the *yanqui* navy, who came to the area as a mercenary for the English settlers on the Moskito coast after the war between the American states. When they could pay him no longer, he went out on his own, captured a steamer, and started to plunder ships.

Fuentes said that the *gringo* had a man named Cadena who was his number two and was like an animal. The girls in Cartagena refused to service him because of his cruelty. He also had a man named Romero, who was as bad. There were maybe thirty men with the pirate, perhaps a few more. Fuentes thought they were based somewhere on the Moskito coast north of Limon, in Costa Rica.

"Is he here in Cartagena now?" seethed Monteblanco in Fuentes' ear.

"I do not know, but Rosas' schooner came in this morning, so he might be on her."

Wake asked, "The American consul, where is he?" Fuentes gave them the location of his office and a few places he visited often.

Monteblanco shifted the knife in his hands, his eyes never leaving Fuentes, then moved closer to the man. Wake realized what was about to happen and pulled Monteblanco up from Fuentes, who was crying and babbling in terror.

"Pablo, don't do it. It will be murder, and then you'll have descended to *their* level."

Monteblanco regarded the quivering shape in the gutter. The

knife was still clenched in his hand, next to Fuentes' carotid artery. Wake saw the muscles in his jaw tense. Abruptly, Monteblanco exhaled loudly and walked away into the street, leaving Wake with Fuentes collapsed on the stone pavement.

Wake took the rag and put it back into the man's mouth, then ripped Fuentes' shirt off and tied his hands behind him. He dragged him to a post and lashed him there. Holding a finger up to his mouth, he said, "*Silencio . . .*" to Fuentes, who nodded quickly. Then Wake left to find his friend.

He caught up with him a block away. They walked briskly toward the docks.

"You did the right thing just then, Pablo. Your father was a man of peace. You did tonight what he would have wanted."

"Yes, perhaps, Peter. But it was not what I wanted."

Wake put his hand on his friend's shoulder. "I know, Pablo. I know . . ." Wake continued, trying to change the subject, "And now we need to get back to the ship and report. This situation is far worse than I thought. What a mess this place is in. Is this entire city sick, Pablo? Is no one here decent?"

They were at the old docks by the *Muelle de Los Pegasos*. Monteblanco stopped and surveyed the scene around them.

"It is especially ironic, Peter, how far *this* city has sunk in human nature. It was once the most famous city in all of Latin America for its pride and honor. In fact, the Great Liberator, Bolivar himself, gave this city a name of honor because of the thousands who died here for independence. I am afraid that he would not recognize it today by its behavior, for it has lost all of its honor." Tears filled Monteblanco's eyes as he turned to his friend. "And do you know what Bolivar named this city, Peter?"

Wake shook his head in silence, transfixed by the grief welling up in Monteblanco for the lost honor of two generations earlier.

"He proclaimed it *La Heroica*. The Heroic City. It was the model for all our people, everywhere."

Monteblanco sighed and descended the steps to a dory where an old man waited to ferry sailors out to their ships after a night ashore. The Venezuelan uttered one last comment as he sat in the stern of the dory and waved his arm over the harbor of Cartagena. "And just look what greed and avarice have made it now."

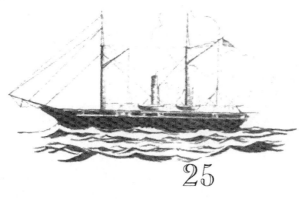

25

Moskito Coast

Captain Russell threaded *Plover* through the maze of reefs along the Nicaraguan coast carefully, for the charts were notoriously inaccurate and the currents confusing. At Punta Perla, Green Corn, and Blowing Rock he was met with distrust from the Anglos, who felt abandoned by their mother country, and apathy from the Indians, who couldn't care less which whites claimed the coast—they suffered under all of them. Both the Anglos and the Indians the British encountered had heard of the *yanqui* pirate, speaking of him with respect in their voices, but none of them had seen or knew anything in detail. Russell did not believe them at all.

When he questioned them further about the American originally fighting as a mercenary for them in '66 and '67, they feigned ignorance, even when he told them he had proof. He had the strong impression that they were in fear of the American's wrath. But still, he could get no one to talk, so it was only his impression.

Russell documented each encounter along the coast, made his required promises and gifts, and moved on down the coast to

Bluefields. At that larger settlement, almost a town, he found more enthusiasm for the Royal Navy, particularly among the Anglo merchants. The animosity against the Nicaraguans was palpable because of their exorbitant taxes, which had never been the case under the British. The local Nicaraguan government tax collector had to be guarded by a company of troops brought in from Managua, and all of them were regarded as occupiers by the local English.

The Anglos were upset that the British had given them to the national government and ended the official recognition of their fledgling colony of Moskitia in 1867, but were encouraged by the potential for a return to the empire represented by *Plover's* visit.

Russell then heard the locals' scheming—a canal could be dug starting just south of Bluefields at the San Juan River, going up to Lake Nicaragua and crossing over to the Pacific. British and American surveyors were already plotting out elevations and routes for competing companies, and there was eager speculation on how much money could be made by everyone from a canal. However, the merchants told him, in the current political climate the construction of a canal couldn't be done as the situation was just too confused by various treaty limitations, financial concerns, and the Managuan government's corruption. But, they said, if only the British Crown would reassert control over the coast, then perhaps the political climate would be stable enough to allow the project.

Russell found himself becoming more intrigued by the idea. It would be one of the wonders of the world, saving shippers months of time and sailors the perils of rounding the Horn. He now understood the glint in the eye of the foreign office man at the Admiralty House that night. The possibilities were incredible, but he knew also that he was on dangerous ground and must not give the Nicaraguan authorities on the coast any reason to be suspicious of his presence. To them he repeated his explanation that he was merely there to search for pirates, a scourge that affected them all. The Nicaraguans, plagued by American and British interlopers for decades, did not appear convinced.

At Bluefields he also found more information about *El Gringo Loco,* who the Anglos said was based to their south, in Costa Rica. The man had not raided their town, but they were concerned he might in the future and wished *Plover* good hunting in her endeavor to end the problem. Piracy was very bad for business, especially business at a potential entry port to a transoceanic canal.

Plover resumed steaming south and entered the anchorage at San Juan del Norte, a small town with a Nicaraguan government outpost that was most definitely not happy to see the Royal Navy. The town was situated at the mouth of the strategically important San Juan River, future gateway to a canal and a very sensitive area for the Managua government.

Russell spent most of his time explaining to government officials that he was merely looking for the *gringo* pirates and had no designs on controlling the coast—a goodwill mission. The commanding officer at the outpost looked doubtful at the explanation.

Russell asked about pirates in the area. The Nicaraguans reported that yes, the *gringo loco* had been there, originally as a fighter for the Moskitia rebels—who were mainly British settlers trying to add a colony to the empire, they added cynically—but he was now a pirate stealing anyone's cargoes and killing men in the process. His last raid was a month earlier. They would kill him if they found him, but as they had no real ships of their own, they had to wait until he attacked a coastal town and hope they could get there in time. Russell thanked the officials and wished them good fortune. They merely stared at him and said good day. The British captain knew they had seen through the ruse, and Managua, and eventually Washington, would be receiving a report of his presence and activities.

Plover left the Byzantine world of Nicaragua and made her way southeast into Costa Rica with Russell feeling relieved that the covert part of his mission was completed and that now he was getting closer to his true quarry, *El Gringo Loco.* He also noticed that the further south he went, the more victims he found and the more information he received about the pirates.

Evidently, the international renegade had been moving his hideous operations steadily toward Panama, Russell surmised as he studied the chart before him. *Perhaps we and our American cousins, and the Spanish allies, can arrange a surprise of our own for this outlaw when we find him.* That is more in keeping with the Royal Navy's mission, Captain Russell decided, reflecting back on his attempt to parley intelligence along the Moskito coast. *Yes,* he thought, *fighting is what we do best.*

Sirena was not welcome anywhere, Captain Toledo was finding out. They had met with the Indians, who traditionally had favored the Anglos over the Hispanics, and gotten nothing from them. Toledo had not expected much, but hoped he would receive a little information about *El Gringo Loco.* That the Indians were protecting the man who had fought for their area's independence was obvious, and it made Toledo wonder why.

Had the *gringo* been decent to them? If so, his reputation for inhuman acts must have started after he left the Indians. It was something he would keep in his mind.

When Toledo's ship finally made her way down the Nicaraguan coast, filled with treacherous reefs, to Bragman's Bluff, they came into contact with the first English. Not the sophisticated men of Jamaica, quite the opposite. The settlers on this coast were the rough descendents of the famous buccaneers of the Caribbean, of Drake and Morgan and Vernon—all of whom the Spanish-speaking peoples in the region considered pirates.

So Toledo was not surprised to get little information from them too, more of a polite curiosity. It had been many years since a Spanish warship had visited that particular coast and the obvious reason why was not readily accepted.

When *Sirena* arrived at Punta Perla he noticed a difference in the reception. The Anglos seemed amused, the Indians perplexed. Finally, a Nicaraguan told the Spanish Captain the reason. A British ship had just been there, inquiring about the relationship of the Anglos to the central government and if they wanted the home country to come back into control of the coast. Obviously some sort of English plot was going on, the Nicaraguan opined, then went on to tell Toledo the name of the British ship, the *Plover*. Toledo acknowledged the information but kept his reaction silent about the British activities.

At Bluefields, Great Corn, and Monkey Point it was the same story. The Anglos were polite, but with a cocky edge, and eventually a local Nicaraguan would tell of the *Plover's* visit a week earlier and her promises to the local English. Toledo also heard of British plans for a canal, possibly in competition against the Americans, which was in violation of the treaty they all signed.

After weeks of patrolling the Moskito coast and interviewing the inhabitants, Captain Fernando Toledo was forced to admit that something sinister was indeed happening. *Plover* was hundreds of miles from her assigned area and involved in another undertaking completely different from going after pirates. But why would they lie? What was their motive? A British move to garner control of a canal across Nicaragua?

Perhaps the suave British were not the friends they appeared to be, he realized. It also made him wonder what would happen when they all did finally meet up with the pirate bandits.

26

Rork's Discovery

A buela slipped out just past midnight on the ebb tide, pass-ing within a stone's throw of the American warship in the darkness. The ex-American pirate even stayed on deck as they passed the *Canton*, watching the navy crew, bored on anchor watch duty, gaze at the schooner glide by in the faint breeze. He saw a young ensign leaning against a pin rail on the afterdeck and remembered that he had stood that same duty many a night. There was no challenge, no gunshot. They didn't know how close their prey was to them, he realized, but by morning they might.

An hour later the schooner slid slowly through the narrows between the forts of San Fernando and San José without an inquiry, the lookouts ashore asleep. Once they were offshore, the *gringo* told the man at the wheel to steer west southwest. They were going to meet with the others at Cayo Holandes. He had finished his business in Cartagena.

El Gringo Loco doubted that he would return to the city—at least as a friend.

Wake and Monteblanco got back to the ship at four, exhausted and emotionally drained. They went aft to report their results to Captain Terrington, who was surprisingly cordial in his reception. He had lieutenants Custen and Connery and the two ensigns roused to join the group. Terrington was looking forward to presenting a *fait accompli* to his cocky executive officer in front of the other deck officers so that they could see who was the truly experienced leader aboard the *Canton*.

Wake wondered the reason for Terrington's almost gleeful behavior and the presence of the other officers, but concentrated on telling what they had found out ashore. When he finished narrating the information they'd gained, Terrington stopped him.

"The consul is in on all of this? The man I met named Swanson Singleton?"

"Yes, sir. The same one who was here on the ship earlier," Wake answered. "He handles cargo sales and protection for the pirate."

"And this man Toro Caldez is in on it too? One of the leaders?"

"Yes, sir. He is related to the local government leadership, has negotiated for the pirates not to touch Cartagena shipping, and transports stolen goods on shore. Evidently he had a cartage business. There is a rumor he was killed tonight. They're all in cahoots with the pirates, sir."

Terrington grew quiet, thinking for a moment, then said, "The Toro man *is* dead. We killed him just before midnight, at a rendezvous in the harbor that Singleton set up." In the corner of his eye, Wake noticed that Connery had shrunk back from the group.

Monteblanco interrupted, "Well, Captain, one more of the scum is dead, and I guess that's good, but the problem is that he was related to, and considered one of, the political head men in this area. That means you killed one of *them*, which means this ship could be detained by the authorities. And, of course, they will not consider one of themselves to be an international outlaw, subject to summary execution."

Terrington's face flushed, his hands reached for the back of a chair to steady himself. "Hmm . . . detained? Yes, it seems the situation has gotten more complicated than I thought earlier. Perhaps we should go—"

Wake held up a hand. "No. Not yet, Captain."

"No? Why?" This Wake was on the verge of damned insubordination, Terrington grumbled to himself. He glared at his number two. "It appears that right now is definitely the time to go."

"Sir, I need to look in the harbor and find this schooner, *Abuela*. If we can't find her, then we need to go ashore and find Singleton. He can tell us more about the leader of this gang, the former American. We need to know more about the man."

Ensign Moe, standing by the door, raised his hand. "Sir?"

"What now, dammit!" blasted Terrington, who was starting to get one of his headaches, the ones that felt like his brain was bursting. He needed his medicine right now, but these people wouldn't leave. They just kept dumping more problems on him. He hated them all at that instant.

Moe cleared his throat. "Sir, I saw that schooner sail out just before watch change at midnight. Sailed close by, sir. I saw the name clear as a bell. I remember thinking it was a strange time to leave. Oh, and sir . . ."

"What?" sighed an exasperated Terrington, who wondered what else would go wrong.

"I saw a man, a tall white-looking man, standing on her deck watching us as she passed by. I'm sorry, sir. I didn't think at the time that it could be the gang leader himself, sir. I've seen several white men on the vessels in the harbor."

"Oh God," blurted out Terrington. "He sailed right by us four hours ago. He was that close."

Moe looked horrified. Wake nodded to the youngster. "Very

good, Ensign Moe. You did well to register the ship and the man in your mind, even though you had no reason to suspect them." Wake then turned to Terrington, who seemed in a trance.

"Captain, I still need to find Singleton. He would appear to be the man who is manipulating things here. I don't have much time before sunrise."

Set on getting the ship out of the harbor, Terrington recoiled at the thought of waiting to leave. "No, the ship must leave, and leave now, before they shut down the exit. Good Lord, I can't allow a United States warship to be *detained* in this God-forsaken tinpot hellhole of a harbor."

Wake persisted. They were close to getting substantial information. He had an idea, risky but potentially productive.

"Captain, why don't you take *Canton* out the main channel now, while Don Pablo and I go ashore." He glanced at the Venezuelan, who nodded agreement. "Then we can meet you off the beach on the Caribbean side of the city after sunrise. Around four bells. We can find a harbor boat to sail us out, they're small enough to make it over the undersea wall at the false entrance so it won't take us nearly as long as it will the ship to go all the way around the outer islands. The timing should work out fine."

"And what exactly do you hope to accomplish ashore, Lieutenant?"

"Find out the real name of *El Gringo Loco* from this man Singleton, sir. Once we find that out, it may be easier to track him down. There must be something unique about him, something he doesn't want anyone to know, that has made him conceal his name so well for these past few years."

Just then Connery stepped forward, "I concur with the executive officer, sir. I think this is a unique opportunity for us to gather intelligence of the enemy."

Terrington darted glances around the cabin, realizing the officers were watching him and waiting. His head was pounding. He needed them to leave so he could take that medicine.

"Fine, Mr. Wake. Have it your way. We'll meet you offshore at eight."

Wake pressed again. "And this time, sir, I want Bosun Rork with us."

"Good, good. I don't care. Just get on with it."

Wake acknowledged the order and told everyone to get to work. As he closed the captain's door after the others had left, Wake saw Terrington's shaky hand open his desk drawer. The captain was searching in the desk as he muttered something about someone's name.

"Remember Rork, you're our *quiet* muscle. Just be ready if you're needed."

"Aye, aye, sir. Quiet as a mouse in church, I'll be."

Roosters were beginning to crow and dogs bark in the early morning gloom of the ancient city as the three made their way from the docks to the American consul's office on the *Calle de la Mantilla* in the oldest section of Cartagena. Fuentes had told them Singleton lived in a room attached to the back of the office. Once they found the building, Rork went around to the back through an alley and waited, while Monteblanco and Wake knocked on the front door. There was no answer to their repeated attempts. Wake was about to tell Monteblanco that they were too late, when the front door was abruptly opened—by a grinning Rork.

"Kindly don't tell me mum, sir. She doesn't know I have such skills. An' the parish priest would have quite the conniption if he knew, too."

"Your secret's safe with me, Rork," said Wake, trying not to laugh while they entered the black interior. Monteblanco struck a match and found a lamp, allowing the three of them to examine the two-room lair. The office part was crude, just a desk and two chairs—as was the back room with bed and dresser. From the lack of personal items it appeared that Singleton didn't spend much time there.

Wake found another lamp, lit it, and immediately began to pull open the drawers of the desk, while Monteblanco went through the man's clothing and bedding. Rork stood by the front door as lookout. Wake found official documents, receipts and manifests mostly, but nothing incriminating. Monteblanco found a pistol and knife, some Mexican silver coins, and a daguerreotype of a man that matched the description Fuentes gave of Singleton. The picture showed him with a woman and child.

They went back through everything again, but found nothing. Wake checked his watch and looked around for Rork, who wasn't at his position by the door. They had to leave now, there was no more time for further searching, but where was Rork? He called out gently for him, not wanting to alert the neighbors, but there was no answer. Monteblanco shrugged his shoulders—he had been absorbed in the search and didn't notice the bosun leave.

Wake, seriously worried, walked out the back door, looking everywhere. He was starting to get frantic when he heard the familiar lilt from the alleyway.

"Lookin' for me, sir?"

Wake was uncharacteristically terse as he whispered, "Yes, dammit! We've got to go. Now. Where the hell were you?"

Rork grinned sheepishly. "Pumpin' me bilge, sir. An' while I was standin' there doin' me business, I happened to ponder jus' where me ownself would be hidin' something o' value around this place. Then it came to me where, sir—as simple as me cousin Jimmy's jokes."

Wake calmed down. "And where would that be, Rork?"

"Well, by the pisser right there in the gutter, sir! Who in their right sane mind would be lookin' in such an unholy place as that? So I tried to see if there was a loose brick in the wall an' lo an' behold," he grinned again, "there was one at the bottom."

Monteblanco had joined them and asked excitedly, "Well, what did you find, Bosun?"

"Can barely make out the writin' in the dark here, sir. Please bring the lamp over a wee bit closer." Monteblanco lifted the lamp up to shine on the paper Rork held in his hand. All three of them read it silently together. Wake was stunned. Rork let out a low whistle and murmured, "Jesus, Mary, an' Joseph . . ."

It was an official dishonorable discharge from the United States Navy.

27

The Black Jesus

Wake was the first to move, and without a word strode back inside and out the front door. Rork and Monteblanco followed, all of them realizing they didn't have much time to get back to the harbor, find a boat and get out to the *Canton*, and all of them pondering their discovery.

By the time they arrived at the docks they were running, all semblance of blending in with the locals gone. Gasping for air, Monteblanco negotiated with a wherryman for a ride out of the harbor. When the old man heard the route and the destination, he smiled and the price doubled. He had rowed many a sailor who had overstayed their shore liberty and knew what they would pay.

As they crossed over the undersea wall at Boca Grande twenty minutes later, Monteblanco grabbed Wake's arm and pointed.

"There is the ship, Peter. We may make it. But what will you do now that you know the secret of the document?"

"I don't know. I just don't know. I do know that for now, this must be kept a secret. I want you both to understand that."

Rork and Monteblanco nodded their assent. The boat was quiet for the rest of the journey, the wherryman groaning with the effort to the point that Rork took an oar for the last mile of the slog through the seas to where *Canton* was hove to offshore.

Terrington was in his cabin when Wake went in. The captain didn't even look up from his bunk, only grumbling in a raspy voice, "I see you're back, Wake. Is that Dago all right? You didn't get him killed, did you?"

It took all of Wake's self-discipline not to walk the five feet to the bunk and jerk the man up and confront him, but he didn't. "Mr. Monteblanco is just fine, sir."

Terrington's words grew fainter. "Find out anything useful?"

For a few seconds Wake debated his reply. He had thought about this moment during the long row out to the ship. "Nothing of import, as far as I know at this time, sir."

Wake thought he heard a sound of relief when Terrington leaned up on an elbow and said, "Really? Well, that's too bad. But the important thing is that we are done here. The man Toro is dead and the pirates' base for selling their loot is gone. We can rendezvous with the other ships at Colón, see what they have accomplished, and go home. I hate this area and I loathe these people."

Terrington, his eyes squinting and unfocused, held up a trembling hand and pointed it at Wake. "And that Dago diplomat can get a packet to his own damn country when we get to Colón. He's just aggravated this whole mess. I'm tired of him on my ship and I want him off as soon as possible. Make sure that happens, Wake."

"Yes, sir," answered Wake, hoping he sounded sincere as he examined the drug addict before him and thought about what they had found at Singleton's.

Romero was not going to wait any more. This place was boring and his men were getting dangerous. Drinking rum all day and night was only good enough for a few days—not the weeks they had been there. They needed some release, some action. And if they didn't get it against someone else, Romero feared they might get it against him.

He had told Cadena as much, but the *gringo's* lackey forbade him to take the boys on a raid, insisting that they all stay together at the island and wait for *El Jefe's* arrival. But Romero had already decided he was taking the old steamer to Porto Bello and they were going to get some plunder and some women, one way or another. To hell with Cadena and his old womanly fear of the *yanqui.*

At two in the morning, after Cadena and the others had passed out from rum, Romero's crew took the old steamer out through the channel in the moonlight. He had planned to hit Porto Bello just before dawn, when the inhabitants were still sleeping.

As they made their way from the island he thought he heard Cadena shout something. Too late, he thought with a smile.

HMS *Plover* had never been to Colón. As she approached the town from Limon Bay, Russell surveyed the buildings through his telescope. He was not impressed. This was the famous trans-shipping point for the Atlantic end of the cross-isthmus railroad, but it looked like the disheveled shanty towns he had seen everywhere else in Central America. Upon searching the harbor front, he noted that *Sirena* and *Canton* had yet to arrive, and that meant staying around this place, known to be pestilential in the summer and dangerous year-round for sailors on liberty ashore. It was not a comforting thought.

Plover moored off the town and Russell had himself rowed ashore, where he reported in to the assistant British consul, a flaccid lump of a man who gave no outward sign of intelligence or initiative. The consul was off at Barbados at some conference. The meeting, during which Russell did not discuss his endeavors along the Moskito coast, centered on what the assistant consul knew of the pirate, which was nothing much. Returning to his ship, Russell decided not to waste time ashore again until the Spanish and American warships arrived.

From the afterdeck of *Sirena*, Toledo saw the mist rising from the jungle along the coast, forming puffy clouds that were then carried inland by the trade winds. No sign of civilization was apparent. The low mountains of the interior could barely be seen, the whole view presenting an ominous picture. So this is the legendary Darien? Toledo saw nothing special, but knew the only value of the area was in what he could not see from this view—the proximity of the Pacific Ocean, only fifty miles away.

The Americans and French already were subtly fighting for position to build a canal here, once they had found a promising route. With what he had found out about the *Plover*'s activities, Toledo was curious how the British would fit into the scheme. And with a sadness, he realized that his country's empire, which once ruled everywhere in this region, was now not even a second-rate player in the grand game.

As they rounded Naranjitos and Toro Points and entered Limon Bay, Toledo saw the Royal Navy warship anchored ahead by the town and sighed. He instinctively knew he was involved in something he could not influence, and wondered where it would lead him and his ship and crew.

Minutes later, with *Sirena* anchored behind the British ship, Toledo was being rowed over to meet with his ally—the one he could not bring himself to trust.

It was so easy that Romero couldn't believe that they hadn't done it when they'd first arrived at Cayo Holandes. He just stopped the engine and quietly glided into the tiny bay, then dropped the hook off the old relic of a fort, built three hundred years earlier after Drake had raided the place. There was no shout of alarm, no gunfire, just a couple of dogs barking when he stepped onto the dock. He had never been to the village and was amazed at his luck. Dawn was still over an hour away and it appeared that Porto Bello was asleep. They won't be for long, Romero mused with a grin, as he ascended the hill to the village. He turned to the thirty men around him.

"Remember, kill the men and boys right away. And the old women—I hate that wailing they do. We go in, get the gold from the church and the girls from the huts, then go. I want this done fast."

A fisherman heading down to his boat saw the crowd coming up the hill and called out to them, "Good morning. Are you here for the copra and banana cargo? You are several days early, *señores*. We did not expect you until—"

The knife was fast, but not fast enough. The fisherman let out a scream, which set off all of the dogs of the village, which woke the people sleeping. The first to come out of a hut was a grand-mother, already awake and getting breakfast ready. Her death was preceded by a scream that included the word dreaded on that coast.

"*Piratas!*"

While the others fanned out through the village, Romero headed immediately for the church at the plaza, knowing there would be gold gilt on the altar, the walls, even the doors. It was the way of the poor villages. The church was their communal source of pride and wealth. And it was there for the picking.

The villagers—mostly *zambos,* part Indian and part African—did not run to the church. Instead, the older people instantly grabbed the hands of their children and ran into the jungle, leaving everything behind in their homes. They ran and ran until they could run no more and, cut and bruised and bleeding, the families spread out and lay down in the bushes and vines, holding hands over the faces of their babies so their cries could not be heard. This instinctual flight was the product of three centuries of raids. It was the first and only thing they did.

The priest did not run. When he woke up in his small room in the back of the church and heard the cry of "*piratas*" from Señora Paloma, Father Damien knew what he must do. All his life had merely been training for this moment. As he walked into the sanctuary, the priest also knew that he could not fight the pirates off, or reason with them to desist.

Romero shook his head when he saw the robed figure emerge from the shadows. "Get away now, priest. I'll kill you easier than the others."

Father Damien knew his body was shaking as he stood in front of the altar, but felt an odd calm in his heart. The decision was already made, the hard part done. He raised his hands and face in supplication.

"Lord, forgive them what they do, for they are the wayward lambs and need your spirit and guidance. Please help their hearts, Lord, for they need your help more than anyone I have ever known." Father Damien turned his gaze to Romero and smiled. "I love you, my son. And Jesus loves you too."

"You stupid old fool," Romero hissed as he walked up and swung his cutlass into the side of the priest's neck. The body spun and fell down at the base of the statue behind the altar. Romero didn't take time to look up at the statue in the dim gloom of the few votive candles. He concentrated on gathering up the sacred golden instruments of the church and wrapping them in the altar cloth.

The front door burst open and three of his men staggered in, laughing maniacally as they pushed a girl down to the floor. Her eyes went to the wall above the altar, to the statue in the shadow. Romero followed her eyes and finally looked up, seeing a statue of Christ, the likes of which he had never seen in his life.

It was a black Jesus. Its gentle face mesmerized the pirate and he couldn't look away, thinking of what the priest had said. Suddenly the whining of the girl became a scream and Romero turned around, seeing the beginning of daylight out in the plaza through the open doors.

"We have to go. Now!" he said to the men grabbing the girl.

"But Romero, this one will be good. *Very* good, *amigo.*"

"I said . . . *now!*"

The men recoiled at his wrath and let go of the girl, who ran to the body of the priest. As Romero followed them through the door he turned, and stared at the Black Jesus, a sneer spreading across his face as he raised his pistol.

"Here's a little gift from the great Romero to you, Jesus."

The first shot entered the black plaster cheek just under the eye and ricocheted into the far wall. The second hit the forehead, sending a crack down through the face.

Then the renegade pirate left the church, rounded up his men, and left the village of Porto Bello.

Word spread faster than it would have with a telegraph—the *zambo* drums echoing every mile or so along the coast in all directions, warning of the pirates' descent upon the region and telling of the outrage upon the Church of the Black Jesus. It went faster than a ship could steam. By the time Romero came up the channel later that day to the remote island where Cadena waited angrily, the native Cuna people of those islands knew what had happened among the *zambos*, and what their own fate very likely would be.

Romero worried when he saw the look on Cadena's face as they met on the beach that afternoon. He had no idea that Cadena would soon be the least of his problems, after what he had started that morning.

The *sayla* peered through the bright sunlight from under the palmetto bush. The distance was great, but he still had good eyesight, as befitting the chief leader of the Cuna people among the little islands at the western end of the 365 islands of the Cuna *Yala*, their domain on the Caribbean coast of Panama. Around the ancient leathery man sat the area's *nele*, or seer; the *kantule*, or historian; and the clan elders of the individual islands—all waiting for his opinion on this unfolding situation. It would be expressed in a chant and translated by the *arkar*, or spokesman, of the *sayla*. The Cuna elders were free to ignore the *sayla's* opinion, but they never did. He was wise from the knowledge handed down to him by generations of repeated chants. The wisdom of *Tiolele*, the great god of the world, was known by the *sayla*. Even the *nele* and *kantule* agreed.

The Cuna men were on an islet a mile away from the anchorage of the two steamers and old schooner, and the carousing of the pirate men aboard the ships and on the beach could be heard even that far. For many days and nights the outsiders had been drinking and shouting and sometimes fighting each other, each night their voices getting stronger, more violent. The sounds were foreign, but the tone was understood. The Cuna were worried.

"These men are not like the others, the traders and labor buyers," intoned the *sayla* to the *akar* as he scrutinized the foreigners. "The others were not good men, but these men are evil. Our ancestors met their kind many moon paths ago. It is told in the chant of the great prophecy. The third chant of the story of *nuu*, the bird, and the *nusu*, the worms."

The *arkar*, *nele*, and the *kantule* nodded their understanding. The coming of the dangerous outsiders was very important and not to be ignored. The chant, one of the very oldest, told of a crisis long ago, and it would render a decisive verdict on what they should do. The *arkar* would wait until the *sayla* sang the chant, then tell the others.

The Cuna had dealt with outsiders for three hundred years, usually through trading or voluntary migrant labor on farms or ships. Outsiders were permitted to enter Cuna territory at designated islands, such as Cayos Holandes just to the west of where the *sayla* was this day, and not to venture beyond them. During those centuries, the Spanish had always looked at the Cuna as simplistic aborigines. The Cuna looked at all the Hispanics as potential invaders, and the arm's-length relationship had continued for centuries.

Occasionally though, the Cuna had used force to defend their area and way of life. Known as hunters, fishermen, and cultivators, they could also be courageous warriors when the situation was severe enough and the *saylas* decided it was the only option left. War was very seldom used, but had been employed skillfully enough that the Colombian district authorities in Panama had learned to leave the Cuna alone and warn settlers against going there. Christian missionaries also were practically nonexistent. The Cuna preferred it all to remain that way.

But the *sayla* could tell these outsiders were not settlers or traders or labor contractors. The *zambo* drums along the mainland had spread the word of what these men had done at Porto Bello. And what seemed far worse to the Cuna than the thefts and attacks on the females was the fact that these outsiders had desecrated the idol of *Cristo*, the one god of the *zambo* people. The Cuna called that god *Ibeorgun*, the great sage and prophet that *Tiolele* sent to earth, and it offended the Cuna, for that was something no one had ever done. No *human* had ever done, the *sayla* corrected himself. It was obvious that these were not humans, but were really monsters who went about wearing human skins as a disguise.

He turned away from the scene across the bay and looked up to the sky, closing his eyes. The chant started soft and low, increasing in volume until the elders were concerned that even the foreigners might hear it at the other island so far away. The chant went up and down in tone, with a rhythmic staccato beat, the *sayla* swaying to the sounds, lost in some other place and time. The elders listened closely but could not understand all of the sounds, they only knew that the *sayla* was entranced beyond anything they had ever seen. It frightened them.

Cadena eyed the man standing in front of him, conscious that dozens were watching the confrontation. Every word, every gesture, would be weighed by everyone there. It was the moment of truth. Either he would stay in charge, or he would die and Romero would take over.

"I told you to remain here. You violated that order and endangered us all."

Romero's worry had turned to arrogance, knowing that this was his opportunity and that most of the men agreed with him—that Cadena had turned into something less than a man by being so scared of *el gringo.*

"Cadena, you act like a nervous woman. Your *yanqui* master isn't here right now. Don't worry. You can relax."

Several of the men laughed at the remark, but Romero noted no smile on Cadena, who remained silent for a long time, then spoke loudly, so all could hear. "We were hiding here. Safe here. Waiting for *el Jefe* to return, so we could go back out there with our fleet of three ships and get even more riches. But no, you decided to endanger us all by going to, of all the places, a town that has roads to Colón! The alarm will spread and our opportunity for surprise is gone."

Romero shifted his stance, seeing several among the crowd nodding as they listened. The men were beginning to separate into two groups, those of Cadena's crew aboard the captured packet steamer and those of Romero's crew aboard the old original steamer.

Cadena continued. "And for what exactly did you do that, Romero? A few pieces of gold in a church? A girl or two?"

"*Amigo*, it was more than we had here. Cadena, this place has nothing. No loot, no women, and even the rum is running out."

Cadena cocked his head, his eyes widening. He looked at Romero incredulously. "Did you dare to call me *amigo?* I am not your *amigo*, Romero. I am your worst nightmare!"

Cadena nodded to a man in the crowd and a shotgun blasted out, cutting Romero down into a lump on the sand. Cadena stepped past the body and swept his gaze around the two groups of men.

"Anyone else feel like being my *amigo?*"

His sarcasm was met with silence and sullen looks from Romero's men as they turned away. Cadena knew they weren't loyal to Romero, or angered at his death, they were sullen because they didn't want to submit to discipline. He would have to watch them carefully.

28

The Prophecy

"There's *Sirena* and *Plover*, sir," reported Custen.

"We'll anchor just aft of *Sirena*. I want minimal steam kept up and a guard detail against bumboats. No liberty and no bumboats alongside. This is a fever port in the summer. Understood?" Wake remembered very well what yellow fever had done to naval crews in Florida during the war. What it had almost done to Linda when she got sick.

Custen acknowledged the order and began preparations for anchoring, the officers and crew very aware that the professionals of two other navies were watching their entry to Colón.

Fifteen minutes later Wake congratulated Custen on a job well done and, accompanied by Monteblanco, descended the side to the gig, to be rowed to *Plover*.

Terrington had not emerged from his cabin since Cartagena, wallowing incoherently in his bed most of the time, and at times truculently demanding his steward. Wake decided to just let it go and gave orders for no one, not even his steward, to disturb the captain. He didn't want the crew to see Terrington this way.

Besides, Wake was the *de facto* commander of the ship, and by this point everyone aboard knew it.

When he got to *Plover*, Wake was told that Russell had been hastily summoned ashore and had left a request for the other naval officers to meet him at an office at five o'clock that afternoon in Colón. The message said that crucial intelligence had come in and they needed to act with dispatch.

"You shot him?" asked the renegade American as the last rays of sunlight shafted into the cabin. They were drinking rum in the packet steamer's captain's cabin as Cadena explained what had happened since his leader had left the hideaway to go to Cartagena.

"Yes," answered Cadena. "As I explained, *Jefe*, he endangered all of us by going to Porto Bello. He had gotten out of control. He still wasn't listening, so yesterday I had Gomera shoot him. The others are still complaining about a lack of women, but they won't step over the line anymore."

"Good. You did right, Cadena. I had to do the same in Cartagena."

Cadena poured more rum for them, then broached the topic he had been considering. "*Jefe*, while you've been gone I have thought about the lack of women here. The men are uneasy, tense. They need a woman." He shrugged. "I know they are not much to look at, but there are women at that Indian village—the one on the island over to the east."

"So?"

"I think the boys should be allowed to go there and get rid of some of that tension, *Jefe*. Otherwise we will have to shoot more of them, and that could become a problem bigger than the lack of women."

"We are supposed to be hiding, you idiot. Laying low, out of sight. Besides, we're leaving tomorrow."

Cadena trod softly. "Yes, but what would be the harm, *Jefe?* The men are lonely. Even an ugly Indian would be better than nothing."

The *gringo* pounded the table. "Dammit, Cadena! All right, go ahead and do your little demented deed, then. I'm tired of arguing. Pick twenty men and take that old bitch of a schooner of Rosas' over there to that island. But you had better be back by the tide at four in the morning. I won't wait for any of you. And don't forget to leave *no* witnesses. I don't need any more problems."

"As you command, *Jefe*. This will make the men happy. Very happy."

"Cadena, you perverted little scum. I know that it'll make *you* happy and that's why you want to do it. Just get it done and be ready to leave at four."

The meeting was held at John Kramer's railroad and shipping company office on Front Street, amongst the seedy hotels and sailors' taverns that faced the harbor, which undulated barely four feet below the level of the dirt street. The squalor of Colón, or Aspinwall as some of the older Americans still called it, was vividly impressed upon Wake by the sight of rotting garbage and animal waste lying everywhere, and by the incredible stench of putrefaction. The smells followed him into the building and up to the second-floor room where the others were already gathered.

"We're glad you're here, Lieutenant Wake, Mr. Monteblanco," said Russell. "Where's Captain Terrington?"

"Sick, unfortunately, sir," replied Wake. "I am here in his stead."

Russell, now the senior naval officer in Terrrington's absence, showed the trace of a smile as he went on. "Yes, well, we are very sorry to hear of that. Anything learned in Cartagena?"

"The head outlaw is, I am sad to report, a former American naval officer named Symons. Presley Theodocious Symons, age thirty, six foot three, dishonorably discharged from the navy. He had people in Cartagena to receive and sell the loot. We didn't find the pirates themselves but did have run-ins with two of the pirates' local facilitators. One is now dead."

Wake waited for questions and glanced at Monteblanco, standing there with a neutral mien, but there were none. He was glad, because though he wouldn't lie to these men, Wake just didn't feel it was the right time to tell them of his own further suspicions. They had ominous overtones for the United States' image.

Russell spoke up again. "Very well. I want to bring you all up to date on what has happened recently. The pirate struck yesterday morning at dawn, quite close to us here at Colón."

The men, including Kramer, who was also the American consul, were sitting in rattan chairs around the room, drinking cooled fruit juice flavored with dark syrupy rum and smoking cigars. Normally, Wake did not like the smell of cigars in confined spaces, but anything that displaced the ambient fetidness was welcome and he lit one up himself. Kramer, in response to a glance from Russell, stood and pointed to a chart on the wall.

"Yesterday morning, just before dawn, pirates in an old steamer attacked Porto Bello, just twenty miles east of Colón. They ransacked the village, raped several girls, and vandalized the church and the statue of the Black Jesus that is revered by the people there. The black inhabitants, mostly *zambos* of African-Indian descent, were outraged and sent word by drums along the coast."

"Where did they go? Anyone spot them after they left?" asked Monteblanco.

"No. We don't know where they are."

Wake was studying the chart as Kramer spoke and had a thought. He held up finger, prompting Russell to say, "Yes?"

"Perhaps we can determine where they did *not* go, though, gentlemen."

Toledo, receiving translation from Monteblanco, smiled and said enthusiastically, "Yes, *señor*, say the idea you possess."

"Well, it's simple really. Through the process of elimination perhaps we can narrow down where to look."

Wake paused, thinking, hand on the position of Colón on the wall chart. He learned upon anchoring when the others had arrived. That gave him a basis for his conclusion.

"Captain Toledo arrived here yesterday from the west, close aboard the coast, just after the time of the attack, and saw no steamer along the coast, yes? Plus, there aren't that many places to hide to the west within thirty miles, correct?" Toledo nodded his assent when it was translated.

"And I came in this morning from the east, but saw nothing coming from Cartagena. We arrived at the coast in the area of Punta Manzanillo, then steamed close by that coast where Porto Bello is, but there were no steamers along the shore and no smoke on the horizon.

"So that tells me that the pirates came from the east, but not from the Colombian mainland by Cartagena, most probably from the coast of the isthmus further east than Manzanillo. And further east than that point are these scattered islands," Wake's hand traced them on the chart as he tried to read the faded print, "called the San Blas. Would that area of the coast be a good hide-out, Mr. Kramer?"

Kramer, hitherto subdued in manner, perked up, his hands spreading in excitement. "Lieutenant, I think you have something there. Those islands *are* secluded. The Cuna people that live there are pretty much left alone by the Colombian authorities, only an occasional trader or labor contractor calls there."

Suddenly Kramer hit the palm of his left hand with his other fist. "And by God, there are only a few islands the Cuna allow outsiders to visit." He pointed to one of the largest of the cays at the western end of the archipelago. "Cayo Holandes is the closest to us. I wonder if they're holed up there?"

Russell stepped forward to the wall chart and waved a hand

northward over the Caribbean. "What if they came in from, and departed back into, the vastness of the Caribbean Sea? We are presuming they made a coastal approach, which I feel may be too presumptive, gentlemen."

Wake shook his head. "You are right, sir. But if they did disappear back out there into the Caribbean, we can't pinpoint them and take action—they are lost to us. If we are to do anything that might have a chance of stopping them, then I think we need to operate on the assumption that they are hiding out on the coast." Wake turned away from the chart and faced the men around him, all of whom were now standing, examining the San Blas coast.

Wake continued. "And I think that Mr. Kramer's information supports that. I say we go to the area of the San Blas Islands, dividing up the chain of islands into search areas between our three ships according to their speed of arrival. That way we can all arrive at the same time and flush them out. The fastest, your ship *Plover*, sir, takes the area farthest to the east, my ship takes the area in the middle, from Iskardup west to Cayo Holandes. The *Sirena* takes the area to the west, between Cayo Holandes west to Punta San Blas. That gives us about ten miles at most between us, easy to hear gunfire and thus to go to the support of each other. We leave tonight and arrive at our coordinated sectors at dawn. If the pirates are there, we'll find and destroy them."

Russell looked pensive for a moment. "I agree with you, Lieutenant. It sounds like a good plan of action. But what about Captain Terrington? We are still under his command on this expedition and he should approve of this plan."

Wake felt the eyes of the others on him. He had forgotten about his captain in the excitement of formulating the operation. "He is, ah, *incapacitated* by his illness, sir. I am certain that he would approve of it. You, sir," Wake glanced at Russell, "would be the senior officer in charge due to Captain Terrington's illness."

The nodding of heads sealed the agreement, and the men took one more round of drinks. As he poured, Kramer made a suggestion.

"How about if I go along with the *Sirena* as a guide and English translator. I speak a little Cuna also. And I have personal reasons to want to watch those bastards die. Those men on the *Colón American* were my friends."

"Excellent idea, Kramer, and yes, of course, we understand your reasons," said Russell.

They drank a toast to success, then made their way to the doorway. Wake heard Kramer mutter something and asked him what it was.

"Oh nothing, just that the pirates picked the wrong place to hide out. The Cuna have quite a reputation."

"What's that?"

"They are diminutive in stature and pleasant-natured. Nice people, actually. Very slow to anger. It takes a lot to get them inflamed. But once they are at war, they're extremely cold-blooded. *No one*, and I mean no one, among their enemies lives."

"Really?" inquired Russell.

Kramer ruefully chuckled. "How do you think they kept independent all these years from the Spanish? The Cuna, Lieutenant Wake, have never been conquered."

The *arkar* felt chills go through him but maintained a monotone as he told the elders what the *sayla's* chant was revealing. He spoke as if he were the *sayla*.

"Last night I saw a strange light in the sky over Iskardup. It came to me in a dream and when I awoke I saw it in the sky. The light was different from the others that cover the night sky, it had great force and was as if on fire. In the vastness of the black sky, it made me think of the power of *Muu*, who forms the children in the vast and dangerous womb of a woman. And that made me travel in my mind to the chant of the story of *Achu Simutupalet*, the dragon who eats the moon once every many days. And that brought me to the story of the *Nusu* worms and the *Nuu* bird—the prophecy of the monsters that will come to us, as they had come to our ancestors. The strange light in the dark sky was a sign. The sign of the prophecy I have long feared.

"When, long ago, the *Nusu* worms were living quiet lives among these islands, there came a monster in the form of a giant bird known as *Nuu*, from the sea. It was the most evil of all evil things and had teeth that could bite and kill any living creatures. It flew from island to island, reaching down and killing all of the worms who had lived there in peace for many generations. The lust of the bird for eating the worms was overwhelming. Nothing could stop this *Nuu*.

"The elders of the worms met one night at sunset, just as we do now. They talked about what they would do. All were fearful. Only one had any hope. He said that the *Nuu* had shown one weakness and that they had to use that against him or everyone would die, one at a time. The *Nuu* was greedy and because of that was always predictable. It would ignore all else to eat worms—that made it weak. It would take courage, he warned them, but they could kill the *Nuu*.

"They waited for the right moment, then they paraded worms who offered themselves willingly out in the open, in front of the *Nuu* as he flew over the island. The giant bird grabbed several of the worms that he saw, thinking of nothing but eating his prey, but other worms were waiting and got on the *Nuu* as he went back into the air. Those that were caught in his mouth died, as a fish eats bait we give him, but those that were not in the mouth crawled to his eyes as he flew and made their tiny bites, slowly eating his vision. The bird could not see any longer and fell to the earth, dying when he hit a coral rock. The worms crawled off the dead body of the bird and returned home, and peace was known for many generations.

"It is a prophecy of these many generations that in time another monster, like the *Nuu* but in different form, will come to us and we will be tested again. The prophecy says that the sky will tell us when. The light in the night sky last night was a sign to me that now is the time. The drum warning from the *zambo* people confirms it—that these are not only bad outsiders, but are truly evil. I had hoped all my life that I would not see the coming of the monster of the chant, but it has come. This monster, which hides in human skin, is more powerful than any before, and we know that it is evil from what it did to the *zambo* people.

"The monsters have been increasing their violent ways, fighting among themselves. Their lust and greed for flesh is getting worse. They have attacked the *zambos*. They will attack us next. They will come for us at our village that is closest to them. They will come to feed off of us. Tonight.

"We are but worms. But even worms can kill a giant bird. Tonight some of us may die, some will be hurt, but we will kill the monsters and make them go away. It is our time. We are the chosen generation."

The sunset had given way to the quick darkness of the tropics, and the *sayla* stood up from the circle of elders and looked to the east, where he pointed to a star.

"The sign of the prophecy is even brighter tonight. By tomorrow morning the monsters will be gone if we are brave tonight. It is so said in the sacred chants and therefore is true."

He sat back down in the sand and spoke directly to the elders, no longer in a mystical chant to be interpreted by the *arkar*. In the calm voice of a grandfather, the *sayla*, two generations older than the elders surrounding him, laid out his plan for how the Cuna would defeat the latest monsters to visit them. The elders were afraid when he told them the plan, but they trusted him and went on their way afterward to carry out their tasks. There was no hesitation because there was no alternative. *Tiolele*, the great god, had sent a sign.

The prophecy was going to come true.

29

"Painted Savages from the Ground"

At midnight the naval vessels departed the harbor as quietly as possible—no one knew if the pirates had spies at Colón—and proceeded out of the bay and east along the coast.

Wake had gone below to tell Terrington of the plan but the man was passed out, so he decided to tell him later in the morning. A guilty feeling touched him as he felt relief at not having to deal with his captain. That feeling turned to dread as he realized the situation was rapidly getting to the point where they might be in battle and Terrington would be in a position to get men killed through his altered state of mind. Wake knew that something would have to be done soon about Terrington, and that he was the only one who could do it.

Custen and Connery were discussing the state of the boilers with Winter, the engineering officer, when Wake came up on deck in the darkness. The boilers were giving the mechanics some problems, and Winter advised Wake that within a month or so the tubes would have to be cleaned and patched or replaced.

"I'm sorry, sir, but that is the state of things. They've got to be maintained or they'll get much worse. We've been steaming hard lately."

"Yes, I understand," Wake acknowledged. "We'll do that when this is all over."

He thought wistfully of the simple days of sail. Then he remembered Terrington's admonition to use the engines as little as possible, in keeping with the attitude of Admiral Porter that sails should be the primary motive power. I understood sail better than steam, Wake thought, but the legendary and all-powerful David Dixon Porter is absolutely stupid for still insisting on naval vessels using canvas for long transits. Steam is more efficient, especially for ships of war.

Wake realized that he had used more coal fuel already in this voyage than the ship was allocated for six months, and would have to justify it. It made him feel very tired just contemplating his professional troubles ahead, not even considering the enemy they were after.

He took a telescope from the rack and surveyed the coast, then the horizon to the east along their course. A star, he thought it Albireo, shone particularly bright in the inky darkness, right along the forestay. Focusing the lens he saw it was really a pair of stars, one fiery gold and the other icy blue. Dead ahead and about twenty degrees above the horizon, in the clear air it looked as if Albireo was drawing them forward with some sort of ominous cosmic energy. It was a beautiful sight, but for some reason made Wake feel uneasy. He kept staring at it, wondering why.

Cadena peered ahead in the darkness. The small island was undisturbed. They would be among them soon and this time there was nowhere for the women to run and hide. His admonitions to stay silent as they slid through the bay in the light of a half moon were unneeded—his men were eager. As they sailed east under jibs only—the creaking gaffs and booms of the main and fore sails were too noisy—Cadena saw a bright star in the sky that he hadn't ever noticed before. Good for steering, he registered in his mind. Maybe I'll use it to steer for Cartagena if we ever go back there.

It took over an hour, but finally they reached the island and doused the jibs, coasting forward until the lowered anchor caught and spun them around to a stop. Slowly they climbed down into the launch and gig and rowed the few dozen yards to the coconut palm–fringed beach, watching the thatch huts for any sign of alarm. There was none.

He could barely contain his rising excitement as he quietly walked up the beach while others pulled the boats further on the sand. "Spread out!" he whispered. "Kill the males and round up the females back here. I get the best."

The *sayla* had last been in a battle four generations before, when he was very young and strong. It was against the *Choco* people who had come into the Cuna lands on the mainland from the east. The *Choco* were known as vicious fighters, but the Cuna kept them away after several fights. The memory of the horror, and of his personal terror during the fighting, had always stayed with the *sayla* during the rest of his life. Now the younger people would know this horror. There was no other way.

He watched as the monsters came closer in their big boat and he thought of the worms and the giant bird. His people were ready. The village was apparently asleep. The dugout log *cayucas* were gone from the island, as if the men were away fishing. Everything looked peaceful. An easy meal for the monsters.

The females in the huts were only those who had asked to help—after they had been told of what was expected of them. His respect for those women was large before—now it was bigger than he had ever had for anyone. He, and they, knew that many would be hurt, and some might be killed. But still they had trusted in his chant of the prophecy. Still they had asked to help defeat the monsters.

His hunters were there also. Only the most skilled were chosen, those who had faced and killed large animals. Each was wearing his clan's color and design on his face and arms, special paintings worn for the most dangerous hunts, put on with colors from the plants among the islands and coastline. The designs made the men more terrifying and not human-looking, with their faces having huge painted teeth. The *sayla* remembered the effect their painted faces had on the *Choco* long ago. Yes, his hunters were ready.

Some were buried in the sands under bushes, flat on their back with only their noses and eyes above the sand, ready to leap up, their bows and arrows or blow dart sticks buried by their sides. Some were under the water in the shallows, using cane sticks to breathe and similarly armed with bows and blow darts. Others in the water were waiting to go onto the big boat, with still others given the task of taking the monsters' little boats away from the island so they could not escape.

All the hunter men had understood and agreed to wait—no matter what they saw and heard—until the *sayla* called out to attack. It would take strong hearts for his men to endure the waiting . . . and the screaming. He wasn't sure they could.

The *sayla* crawled back into his hole under the bush. The monsters were here. The time of the prophecy had come. It was time for the worms to kill the giant bird again.

The first shriek was quickly followed by a dozen more. The village was small, only eight or ten huts, and it was all over in a minute. But to Cadena's surprise there was no one to kill. The men were all away on their fishing boats. The pirates, already drunk with rum from the anchorage across the bay, howled with delight at their good luck.

The women—there were no young girls—were dragged to the beach where Cadena stood. He examined each of them, then picked the youngest, who was probably a grandmother. He grabbed her hair and began dragging her to a hut, setting off a frenzy as the others seized other females and started toward huts. The women began wailing but did not fight. Soon, none of Cadena's men was focused on anything other than the woman in front of him, lust and rage combining to deny him hearing and peripheral sight.

The *sayla* waited. What he saw and heard made his soul hurt more than ever before. His eyes were crying, but he waited. He glanced around and through his tears saw no movement from his men, knowing what it was taking for them not to attack.

But he knew that the monsters must be attacked at the correct time, when they could not reach their guns. The loud wails and shrieks of the women became muffled whining as the shouts of the monsters ended. The monsters were now away from their guns.

It was time.

Cadena had flung her down, ready to end the building rage he had felt about everything in his miserable life. The Indian was barely human, yes, but she was a female.

From somewhere outside the huts he heard an animal sound, deep throated and gaining in volume as it continued. The sound was like an animal in pain, lashing out.

"*Ahhh . . . Reee!*"

Disoriented in the dark, Cadena struggled with his trousers, angry that one of his idiots was making him stop right now, of all times. He stumbled out of the hut, about to ask what the hell was going on when he stopped, stunned at the sight around him.

Tiny men with grotesque faces were coming up out of the ground and shooting darts and arrows. Others were coming out of the water stabbing Cadena's men with knives and shooting arrows into them. The little men were everywhere, taking aim and killing his men. Cadena stood there, for a moment unable to understand it, then felt the deer bone knife plunge into his back and go upward, twisting as it made its way inside him. He turned to see the woman from the hut smiling at him just before she ran away, taking the dripping knife with her.

Cadena staggered around behind the hut, looking for the schooner's boats, but they were gone. He made his way into the water, collapsing in the shallows. Suddenly a flash of flame erupted from the schooner, the lantern oil cask having been opened and poured on the deck. Within seconds the rigging and sails were ignited and the whole vessel was a floating bonfire, illuminating the scene on the island.

Cadena thought it a scene from hell. Painted savages were running around crazed, hacking the pirates' bodies into pieces. None of Cadena's men were still standing. One ancient man, nearly naked, was standing in the middle of it of all, singing at the top of his lungs, clearly urging the Cuna on in their search for any who had not yet been found and killed.

Cadena knew he had to get away quickly, before they found him, and slid further into deep water. The pain was excruciating now, the salty water entering his body, but he forced himself forward through the water until he was in water he couldn't stand up in. Slowly he swam, every stroke bringing a gasp, gaining more distance from the nightmare of the island.

A plank from the schooner floated into him and he thanked God aloud, not even registering the incongruity. Using it for flotation, Cadena was able to increase his speed away from the screeching and yelling still coming from the island.

The *sayla* first tended gently to the women, his joy at seeing that none were killed almost overcoming him. He told them how much he respected and loved them, how all Cuna would also. Several were injured with cuts, some had bruises, all were shaking with the memory of the monsters and were given the special drink that would calm them and take away the pain. *Cayucas* came from the nearby island and took the women to safety, honored heroes who would have their own chant for generations of Cuna to hear forever.

Then the *sayla* turned to the grisly task at hand. All the monsters had been taken by surprise and killed. Most without even a fight. It had been easier than he had thought possible. No hunters were killed, for which the *sayla* was very grateful. Two of the hunters were injured by knives, but none of the monsters had been able to use their guns.

The sayla gathered the hunters and told them what must now be done. He ordered that the bodies of the monsters were to be cut into pieces and put into the *cayucas*, then taken out to the reef in the morning and fed to the fishes. All of the items that belong to the monsters, including the dreaded guns, were to be taken out to the deep blue water and dropped in. Even the blood-soaked sand from where the monsters were killed was to be dug up and taken out to the deep water also. The monster's big boat was to be destroyed completely, the last remaining parts that could not be burned to be taken out to deep water too. Nothing showing there had been a battle at the island was to remain. Every vestige of the monsters was to be purged from the domain of the Cuna. The work of carrying out the *sayla's* orders was given to the young hunters, so that they could see what their elders had done for the Cuna people.

And finally, the *sayla* ordered that the island would never be inhabited again by the Cuna, that it would forever be a shrine, a sacred place, and that no one would ever go ashore there again.

After all the men had started on their tasks, the *sayla* sat down on the sand, his strength ebbed. He cried for his women, but knew he had done the correct thing.

The prophecy was right, the worms could kill the giant bird.

"What the hell was that God-awful noise?" said the *gringo* as he emerged on the deck of the captured packet steamer and looked around. His pale skin, accentuated by the sunburned face and arms, made him look ghostly in the dark.

"We do not know, sir." The lookout was peering across the bay. "It's coming from the island where Cadena took the lucky ones tonight. Something is going on there. Maybe the party is getting better!"

The noise coming across the water got louder, a mix of rage and fright. Suddenly a light erupted on the horizon. The old schooner was in flames. The renegade American instantly knew the party wasn't getting better.

"Get steam up. Now!" he said as he dashed below to his cabin for weapons.

"Yes, *Jefe*! We will start the fires and get the boilers stoked immediately!" cried out the leader of the anchor watch to *El Gringo Loco*'s back.

The *gringo* got dressed and put on his pistols and daggers. It would take almost an hour to get the boilers steamed up enough to get under way, and in that time they might be attacked. By whom, he did not know, but he was going to be ready. Was it Indians? Could Indians overwhelm armed men like Cadena's? That damn fool Cadena had somehow walked into a trap and endangered all of them. Worse, he had taken almost half the men with him, so the two remaining steamers would be shorthanded if those men couldn't get back. He roared out a graphic epithet as he slammed a fist down on his table, splitting the wood.

Cadena could see the steamers now. The loss of blood and the pain had halved his ability to make speed, but he kept paddling with his arms while riding on the plank. He saw movement on the decks and knew that they had been alerted by the schooner going up in flames. *Even now they are probably getting the fires started. I have to make it to the ship,* he told himself. *The ebb tide is helping me. I just have to stay strong. If I am caught here in the daylight those Indians will kill me.*

He clenched his jaw and pushed himself harder, grunting with the pain, each grunt becoming part of a rhythm that kept him moving, his eyes always on the ship anchored closest to him, the packet steamer.

The *gringo* paced the deck, almost growling with anger at their inability to move until the boilers had enough steam. The old steamer anchored close by was already getting some steam in her pipes, the capstan starting to clank up the chain as they weighed anchor. He had told them to go ahead and get out of the anchorage, get away and meet him out at sea.

On the eastern horizon he saw that the fire had died away and no sounds came from the island where Cadena had taken his men. *Dark and silent. What happened over there?* A voice disturbed his thoughts.

"We have steam up, *Jefe.* We are ready to engage the shaft."

He looked at the mechanic in front of him, wanting to kill

him, to kill someone. The man shrank away in fright as the *norteamericano* hissed a reply.

"Then get the damned shaft engaged, you idiot. Get it the hell done."

The *sayla* heard one of his men call out and point. He looked at the anchorage where the monsters had their large engine-driven ships. One was leaving and the other had lights and movement. Good. By the sun's arrival this would all be over.

He was tired and wanted to lie down, but he had to stay up, walking around and encouraging the others, as an example to the younger men. He sighed with the effort.

It had been a long time but he was making it, now only a cable's length away. Cadena heard the old steamer, his steamer, weigh anchor—each clank of the chain in the capstan pawls another spur to make him keep up the pace of his paddling. Then he saw his steamer slowly move, bound out the channel, for a moment coming closer to him before they made the curve around to the north toward the open sea. Then they were past him, gone into the dark northern horizon. The packet steamer with *el gringo* aboard was also now hauling its anchor.

They were leaving him.

He yelled, "Stop, I'm Cadena!" at the top of his lungs, but ended up with a mouth full of salty water. Crying out in pain he tried to paddle the plank faster, desperate to close the gap between him and the departing ships.

He kept screaming and finally saw a man's head turn, then an arm point in his direction, but the packet didn't slow down. They were a hundred feet away now, coming toward him in the channel bend. He screamed out with every stroke, lashing the water and driving the plank forward, using his rage to get him closer.

"I'm Cadena! Pick me up!"

The ship was charging along now at five knots, about to run him over. Cadena could see the razor sharp barnacles slice into his arms as he pushed himself up off the plank and lunged toward the main chain plate on the starboard side, the bow wave lifting him up. He hung there, one arm crooked around the rigging chains, trembling with the effort and the pain, bleeding from the hole in his back and the gashes on his arms, as the water rushed by inches below him.

"Help me!" he cried out, but no one came down over the side from the main deck to assist him up. Cadena looked up and saw them leaning over, watching him. He thought he heard a laugh, a bet on how long he could hold on. That was a mistake, he promised silently. I will make you pay for that. A surge of malevolent energy filled his arms and he propelled his body up, arms locking over the gunwale at the main deck. With his last ounce of strength and a primordial scream, Cadena pulled himself over the gunwale and fell in a heap on the main deck, gasping for air. The crowd around him was merely staring and no one was helping. He heard someone order full speed ahead and he knew they were past the reefs and safe at sea. He had made it. Survived.

El Gringo Loco had a sneer on his face as he walked up to Cadena and kicked him over onto his back. The crowd of seamen closed in to watch what was about to happen. No one moved to Cadena, who lay there limp, only his eyes moving.

"You're late, Cadena, you stupid piece of dung. You just wasted half our men, killed by tiny Indians half your size."

Cadena tried to explain, the words hoarse, weak.

"Nightmare . . . all dead . . . savages . . . painted savages."

"Leave this worthless piece of trash right where it is on the deck. If he's still alive in the morning I might let him live until noon." The American then spit on him and walked away.

Cadena saw them all turn away as he was still trying to explain, but they weren't listening.

"No . . . no. You don't . . . understand." He struggled for air, desperate to breathe.

"*Painted . . . savages.* They came from the ground."

30

The Demons Within

The sun was still more than two hours away, the dark of the Caribbean night cloaking the sea. *Canton* charged onward to the east, the bright star having risen in the sky until it was now high above the foremast. Wake paced the deck, debating what to do with Terrington during the coming battle. He could not call for a meeting of the officers—the debate in his mind would be called mutiny if expressed aloud. So he paced the deck and tried to reason it all out.

He understood that Terrington was in no shape to command during an engagement, and even if ignored and left in his cabin, would probably burst onto the main deck and interfere once the guns started firing. The guns would wake him even if he was passed out on the laudanum. He would likely interfere, contradicting orders and raving like a lunatic. The crew would be confused, the officers humiliated, the fighting efficiency of the ship destroyed, and American sailors killed or wounded because of it. And, in the process, Terrington himself might be killed.

Two hours to decide. What could he do? What should he do? Logic and reason, he counseled himself. Do the logical, reasonable, and *right* thing.

Terrington would only stay out of the way if he was unable to get out of his cabin. That meant locking him in. That was either helping a sick man by protecting him from harm, or it was mutiny against the captain of a vessel of war. And that conclusion would be made by a court-martial, months from now, back in the United States, far away from the danger and uncertainty, and long after what I do this morning. Would they understand?

"Are you all right, sir? You don't look well." Connery, the officer of the deck, had come up to Wake unnoticed.

Wake looked at the gunnery officer. It wasn't anyone's responsibility but his. Connery could not make the decision or even know of it beforehand. "Just thinking about some decisions this morning."

Connery smiled, thinking of the coming fight. "Yes, sir. It'll be a very *decisive* morning!"

Wake returned the smile, nodded, and went down the after hatchway. It was time to get it done.

He went into the petty officer mess and told the steward to pass the word for the surgeon's mate to meet him at the captain's cabin in ten minutes, exactly. Then he went aft and entered Terrington's cabin. Lighting all the lanterns, he turned to his captain, who was sprawled on his berth, an empty rum bottle below rolling with the motion of the deck.

"Get up, sir. I need to talk with you."

Wake shook Terrington's shoulder until a grunt was heard. He shook it again until finally the captain opened his eyes, leaned up on his elbows, then fell back face down. Wake shook him one more time.

"Who is it? Wake?" mumbled Terrington. "Wake, is that you? What the hell are you bothering me for?"

"Captain, we need to talk."

"Get the hell away from me, you fool. Wake, just get the hell away and leave me alone."

Wake took both of Terrington's shoulders in his hands and forcefully lifted the captain up. Terrington's eyes were unfocused, his hands trembling.

"What's going on? Gawd, give me my medicine. I need my medicine! Where is it? There!" His fingers reached out to the shelf above the bunk for the little blue bottle. He poured the thick liquid into a glass, then raised it, quivering, to his lips. Groaning, Terrington drank it in one gulp while Wake watched.

"What in hell do you want now, Wake?"

Wake glanced out the stern gallery and saw the sky was lightening. He needed to get back on deck. They would be getting close and this had to be done.

"Captain Terrington, you are incapacitated by your illness and it is not reasonable or professional to expect you to be able to fulfill your responsibilities of command. You need expert medical care, sir, and we can't give that to you until we reach home, after we've accomplished our mission—"

Terrington's head swayed as he held up a hand and interrupted him. "Gawd, Wake, can't you talk slower? I can't understand a damned thing you're saying. In fact, just stop talking altogether and leave me alone. Get the hell out."

"No, sir. I'm not leaving until you understand that you are no longer in command. I am relieving you as of this moment because of your illness and inability to function as captain."

Terrington cocked his head and leaned forward toward Wake. "You are doing *what?*" he asked, incredulously.

"Relieving you, sir. You are sick and no longer in command."

Terrington's eyes went wide and he launched up out of the berth, his body trembling with anger as he pointed a fist at Wake.

"*The hell you say!*"

Terrington stumbled and sat down again, his face grimacing in fury. "How *dare* you even *think* those words, much more say them. By God, I will see you hanged for that comment. *Hanged!*"

Wake expected it would unfold this way. He sighed and pulled out of his pocket a piece of paper, then laid it on the berth. Terrington glanced at it, not comprehending.

"What is that?"

"A dishonorable discharge of commission from the United

States Navy. It belongs to the renegade American naval officer we are looking for. I found it in Cartagena at the office of Singleton, the consul. Evidently the note in the margin stating that it's *El Gringo Loco* is Singleton's. Read the name on the discharge. I think you know it well. I think you've known about this the whole time."

Terrington picked up the paper, the anger in his face disappearing, replaced by dread. He dropped the document to the deck; which Wake immediately picked it up.

"Captain, the name on this document is Presley Theodocious Symons. The description listed is the same as that of the pirate. And of you. Even a shared susceptibility to sunburn. The wounded merchant marine officer in that Jamaican hospital said the pirate looked just like you. And your middle name, sir?"

Wake pulled over a chair and sat directly in front of Terrington, who was sitting there mute, his eyes moist.

"What is your middle name, sir?"

"Parker . . . Theodocious . . ."

Wake reached over and put his hand on Terrington's shoulder. "Parker, Symons is your brother, isn't he?"

Terrington slumped down, tears flowing, his voice muffled between sobs.

"My half brother. We share a father. You don't have to tell anyone, do you? Please don't tell anyone. . . ."

"Tell me what happened, Parker. According to the note in the margin, Presley went to the academy, just like you. He graduated three years ahead of you, in fifty-eight. What happened?"

Once he started, it came out in a torrent, like an emotional dam had burst inside Terrington. "He was always bad. He was smart, smarter than me, but looked at everything different, like he was angry at everything. Always in a lot of fights. He liked to hurt them, you could tell. He liked to hurt me, too. Father got him into Annapolis through his political friends, but he barely got through, so many infractions.

"In the war he did well at first, then they gave him his own ship, a gunboat. Did some sort of assault on a sailor, beat him nearly to death for some minor thing. Removed from command, then worked ashore at Farragut's depot at Ship Island. Got caught doing something sick with a boy seaman, hurt him too. They kicked him out. Didn't want a public trial.

"I heard he was in Mexico in sixty-five but the French didn't want him. Lost track of him after that. Hoped he was dead. God help me, I hoped my own brother was dead."

Wake heard a knock at the door.

"Sir? Surgeon's mate Pullwood as ordered."

"Come back in five minutes, Pullwood." Wake returned his attention to Terrington, now curled up in the berth.

"Parker, when did you know Presley was the pirate we were sent here to stop?"

"I suspected it was him when I heard the stories and read an article in Washington. I hoped it wasn't, but had this feeling it was."

"Why didn't you tell them?" Wake asked, but instantly knew the answer.

Terrington looked at him. "It was a command. I waited for years and finally got a ship of my own. I couldn't let them know. I still can't. They'll take my ship from me. They can't know. . . ."

"The laudanum, Parker. When did that start?"

Terrington suddenly sat up, wary, his eyes darting toward the door, then to the skylight overhead.

"What do you mean? This is just medicine. I take medicine."

"You take it all the time. You're an addict, Parker. And you mix it with rum. You are out of control and unable to function as a naval officer, much less a ship commander. Now when and how did this start?"

"I don't know what you mean," Terrington said indignantly, his chest inflating.

"You are a drug addict! Don't lie to yourself. You know what you are and that you need help. When did you start taking laudanum?"

Terrington's body drooped again. "Back in sixty-four, on that damned tub I was assigned to. Hell, we were all drinking rum in the wardroom. Some of them were lacing it with laudanum, let me try. Dulled the heartache when we were feeling lonely. Then it got to where we would meet off watch and just take a little laudanum to get to sleep. Every day."

"And ever since." added Wake.

"Yeah, and ever since."

Wake thought it was time to tell him what was about to happen. "We are going into an area of small islands after the pirates in just a few minutes. I am now in command and will tell everyone you are incapacitated by illness and that I have relieved you. You need to stay here. The surgeon's mate will come in, make you comfortable and watch over you, unless he is needed for any wounded. Do you understand that?"

The answer came in a sigh. "Yes."

"Parker, I will do everything I can to help you, and help your reputation and career. Now stay here and rest."

Wake didn't receive a reply, just a vacant nod of Terrington's head. He left the man still slumped on the bed, staring out the stern gallery windows at the sea.

Pullwood was in the passageway when Wake came out.

"Pullwood, the captain is very sick and has been for some time. Hallucinative and invalided. I have relieved him of command. Go in there and get him comfortable in bed. You may give him a sedative, but not too much. He's already had some laudanum. Stay with him for a while. We may go to action stations if we sight the pirates, but until then stay with Captain Terrington."

Pullwood's acknowledgment was nonchalant. Probably trying to listen at the door, guessed Wake as he turned to ascend the ladder to the main deck. He stopped and asked Pullwood, "Were you treating the captain for any illness?"

"No, sir."

"Did he use any of your medicines?"

"Why no, sir."

Pullwood's attitude bothered Wake. The man wasn't acting surprised at all. "Very well. Lock the door to his cabin when you leave him, Pullwood. I don't want him to accidentally wander around. He could get hurt that way when we're in action. Understood clearly?"

"Aye, aye, sir."

Cadena woke up when a shot of fire went through his back as he tried to roll over. He was covered by a canvas tarpaulin but still shivering cold. The sky above him was gray which meant he had lived until dawn. I will live long enough to see these bastards in their graves, he vowed.

The *gringo* walked up minutes later. "You're stupid as all hell, but you're also tough, Cadena. I'll give you that. I've decided to let you live, if you can recover from that big friggin' hole you've got in your back."

Cadena then heard him say to someone, "Get him below to his cabin and patch him up. I want him standing watch in three days."

Cadena summoned his strength and asked, "Where are we, *Jefe?*"

"Headed back to our old hunting grounds, Cadena. Bound nor'west to the Moskito coast."

31

The Needle in the Haystack

Wake spoke to the assembled officers quickly, the lantern suspended from the overhead swaying its dim light around his cramped cabin.

"Gentlemen, we don't have much time, so let me be brief. I have just relieved Captain Terrington from command due to his incapacitating illness that has required him to use sedatives."

Wake paused, expecting questions or at least a reaction of some sort, but the officers said nothing, maintaining a neutral mien. The only sound was the creaking of the ship as Wake continued.

"He will stay in bed in his cabin. Pullwood is with him now. When we complete our mission we will put him ashore at the first American naval station with a hospital.

"Now, as we discussed last night, very shortly we'll enter the San Blas Islands, here at Iskardup, then work our way west toward Cayo Holandes. *Sirena* is to our west, *Plover* is to our east. Remember, if you hear any gunfire, pinpoint it and immediately head that way. Don't wait for orders, just do it right away.

"When we do come into contact with them, we treat them as

we would any enemy—taking no chances at all. They are very dangerous and have no sense of decency or honor. Understood?"

All the heads nodded assent, some of the junior officers commenting among themselves.

"All right then, any questions?"

Moe held up a hand, then winced as an elbow jammed into his ribs. "Hey, he asked," he said to someone near him.

Wake said, "Go ahead, Ensign Moe. Never worry about asking questions. It could save lives later."

"Ah, sir, what do we call you now? Captain?"

"That's a good question, Ensign. No, don't call me captain. Continue as you were. And continue as you were with Lieutenant Commander Terrington by calling him captain. He will be shown the utmost respect and deference."

The *sayla* was pleased. Everything was completed. No sign of the monsters was left on the island. Parts of the hull of the big boat were still in the clear shallow water but would be removed later in the day after everyone rested.

Surrounded by the elders, he sang a final song of praise. Then they all paddled their *cayucas* away from the island, which would forever be proudly known as *NuulbeorgunDup*, the island of the great prophet's worms. The *sayla* hoped the *zambo* people would be pleased.

"They were here, all right. Look at the debris. Good Lord, look at the rum bottles," exclaimed Connery as he surveyed the beach where the pirates had erected a crude camp for several weeks. Hundreds of rum bottles were strewn everywhere. Among the debris was a broken china plate, bearing the name of Captain Phillip Underhill, late of the *Colón American.*

"Not long gone, sir," called out gunner Durling in a low voice to Connery. "This fire's coals're still warm. Less than ten hours, I'm thinking."

"Such a sad waste o' rum, on scum such as them. More's the pity," lamented Rork, shielding his eyes from the bright morning sun. Rifle in hand, he was leading the landing party around the island searching for clues about the pirates. They found nothing living anywhere.

Wake landed moments later in the gig. After walking through the abandoned camp he called Connery and the petty officers over.

"Mr. Connery, I want well-armed boat parties to take every ship's boat we have and check all of the surrounding islands. I want that done immediately and completed by two hours from now. Then we'll weigh anchor and meet the other ships. Signal by gunfire that we have found the pirates' camp."

The chorus of "aye, ayes" was followed with shouts to the men to return to the ship and get ready to shove off for more searches.

Cadena climbed the ladder up to the deck, semi-drunk from rum to dull the pain. The sun glared into his eyes, worsening his headache. The *gringo* was standing in the shade of the boom awning. Behind them steamed their old original ship, the one with no name.

"So Cadena, you're alive? Oh yeah, now I remember. It's only the good that die young."

"Yes, *Jefe.* I am still alive. It is good to be alive."

"There's a bunch of our men that don't have that benefit because of you, fool."

"I was surprised by Indian warriors. It was a trap. I will not fail you again, *Jefe.*"

"We're going to be at the Moskito coast in three days, Cadena. I want you in charge over there on the old steamer tomorrow and I want you ready to do what I tell you. You fail again and I will personally rip your guts out and watch you die."

"I comprehend, *Jefe*," said Cadena, averting his eyes lest they give away his thoughts. And someday when I am strong again, Cadena pledged, I will cut your throat and watch you drown in your own blood, you self-centered dog.

"You searched the surrounding islands and that was all you found? Nothing on the little island next to it, you say?" asked Russell.

"No, sir, nothing. Just the remnants of the hulk in the water. The char marks looked very recent. We checked everywhere close by, but found absolutely nothing. I have no idea where the rest of the vessel is. She's stripped, but I don't know what they did with what they took. Looks like maybe a schooner, but most of it's gone," reported Wake to the others standing around a table in Russell's cabin, each man drinking a glass of Royal Navy port wine. The three naval ships had rendezvoused at Cayo Holandes that afternoon. *Sirena* and *Plover* reported finding nothing in their sectors.

Kramer rubbed his chin. "The Cuna probably will never talk about this, if they were involved, but it has the sound of a Cuna attack. They leave nothing of their enemies. Maybe the pirates tried to raid the island."

"Bows and arrows against pirates' guns?" asked Monteblanco. "They must have lost many warriors."

"Yes, I would imagine they did. Well, the main question is where are the pirates now," said Russell. "We seem to be consistently one step behind them. We must find them. Where will they go now?"

A chart of the lower Caribbean was spread out on the table. Toledo leaned forward and spoke in Spanish, Monteblanco translating.

"Gentlemen, I propose that they will not go east toward Cartagena, since they are well aware *Canton* has been searching in that area. Nor will they stay here on the coast where the Cuna are evidently already angry at them. They will not go west since they know that coast is alerted because of the attack on Porto Bello. They were not welcome at all in Costa Rica either. I think that leaves north, my friends."

"North where?" asked Wake.

Toledo raised an eyebrow and shrugged his shoulders. "Maybe the little islands we searched off Nicaragua. Maybe the Moskito coast itself. Many of the people there were supportive, I think. The pirate leader was careful to attack shipping along the coast there, but not to actually raid the villages. I think he wanted to keep it as an area of refuge. But, of course, it is all merely my conjecture."

"Mr. Kramer, can the *Colón American* burn wood if she can't find coal?" inquired Wake.

"Yes, she sometimes had to do that, but Captain Underhill hated it because of the fouling it would do in the flumes of the boilers. It affected their efficiency greatly, and the wood burned much faster than coal does. Their range was therefore much shorter."

Wake thought about the distances on the chart. "I think Captain Toledo is correct. I think they are low on coal. Remember, that ship normally coals at Jamaica on her route north to the States. She steams fast and uses it fast. The pirates probably don't have enough coal to go anywhere far and there weren't many trees on these islands suitable for a steam ship to consume."

"What about Jamaica? Might they head there?" asked Russell, prompting everyone to look over at that area of the chart.

"Too far," said Wake. "At least nonstop. They could get there if they refueled with wood at Moskito coast though."

Russell exhaled a long breath. "Then it's Nicaragua for us. They have a day's head start, but when they get wherever they're heading they'll be staying for a few days to find fueling wood, so with luck we can find and engage them."

Russell asked if all the naval vessels still had sufficient coal after topping off their bunkers at Colón and was told that they did.

"Search pattern as we did on this coast, each ship ten or fifteen miles apart?" asked Kramer. "By the way, I'm staying with you gentlemen." He grinned at Toledo and shrugged his shoulders. "I might be able to help. Who knows?"

"Very well, John. We're glad to have you. The search? Yes, but farther apart. There's more coast to search," said Russell as he spread the dividers along the coastline of Nicaragua and compared it to the latitude scale. "Two hundred miles from Cabo Gracias a Dios down to Monkey Point. That gives each of us sixty-five miles. We'll be on our own if we confront them."

"We were before when we searched that coast two weeks ago," commented Toledo after the plan was translated, still wondering what the Englishman's real motives were on that coast.

In the end they decided to do it—steam directly for Old Providence Island, rendezvous one last time, then search the Moskito coast. The Spanish would take the northern part, the Americans the central, and the British the southern section.

Then Wake took advantage of a lull, drew in a deep breath and told the others about his relief of Terrington. He explained that Terrington's illness had incapacitated him and he had been resting in his cabin since then. Wake added that he had prepared a report to his superiors and was sending it via Colón and Jamaica. They quietly listened, each knowing exactly the legal danger Wake had entered.

"Yes, well, good luck on that endeavor, Lieutenant Wake," said Russell with a concerned look. "It is a very serious step to take, but it sounds like it was necessary."

"It was," Monteblanco added in support of his American

friend. "Captain Terrington was extremely *unwell.*"

Russell straightened up from the chart. "And now, we'll be on our way, gentlemen. Before we do, I propose a toast."

All the men raised their glasses and looked at the Englishman.

"Gentlemen, to the wide Caribbean Sea. May God help us find the needle in that haystack."

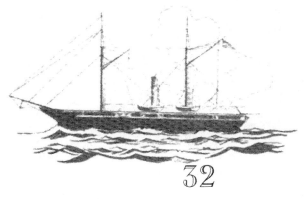

32

Sea Lawyers and White Mice

July 1869

The three ships rolled in the swells at Bahía Santa Catalina on the northwest coast of Old Providence Island. Officers from each ship were ashore buying fruit and vegetables, knowing this might be the last chance to stock their ship's larder.

The meeting in Russell's cabin was brief, just a last minute confirmation of the plan, for they were weighing anchor in an hour. As the others filed out, Russell touched Wake's arm and asked him to stay a moment.

"How is it going with Terrington?"

"He is staying in bed. Sleeps mostly," replied Wake.

"You're on extremely dangerous ground, Peter. Be very careful. I've seen this before."

"Yes, I know about the legal situation, Commander. But I'm following regulations as to the proper relief of an incapacitated superior."

"Regulations have different interpretations at headquarters. Peter, we all know that you have been in real command of

Canton, and we know that Terrington's sickness is self-generated. Just beware. I'll be a witness, should you need me. So will Toledo and Monteblanco and Kramer. Remember that."

"Thank you, sir. I'll remember that."

His stomach cramped into a knot as Wake departed the cabin and thought about Russell's words. Pirates would be easy compared to explaining to his own navy why he removed the captain from command.

One battle at a time, he thought, as he went down the side of the *Plover* to his gig. He noticed that they did not pipe him on or off the ship, as they would the captain of an allied naval vessel. Well, I'm *not* the captain—I'm not sure exactly what my position is anymore.

"He's gone? Well, find him! Now!"

"We're looking now, sir," explained Connery. "I've got the officers and senior petty officers searching the ship."

"Dammit all to *hell!*" Wake instantly regretted his outburst, but his anger had gotten the best of him. Moments after he returned to *Canton*, Connery reported that Terrington was missing. The surgeon's mate, Pullwood, had left him sleeping after giving him a sedative. When he had checked in on him an hour later, the captain was gone. Now they had weighed anchor and were heading out to sea. "Very well, Mr. Connery. Keep me advised. And send Pullwood in here."

Pullwood, the only medical man aboard since the ship's surgeon had taken sick and disembarked at Key West, arrived and stood rigidly at attention. His eyes were neutral but unafraid, which bothered Wake. Normally, being summoned to the executive officer's cabin was a cause for anxiety among enlisted men, especially given the current circumstances.

"Pullwood, what was Captain Terrington's demeanor when you last saw him?"

"Asleep, sir."

"All right, when you last saw him awake."

"Sleepy, sir."

"Sleepy from tiredness or from drugs?"

Pullwood glanced at Wake's eyes. "He was tired, sir. He's been through a lot."

"Did he ever speak of hopelessness or suicide to you?"

"No, sir. He's not the kind of man to say such a thing."

"After I relieved him, I searched his cabin, Pullwood." Wake leveled his gaze at the surgeon's mate, who remained unintimidated. "I found his stashes of laudanum and rum and have secured them, so I know he didn't have any of his own left. You were to give him sedatives only as a last resort, and then as little as possible. Have you done that, Pullwood?"

"Yes, *sir.* I have taken care of my captain, Lieutenant. I would have even without orders from the executive officer."

"You sound angry, Pullwood. Almost arrogant."

"I'm not allowed to be arrogant, sir."

"You're correct on that, Pullwood. Present a report to me in ten minutes listing all medications dispensed in the last month. You should have that handy, since it's part of the regular supply statement. Dismissed."

After the surgeon's mate departed, Wake called for Connery to come to his cabin.

"Immediately do a *personal* inventory of the drugs and medicinal liquor in the medical chests. Have it here in fifteen minutes."

"Aye, aye, sir," acknowledged the surprised officer. Suddenly a shout came aft to them from forward, relayed from man to man.

"Call for Lieutenant Wake, right away!"

Wake couldn't believe the scene in the galley storeroom, dimly lit by lanterns that swayed with the roll of the ship. Lieutenant Custen was staring at a bread locker in the corner. Rork was standing beside him, a belaying pin in his hand, and Durling was glaring at the crew who had gathered in the passageway, keeping them back.

"Captain Terrington's in the bread locker, sir. He won't come out and says he'll fight anyone who tries to make him," reported Custen.

"Clear this area," said Wake as he approached the bread locker. Durling and Rork pushed the men back down the passageway, leaving Custen and Wake in the small compartment.

"Captain Terrington, it's Lieutenant Wake. I need to talk with you, sir."

The reply sounded as if from a child. "I hate you, Wake. Get away."

The ship rolled off a wave and there was a tumble inside the locker, prompting Wake to make his move. He flung the door open and entered the small space, Custen following. Terrington had fallen and was trying to stand when Wake took his wrists and held them tightly, pulling him out into the main stores room. Custen held Terrington's shoulders.

"Captain," said Wake in a firm tone, "you are ill, sir, and need to get back in your berth. Let us help you, sir."

"You stole my ship! I'll see you hanged at the first American port." Terrington bowed his chest up, arms suddenly like steel as his voice raised. "You stole my ship. You stole *my ship*, damn you!"

"Captain, please, sir." Custen was shaking as he tried to calm Terrington. "You're sick. Lieutenant Wake didn't steal anything. He just relieved you because of your sickness. You know that, sir."

Terrington turned to Custen, his eyes glistening, lip curling. "You'll swing too, you spineless puddle of bilge scum. You should have supported your captain when this mutineer took the ship! I won't forget you, and this moment, Custen."

Wake tightened his grip and pulled Terrington again toward the passageway, worried that Custen might loosen his due to the tirade. "Captain Terrington, I am taking you back to your cabin right now. Lieutenant Custen, summon Bosun Rork in here."

Rork appeared instantly. "Couldn't help but hear, sir. Let me help ya with this burden," said Rork as he seized Terrington's right arm and smoothly pinioned the man's wrist back, all the while showing an innocent smile. The bosun looked at Custen, who was obviously shaken by it all. "Lieutenant Custen, perhaps you could clear a way in the passageway for us, if you would, sir? It would help Captain Terrington make his way. I'm a'feared he's feeling a wee bit poorly right now."

As Custen walked ahead of them, Rork leaned over and whispered something in Terrington's ear. Wake felt an immediate weakening of the captain's resistance. Terrington grew silent, his eyes locked on Rork as he was swiftly escorted out of the room. They strode down the passageway and into officers' country, through the wardroom and into Terrington's cabin, where Rork firmly set the man down onto his berth, then stood at parade rest, his eyes never leaving Terrington. Custen stayed outside, guarding the door.

Wake locked the door and said, "Captain, I am going to post an *escort* for you here twenty-four hours a day. Everything you need will be provided. You will not need to leave this cabin."

Terrington was still defiant. "You're going to die, Wake. In a ceremony in front of everyone on this ship. They're going to hang you, and everyone who helped you, and everyone who did not help me."

Rork was at Terrington's ear in an instant, saying something that made the captain's eyes go wide and his body recoil. Rork nodded at Terrington, then looked over at Wake.

"Sir, Captain Terrington will remain in his berth, snug an' comfy as a bed bug, an' not cause even a wee problem. I know you have some heavy responsibilities right about now. Nary worry a bit, sir. I'll be honored to assist Captain Terrington here an' make sure his every need is taken good care of. I'll take the first trick. No problem."

This had gone beyond relieving a sick captain, Wake knew. Now he had used force against his duly appointed superior. How many in the crew heard the shouts? How many thought it was mutiny? How could he command with credibility?

Wake had seen men hung by direction of a naval court-martial during the war. He recalled that vivid scene in Key West in 1865, the bodies jerking up the halliards, then swaying with the ship all day long as every sailor in the squadron watched. He had felt no remorse then, they had deserved it. Would anyone feel the same for him?

And he had dragged Rork and Durling and the officers into this mess. They would all suffer, particularly Rork after what he had done. Well, what's done is done. Wake nodded his approval to Rork and walked forward to his cabin, ignoring the stares along the way.

"What?" exclaimed Wake, sitting at his tiny desk. "Explain that again."

Connery shook his head. "There's damn little laudanum left, sir. The chest has only three bottles. The medicinal brandy is gone, too. The reports have been falsified. Faked."

"How the hell did that happen?"

Connery sighed, eyes downcast. "Because I received the monthly reports, sir, but I did not physically check the stock. I regret to report that I trusted the surgeon's mate."

"How did he explain on the medicine log the depletion of the laudanum?"

"Various ailments with various seamen, sir. Sometimes they were given a little laudanum, but he would put down that they were given more. He never put down that he was getting low. I've now talked to several of the seamen, sir. They told the truth. I also had Pullwood into my cabin, where he admitted what he did."

"And how did he do it?"

"He and Captain Terrington were shipmates in sixty-seven, in the Med. He supplied him with the drug then. In exchange, Terrington got him privileges, extra liberty, wardroom slops, that sort of thing. Terrington asked for him to be on this ship. Pullwood kept him supplied all along."

"Amazing. Anyone else?"

"Yes, sir. Quartermaster Johnny Castle and Steward Morely, sir. Both on laudanum. Both from Captain Terrington's old ship. Both requested to come aboard with him. I've wondered about Castle for some time now, but thought he was sneaking rum. Pending your decision, I've got them all under arrest, put 'em under guard and separated them."

"And their view of all this?"

"Morely came clean pretty fast. He appears to be the lackey of the group. Castle was the ring leader, according to Morely. The steward said that Terrington—excuse me, sir, Captain Terrington—was having regular meetings with his cronies and that Castle would take laudanum right alongside the captain. Said that he never saw Pullwood do that, but they'd all drink rum together. Turns out that Morely can write, too. I had him write out a statement in his own hand. It'll be good evidence. Pullwood wrote his also, but it's not as detailed. Says he can't remember much."

"What about Castle?"

"Castle isn't talking, except to sound like a damned sea lawyer. The fool told me, all respectful of course, that I was the one who should be concerned, since I was the one who'd swing from a rope. Said I'd violated Article Thirteen of the naval regulations. Mutiny, a death offense, he reminded me—as if I didn't know the articles by heart. Thought I saw the start of a smile on him when he said that."

"Does he know Morely and Pullwood talked and the game is up?"

"Yes, sir. I confronted him with that, but it didn't shake him a bit. Called 'em both the *white mice* of the ship, sir. Informants."

"Hhmm . . . I see. Anyone else in on this damn thing?"

"Not that I know of, sir."

"When you leave here I want you to write a full report—

including everything anyone said. Bring all you have to me. I want it completed tonight."

Connery acknowledged his orders and departed the cabin, leaving Wake alone with his thoughts. There was no doubt now that when they returned to the United States a court-martial would be called to decide upon his actions.

Would he and the officers and petty officers be convicted of mutiny? Wake was sure that he did the right thing, but would the senior officers of the court understand? Or would they take the word of Terrington?

God help us all now, he thought. It might all boil down to the testimony of sea lawyers and white mice.

33

Jungle Lair

El Gringo Loco found it two years earlier while working as a mercenary for the grandiosely named República de Moskitia. He had filed it away in his mind as the one place of refuge to go to when things got really difficult. It was perfect for his present purposes.

The Bomkatu River was not on any chart. The Nicaraguan government didn't know it existed, even Moskito Indians twenty miles away at Uani had never heard of it. Ships transiting the coast could only see the entrance when they got within a mile—but most stayed far away from the reef-strewn shoreline—and the channel across the bar was unmarked. It was as secluded a location as he knew of in that part of the world.

The two steamers were nested together and tied to the mangroves and jungle trees on the bank. The upper masts had been lowered, and only the tips of their lower masts protruded above the treeline. For all intents, they were invisible from anyone searching for them.

For the previous two days they had been making minor repairs and taking all the dry wood they could find for fuel. But there wasn't much dry wood. It was the rainy season, the forests were soaked, and the only cache of dry wood in the area was at Uani, a tiny village a few miles down the coast. The village had a pile of wood, cut for use in steam engines' fireboxes, in a thatched shed. It also had food, which the two steamers had run out of upon arrival. Since then they had killed every animal on the river bank they could find. Now there weren't any left.

Cadena was mending slowly, but still strong enough to stab one of the men in the eye for insubordination his second day on board his old steamer. Cadena knew that he would have to hurt someone, just to show the rest who was boss. When one man was less than respectful he had his chance and struck without warning or mercy. Now Cadena was standing in front of the *norteamericano*, visualizing the same act on him. It made him smile, even though he had bad news to report.

"The rum is gone too, *Jefe*. We must do something."

"Food first, then fuel. Rum counts as food. Uani is close by. We'll go there."

That made Cadena smile more. "Ah yes, *Jefe*. The Indians here are far more friendly."

"Cadena, since when have you cared whether they liked you or not?"

"You told us to pay on this coast, not to take against their will," Cadena protested. "I was only remembering your orders, *Jefe*. You wanted this to be our refuge and we should not anger the locals."

"Yeah, well that was then and this is now. I don't care what you do here because we'll be gone soon enough. By the way, this time we're not paying—we're taking. I'm not wasting money on 'em. And we're not coming back to this area. This part of the Caribbean is getting too crowded with navy ships. Time to go elsewhere to have our fun. Somewhere we aren't expected."

Cadena was intrigued but knew enough not to ask. The *gringo* would tell him when he wanted to. Not before. "When do you want to go to the village?"

"Tomorrow, before dawn. We'll go down the coast in the small boats, raid the place, and come back. I want to be under way as soon as possible after we get back and load the steamers. That means no lollygagging in the village, Cadena. Go in, get the stuff, and get out. No parties with your boys."

"Yes, *Jefe*. I will lead the attack and be back here by early tomorrow afternoon, full of fuel and food. It will be a great success. You will see."

The *gringo* stood up and grinned. "Oh yes, Cadena you little *gusano*, it will be a success—I'll be leading it just to make sure, and your crippled little self will be right alongside me where I can keep an eye on you. Now get the men ready. We leave at two o'clock in the morning."

Sirena was going slowly. The reefs formed a mortal maze at Cayo Muerto, and Toledo didn't want one of them named for his ship. The maze extended twenty miles to the west, where the coast of Nicaragua lay waiting for them.

"Didn't you go through here before?" asked Kramer in Spanish.

"No, we closed with the coast from the northeast, a deeper approach, not from the southeast. This time we have to come through the maze. It will add a day, I think. We must take our time among the reefs," said Toledo as he pointed to a brown patch of water next to them.

Kramer watched as the coral head slid by to starboard, its top barely five feet below the surface. "Yes, my friend. I understand completely."

Toledo laughed at Kramer's concern. "In order for us to kill these pirates, we have to be able to find them, in a ship that floats!"

"Yes. Well said, *amigo*. Well said."

The *Plover* made Greytown on the southern coast of Nicaragua with little problem. Upon their arrival Russell greeted the local Anglos—he still had trouble considering these disheveled quasi-renegades truly British—as a returning friend, hoping for information about the current political situation as well as about the elusive pirates. He got neither. What he did find was a cold hostility from the Nicaraguan authorities, who called the place San Juan del Norte and refused to use the English name. In fact, they were even more hostile than his previous visit.

In the person of a *mestizo* decked out in colorful sash over a ragged suit, who insisted upon being addressed as "Your Excellency," the Nicaraguans demanded his ship leave an hour after she had dropped her hook, saying that there was no reason for him to stay longer. Though they had no military power to force him to leave, Russell complied, imagining how many rounds it would take to destroy the town as he departed the anchorage. He gauged it at around ten, maximum.

"Course to the north, sir?" asked his executive officer.

"Yes, make it so, Number One," replied Russell as he stared out at the limitless eastern horizon, his mind filled with images of the green hills of England.

"Steer small, damn you!" yelled Custen at the helmsman, who had allowed *Canton* to slew off a wave as they approached Punta Perlas from the southwest, around the reef. It was a tricky path through the inner reefs and everyone was nervous.

Wake watched the landmarks on the shore line up for their entry into the channel, then snapped the telescope shut. "Ring bells for dead slow. Come right to nor'nor'west."

The helmsman and lee helmsman acknowledged the orders, their eyes locked on the wheel and the engine telegraph, their voices monotone. Wake caught Custen's eye.

"We're out of the worst part, I think, Mr. Custen. Have the foc'sle party prepare for anchoring. Have the coxswain get the gig ready for me. I'm going ashore."

Twenty minutes later Wake was stepping out of the gig onto the beach in front of the village, Monteblanco beside him. A man with the confident air of command stepped up to them and spoke rapidly, Monteblanco translating.

"He says he knows why you are here. You are looking for the *gringo* pirate, but that person is not here. He also says that the government in Managua has been warned that foreign ships already have been searching the coast and has ordered that they be refused hospitality. They are to leave. Managua doesn't trust foreign warships."

"But we are here to help, to find and destroy the pirate."

Monteblanco raised his eyebrows. "You are talking logic, Peter. They are talking ego and honor. They have memories of the man named Walker, who also said he was here to help them."

"The filibusterer? The one who tried to overthrow the government?"

"Yes, my friend, the same. They equate all *gringos* with him now."

Wake rubbed his eyes and shook his head slowly. "Pablo, do you believe him when he says they haven't seen the pirate?"

Monteblanco nodded. "Yes, I do for some reason. If the pirate had attacked here, that would be more important than some decree from far-off Managua. They would have told us, to get revenge, if for no other reason."

"Then I guess we go."

"Yes, *amigo*. We can continue north, toward *Sirena's* area."

In the next several days *Canton* stopped at Caralaya, Río Grande, Huanclua, Huaonta, and Puerto Cabeza with similar results. No one had seen the pirates, and no one wanted the foreigners around. Wake had the same eerie feeling he got when he had seen the star off Panama, as if some type of fate was drawing him northward faster and faster.

"All right, set a course for Punta Gorda. We should see *Sirena* soon."

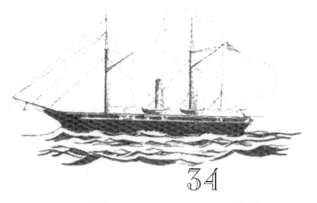

34

Destiny of Honor

The Moskitia Indian village of Uani was a crude collection of twenty-two thatched huts, three clapboard structures, two open-sided sheds filled with fuel cordwood, and a rickety dock. The dark jungle was stark against the white sandy beach in the waning moonlight. *El Gringo Loco* had been there before and greeted as a friend, since he always brought gold to buy the food and items he sought.

Been a while since I was on a raid myself, he mused as he steered for the beach. A leer crossed his face. They won't think of me as a friend anymore.

The five boatloads of men grounded their craft on the beach and ran ashore, bursting into each hut and rousing the families out at the point of a cutlass. It was accomplished in minutes, without any bloodshed. When all the villagers, mostly Indian but with a few *mestizo*, had been assembled on the beach and were under guard, the loading of the wood and food commenced. Several of the outlaws eyed the girls longingly, but the *gringo* had only to glare at them and they got back to work. He forbade any fires to illuminate their work, worried that any patrols along the coast would see lights and wonder why. The moonlight was enough for their purposes.

But not all the villagers were captured. Consuela and Pietro Estelo, ages eleven and nine, slipped out of the back of their hut in the confusion and ran away from their parents, who were now frantic with worry. The siblings hid under a bush and watched the rounding up of the people. They had never seen anything like it before. These were the dreaded pirates they had heard the adults speak of, the ones who had been friends, but then had done bad things to other villages on the coast. They also knew that something bad, very bad, was going to happen here, to their family, their friends.

Consuela turned to her little brother and put a shaking hand on his shoulder. She was frightened but tried to sound brave. "We have to run to Dacura and get help. They will know what to do. We have to run fast, little brother. Now. Keep up with me."

Consuela didn't wait for a reply, but started running down the path to the south, toward Dacura village and help. Pietro followed with a quiet yelp and both were soon gasping as they followed the winding path through the coconut trees, just inland from the sandy shoreline. Consuela didn't know how far it was to Dacura, she usually rode on the donkey cart that took coconut husks there, but it was the closest village she knew. When she heard a scream from their village behind them she made sure Pietro was with her, then kept on running.

After many minutes they reached the hut of a fisherman and fell through the entryway, waking everyone inside. As the fisherman lit an oil lamp, his old wife immediately gathered the two children to her, sensing they were frightened to death and calming them enough to tell their story. It was a wild story, but the old couple had heard of the pirates and believed the tale.

"It will take too long to run the path to Dacura," the fisherman said to his wife. "I'll go there by boat. Much faster. I will take the children too, so they can tell the story to the *alcalde* in charge there." He looked at the woman he had shared life with for more years than he could count and grimly added, "I want you to take our things and hide among the trees and bushes. Wait until I come back. *Do not* come out until you see me."

The sun was lightening the sky when the fisherman slid his *cayuca* into the water and paddled his way out beyond the reef. Once there Consuela helped him step the tiny mast and raise the husk cloth sail. A moment later they were moving briskly southward.

"Nothing to report, sir," declared the young ensign as Toledo and Kramer emerged onto the main deck of *Sirena*. The sun was just coming up, illuminating the lush green-clad hills on the coast a mile off to the west.

"Position?" inquired Toledo.

"Twenty miles or so south of Uani, sir."

Toledo considered that. They had taken three days to transit through the maze of reefs from Cayo Muerto to Cabo Gracias a Dios, far longer than he had anticipated. From the Cape they had taken two days to search the shoreline southward, seeing nothing of value. During the night they moved slowly, ever alert for the grinding jar of *Sirena* finding a coral reef, by necessity farther offshore than he would have liked.

Had they missed something in the dark, especially this far away from the beach? Should they go back and search closer in the daylight? Toledo had a feeling he couldn't define, but just knew in his guts that the pirates would be here, on this coast, its remoteness the key to their escape and survival.

Toledo was searching the shore behind them, to the north, when the shout came down from aloft. "Deck there. Small sail ahead one league. Looks like a fishing *cayuca*."

To the ensign's questioning glance he nodded, and *Sirena* altered course two points to the starboard to come alongside the canoe in the distance.

"About twenty minutes at this speed, sir," said Lieutenant Dulce, the executive officer who had arrived on deck in response to the lookout's report.

"Very well. Have the fisherman brought aboard and treated well. I want to know what he knows."

Toledo turned to Kramer. "I trust a fisherman more than one of the chiefs or a government man. The fishermen have no political agenda, John. They just want to be left alone to catch their fish and feed their families, and frequently speak the truth more than the landsmen I meet."

Good point, thought Kramer, impressed one more time by the Spanish officer who had become his friend.

"Don't just stand there, get the last of that wood in the boat. We need to go, the sun is rising and I want to be gone from here." The *norteamericano* was in no mood to tolerate any slackening of the pace of loading. Some of the village prisoners were pressed into loading the boats too.

Finally the boats were loaded and floated in shallow water. Cadena limped over to the *gringo*. "Witnesses?"

The one word answer was what he expected.

"No."

Cadena said nothing, walking over to his men and whispering. The villagers were taken to the far side of the huts, put in a line and told to turn around and walk into the jungle and hide, not to come out for an hour, by which time the raiders would be gone. Some of them believed they were going to be let go, others wondered what was going on.

Standing in the water by a boat, *El Gringo Loco* heard the ragged volley of gunfire, then a few isolated shots. The men coming back to the boats were neither excited nor depressed, it was part of their life and they understood that leaving no witnesses meant they might live a little longer.

"That took too long, Cadena. You're getting weak-willed as well as crippled."

Cadena looked at the man he followed, but also hated. The morning sun made the red sunburned splotches on his face and arms stand out. It will be a pleasure to kill him someday, Cadena imagined as he replied.

"I am still strong enough to kill, *Jefe*. There are no witnesses."

"Good. Let's go. I want to be back by late morning so we can load the food and wood and be gone this afternoon."

"I thought we would leave tonight? The men will need rest."

"You thought wrong, Cadena. We'll leave this coast as soon as we can. We just killed the last friends we had here."

"Uanlay? And where is this village?" asked Toledo of the fisherman sitting at his table, downing his third glass of rum in five minutes. The children, wide-eyed at the commotion and machinery of the ship, stood beside the wrinkled man, nodding their agreement as he told the story they had told him.

"It is named Uani, Captain. About two leagues to the north. You must have passed it in the dark. A small fishing village. My brother married a girl there and his family lives there. Please go quickly."

"We will, sir. We will go now."

Amid the subsequent calling of bosun pipes and shouting of orders, Toledo stole a glance at the fisherman and the children as they carefully climbed down the side of the ship to the *cayuca*, laden with canned food from the galley. He hoped the children would find their family safe and was glad they were in the care of the fisherman. The old man had a quiet dignity and reminded Toledo of his own father back in Spain. Beautiful, civilized, and majestic Spain. How he wished he were there, with his parents, sipping wine on the patio and discussing events around the world.

"Full speed, sir?" asked Dulce, breaking Toledo's trance.

Full speed was very dangerous on this reef-filled coast. What good did it do to go fast if you wrecked and never made it? And what if you got there slowly but safely, but everyone was dead and the pirates gone?

"Yes. Full speed ahead. Triple the lookouts for reefs."

"Row, you bastards! Row like you're men, dammit." The sun was making the *gringo* feel uncomfortable, clammy and baked, even though he had covered his arms and neck, wore a broad-brimmed hat, and had an awning spread over his seat at the stern of the lead boat.

They were heavily loaded with cordwood, the food stacked on top of that. Several of the *cayucas* from the village were taken and carried the extra members of the gang and even more food. Cadena, on the last boat in the line, was urging his men to keep up with the rest. They had all gradually slowed down though, the heat and exertion taking its toll.

Cadena stood up and looked ahead, seeing far up the coast the slight point of land that sheltered the mouth of the river. The whole flotilla, laboring hard in the rising sea breeze and accompanying waves, was now only three miles from Bomkatu River and safety. It looked like they would make it.

Hamilton Fish, newly appointed secretary of state since March, stroked his jawline beard and looked across the massive desk at the newly appointed secretary of the navy, George Robeson, who had been in that capacity all of five days. Robeson had just moved into the office and was pleased to host Fish when the secretary of state had sent a note saying he had something to discuss.

Fish, a consummate Washington politician from his decades in Congress, didn't want to give the bad news up front. Better to be gentle, play the role of elder statesman and start with good tidings.

"Congratulations on your appointment, George. Very glad to see you here in Washington. We can certainly use some new blood from beyond the District. New Jersey's loss is our gain."

"Thank you, sir. But I must admit, after finding out the mess Borie made while here I don't know if it's much cause for congratulations, Mr. Secretary."

"Yes, well, old Adolph had some problems that Sam didn't know about when he nominated him," said Fish, referring to Adolph Borie's prodigious drinking and President Grant. "I think the incident with the Parisian was the final straw, though I don't know if it's true, of course."

"Yeah, well he wasn't even competent here in this office. He only lasted, what, three months? But did he ever cause problems here. None of the senior staff respected him—you should hear what Porter says about him. Now I've got to get things back to normal around here."

"I have no doubt that you will, George. But I'm afraid I have to add to that burden, my friend."

"Oh? How so?" Robeson grew wary. He didn't have to be a Washington veteran to know that Fish wasn't there just to say hello. Something was wrong and the secretary of state was probably going to dump a load of manure in the navy's lap to take care of.

"Complaints from the Caribbean, George. Colombia to be exact. Seems their ambassador got word from their president to send a protest to our diplomats about an American warship that went to Cartagena and started killing people that might possibly be pirates."

"What? You must be joking!"

"No, actually George, I'm not. The USS *Canton* is one of

your boats, I believe. She was in Cartagena a while ago and assassinated a local—according to the Colombians, really assassinated him, as in ambushing him in the harbor one night in a small boat—then fled the scene before any investigation could be done. The ship then showed up at their district in Panama looking for more people to shoot."

"This is ridiculous. Preposterous." Robeson couldn't believe it. Assassination ordered by an *American* naval officer?

"Perhaps, but the gentleman diplomat from Colombia is rather upset and says that they demand the captain of the ship be sent back for trial on charges of murder. Evidently that man they shot was a prominent citizen and family member of the senior authorities there. Their ambassador says honor is at stake."

Robeson started to speak, but Fish raised a hand.

"I explained to him that I was not in charge of sailors and ships, but I would surely pass along his complaint to the man who was, which, of course," Fish smiled sympathetically as he laid the protest document on the desk, "is *you*, George."

"Gee, thanks, Hamilton."

"Oh, by the way, I haven't told Sam about this yet. Thought since it's your bailiwick you'd want to do that."

Robeson studied Fish, whose face showed only apparent sincere concern for his fellow cabinet member. Robeson had the sudden urge to reach across the desk and hit him.

"This is just the last of several complaints I've gotten in the last three days," said Robeson. "The Spanish are angry about some damned sailor brawl at Cadiz, the French have told us to stay out of Marseille because of a perceived insult we did to their women, as if that is even possible, and the Brits are in a twit over some problem we caused in Honolulu with a native king, of all things." Robeson moaned. "And now this."

Fish stood up, waving a hand in pleasant farewell. "Well, I must be off. Again, good luck, George. I'm always here if you need help. I'll see you around. Maybe drinks over at the Willard some evening? I'll buy." And with that he exited the room before the brand new secretary of the navy could think of an appropriate response.

Robeson summoned his naval aide, an addled commander on temporary assignment, asked him for the current orders and disposition for a ship called the *Canton,* and settled back in his chair, wondering why he had ever agreed to Sam Grant's request to come to Washington and run the navy for him.

When the aide returned with the paperwork Robeson scanned it quickly and saw that, yes, the ship was assigned independently to go after pirates, possible ex-Americans, in the lower Caribbean and that it had been down there for months.

"Get a recall order out to that ship," he ordered the aide. "And when they get back, I want to see that captain. There's no telling what else has gone on that we don't even know about yet."

"Ah, sir, they aren't anywhere near our regular dispatch routes. It may be a while."

Robeson took in a deep breath. "Commander, just do what the hell I say."

"Aye, aye, sir."

It was high noon when they got back to the steamers, collapsing on their oars and drifting the last few feet. The *gringo* was miserable, getting burned badly in spite of his precautions, and in a foul mood when he climbed up the side of the *Colón American.*

"You there! Get these poxy-brained idlers working!" he yelled to the man in charge of the deck, who promptly yelled at the men who had not gone on the raid to begin unloading the boats. The skin on his face was already blistering when the renegade Yankee shouted across the deck to Cadena on the old steamer.

"We leave in four hours! No more. Get 'em all working—every damned one of them!"

The crew stared at him as he disappeared below. They hated

him and he knew it, but he had kept them out of gaols and off the gallows, given them women and gold, and a sense of power they had never felt, so he knew they would take his abuse and get the job done. They might even do it faster because of the hate.

When he got down to his cabin he stripped off all of his clothes and lay naked on the bed, the small waft of air through the skylight cooling his ravaged skin. He closed his eyes and remembered a night in Havana when a soft-skinned girl with an angel face had caressed him with a botanical lotion, soothing his sunburned body until he fell asleep. She was a prostitute but not predatory like the rest, and he wished she was here now.

The village of Uani was empty, the huts with items strewn about, as if ransacked and hastily abandoned. Toledo walked around, pistol ready, getting angrier by the minute, but there was no one to fight. The whole place was devoid of people.

It was clear that the cordwood in the sheds had been stolen. The locals stored it there to keep it drier during the rainy season and sometimes to sell it as fuel. The food stocks were also gone. Lieutenant Dulce walked up to Toledo and Kramer, stretching his arms out.

"No one, Captain. Everyone is gone. Would they kidnap them?"

"Maybe they escaped after the children ran away?" offered Kramer.

"It is possible, but not likely, John," said Toledo. "Why would they not return then? Especially when they would see us arriving here as protection."

A petty officer on the jungle side of the village groaned loudly, causing the sailors to look his way. Then he called for the captain, saying that he had found them, the whole village.

"Oh God. Oh merciful God." Toledo was almost overcome

by the sight. Men, women and children. Families huddled. All were dead. Tears flowed down his cheeks as the Spanish captain walked among the bodies, muttering "Why . . . why?"

In a shaky voice he ordered the men back to the boats, to get aboard *Sirena* immediately. When Dulce protested, saying that their Christian duty demanded they bury the dead right away, Toledo scowled.

"This was done this morning, only a few hours ago, and the animals who did this are close by. They are not to the south or we would have seen them. They are holed up somewhere close to the north. In a cove or a river. We must have passed them in the night last night. We go now and find them. Later, when we are done, we can return and bury the dead."

Conscious that his men were listening to his every word, Toledo went on, speaking louder. "Right here, right now, men, is our destiny. We, of the *Sirena*, and the Navy of the Most Catholic Kingdom and Empire of Spain, have been chosen to be the ones. The vermin who did this are nearby and it is *we* who will find and vanquish them and send them back to hell. And we will do it this very day."

He lifted his sword, the ceremonial one he had carried since the academy years ago. The others lifted their cutlasses and rifles as he shouted.

"It is our destiny men—*a destiny of honor!*"

A cheer erupted, growing into a guttural growl of commitment by men who were ready—eager—to kill.

35

Battle at Bomkatu

The reality of his present life intruded into the *gringo's* prostitute fantasy with a knock at the cabin door. It was a messenger from the main deck, nervously begging *Jefe's* pardon but that the lookout had spotted a steamer five or six miles away, coming north along the coast. A moment later he was on the deck in his trousers and climbing the ratlines, startling the crew, who had never seen the pale *gringo* go aloft.

At the main crosstrees he climbed over the shrouds and swung his telescope to the south. There she was. Coming fast, maybe eight, nine knots, a medium-sized gunboat, less than a half mile off the shore and five miles away. Cadena appeared next to him, breathing hard from the climb and holding his wound as he spoke.

"Warship?"

"Yes," came the answer they all dreaded. "She's a gunboat. Inshore and searching." The gray eyes leveled at Cadena, unnerving him. "Did you eliminate all the witnesses? *All* of them?"

"Every one of them, *Jefe*. There was no one left to talk."

"All right, it was luck of the draw. Doesn't matter. We've got a little steam up already—get it topped up, quickly. I want enough steam to get under way by the time that gunboat arrives, but don't let the flue open before then. I don't want them to see smoke until the last minute. I think we'll have enough time."

"Yes, *Jefe*. Get the steam topped up. What will we do when they get here?"

"Surprise them."

Cadena waited for more explanation. "*Jefe*, you mean fight them? A warship?"

"Yes, between the two of us we can maneuver around her, confuse them, and damage or cripple them. We won't be able to sink her, but maybe get in some lucky shots to slow her down enough so we can outrun her.

"With the small gun on the old steamer's deck you can nail her quarterdeck and go for the helmsmen and officers. Riflemen in the tops can shoot down on her decks. I'll use the packet steamer's speed to run around her and engage from the other side with the small pop gun we've got."

Cadena didn't like the sound of it. Warships were too strong for the small caliber guns they carried, and naval crews didn't give up like the merchant seamen. He started to object but the *gringo* cut him off.

"I don't have time to hear your whining, Cadena. Just get ready to get under way and follow my orders. And stop being an old lady about this. Show your manhood for once. Now get back to your ship."

Toledo stayed on deck, and sometimes perched in the main shrouds, scanning the shoreline with his telescope. Every officer did the same and every deck petty officer was aloft peering north and west. The crew was tense, ready, and they jumped when the word came.

"Deck there! A mast! Two masts, three . . . no, four masts. Four masts behind those trees, four points off the port bow, back in the jungle."

Half a dozen telescopes turned in unison toward the shoreline, one by one the officers calling out that they saw the masts, not a mile away, forward to the north and about a quarter mile behind the beach.

"A cove or river, sir. Just as you predicted," observed Dulce, admiration showing.

"Deck there! River entrance just up the beach. I see a channel with sandbars extending out."

Toledo put a hand on Dulce's shoulder. "Go aloft and tell me what you see."

The lieutenant leaped into the ratlines and raced upward, calling out from the topmast spreaders. "Go right two points, sir. The sandbar comes out in front of us."

"Beat to quarters," ordered Toledo. Kramer, standing beside him, marveled at his composure. Toledo continued. "Slow engine to dead slow. Standby the boarding party for the ship's cutter and launch." The bells of the engine telegraph and the bosun's pipes shrilled out as sailors ran to their stations.

They were almost up to the mouth of the narrow river, the water coming out of it staining the clear Caribbean brown, when a burst of smoke came from the treeline, then another. "Deck there! The masts are moving! They are coming out!"

That caught Toledo by surprise. Pleasantly by surprise. He thought they would have to fight their way in and board the pirates in the river. This would be simpler. Much simpler.

"Deck there! Two steamers coming out." The lookout's report was no longer necessary. Toledo could see it all, for they were only a mile from the river entrance, the first steamer coming out the channel at full speed, black smoke roiling from her stack, a puff of gray smoke coming from her foredeck. A small splash erupted in front of the ship, causing derogatory comments from the gun crews.

Toledo called out, "Send up the battle ensign. Fire number one gun when the first target bears."

Flapping madly in the breeze, a giant Spanish naval flag, as big as a sail, streamed out above the sailors, causing everyone to look up, then return to their duties with obvious pride. They may have been born in colonial Cuba, Toledo realized with emotion, but they are Spaniards this day.

The ten-inch caliber gun had already been laid into the target, turned on the pivot to point over the port bow. The *boom* was followed by a cloud of acrid smoke floating aft along the deck and a fountain of water that went up right next to the first steamer. Another *boom* blasted out, the concussion sucking the air away on the deck, the gun crew reloading even before the smoke cleared.

A cheer went up from the navy crew as a mass of debris exploded on the steamer's foredeck and the foremast leaned over, hanging in the rigging for a second before crashing alongside. But Toledo saw that it was still coming toward them, and that *Sirena* was passing the river entrance. The pirates would try to get out behind them.

"Come right full rudder to due south," he ordered, turning the *Sirena* around so that she could reverse course and rake the pirate steamer again, this time over the gunboat's starboard side.

The second steamer was now at the opening of the river, coming out twice as fast as the first one.

"God above! That's her, the *Colón American*. Captain, that's our Panama packet steamer!" cried out Kramer in English, gripping the rail, practically jumping up and down in rage.

"Shift fire to second target when it bears to starboard," Toledo said calmly, ignoring the yelling American beside him.

Sirena was turning now to the northeast then the east, her stern toward the steamers and her starboard side beginning to present itself. The starboard broadside 32-pounder batteries' gun captains were holding up their hands, signifying their guns were loaded and laid on the target even as she turned. So far the 32-

pounders had not been used, only the forward pivot gun.

Crash! A round from the pirates' small cannon came in through the transom, splinters flying in the air. The gunboat kept turning beyond east to the south, Toledo never taking his eyes from the lead steamer that was closing fast.

"Switch 32-pounder loads to grapeshot."

A bustle of activity began as the gun crews unloaded and reloaded with the close-in deadly scatter munitions. *Boom* came from the pivot, the shell exploding the bow of the steamer only three hundred yards away. Toledo could see a man in the main shrouds, apparently her commander, directing men on her deck. The steamer shifted course as *Sirena* came around and steadied due south. Toledo shook his head in disbelief. They were ramming.

He had to try to destroy her before they hit.

"Rapid fire with the number one gun. Broadside volley with the 32-pounders. Fire!" Toledo saw that Dulce was next to him and ordered the ship to keeping turning. It would lessen the blow when it came.

The four side guns roared out a hail of one hundred and twenty-eight one-pound lead balls into the approaching steamer, ripping away the planking on her bow and stripping her foredeck of every man standing. But Cadena's steamer still kept coming, her engine untouched.

Toledo, immersed in the lust of battle, knew that this was the moment he had trained and worked for all his life. Unconcerned by the death flying through the air around him, the officer drew his sword and held it high above his head, shouting to the sky.

"*For the honor of Spain!*"

Cadena stood atop the port side caprail, his aching wound forgotten in the lust of the action, ordering all hands to lie down on the deck for the coming collision and then be ready to swarm aboard the gunboat. *El Gringo Loco's* last order to him, as they were unmooring the steamers for the run out the river mouth, was to ram and then board the gunboat. Once the old steamer had immobilized the gunboat, then the gringo would swarm her from the other side, and they would have a warship, a real warship, of their own.

Cadena loved the idea of it. He saw the white and gold ensign of Spain on her mizzen, billowing out from the smoke pouring out of her stack. You won't be Spanish for long, he promised. Not for long, you Spanish whores.

They were close now, seconds away from the collision. Cadena looked back and saw the *Colón American* charging out the channel toward him, doing every bit of fifteen knots, small puffs along her rail where men with rifles were peppering the gunboat's decks. He waved to her quarterdeck and saw the figure under the awning wave back. The plan was working. They would do it!

A movement on the gunboat caught his eye—her captain was shouting something. Then the invisible wall of lead grapeshot hit him before he even heard the sound of the guns that fired it. He registered the impact without fear, noting that it was as if he had been thudded in the chest and right leg with sledge hammers. He could feel the bones shattering inside him, the limbs contorting unnaturally, his body curiously crumpling with no control. Splinters by the dozen dug their barbs into his face and torso, but he felt no pain and didn't understand why. It was all unreal, so very unreal, as he lay on the deck, blood pouring from wounds everywhere. The steamer smashed into the gunboat's bow on an angle from behind, instead of the decisive blow he had planned.

Chaos erupted. The masts and rigging were falling, broken by the force of the crash. Rending wood was shrieking as the two ships bounced away a few feet then smashed together again. Pistols and rifles exploded randomly. Screaming epithets in various Indian dialects and Spanish, the few men in the crew who could stand ran forward to board the gunboat. Desperation drove them, for they knew what would happen if they were captured.

Crying out in pain, for suddenly it was overwhelming now, Cadena pulled himself up to the gunwale and onto the caprail, swaying unsteadily. He could no longer stand and leaned there, watching as his men were shot down by the Spanish sailors.

He swiveled his head around to search for the packet steamer. They should be boarding the other side of the gunboat now. He saw her, but it was her stern. They had passed by and were steaming fast out to sea. Leaving him. Running away. He raised himself on an elbow, squinting in the pain to find him, to see him. Cadena finally saw the white clad figure under the awning, standing at the stern, hands on the rail, watching the battle. Watching Cadena die.

Another blast of grapeshot from the gunboat swept the deck. Cadena's last conscious sight was the explosion of the small arms ready ammunition box on the deck near him, as a sheet of flame covered him. He didn't feel the ricocheting bullets that fanned out. He was already dead.

The forward pivot gun had been making hits on the fast steamer, but she wasn't slowing down and now the pivot wouldn't bear, the collision having turned them toward the beach. Toledo shouted for his men to fend off and disengage the pirates, to go after the packet, but no one could hear him above the incredible noise. Eve ryone on *Sirena's* deck, including Kramer, was firing a pistol or rifle into the pirate steamer alongside to starboard.

Toledo climbed up on the gunwale to get above the confusion and smoke. He had to see about getting away from this steamer in order to destroy the one escaping. Peering over at the steamer next to him, he saw they could back away in reverse and clear the wreckage. Then they could bring the gunboat's bow around to the west and get the pivot gun into play. That way he could still stop the fast steamer. Toledo turned to give the order to the quartermaster at the same moment the broadside 32-pounders lashed out and the pirate's ammunition box exploded, only fifteen feet away.

Kramer, standing by *Sirena's* stack and looking aft, saw it happen. He would remember it for the rest of his life, and cry every time. The captain was engulfed in an explosion.

By the time the American reached him, Toledo was being gently set down on the deck by a burly petty officer. The Spanish captain still had the ceremonial sword gripped in his right hand, chin quivering from the agony of his catastrophic wounds, abdomen laid open and oozing gore. Kramer knelt on the deck and cradled his friend's bloody head as the Spaniard slowly tried to form words.

"Tell my father . . . tell him . . . say, that I died . . . as a . . . naval officer . . . should."

Kramer fought back the tears as the hand went limp and the sword dropped on deck. "I will, Fernando. I will . . . *amigo* . . . for the honor of Spain."

A rumble came from below deck when the engine went into reverse, gaining power until the deck vibrated violently as *Sirena* backed away from Cadena's sinking ship. Lieutenant Dulce strode by, calling for the pivot gun to rotate to port and fire at the diminishing shape of the packet. More shots went into her, bringing up smoke, but didn't stop her. No chase was started, for even when she was newly commissioned, *Sirena* couldn't keep up with the packet's kind of speed. The sailors swore blue oaths and pounded fists, frustrated at their impotence, devastated at the death of their captain.

Kramer was still holding Toledo when Dulce knelt down next to them.

"We killed them all, but in addition to Captain Toledo we lost three ourselves. Eight wounded. The packet steamer is too fast for us. We must wait for the *Canton* to come, then give her the information so they can continue the chase."

Kramer didn't answer. It was all just too much for him.

36

Searching

It took *Canton* a day to get there, with *Plover* a day behind.
Treating the wounded, repairing the ship, and searching for
escapees filled the time for the Spanish sailors. Their lieutenant
explained to Wake, Russell, and Monteblanco the horrific scene
they had found at Uani and the subsequent battle at Bomkatu
River. Tears filled Dulce's eyes as he described their friend's death
and how the packet was damaged but had escaped. His guns had
hit her solidly several times, he explained, bringing down rigging
and sending up smoke, but failed to stop her completely, though
he did not understand why not.

He also explained that since the packet was so much faster
than *Sirena*, he had decided to stay where he was and round up
the outlaws who had made it to the beach. Three more Spanish
Navy sailors had died while pursuing the renegades ashore, but
they thought that in the end they had gotten them all. They had
aboard four in irons, locked in the hold.

He ended his report with the butcher's bill, as naval seamen
everywhere called the casualty list. Captain Toledo was joined in
death by six sailors, and eight more sailors were wounded, all by

rifle fire. Wake and Russell thanked the lieutenant and suggested that he take his ship home to Cuba where the men, both alive and deceased, would be considered heroes. The prisoners could be transferred from there. Kramer, distraught and exhausted, requested that he be allowed to find passage back to Panama.

An hour later *Sirena* weighed anchor and made her way through the reefs north toward Cabo de Gracias a Dios, then northward toward Cienfuegos, on the southern coast of Cuba. Leaving at the same time, *Canton* and *Plover* steamed northeast along the course last seen of the *Colón American*.

"He was a good man, Peter," said Monteblanco as he watched the Spanish warship disappear on the rolling horizon. "He reminded me of my father. A true gentleman of the old school."

"Yes, he was good man, Pablo. And from your descriptions of your father, I can see the similarities."

"But this is not really a fight for a *gentleman*, is it?" Monteblanco sighed.

"No, Pablo. I think I disagree there," answered Wake as he shook his head sadly. "This is exactly the kind of fight where a gentleman is needed—lest we descend to the enemy's level. It's what sets us apart from them, my friend."

The men thought it was hopeless, but *El Gringo Loco* knew better. He had always been amazed by the ingenuity and audacity of the Confederate raiders. Now he would do them one better.

The *Colón American* was a wreck, not destined to float for much longer after being torn apart by the Spanish Navy's guns. She was leaking everywhere and they had gotten the fires out only after much work.

Out of fuel, for they had not had time to completely load her at Bomkatu, they were limping northeastward under jury-rigged sails into the shipping lanes outside of Jamaica to wait for the crew of a merchantman to come along and rescue them. That would be no problem, for they would portray themselves as the victims of—a sly smile crept over his face as he thought of the delicious irony of it—a pirate attack. He did not think they would have to wait long either, the area between Rosalind Bank and Jamaica was a major thoroughfare for shipping. And as he well knew, seamen always stopped to help brother seamen in distress.

Yes, once he got off this tub and had another ship, they could have some fun along the coast of Jamaica, maybe three days' worth before the Royal Navy got word. And by the time the Limey sailor boys got to where he had been, *El Gringo Loco* would be long gone, heading to his new home base—a place totally new and unexpected. He wondered how his crew would like it there and realized with a grunt that they would like it anywhere they could get drunk and laid.

He admitted grandly to himself that he liked the plan, especially the impudence of it. The brass bottoms in Washington and London would be clutching the ulcers in their guts when they heard of his escape and raid along the Jamaican coast. He hoped the pompous fools in the Navy Department would be apoplectic.

And his new hosts and countrymen? They would welcome his money, probably more money than most had ever seen in their miserable lives. He would live like a king among the natives. Ah yes, a great white king.

As his men strained at the pumps nonstop to keep the ship afloat, he sat there in the shambles of his cabin grinning to himself at the vision of his future.

Exactly how is it that you say *El Gringo Loco* in French, he wondered?

Wake and Russell decided to split up. Each gunboat could handle the lone packet now, if not with speed, definitely through gunnery. *Canton* would search from the islets at Serrana Bank northward to the coral cays of Serranilla Bank. *Plover* took Cay Gorda at Gorda Bank to Roselind Bank. In four days they would rendezvous at Southwest Rock on Pedro Bank, after having searched the entire area north and east of Cabo de Gracias a Dios as well as they could.

The nights were filled with self-doubt for Wake, particularly when he was alone in his cabin. In the confines there, by the dim light of the swaying lantern, he was given to reflection, which was not a positive pastime lately. Everything had gone wrong on this operation. What started out as a simple mission to apprehend maritime outlaws had become a chase in which the enemy left a trail of dead bodies. The grisly results of Symons' path through the lower Caribbean were disgusting, but a constant spur to persistence and vigilance. They must continue and find him.

Then Wake thought about his other problem. Terrington had been quiet. Too quiet. The ensigns reported that he was racked with incessant pain from being deprived of the laudanum, but that he had tried no escape or violence. To his repeated pleas for medicine they said no, that they were not allowed. Now he wasn't even asking. He was eating less and less and getting quieter and quieter. Wake wondered what was going on in the man's tormented head.

The other prisoners were quiet too. Kept far forward in the lowest, darkest part of the ship, they survived on the same rations as everyone else, but were cut off from the rest. The crew had no sympathy for them.

Unbeknownst to Wake, over the past months the crew had heard from Durling and Rork of the lieutenant's concern for his crews in the past, his intense loyalty to those who served with honor, and his ferocity when aroused to anger. The men were willing to back Wake and follow him, even through this bizarre voyage, the likes of which none had ever seen. No one in the crew had ever seen a captain relieved of duty, and they were awed by Wake's decision to do it.

As he sat in his cabin writing his log and reviewing reports, Wake did not know what the men of the *Canton* thought of his actions. He only knew what their behavior displayed, and that indicated that they were as anxious as he to find the pirates and end the terror. He realized it was their reputation on the line as well as his. For years in the future, in sailors' haunts at navy ports the world over, the men of the *Canton* knew they would be asked, "Say, were you aboard her when they went after that madman pirate back in sixty-nine?"

He remembered what he saw happen to the men of the *Sacramento*, three years after she and another warship had refused to respond to the challenge of a lone Confederate raider off Spain in '65. The barroom fight was quick and vicious after they had been called incompetent cowards. The accusers had lost, but Wake never forgot the look on the face of the *Sacramento*'s crew when it had been brought up.

And this was even worse, for innocents were being slaughtered. He would find Symons and kill him, Wake vowed with a tightening grip on his logbook—not for bragging rights or honor, but to prevent future victims.

All was ready. The name *Colón American* on the transom had been painted out and replaced with *Lorena*. The men had hidden their pistols in their pockets and were looking despondent, which the *gringo* thought with a grin was very appropriate, for the water in the holds was gaining and the few sails they could set were barely moving the ship. The ruse was perfect.

The merchant steamer approached with her boats swayed out and lowered in the falls, ready to assist in any way. She stopped her engines and drifted alongside, the captain leaning over the rail with a speaking trumpet.

"Ahoy, *Lorena*. What say you, sir? Do you need assistance?"

"Aye, we do," shouted the *gringo* back. "We've been destroyed by a pirate gang off Nicaragua and are sinking. Can you help us, for the love of God, sir?"

There was a hurried discussion on the other ship. Then the pirates saw her boats being dropped into the water and knew it had worked.

"Of course, Captain! We will be right over," the other captain shouted into the trumpet.

"Where are you bound?" the American renegade said as innocently as he could.

"We are the *Diana*, sir, bound for Kingston with a load of cane and corn from Belize. We'll be there tomorrow."

"Thank God for you, sir," said *El Gringo Loco*, as he cocked an eyebrow and realized how much his relief was real.

The *Diana*'s men were almost to them when he pulled aside Bajo, his new Cuban number two since that idiot Cadena had been killed at Bomkatu.

"Remember, wait until we get up on their deck and I give the signal."

Bajo acknowledged the order and went forward as the rescuers climbed up, amazed at the wreckage and staring at the men aboard. The *gringo* hugged the one who looked to be in charge and cried out, "You saved us. We'll live now."

The crew of the *Diana* were mainly black Jamaican and Belizean and were happy to be hailed as heroes. They helped the men carry bundles of personal possessions down into the boats and rowed them over to the smaller steamer, where her captain greeted them. The *gringo* could feel his skin already burning in the glare of the noonday sun.

"I'm Captain Collins, sir. Devon Collins, from Exeter. "What do you want to do with your ship, Captain . . .?" The steamer's skipper asked the *gringo* as the other stranded men were helped up on *Diana*'s deck.

"What? Oh, yes, well I'm Captain . . . Darien. And we can leave her. She'll be under in an hour now that the pumps aren't being worked."

"Yes, yes. Well, come below, Captain Darien, and we'll get a spot of rum in you. Do you good after what you've been through. Now tell me about these pirates, sir," said Collins as he led the way. The *gringo* stopped and looked forward to his men, catching Bajo's attention. He nodded, saw Bajo's nod back, and turned around to see Collins waiting by the after hatchway, waiting to hear his story.

"Well, Captain Collins, these pirates are the kind of scoundrels who would pose as victims, then kill everyone in the ship that rescued them."

The confusion on Collins' face lasted a fleeting second—his look changing to terror as the man he had just saved raised a large revolver and shot him twice in the chest.

Shots banged out on the deck for a few seconds. Then several of the gang went below to the crew's berth while others went charging into the engine rooms. None of the victims had a chance. Within a minute, every man in the *Diana's* crew was dead.

A cheerful Bajo reappeared on deck, reported to his leader that the entire ship was theirs, congratulated him on his victory, then received his orders—steer north to the coast of Jamaica, fifty miles away. *El Gringo Loco* gazed around the horizon, stopping to watch the packet steamer as she settled lower in the water and wallowed in the swells.

"You served me well, bitch," he muttered to the wrecked hulk, "but this little darling will serve me even better."

As he descended the ladder he called out to Bajo and pointed to Collins' body.

"And get this mess cleaned up, Bajo. I like a *clean* ship, damn it."

"As you command, *Jefe*," responded Bajo quickly, knowing enough to never question the *norteamericano*, whatever the hell his real name was.

"I need to go to Kingston, Peter, and report in to my command-er. Why don't you come there too. You can reprovision and com-municate with your superiors," suggested Russell as he sat on the bench seat in his cabin, the *Canton* visible out the gallery ports. Once the ships met at the reef at Southwest Rock on Pedro Bank, Wake and Monteblanco had been rowed over to confer with the British captain.

Days had been lost on fruitless searches of the small islands off Nicaragua and the men were in low spirits. None of them had a strong theory on where the gang had taken the packet steamer. The pirates had disappeared.

"I hate to waste any more time, though, Rodney. Symons already has a week or more on us," replied Wake, clearly frustrated.

"Peter, I need to go into Kingston also," Monteblanco said gently. "I have delayed my return to Caracas for some time now, but I need to go home and report to my own government. It is time for me. I truly think you need to do the same, my friend." He paused and raised an eyebrow. "For you have more to report than all of us."

"Yes, you're both right, of course," Wake sighed. "I'll take you into port at Kingston, Pablo. *Canton* can reprovision and fill her bunkers and I'll report in at the consul general's office and tell them what's happened so far. They've already received my initial report about Captain Terrington and have forwarded it to Washington, I imagine."

"It is best," agreed Monteblanco.

"And after my ship is readied and I've sent my report off, *Canton*'ll go back out and search again for Symons," added Wake in a determined tone, causing Monteblanco and Russell to exchange glances.

"Peter, old chap," said Russell, "I appreciate your persistence, as does Pablo here—who has the most serious reasons to gain justice of any of us—but remember to think clearly. You need to resolve some of the other issues you've got to deal with also. Namely, removing your captain from command. Some uncharitable gentlemen might consider that *mutiny*, my friend—even in your rather enlightened navy. Going off half-cocked is not the answer and will only lead to your dismissal, or worse. Your navy, or ours, will get Symons and soon. I have no doubt."

Wake smiled. The British captain was being polite, but he was right. Wake needed to take care of the issue he loathed thinking about—Parker Terrington.

And then he would resume his search.

The *Diana* was drifting five miles offshore of Black River on the southwest coast of Jamaica the next sunrise with the *gringo* standing on the main deck surveying the horizon with a telescope. He was just tightening the focus on an object to their west when the lookout called down, reporting it.

"Schooner to the west, tacking inshore."

He could see that she was relatively large, heavily laden, and probably coming in from Cuba. Watching her tack through the wind and settle on an offshore course, he decided she would do and, unless some better target turned up, he would let her sail to him, then take her.

A moment later the lookout called down again. "Another one . . . no, two . . . to the east by that headland. Sailing downwind to us."

Snapping his telescope back open he turned around and examined the schooners to windward. They were surging westerly down the waves with their sails out on either side, wing and wing, rolling in the small seas, coming around Great Pedro Bluff.

Incredible, he thought, here at Jamaica they come to you. Not even any need for searching.

37

Her Majesty's Crown
Colony of Jamaica

During that same sunrise, fifty miles to the east of the *Diana*, HMS *Plover* and USS *Canton* were letting go their anchors into the clear waters off the Royal Navy's station at Kingston Harbor. Every man aboard each ship was looking forward to the possibility of going ashore and relaxing with drink and women. Wake, who was definitely going ashore, dreaded the upcoming experience, and the possible consequences.

He walked up the hill to the American consul general's office on Oxford Road and introduced himself to the clerk, who went into another office and came out with a superior. The tall, thin man who appeared stared at Wake before speaking in an easy Midwestern drawl, an incongruous sound in the tropics of the Caribbean.

"Yes, well Lieutenant Wake . . . ah, welcome back ashore in Kingston. We met at the reception when you were here before, but let me introduce myself again. My name is Randall Collmer, from Indiana, and I'm Consul General Clingenpeel's assistant. Unfortunately, he is away right now in Cuba, so I'll be your liaison.

"Ahmm . . . Lieutenant, we've received some rather, ahmm . . . unusual . . . correspondence from the Navy Department regarding you and the *Canton,* and were wondering if you would come back this way. Say, were you able to get that renegade naval officer down there?"

"No, we haven't got him, yet," answered Wake. "I've come to send my report to Washington on that, and other developments, and to advise your office on the situation in connection with the pirate. We also need provisions and coal."

"Oh, I see," said Collmer without showing his opinion. "Well, please come in and have a chair, and I'll find that correspondence for you to peruse. Provisions and coal we can do right away. I'd also be interested in hearing of your view on the situation in the Central American countries."

Sitting in the offered chair as the diplomat left the room, Wake looked out at the magnificent view over the anchorage in the bay, thinking about the conversation he'd just had. Collmer was very polite and helpful, but there was something strange in his demeanor. Then Wake realized ominously what is was that bothered him—the man had never even asked about Captain Terrington. He already knew?

"Welcome home, Captain Russell," offered Commodore Forester. *Plover's* commander stood from his chair and said, "Thank you, sir," as his superior entered the office and sat behind the huge mahogany desk.

"I do not see a captured vessel in the port, so may I presume the pirate's ship is destroyed?" asked Forester pleasantly. Russell was sure the commodore already had the news from his staff that Russell had briefed downstairs, but answered the question.

"Two of the pirate's vessels have been destroyed, sir. Captain Toledo of the *Sirena* was killed in the process of destroying the second one a week ago at Nicaragua, along with several of his men. The third was damaged but escaped, with the pirate leader—Symons is his name—aboard."

"I see," said Forester, folding his hands in a steeple and pursing his lips. "And where was his last position?"

"By Cabo Gracias a Dios, heading northeast. A week ago. We, *Canton* and *Plover*, searched the islands offshore there but found no recent sign of him."

"Hhmm . . . And your opinion of where he went?" Forester's eyes bored into the ship captain.

"Ah, I just don't know, sir," admitted Russell, trying desperately to project an air of professional confidence.

"Conjecture?"

"Maybe west to Yucatan, maybe east to Venezuela, sir," ventured Russell. "He'll not be welcomed on the Moskito or Panama or Colombian coasts, sir."

"Oh? And pray tell why not, Captain Russell?"

Over the next twenty minutes, Russell proceeded to tell the commodore in detail what had happened with the search for Symons and his men on those coasts. Afterward Forester rose from his desk.

"One last matter, Captain Russell. Your special mission for the foreign office. What was the outcome of that?"

"My confidential report was sealed and given to your aide, sir, but the simple truth is that the English people of the Moskito coast are out for themselves, have no real economic viability, and in my opinion, are not trustworthy. They smell potential money from London in regard to a possible canal project and will tell the bureaucrats back home what they want to hear. In fact, many supported this pirate, directly or indirectly, until his atrocities on their coast."

Russell knew what he had just said was explosive and not what was expected, but the naval officer also knew that somebody had to give the true picture of the situation. He went on as Forester digested the previous information.

"Another truth is that the Moskito Indians are simple people who just want to be left alone by everybody, English and Nicaraguan. They are subsistence fishermen and farmers, sir, nothing more."

"And the Nicaraguans?"

"The Nicaraguans are very concerned about British movement in their area and watched our actions closely. They will not hesitate to complain to Washington if they sense we are trying to reverse the Clayton-Bulwer Treaty's provisions, sir."

"How strong is their control over that coast? Would, and could, they fight for it?"

Russell paused, understanding the latent consequences of his answer and how it would be viewed in London.

"Their day-to-day control is not strong, but they could reinforce rapidly and, yes, they would fight, even against us or our surrogates. Latin honor would compel them. Remember, sir, Symons was one of our surrogates in their eyes when he originally arrived there and fought against them for independence of the area." Russell stopped as he saw Forester's objection coming, held up a finger and continued. "Yes, sir, I know that London did not officially support the Moskito coast uprising last year, but no one in Managua believes that."

"Could the English settlers hold off the Nicaraguans?"

"Not without our help, Commodore, and even then it would be a protracted conflict in a terrible jungle. Diseases would wipe out large numbers of our men."

Forester grew pensive, remembering similar wars, then nodded his head in agreement. "And your assessment of the feasibility of a solely British canal in Nicaragua, Captain?"

"Not good, Commodore. The Panama route would be easier, but if London is determined on a Nicaraguan route, I think it should be a joint project with the Americans, as the Clayton-Bulwer Treaty envisioned as a possibility. I hear that President Grant is very interested in not having an outside power controlling that canal, for it would be the sea route to their western states."

Forester regarded Russell quizzically for a moment. Then he spoke without smiling. "Your opinion of Americans seems to have changed lately, Captain Russell. I remember it was not so long ago when you commented that they weren't as much competent as they were lucky. Overrated, I believe you said."

Russell thought about that and realized that his opinions about a lot of things had changed in the last month. "Yes, sir. I was wrong. Now that I have seen them in action, I would never underestimate the Americans, Commodore," admitted Russell. He thought of his friend Wake and the difficult decisions that man had made.

"Especially their navy . . ."

Wake opened the dark blue Navy Department pouch Collmer handed him, noticing that the seal appeared unmolested, and pulled out two envelopes. One was addressed to him personally from the secretary of the navy. The other was to Captain Parker Terrington, which Wake would have to deliver. He opened his as Collmer sifted through other papers on his desk.

Getting past the usual official introductory language, Wake read the main body of the missive.

Lieutenant Wake,

> *In response to your report of June 1869, sent from Panama through Jamaica—you are hereby ordered to bring the USS* Canton *back to a United States port, taking care to document all of your previous and subsequent actions and those of your men.*

> *Upon arrival at such port, Captain Terrington and you are ordered to travel by the most expedient means possible and present yourselves, and the aforesaid documentation to this office. Lieutenant John Connery will assume command of* Canton *at that point in time. Your*

request for a Court-Martial decision is granted de facto, as it would be ordered in the event, regardless of your wishes.

The Department looks with great dismay upon the events of Captain Terrington's removal from command, and expects that this unprecedented, and embarrassing, action on your part will be accompanied by overwhelming evidence.

This directive is being sent to all ports within your region. Upon receipt you will instantly send a response describing your immediate compliance with the aforementioned order, the first United States port you intend to arrive at, and the estimated date of said arrival.

Until you come under the direct control of a superior officer who can assess the situation, the Department expects you to maintain a respectful relation with Captain Terrington, and accord him all of the rights and privileges accustomed to his rank.

Wake felt the blood draining from his face. He expected this kind of response, but still, actually seeing it was chilling. The directive was signed by the secretary of the navy himself, but it was a different one, someone named Robeson. Wake had never heard of him.

Wake looked up to see Collmer observing him.

"Mr. Collmer, I will need to send off some communications to the Navy Department as soon as possible, then make arrangements to get the ship reprovisoned and recoaled. I want to be under way tomorrow, at the latest."

Collmer was surprised. "Leaving that fast? Well, yes, we can do that, Lieutenant. It's very unusual, though." He smiled while watching Wake's eyes. "Here in the tropics things often go at a slower pace."

"The situation is complicated, Mr. Collmer. I am sure you know of the unfortunate events regarding Captain Terrington," Wake paused as Collmer nodded neutrally, "and I have been ordered to expedite my return."

"Then we will assist all we can, Lieutenant." A look of concern began to show on Collmer's face. "You can write out the telegraph message, and I will have it sent immediately via the new cable to Havana, thence by ship to Mobile for further telegraph. And I wish you good luck in those distressing professional matters."

The consular official continued, now smiling as if nothing unpleasant had just been discussed, "While I have you here, can you give me intelligence of the situation in the Central American region? I am particularly interested in Panama and Nicaragua and your candid assessment of the . . . *atmosphere* . . . there among the expatriate Americans and British, if you would be so kind."

Wake grew wary of the man in front of him who could hide any indication of personal emotion or opinion. He's like a professional card player—always receiving information and never sending it, Wake thought, as he gave his opinion of the confusing scene in the Isthmus, where nothing ever was as it first appeared.

Ironically, it turned out to be an assessment quite similar to the one that Captain Rodney Russell had already given his superior half an hour earlier, suggesting cooperation with the British instead of competition.

While still at anchor on the following day's afternoon, a grim-faced Connery came to Wake in his cabin and reported he had urgent information from shore. After just dealing with Terrington's complaining for the third time that day, Wake was in no mood for bad news, but told Connery to come out with it.

"Sir, two things to report. First, the coaling is done, finally. The ship is ready in all respects for sea. The second is bad news, sir. Very bad news."

Wake braced himself, wondering what was next. "Go ahead."

"Symons evidently struck several ships in the last couple of days. Two are known destroyed with no survivors and there are two missing that should have arrived here—"

"Where, John! Where were they?"

"Right here, sir. On the south coast of Jamaica."

Wake was stunned. "Good Lord. He hit here."

"Commodore Forester has asked for you to come to Admiralty House immediately, sir."

"Yes, of course," said Wake absently, his mind working the new possible locations Symons could have gone. "While I'm gone I want *Canton* hove short, steam built up and ready to get under way the moment I am back aboard."

"Aye, aye, sir."

Wake could tell that Commodore Forester was enraged but attempting to stay calm. The man's face was dark-hued and his voice level. There were no niceties upon arrival.

"Lieutenant Wake, come in and please sit down. You know everyone."

Wake did as asked, sitting at a table with a chart of the Caribbean spread out on it. Russell was there and, to Wake's pleasant surprise, also Monteblanco. They nodded their hellos but said nothing. He hadn't seen his Venezuelan friend since the morning of their arrival in Kingston, when he had left for his country's consulate. Next to the somber-looking Royal Navy commodore, Forester's young flag lieutenant stood nervously in the corner with arms crossed behind him, waiting for orders.

The commodore wasted no time, calling the lieutenant forward to present his information.

"Yes, sir. Gentlemen, I am Lieutenant Stonewell. Here is the situation as it has unfolded and we know it. This morning we were notified by fishermen that two schooners were seen burning about ten miles off Portland Point, and just twenty miles southwest of Kingston. When the lifesaving cutter got there they found both vessels burned to the waterline with debris and bodies in the water. The bodies had bullet holes. No one was found alive. The cutter spoke with a brigantine in the area who saw a steamer moving from that area northward, in toward shore. And a small sloop found debris off Starve Gut Bay, by Black River, that had the name *Colón American* on it. All of this happened this morning. A coastal alert has been sent out around the island."

Russell interrupted. "Description of that steamer, Lieutenant?"

"Nothing other than single stack, schooner rig, no square sails on the foremast."

Russell glanced at Wake, who raised an eyebrow as Stonewell continued.

"There's more, gentlemen. A steamer, the *Diana,* bound from Belize to Kingston, had been registered by the observers when she made Negril Point on the west end several days ago. She should have been in the harbor here at least two days ago. She's missing, and she matches the general description of the steamer from this morning."

Stonewell took a breath and went on. "We also have a schooner missing from Savannah la Mar on the west end of the island. She was bound to Kingston also. Should have been here two days ago.

"Our analysis is that the *Colón American* has sunk and the pirates have transferred to another vessel. Most likely the steamer *Diana.*"

Stonewell ended his report and backed away as Forester spoke.

"All right, gentlemen. I have asked you all here for your opinions of this information. The three of you understand this Symons fellow better than anyone else. Do you think it's him?"

Russell answered first. "It sounds like him, sir, but have we checked to make sure it's not a repeat of sixty-five and another uprising?" He saw Wake's questioning look and explained.

"Peter, in eighteen sixty-five there was an uprising here that got so bad the island lost its status as a self-legislative colony and was reverted to a crown colony, governed by appointed governors. I was just thinking that might be a possibility—that the anarchic types who did that might have tried again."

Lieutenant Stonewell answered quickly. "No. We thought of that too. No indications ashore of that at all."

"Very good, Lieutenant. Well, Commodore, we haven't had any piracy here for a long time, so I think it's Symons," said Russell. "No doubt."

Monteblanco agreed, adding, "He has nowhere to go to the south. He is heading to new areas. Target-rich areas."

"Thank you, Don Pablo. I value your opinion, and also thought you had a right to know the situation," said Forester, who then turned to Wake. "Lieutenant, what's your opinion of this?"

"It's him. He's displaying his prowess. But how many ships does Symons have now? And where is he headed?"

"Precisely the questions we need to answer, gentlemen," said Forester. "Now, here is what we in the Royal Navy intend to do. I realize that you are in a difficult position, Lieutenant Wake, with serious obligations to return to your country, but perhaps you might assist in a minor way."

"Of course, Commodore. I'll assist in any way that I can," responded Wake while wondering how Forester knew of his orders. Was nothing secret in the Caribbean?

"Excellent. Here is the plan," explained Forester as he pointed at various locations on the chart. "Captain Russell will take *Plover* out to sea after the meeting has concluded. He will work his way west along the coast, circumnavigating the island clockwise. HMS *Harpford* is at Falmouth Harbor on the north coast. They received a telegraph from me to commence a search starting there and working clockwise as well, around to Kingston. In addition, all cutters in Her Majesty's Excise Service and all the lifesaving boats have put to sea and are scouring the coasts of the island."

Forester then turned to Wake. "And if Lieutenant Wake could be so kind as to examine the southeast coast and east end of the island while he is transiting homeward, we would be greatly in debt. I understand sir, that your ship is ready to get under way at this time."

Wake tried not to show his amazement at Forester's knowledge. "Yes, sir. I will weigh anchor upon the conclusion of the meeting and will be honored to assist by checking the coast along my way."

Forester looked at all of them. "Then it is a plan, gentlemen. Let us make it happen as soon as possible."

Monteblanco raised a hand and asked, "Commodore, what will you do if you find he has gone from Jamaica?"

"My first concern is to protect Her Majesty's Crown Colony of Jamaica, Don Pablo. After that," admitted Forester with obvious frustration, "I don't have a bloody notion of where the bastard is or how we'll get him."

38

La République de Mort

August 1869

Staying inshore, *Canton* examined all vessels along the south-east coast of Jamaica while on their way home. Out of the thirty-one ships they observed from Kingston Harbor to Morant Point at the eastern end of the island, four steamers looked suspicious enough to send boarding parties. The captains were quickly told that the American warship had special permission from the Royal Navy and were shocked when told that piracy had occurred in the area. All of the steamers were legitimate, however, and none had pertinent information.

The atmosphere aboard *Canton* was tense. All aboard knew that Wake faced charges of mutiny and that the court-martial would end in the humiliation of one man or the imprisonment of the other. It was a voyage unlike any other in the memories of the officers and men, and no one made jest of the matter.

The day they left Kingston, Wake delivered the envelope to Terrington, who was looking worse than ever. He had started to eat again, broth and porridge, but his body had undergone stark changes. Sunken eyes stared out from hollow cheeks the color of old parchment. The voice was merely a croak and the man was unsteady on his feet.

Terrington's hands had shaken as he fumbled with the envelope, finally getting it open, then holding it to his chest so that Wake could not see the contents. Wake had excused himself, glancing at Terrington when he left the cabin. The man was sitting on his berth, bent over with the paper close to his face, mumbling as he read the contents. It had been pitiful and disgusting, Wake remembered the next day as he climbed the after ladder to get some fresh air.

The engine, boilers having been temporarily repaired at Kingston, was pushing them at an easy eight knots into the swells from the east. Looking around the darkening horizon he saw nothing but the small puffy clouds of the trade winds and the panoramic display of a Caribbean sunset. Normally he would revel in the sight, but he was not in the mood.

Their course would take them to the area of Cap Dame Marie, Haiti's southwesternmost point of land. From there they would head north into the Windward Passage, rounding Cuba and heading to Key West, the nearest United States port. His report to the secretary of the navy had estimated their time of arrival at a week or so, in late July. A week in which to ponder his fate, Wake rued, and to go over all his decisions and see where he had gone wrong in the chase for Symons.

Every decision seemed at first glance to be the wrong one. But the one to go to northeast Nicaragua had been the right one after all, hadn't it? And there had been some success, for two out of Symon's three vessels were destroyed, albeit one by the mysterious means of the Cuna Indians. The price of the Nicaragua decision to split their force had been steep, but still, Wake felt that it had been correct, based upon what they had known at the time.

All in all, he told himself, he had conducted the operation as well as anyone could have, so the court-martial would not find fault there. The decision to relieve Terrington was another matter though, one that would be harder to justify in the calm, safe rooms of the Navy Department, three thousand miles away from where the events took place. That fight, Wake knew, would be the toughest of his life, and there wasn't anything he could do about it right now.

He wondered what was in the orders for Terrington and concluded they were probably a near copy of his own. But what would Terrington be thinking? It would be hell on him too, probably worse because of the humiliation already suffered at his addiction being made public knowledge.

The sky was painted a faint pink, the molten copper sun having disappeared. Wake breathed in the salt air and felt it calm him. Come what may, he had no regrets. Terrington had brought it on himself.

Diana was a good little ship, *El Gringo Loco* decided. Not as fast as the Panama packet had been, but fast enough, and useful for his purposes. The quarry along Jamaica had all succumbed quickly once he rammed alongside at the last minute, after hailing them to come close for a friendly gab. Usually within seconds he could have enough men aboard the other vessel to persuade them to surrender. Not that that did them any good, he reflected with a laugh. The stupid dupes thought he would let them go in their ships' boats! What fools. He didn't even keep their ships afloat, so why would he keep them alive?

But the really delicious part was that he was making the vaunted Royal Navy look incompetent. He could just imagine the senior officers raging about it now in Kingston. Hit them in their own backyard, just like those Confederate raiders hit us in New England in '63. And thinking of that—where was dear brother Parker Terrington and the U.S. Navy? Probably still in Cartagena, he imagined, looking in vain for the *Abuela*.

The Limeys would, of course, thoroughly scour the lower

Caribbean, every bay and river, every island. But *El Gringo Loco* wouldn't be there, for there were much greener fields in which to hunt. When his men finally figured out where they were going they had cheered, for they would make a lot of money off the fat targets in this part of the world, and those dusky girls were all right for what they needed too. The main shipping route for the Caribbean ran right past their new lair, and no one would know their location, for their lair was a place that no one wanted to go. In fact, everyone went out of their way to avoid it.

He was surprised about how easy it had been, really. He had chosen the village of Colline Pauvre, on the Bay of Henne, on the north shore of Haiti's Golfe des Gonaives from its position on the chart. He found the entrance deep and without dangerous reefs. Coming into the strange bay, he had asked for the headman, who turned out to be some local thug named Henri Muret, who luckily spoke some English and Spanish.

Within seconds he knew Muret was the kind of man he could deal with. Within two hours he had "an arrangement," as Muret termed it, allowing him to use the little village as a base of operations in return for a share of the cargo obtained. They could even handle larger sales of the stolen merchandise to factors in the bigger town to the east. And Muret did not want to know details of the piracy operation, only the results, which was just fine with the renegade *gringo*.

His plan was simple. Steam out into the shipping lanes of the Windward Passage in the night, in the pre-dawn light make the capture, and in the morning race back. By noon they would be back at the village, offloading the items that were of value for resale. The ex-American deduced that he could keep this little operation going for about a month, before he would have to move on. But in the meantime, it would be very profitable.

And they would start that very night.

The morning found *Canton* with the end of Haiti's northern pincer, Cap Foux, on their starboard bow, distant ten miles. The Windward Passage was living up to its name—the breeze was roaring through from the east northeast—but they were slogging upwind and making good speed with the sails assisting the engine.

The rising sun was made blood red by the smoke that covered the eastern horizon from the farmers' slash-and-burn fires ashore on the Haitian mainland. The red disk rising up looked ominous, a celestial sign commented on by the deck watch.

Wake was at the starboard waist watching it too, when the cry came down from aloft.

"Deck there! I think there's some sort of wreckage a mile on the port bow."

He walked aft and took the proffered binoculars while Custen used the telescope. Wake focused on the dark spot among the waves but couldn't make it out. Was it really wreckage, or deck cargo that had washed overboard?

"Deck there! Sail to port. Looks to be a brig, five miles off, southbound. Another sail on the port bow, five miles, schooner rig, northbound."

They were in one of the most crowded shipping lanes in the Western Hemisphere, and Wake realized that as the sun rose and visibility increased there would be plenty of sightings. As if reading his thoughts, the lookout added two more sailing ships as Custen shook his head and reported, "It's wreckage, sir. I can see it now."

His evaluation was confirmed by the lookout a moment later. Wake ordered *Canton* to be steered to the debris, the lookouts to be tripled, and all hands to watch for survivors. Walking forward in his nervousness, he came upon Rork standing by the mainmast. The bosun, who had already called for the coxswain to ready his boat crew, was also eyeing the flotsam.

"Not a good sight for a sailorman to see, sir. I've a nasty feeling in me gut about this. Nasty indeed."

"Your Irish intuition hoisting a signal again, Rork?" asked Wake. Though he often joked with his friend about his Gaelic sense of forewarning, he always paid attention when Rork gave voice to it.

"Aye, sir. I can feel it in me blood, I can. 'Tis chilled like the Mull o' Killarney right now, sir. Aye, we'll find bad things in that wreckage, or I'm not a son o' the Sainted Isle."

His prediction came true ten minutes later when they hove to next to the wreckage, which turned out to be the ship's boat from the *Connie Kate*, port of Nassau. The boat was swamped, holes having been cut through the floorboards and hull, and part of the bow was charred. Other debris was scattered nearby, the *Canton's* cutter investigating each piece for a sign to indicate what had happened. The sailors were already speculating that it was no accident or storm that caused it, but Symons the pirate. Wake kept his opinion quiet, waiting for proof.

When they found two bodies, one headless and the other with a large hole in the chest, both in relatively fresh condition in the warm tropical waters, they knew for certain. *El Gringo Loco* had been right there, and not long ago.

Wake went to his cabin and examined the chart, accompanied by Custen and Connery.

"All right, gentlemen. It's got to be Cuba or Haiti. Which do you think?"

Custen leaned over the chart, shaking his head. "Not Cuba. That's a rugged lee shore. The only harbor close to the Windward Passage is at Caimanera, on the Bay of Guantanamo, and that's more than a hundred miles from here. Those bodies are fresh, not more than four or five hours at the very most, sir. No, my bet's on Haiti."

"The Spanish Navy would be aware of them at Caimanera or

Santiago, anyway, David," added Connery. He ran a finger around the giant body of water that Haiti bordered on three sides, "But where the hell in Haiti is he? He could be anywhere in this Gonaives Gulf."

"This northern peninsula, I think. Probably along the shore-line," said Custen placing his hand on Haiti's northern pincer. "I'm not familiar with it, though. Never been there, have you, John?"

"Me? No. And neither has anyone I know. No reason to go there and a lot of bad stories—African witchcraft and such," answered Connery.

"And the steamer smoke would have been hidden in the smoke from the fields!" exclaimed Custen suddenly as he pound-ed the table. "Damn! That's why we didn't see anything to the east. They blended in. They could do that every day. Dash out for a victim, dash back in to their hideout right after. Haiti's always had a smoky horizon because of the farmers burning off land."

"Exactly," concurred Wake, intrigued to see his officers' exam-ination of the facts. "All of which makes it a perfect place for the likes of Symons and his gang of cutthroats, doesn't it, gentlemen?"

The two officers agreed. It was so simple. Why didn't they think of it before when in Jamaica?

"Very good, gentlemen. Mr. Custen, alter course to star-board," ordered Wake. "Steam due east and let's examine that coast right now."

Connery raised an eyebrow. "Ah, sir. What about your direct orders to return as soon as possible to the nearest American port? You're already facing a court-martial, sir. I think that adding a charge of failure to follow the direct order from the secretary of the navy would not help your cause any. Now, it might be better for you if we report this information when we get to—"

"No, John. Thanks for thinking of me, but my career is prob-ably done anyway and we need to do this right now. It's the right thing to do, and even the leadership in Washington should rec-ognize that."

"I hope you're right, sir," said a dubious Custen. "I hope to hell you're right."

It was the easiest one they had ever gotten. Came right up on her from behind in the dark. Two minutes and it was all over. Main cargo was a shipment of farming tools and turpentine barrels, but the real catch was in the after hold. Bajo found four large cases of British Enfield rifles and two cases of Armstrong pistols, all with ammunition. It would be worth a fortune.

By the time the sun tried to penetrate the haze to the east, they were already back in Haitian waters. By ten in the morning they were at the rickety dock and the *gringo* was sitting in what passed for the local bar with the headman, describing the cargo he had to offer. Muret was impressed. The factors in Gonaives would pay dearly for this treasure and he would arrange it all. The warlords in the northern part of the country would salivate once they heard the weapons were available for purchase. When he said it was a very *apropos* cargo for Haiti, the white man asked why.

Muret explained to the ex-*Americain* that Haiti had no real central government, that the last national leader they had had was General Fabre Geffard. Geffard had controlled Haiti from 1859 until 1867 and was the first in generations to open the country to trade. He finally had gotten recognition by the United States in 1864—sixty years after independence—and had regularized relations again with the Vatican, which had been severed for some time. Money had started to flow from foreigners again.

Muret went on to relate how Geffard had restored the republican form of government, built schools, and started to export crops—then made a big mistake. He reduced the size of the army in 1867, and three months later a barracks revolt deposed him. Since then no one had been in charge and the warlords had divided up the country, and hundreds had been killed everywhere.

Anarchy reigned. Now, two years later, the only thing left of the hard work of Geffard was in the name of the country: the *Republic* of Haiti.

And even that had become a jest among the people, Muret said. It was now known jokingly as *La République de Mort.* The Republic of Death.

The *gringo* took another gulp of rum and leered at the short, dark man across from him at the table. "Muret, this sounds like the perfect home for a man like me. Now, how is it that you say *El Gringo Loco* in this Haitian lingo of yours? That's what they called me in Spanish."

Muret studied the white man, feeling uneasy. That the man behaved oddly was obvious, but he showed signs of being crazy too. And now he was asking how to actually say it? Oh well, he thought. The money is real.

"The closest would be *Le Blanc Fou,*" said Muret. He watched the man's reaction closely as he explained, "It means the crazy white man."

"*Le Blanc Fou*—a catchy sound. Spread the word that that is my name," replied the renegade pirate, laughing at the surprised look on Muret's face as he added, "Oh yes, *mon ami.* I'm gonna like it here just fine."

39

La Sorcellerie Noire

The factors in Gonaives were most definitely interested, asking Muret detailed questions about the items for sale, the proposed price, and how to effect the transfer—none of which he answered, of course, for this involved far more than the art of the deal. It involved his life.

If he handled this correctly, he would make more money than he had ever seen, and *Le Blanc Fou* had promised him that there was more, far more, to be had. If he was not careful, though, the warlords would come, kill him, and take the guns without ever paying a *centime*.

Later that day, a worse than usual thunderstorm came through the area from the mountains to the north, the winds rising quickly and the waves out to sea becoming dangerously high. *Diana* had anchored off the beach, her crew closely watching the wind direction. If it came out of the south they would weigh anchor and get away from the leeward shore. Muret braved the weather and reported to *Le Blanc* aboard the anchored steamer that he would go to meet the factors again that very night, bringing a sample part from one of the weapons. The deal should be concluded within a week, future transactions taking less time.

In the pitching cabin the pirate considered the information and nodded his head, agreeing to send a part of one of the Enfields. He also decided he would stay at the village that night instead of raiding out to sea, and that the guns would stay aboard, not ashore under guard as Muret suggested.

"Muret, they'll be safe here on this ship. And should anyone approach in the night, *ami*, they will receive a demonstration of the effectiveness of the rifles. *Comprenez-vous?*"

"Completely, *monsieur*," said Muret, more than a little sick from the motion of the steamer at anchor. "I understand completely."

They knew without doubt that they were on the right track, for when they went ashore to inquire if anyone at the village of Poisson Rouge had heard of a steamer coming into the area in the last day or two, they got a terrified look and nervously shaking heads in response. No one would admit to knowing anything, but their eyes gave them away. Wake was determined to examine eve ry bay and river. Symons was close. The gunboat got under way again and steamed east, searching every beach, every indentation for signs of the pirates. By the afternoon they were approaching a high point of land and cautiously began to round it.

The storm caught *Canton* without warning. It swept over the mountains, descending the slopes rapidly. One moment it was sunny as they steamed along the coast, ten minutes later it was cloudy, then it grew very dark very quickly. The wind coming down off the mountain was cold, dropping the temperature more than twenty degrees.

Visibility shut down instantly and Wake, standing in his flailing oilskins on deck and holding onto the main shroud, gave the order to bear away from the coast and steer south. He didn't want to be caught on a lee shore if the wind veered to the east or south.

Wake took a bearing on the point of land, then went below to study the chart. Their departure from the coast was at Pointe Palmiste, he saw, just west of a bay called Henne. He decided that when the storm abated they would close the coast again and look into that bay. The chart said there were two villages there.

The visibility was so bad that the transition to night was not apparent. Wake stayed on deck through the dog watches trying to get a feel for the weather. This was something more than an average tropical afternoon storm. It was not letting up, the wind from the north continuing unabated as the steamer hove to with her bow into the seas. Wake estimated his position as thirty miles off the Haitian coast.

All night they steamed slowly ahead, keeping the bow into the waves, attempting to maintain their position. In the morning this will let up, hoped Wake as he tried to sit at the desk in his cabin. He surveyed the chart again in the swinging lantern light. He could feel it—in the morning they would find Symons.

Muret came back early. At three in the morning the rain was still coming down as he was rowed out to the *Diana* and brought down into *Le Blanc Fou*'s cabin.

"What the hell is wrong with you, Muret? You look like you saw a ghost or something," growled the white man as he poured rum from a bottle into a filthy glass. Muret's eyes bulged in fear, knowing his report would anger *Le Blanc*, and in addition, the insane motion of the cabin was making him sick. He was afraid of the sea.

"We have problems. Big problems . . ."

"Well, then tell me about them! Don't just stand there like an idiot and make me guess," bellowed the *blanc*.

"There is an American warship on this coast, not ten kilometers from here, searching for you. They asked at the village to the west of here, but no one told them anything, though everyone knows you are here."

"Son of a *bitch!*" A red fist smashed down on the table, capsizing the glass of rum. "Where's the warship now?"

"It disappeared in the storm. But there is another problem." Muret hesitated, the anger of the man was more than he had thought. "Also a big problem."

"And what the hell would that be?"

"The factor put out the news that you have weapons—good English weapons—to sell and that he would be the broker. The general in Cap Haitian was upset that he did not get the first exclusive opportunity to buy the guns. He said he has been insulted and will stop anyone else from buying them. That means Colonel Ceder of St. Marc, and the colonel in Gonaives."

"So? Who cares what the little bastard says, as long as his money's good."

"There is more. The general in Cap Haitian has spread the word that *Le Blanc Fou* will die when the sun rises, that he has had the *prêtre gran voudou* declare you a dead man. No one will work for you to carry the guns or do anything for you. I think the general will send men here to capture the guns."

"Oh, yeah? That I'd like to see. Now, what is this *voudou* thing about? One of your savage little African myths from days gone by?"

Muret could tell the *Americain* did not understand. "It is very real. You have been sentenced to death."

"How the hell am I supposed to die? Did the black son of a bitch include that in his proclamation?"

"You will drown. Everyone believes in this here. No one here will associate with you."

"Then why the hell are you here, Muret?"

"Because I am to die also," muttered the Haitian.

"So what do you suggest we do?" asked *Le Blanc Fou* as Bajo entered the cabin to see what was happening.

"Get away from here at sunrise," said Muret. "We can escape the American warship and the general's men. Go to Miragoane in the southern peninsula of Haiti. I have contacts there. We can sell the guns easily through them."

The white man thought for a moment, then nodded and spoke to Bajo. "Weigh anchor an hour before dawn. We'll steam due south . . ." he paused as he checked the chart, ". . . around the west end of Gonave island, then southeast into that port of Miragoane."

Bajo got up to get the ship prepared but stopped when his leader said, "And Bajo, get those rifles ready to use, just in case some Haitian general's little army shows up before we leave."

"Yes, *Jefe.*"

"Looks like you're in the crew, Muret. I hope you like to kill people." *Le Blanc Fou* grinned. "It's what we do best."

Muret didn't answer—he just looked at the white man's wild eyes and wondered how he had gotten into this situation in the first place.

Two hours later he was on deck watching his home village disappear in the rainy mist as the pirate steamer moved away from the land, headed to a part of the coast where he had never been and knew absolutely no one. It had been a necessary lie to the white man in order to get away from this place where Muret knew he would most certainly die, if not from the curse, then from the general's men when they wouldn't find the guns.

Now he wondered what would happen when they arrived at Miragoane. He looked around at the crew and could see that *Le Blanc* had not been joking. These were the kind of men who liked to kill—he could see it in their faces.

The storm had lessened enough by the end of the first watch that they were heading north again. Wake estimated that they had drifted off to the west ten miles or so, and that therefore they would see Pointe Palmiste in three hours, or about seven o'clock in the morning by his watch. Right about sunrise.

As they steamed north, the rain stopped and the wind started to pipe down, decreasing the spray that had been bursting from the bows and deluging everyone. After a couple of hours the stars were visible, and Wake began to hope that perhaps his luck was changing as he went to his cabin to get a quick nap.

A few hours later Lieutenant Custen was on deck as the sky lightened. "Well look at that," he exclaimed as he gazed east.

"Like a different coastline." said Connery.

The horizon was completely different, for the storm had washed away the smoke that usually hung in the air. It was a beautiful morning with a light northerly breeze; they could clearly see mountains to the east and north.

"Deck there! Steamer three points on the starboard bow! Against the coastline. Range is about five miles."

"Damn! I think that's her! Steer nor'easterly and ring up full speed," yelled Connery, his enthusiasm getting the better of the quarterdeck protocol expected of the officer of the deck. "Messenger! Present my respects to Mr. Wake and let him know that a steamer—"

"No need for that, Mr. Connery. I'm here already," said Wake as he emerged from the hatchway. "I see we have a steamer to look over. Sound quarters and clear the ship for action."

The shrill bosuns' pipes and deep ringing of the ship's bell— *Canton* didn't rate a drummer—produced a flurry of commotion. Within seconds the main deck was a mass of men moving to their gun positions, others taking up small arms from the ready boxes, still others attending to the boats, helm, and rigging. Wake turned to see three helmsmen, the extra in case of casualties.

"I have the deck, Mr. Connery. Helmsman, steer east nor'east."

The helmsmen acknowledged the order as Wake did his best to remain calm and work out an intercept course in his mind should that vessel be Symons' steamer and he elected to fight. The vessel was about four miles away to the northeast from *Canton*, steaming to the south at what Wake estimated to be about ten or twelve knots. He figured the time to half shot range, then turned to Moe, standing next to him in his battle quarters position.

"Mr. Moe, what will be the time of our intercept, at five hundred yards range?"

"Wha . . . what, sir?" the startled ensign stammered. He had been mesmerized by the sight of the steamer in the distance.

"Mr. Moe," Wake continued in a paternal tone. "You are an officer, and the people are looking to you for your example. Now is the time to show them. Please work out the intercept in your mind and tell me. Now."

"Ah . . . yes, sir. The time to intercept . . . is . . . ah, eighteen minutes?"

"Was that a question or a report, Mr. Moe?" asked Wake, still in a gentle tone.

"A report, sir. The intercept should be in eighteen minutes at this course and speed," stated Moe with more confidence.

"Very well done, Mr. Moe," Wake smiled at the relief on the young man's face. "The same as my calculation. I certainly hope *we* are right."

Custen stepped up and announced, "The ship is cleared for action, sir. Mr. Connery is at his guns, Mr. Noble is below with Captain Terrington and the prisoners are locked in. The cutter is swayed and Bosun Rork is ready with the boarding party, should they be needed."

"Very good, Mr. Custen. You may send up the colors. The battle colors, please."

Seconds later the large battle flag ascended the after peak halyard, the Stars and Stripes streaming out aft and gleaming in the morning light as the *Canton* charged toward the rising sun.

It was a sight that stirred every man on the main deck—one they would remember for the rest of their lives and describe in bars and pubs and homes for years.

Bajo jumped down the hatch and ran into his leader's cabin without knocking. "*Jefe,* come quick!" he said to the nude sleeping form on the bunk. "There is a steamer off to the southwest, and she just sent up a big *gringo* flag."

"Son of a whoring bitch," muttered the *gringo.* "I'll be right there."

By the time he got up to the deck and was able to focus the glass in on the other steamer, the distance had diminished considerably. He groaned. It was a U.S. Navy gunboat, that same one he had last seen in Cartagena. So Parker had found him after all. And that fool Bajo hadn't turned away immediately, costing a mile already in a chase. In addition, there wasn't any smoke haze in the sky—that storm had blown it away, he realized.

"Turn her now and steer east, damn you," he yelled to Bajo. "And tell the boys below to stoke as if their miserable lives depended on it, because I assure you, that they most definitely do."

At that point he sensed someone behind him and saw Muret staring at the warship. "Well, Muret, it's your lucky day, my friend," he shouted above the wind. "You may get to watch a real sea battle, close up and personal."

Muret said nothing in reply, but started some sort of low tribal chant. It came out softly at first, then rose in volume as he gazed at the warship that was now astern of them.

"What in the hell is that African jabber you're mumbling, Muret?" demanded *Le Blanc Fou.*

The Haitian looked at the white man as if he had just noticed him. "*La malédiction de la sorcellerie noire.* The curse of the black sorcery, of the *voudou,* has come true," said Muret as he pointed toward the ship flying the huge red, white, and blue flag.

"That is our death, *Le Blanc Fou*—come to visit us on the sea, at sunrise."

40

Yankee Ingenuity

"Set the foresail, jibs, and mizzen staysail," ordered Wake. Custen relayed the orders as Wake went forward to confer with Connery and Durling.

"Mr. Connery, what range would you like to commence firing for effect?" Wake asked as he held on to the barrel of the forward pivot gun, the 110-pounder.

"In this height of sea, sir? Gunner Durling here can hit her with no problem in this sea at a mile, sir. Outside effective range," he glanced at Durling, "about two miles."

"Very well, I'll want a blank shot in just a moment, then a warning round over her bow. Then, when I tell you, fire for effect on her transom. I want the rudder disabled first."

Connery and Durling both acknowledged the orders, with Durling adding slyly, "Going to do a bit of a *Kearsarge* to her, sir?"

"You've read my mind one more time, Durling," answered Wake. "Yes, we'll try to do her like Winslow did Semmes. I also want the secondary battery double loaded with grape. I think they'll try to ram or board or both. The secondaries will have to stop that."

"Aye, aye, sir."

"Mr. Connery, once the action gets going at close range, do not wait for orders, just keep all guns firing. I want as much metal hitting her as possible. I want them destroyed."

Wake turned and strode aft, then eyed the other steamer as Custen commented, "I'm sure she's the *Diana*, sir. Matches the description and there aren't many steamers at all this far into Haitian waters these days. That's Symons. I'd wager he thinks he can run her away from us."

"Yes, I agree on her identity and see that we aren't forereaching on her. Send up every inch of canvas she'll carry, Mr. Custen. I want to close the gap as soon as possible. Now let's have a blank shot for her to heave to—just so we can report later that we did."

Custen laughed as he passed along the order. The sound and smoke of the signal shot flew away downwind as soon as it was fired.

"Deck there! The steamer is setting all sail."

"That's her answer, sir!" shouted Custen from the starboard secondary battery.

A dozen tanned and patched sails appeared on the spars of the steamer ahead as she heeled over on a broad port reach with the additional press of canvas. Both steamers were now racing east at their fastest speed, further into the Gulf of Gonaives toward the port of Gonaives, twenty-five miles distant.

The rush of the water on the lee side was overwhelming all other sound except the rhythmic pounding of the steam engine's cylinders as *Canton* surged forward through the beam seas. The enemy ship—for that is how Wake thought of her now—was squarely in front of the gunboat and therefore safe from the fire of their forward gun, which needed to shoot ten degrees on either side of dead ahead in order to miss hitting their own forestay rigging. It would be an interesting problem in dynamic geometry, thought Wake as he estimated the firing angles by eye.

"Mr. Custen, I want the helmsman to bring her one point to windward upon my word and hold her there while we send off two shots. Not until I give the word, mind you. The timing will be important so we don't lose ground on the chase."

"Aye, aye, sir," replied Custen as he went to brief Quartermaster Morrow, who was personally manning the helm.

Connery came aft in response to Wake beckoning.

"Mr. Connery, we'll bring her up to windward a bit to give you a firing bearing over the starboard bow. The helmsman will try to hold it long enough for you to have Durling send off two rounds. Remember, the first I want over her bow, for the record. But we know she won't stop. The second I want on her stern, from the main deck down, twixt wind and water if he can."

The ship lurched over a wave and slid sideways for an instant, making everyone grab onto something close by. The wind appeared to be rising, the seas gaining in height. Wake cast an eye aloft to check the strain on the rig. With the forward speed of the engine and the apparent speed of the wind over the sails, he worried that it might be too much. She was going at least twelve knots, two knots faster than her fastest designed speed. The rising seas would make the gunnery more difficult too. The wind and sea conditions were favoring Symons more and more.

"We are keeping the same distance, *Jefe*. Maybe they will tire," suggested Bajo as he held onto the windward rail.

"That's not the damn *guardia costa* back there, you fool. That's the U.S. friggin' Navy. They won't tire or go away, Bajo. They want to *kill* us, you dumb son of a worm," growled the *gringo* as he tried to get a fleeting glimpse of the gunboat's quarterdeck. It was difficult to get a clear view, but he didn't see Parker on the deck. Whoever was commanding her, he was good, begrudged the former naval officer. Very good.

He waited for them to luff up to windward to get a shot over the leeward bow—that's what he would do if he were over there. He called Bajo over.

"Any minute now they are going to bring her bow up to windward to clear her forward gun for a shot over her starboard bow. Keep your eyes glued to that gunboat, Bajo. When you see her swing up to windward, then luff this bitch up too. Instantly. We have to keep her forestay masking her gun. Do you understand what I mean?"

"Yes, *Jefe*. I see what you mean. The moment she alters course, we will too."

The *gringo* was already feeling the sun on his skin. He was standing in his under-drawers only and knew he had to cover himself up. Just as he got to the hatchway to fetch his clothing in his cabin he felt the *Diana* swerve to the left and upwind. He looked aft to see that the warship had done the same and saw a puff of smoke from her lee bow, the sound blown away on the wind. The round screamed overhead and geysered in the water two hundred yards ahead of them off to starboard. A warning shot, he thought incredulously? That was something silly Parker would do—maybe he *was* in command.

A second puff showed, followed by another miss to leeward, though this one much closer in range.

"*Jefe*, you were correct! You knew what they would do," called out Bajo with obvious admiration.

"That's because I used to do that myself, Bajo," replied the *gringo* as he went down the ladder, "—back when I was respectable and I used to chase scum like you."

Then the steamers slid back to their original courses as the *Canton* tried to reduce the gap again.

"He knew that trick, sir," said Custen.

"Yes . . . We'll have to come up with another trick. Have Durling and Mr. Connery come aft with you, if you would please," requested Wake.

When the three gathered, Wake included Moe also. This would be a good education for the young ensign.

"All right, men. Ideas?" Wake asked.

"At this speed, sir, Symons'll be in that port of Gonaives in a little over two hours," offered Custen. "He could run her into the port, smash her into a dock or run her ashore, and make off on foot. We'd have to slow and anchor or come alongside, and they'd get away."

"Very good point, Mr. Custen," commented Wake. "That would appear to be their hope, for we're chasing them into a cul-de-sac."

"Not necessarily, sir," suggested Connery. "They could still go southeast around the east end of Gonave Island, by Port au Prince, then exit the Gulf by the southern peninsula."

"Then they should have altered their course already, Mr. Connery," countered Wake. "No, I think Mr. Custen is correct. They are heading into Gonaives to get away ashore. Now, gentlemen, how do we stop them?"

"Continue to alter ten degrees and fire, sir," said Custen.

"All right, but this time we'll change the tactic. Use a bit of a ruse. Listen carefully," said Wake. "We'll start a swing to windward, but then instead turn to leeward. They'll probably take the bait and bring their vessel up into the wind to port, while we increase the angle by altering to starboard. That should give you a decent firing angle over the port bow, Durling."

"Indeed it will, sir. If 'n the slimy bastard plays the game and takes the bait."

"Well let's try anyway. He just might."

Now he was wearing a full-sleeved white cotton shirt buttoned to his throat, white cotton trousers, and a white kepi hat with stern cloth protecting his neck from the sun. His skin still hurt, but the *gringo* felt he could stand it, for he knew he had to be up here on deck and make the decisions.

He tried to anticipate the warship's next move. It was too bad they were out of effective rifle shot—his Enfields, even in the hands of these useless idiots, could be helpful in disrupting the gunboat's actions. Even so, he only had to hold on a couple hours more, then he'd be ashore—in some backward bilgewater of a town among tribal savages. But still, he knew he could escape the U.S. Navy once ashore.

What would they do next, he pondered as he held onto the weather rail?

"*Jefe*, they are doing it again!' Bajo yelled. "Bringing it up to windward. I will too—"

"No Bajo, it's a feint! Slide her a point to leeward. Now!"

He could see the gunboat's bow swinging quickly in reverse of her original turn. The *Diana* stayed dead ahead of the warship's forestay, though. A shot penetrated a wave to windward, twenty yards off *Diana's* port side. Then another round exploded in the same place—the spot where the steamer would have been had they followed Bajo's idea. It had been a close call.

"Damn, but he's a crafty bugger that one, Bajo," shouted the ex-naval officer. "But not as good as *El Gringo Loco!*"

It couldn't possibly be Parker in command of that gunboat, he decided—this commander was too dogged, too cunning. No, Parker was probably in a club in Washington, telling made-up sea stories to fawning ladies. That was his style.

He knew that sooner or later he would guess wrong, and the shots would hit. They just had to keep up the speed and get this tub into that harbor. The natives would get a show when the ol' *Diana* arrived, he thought with a grin, picturing in his mind ramming the steamer into a crowded wharf and watching the people scattering. It would be easy to get away in *that* kind of confusion.

"He's good, sir," said Custen, shaking his head as the shots went harmlessly off to the port side of the target.

Wake sighed and ran his hand through his hair. They were not closing the distance, and this swerving of course wasn't helping narrow the gap.

"Yes . . . that he is. You can tell his naval experience."

Connery and Durling came aft again, clearly frustrated.

"I'll put a shot right up his *poxied ass*, sir. It may take a while, but I'll get that renegade bastard son of a bitch, if it's the last damned thing I do!" swore Durling as he pounded a fist into his other hand.

That comment, and the enraged look on Durling's face as he made it, broke the tension and they all laughed at the gunner, who reluctantly joined in.

"Gunner Durling, I'm glad you're on our side, by God!" said Wake. "Now, does anyone have any new ideas, other than continuing what we've been doing."

No one had, so he continued. "Very well, then I do. But I need to know if you two think we can do it," he gestured at Connery and Durling, then went on.

"We can't fire the forward gun dead ahead because of the forestay and we can't take down the forestay because of the masts and sails, right, gentlemen?"

They all agreed with that assessment, but failed to see where he was going with his theory.

"Then gentlemen, if Mohammed cannot go to the mountain, it's time for the mountain to come to Mohammed."

He got confused looks in response to his parable, so he explained. "We move the damned gun, gentlemen—to the windward side of the foredeck so it will fire over the port bow without us having to alter course."

Connery spoke up first, an uncomfortable look on his face. "Ah, sir. That gun is on those special pivot tracks. We'd have to jack it up out of them, then manhandle it up the incline of the deck and lash it down to the bulwark."

"And the little darlin' weighs six and a half *tons*, sir! Thirteen thousand pounds. This ain't no 9-pounder that we can lift easily," added Durling.

"Yes, but having it on the windward bow would also help our lee helm and maybe our leeward drift," offered Custen, to the negative reactions of Connery and Durling.

"Just how the hell would we get it up there, sir? All respects intended, of course," asked Durling.

"Not really sure yet, Gunner. But we have," Wake looked at his pocket watch, "an hour and a half or so to figure it out and get it done. A little Yankee ingenuity perhaps?"

The chorus of "aye, aye, sir's" was less than enthusiastic, but Wake was absolutely confident that if anyone could solve the problem, Durling and Connery could.

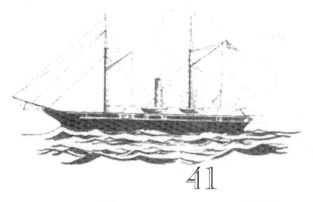

41

Journey to Hell

Muret had been silent the whole time, as if waiting reverently for his death, but now when he heard the lookout shout that there was a harbor up ahead, he shook himself out of his trance. Perhaps they could survive this after all. He heard the white man tell the Spanish man his plan for running the steamer into a dock and escaping ashore. It sounded better than trying to elude this warship that was staying on them. Anything sounded better than remaining on this boat. Muret intended to be the first off.

"Bajo, pass the word to all hands," said the *gringo*. "We'll run the steamer right into the wharf—forget the vessels that are tied up—then everyone runs ashore in different directions. In the confusion, they'll get away. No problem."

He could see the harbor himself now. Not long to go. He had been in bad spots before and would get through this one. And when he did, the fame of *Le Blanc Fou* would spread even further. They couldn't kill him. No one could.

"The man with nine lives!" he shouted to the sky.

The number two hawser was heavy by itself, but it was the only line they had that could take the strain of the huge gun. A bight of line passed around the main gun carriage, after they had jacked it up off the pivot slide tracks, was led to the only block aboard with a large enough sheave. The block was secured to the port anchor cat and placed on the windward foredeck bulwark. From there the hawser led aft around the secondary capstan, hence forward to the primary capstan. Twenty-three men were on the capstans ready to winch the gun the fourteen feet it needed to go— uphill on the steeply heeling deck.

Durling looked at Connery, who nodded, then shouted to the men. "All right, men—haul your guts out and get my iron daughter up to windward!"

As they took up the slack, Rork called out the cadence as the men strained to push the bars that jutted out from the capstans, their feet stamping the deck. "*Heave!* Ho. *Heave!* Ho. *Heave!* Ho."

For the first few seconds nothing happened, then as the ship plunged into a trough and smacked down onto a wave the gun moved. The jolt was just enough to break the inertia and the metal beast inched over to the port side, slowly but steadily.

Canton hit another wave and the gun tilted back to leeward, the sailors behind it holding jack irons wedged underneath, and ready to run if it broke loose and fell down among them. But the same wave that caused the tilt rolled the hull for a fragment of a moment to windward, and the gun recovered and resumed its climb up the tilted deck.

Wake consulted his watch again, then looked ahead at the coast beyond the pirate vessel. At this rate it would take hours, and they only had less than thirty minutes, by his estimate, until the enemy would make the shore. It was time for a drastic measure. He called Custen and Connery over again.

"This is doing well, but we need to speed it up. When I give the word, Mr. Custen will have the sheets freed and luffed. That will make her roll to windward and eliminate the heel for a moment. At that instant, Mr. Connery will have a maximum effort to move the gun. Then we'll haul the sheets again. The gun should be in position at that point. It will slow us down a bit, but I'll take that chance. Any questions? No? Pass the word to all hands so they understand. Let's get on with it."

They were minutes away from the harbor and escape ashore. *El Gringo Loco* felt the exhilaration flowing through him. He had bloodied the Spanish Navy in Nicaragua, eluded the Royal Navy in Jamaica, and now would humiliate the American Navy in Haiti. He was the scourge of the Caribbean and it felt great.

He gauged their speed by eye as they raced past a decrepit channel buoy. He had no chart of the channel and was trusting luck and following where he had seen deeper draft schooners sailing ahead of them. There was no alternative. They must keep up the speed in order to prevent the warship from being able to bear off and fire.

He saw the crowds of black people on shore gathering to stare. Everyone was watching. He gave out a howling laugh and climbed up on the bulwark, oblivious to the pain in his burned skin. He would give them a show they would talk about for centuries—the day *Le Blanc Fou* came to town.

Native Haitian fishing boats in the channel, seeing the chase, scurried as fast as they could under oars to get out of the way. Other boats stopped where they were and watched the contest.

Ashore, the people along the waterfront were pointing out to sea and conjecturing wildly about why an American ship was chasing the steamer. And who were they chasing? Soon, wagers were being made on the outcome, with most favoring the quarry.

At the wharf—Gonaives had only one large pier in deeper water—schooners were tied up along every foot of available space, most with another schooner moored outboard alongside. The seamen and laborers halted their work of unloading the various cargoes and stared to the west as the two steamers entered the outer channel at full speed, rushing past the old French buoy toward the inner harbor. Everyone was asking, "Where will they stop?" and "How could they stop anywhere in time not to hit an anchored vessel?"

Among the experienced seamen in the port, doubt, then fear, began to grow. This chase was deadly. It was crazy. People were going to die when those steamers hit something.

Most of the townspeople had no such concern. They only knew that this was the most exciting thing that had happened in years, and thousands began to line the shore, crowding into every location with a view of the action. The wharf was jammed with people, some spilling over onto the schooners alongside, all of them turned into excited spectators of the chase.

No one was listening to the few seamen who said to get away from the wharf.

"Ready. *Now!*" yelled Wake.

Custen gave the order to let fly sheets and a dozen men cast off the lines controlling the loose edges, or leeches, of the sails. *Canton* abruptly righted herself from the twenty-five-degree list as the pressure of the wind on the sails vanished. She also dropped speed quickly as the engine alone carried her forward.

But the men on the capstans no longer were pulling the massive gun uphill, and the 110-pounder moved on the canvas matting smoothly to the port side of the ship within thirty seconds. It amazed everyone, especially Wake.

"Haul in again, Mr. Custen!" he said as he walked forward to the main gun.

The gun was already being chocked, lashed and loaded as the sails once again felt the pressure of the wind and their speed increased. Wake saw that they had lost perhaps a quarter of a mile in just that short time, but it didn't matter, for Durling was sighting the gun, waiting for the last part of the loading drill to be completed.

"Gun One ready!" the old gunner cried as Wake arrived beside him.

Wake studied the target background of Symons' steamer. If Durling missed, the shot would plow into the wharf, exploding among thousands of people. Should he give the order to fire and risk those deaths on his conscience? It wouldn't take much to miss the target and kill innocent people. Wake felt his heart pumping so hard his ears pounded. Connery, Durling, and the gun crew were waiting.

Wake looked again. Symons was only moments away from the wharf, his intention clear. The crowd had started to panic and everyone was trying to get away. The seamen aboard the schooners were scrambling up to the deck of the wharf, some jumping overboard and attempting to swim out of the way.

Wake glanced at Durling, who stood, jaw set, firing lanyard in hand, eyeing the gunline to the target. Waiting.

Wake made his decision. "Fire for effect on the stern!" he shouted, louder than he wanted.

Boom!

The stern of the enemy steamer exploded in a blast of fire, smoke, and planking. Durling was calmly counting out the reloading drill as if he were teaching a class.

" . . . Three—sponge out. Four—dry rammer. Five—cartridge man. Six—shell man . . ." At the end of his drill count he yelled "clear!" and pulled the lanyard again.

Boom!

The pirate's stern erupted again as Durling again called out the cadence of the drill to his men. Wake saw the *Diana* slow, then slew a bit to port, still within the firing angles of the gun. Black smoke was roiling up from what was left of her transom.

Boom!

The after mast fell on Symons' ship as she continued her turn to the port. Wake suddenly realized he had to slow down *Canton* or they would smash into the Haitian vessels or wharf themselves.

"Cast loose sheets and ring for engine stop!" he shouted aft to Custen, who had men standing by in anticipation of the order. Among the cacophony of shouting Wake heard Rork urging his men as they let the sails go and the ship slowed.

Wake started to make his way aft as another *boom* blasted out. He caught a glimpse of *Diana*'s port quarter being ripped apart just above the waterline, then ran to the helm.

"Follow that steamer around to port and lay us between her and shore, Mr. Custen."

"Aye, aye, sir," said Custen, almost breathless from the tension as he told the quartermaster at the helm to bring the *Canton* along the starboard side of the pirate vessel.

Diana's sails were no longer being handled and now that she had turned left and was heading northerly into the wind they acted as a brake, almost stopping her. The engine had ceased functioning when the shaft was severed by the explosion of one of Durling's shots, and water was pouring into the after hold and engine room. She was settling by the stern rapidly as she drifted forward.

"Fire the portside secondary batteries into her as soon as they bear, Mr. Connery!" Wake said to the gunnery lieutenant, who had come aft to the 32-pounders for that very purpose.

"Engine back full, Mr. Custen," he said. "I want to have us stopped right along the steamer where we can finish this."

The sails were flapping loudly as they turned to port and

luffed upwind and stopped, ten yards from the hull of the *Diana*. Even before *Canton's* forward movement ended, the pirate gang was firing the Enfield rifles, the bullets whizzing audibly through the air and splatting into the wood deck and spars around Wake.

"Sir! Get out of the way!" screamed Custen. "They shooting at *you*!"

The blast had caught him unprepared and the *gringo* was thrown into the helmsman knocking both down to the deck. Stunned, he looked aft past the wreckage of the transom and saw the gunboat was still directly astern, and there was more smoke from her port bow. So they moved the gun—good decision, he admitted as he tried to stand up just as the second shell exploded in his cabin below. An invisible wall of heat seared his flesh, then a cloud of black smoke engulfed him.

The steamer heeled to starboard as her rudder jammed over to port and *Diana* slewed around to the left, the helmsman spinning a useless wheel. The cables had been parted and the rudder itself was jammed. The men started to panic and scream for the helmsman to do something.

Another shell exploded the port side of the main deck and hull into pieces of wooden shrapnel that scythed across the deck impacting everything there.

The *gringo* was bleeding from splinter wounds all over his chest and arms and his charred shirt was hanging in shreds, but he was still composed enough to assess the situation. The steamer was on fire aft, her stern was down, and she was almost dead in the water, parallel to and fifty yards off the beach. He could still escape. Only fifty yards.

Shaking his head clear of the ringing in his ears, the *gringo* stood and saw Bajo standing there dazed, blood pouring out of a wound across his face.

"Bajo, tell everyone to grab a rifle and shoot that damned captain," he shouted as he pointed toward the stern of the gunboat coming up on their starboard. If he could get his men to distract the sailors on the warship for just a moment, he could swim to the beach.

Several of the gang started shooting at the *Canton* as the *gringo* grabbed a shotgun lying on the deck and stumbled aft into the disintegrated ruins of the stern. Smoke was rolling out from below decks where the lamp oil cask had set alight the surrounding area. Intense heat from the flames burned his sensitive skin as he made his way through the wreckage and descended closer to the rising water. Glancing over, he saw that the commander of the gunboat was in full view, but it wasn't Parker Terrington. Then he climbed down into what had been his cabin and felt the water around his feet.

The gunboat halted right alongside of them, the *gringo* looking up at her and grudgingly admiring the work of the other commander in getting his ship in precisely the correct position. His mind registered the blast of a doubled grapeshot broadside an instant before he felt the concussion sweep over his head as the gale of metal obliterated everything and everyone up on the main deck.

And then it got quiet, for the *gringo* could hear nothing, his eardrums having been imploded by the detonation above him. He tried to get up as the water rose above his waist but his head was dizzy, the spasming pain inside incredibly intense. He let the water take him off the deck as the ship settled downward, still holding the shotgun in a death grip in his right hand as he floated away, his eyes on the beach, the ringing in his ears making it all seem unreal.

Fifty lousy yards, you bastard, he swore to himself.

Stroking slowly with his left arm toward the beach, he looked up at the transom and stern gallery of the gunboat, her name *Canton* carved in large gilt letters below the ports. Thirty yards now, he thought as he felt the presence of someone above him and rolled to his left, bringing the shotgun up out of the water toward the gunboat's stern.

He couldn't believe it. His brother Parker was there, leaning out of the stern gallery port and saying something. Parker looked angry and was pointing his finger at him.

"Too late now, you worthless pompous ass!" Symons muttered as he pulled both of the shotgun's triggers, sending two loads of buckshot the fifteen feet into Terrington's face.

He dropped the shotgun and swam as hard as he could. The blacks had run away from the beach to the shacks, their faces peering at him from the windows as his feet found the muddy bottom, then got traction.

Just five more yards, he willed his pain-wracked body. Almost there.

The aftermath of the roar of the thirty-twos stunned everyone aboard *Canton*. One minute they were engaged in a deadly fight with desperate men, the next there was silence. Then the gun crews' training reasserted itself and they mechanically went through the motions of reloading their guns.

Wake stood there, numbed by the blast, trying to contemplate the destruction they had just wreaked upon the other steamer. Every piece of wooden accoutrements—pin rails, cleats, hatch rails, binnacle, chart table, sheet traveler, everything—was gone from *Diana's* main deck from amidships aft.

And no human being was left alive on that deck either.

Body parts, some unrecognizable, were scattered everywhere. No enemy was in sight. Wake saw the sailors of the *Canton* looking at him, wondering what to do next. There was no hesitation in his mind, for there might be some of the gang hiding below the other ship's main deck.

"Depress muzzles and fire again down into her!" he said. The roar erupted immediately afterward.

As Wake walked aft to get a view of their position in the harbor, he stretched his jaws trying to get his hearing back. He suddenly felt drained and weak, wanting to just sit down—then he noticed Custen staring at him wide-eyed.

"They shot you!"

"What?" said Wake as he began to feel an ache in his left chest. He looked down and saw blood dripping from the sleeve cuff of his left hand and followed the discoloration to the shoulder of his uniform, which was covered in a dark stain. At that moment the pain hit him and he felt himself get disoriented as Custen reached for him. He saw Rork standing there too, holding a rifle and looking concerned, as Custen started to unbutton Wake's tunic.

"I tried to warn you, sir," Custen said. "They were aiming right at you. Here, sit down and we'll get your coat off. Ah, it looks like a ricochet wound—not bad."

The sound of a smaller blast interrupted. It was from the water directly aft and Wake turned to investigate, but Rork was already striding to the transom. Wake saw him peer over and down into the water below, shake his head sorrowfully, then steady his rifle on the railing and aim at something.

"I'm sorry, sir!" Ensign Noble cried out in dread, a smear of blood across his uniform, as he emerged from the after hatch and ran up to Wake. "I tried to get Captain Terrington to stay from the gallery ports. I *did*, sir. But he pushed me away and looked out the window." The youngster was almost in tears he was so distraught.

"That's when he shot him. Shot him in the face, dead, sir. I'm sorry."

Symons watched their simple little faces turn to terror when he came out of the water and sneered, as he staggered toward the line of huts. He loved that feeling of domination, of seeing the abject horror in their eyes as they beheld his strength and realized his power over life and death. They obviously feared him, as they should, and now he would have them fetch him some new clothes and hide him so he could rest awhile.

"*Le Blanc Fou* has arrived, you savage sons of Africa! Now get over here and bear a hand."

When the shooting ended, a crowd formed on the beach, gaping in terror at the vision of a bloodied white man with reddened arms and face, rising from the harbor. He yelled at them again, but none of the Haitians moved. Symons, bleeding from gashes everywhere, clothing in rags, stumbled over a bush but kept walking, his skin beginning to send waves of agony to the dazed brain. His ears could barely distinguish a voice behind him call out.

"Aye, Symons! So ya wan' a wee bit o' help, do ya?"

He wondered who would be calling him by that name? It had been so long, so very long, since he had heard it used. He turned slowly around and saw a tall petty officer on the stern of the gunboat, thirty yards away—those same thirty yards he had just forced himself to swim to his new freedom. The petty officer was leaning over a rifle laid on the transom railing.

It was aimed right at him.

"Well, here's some help from Uncle Sam, Symons. Enjoy your little journey to hell. . . ."

Presley Theodocious Symons was still trying to comprehend what was happening when Bosun Sean Rork's 1865 model, .58 caliber, United States Navy Springfield rifle sent its minie ball thudding into the center of his chest, where it exploded his heart, the exit wound in his back spraying tissue and gore over the beach.

El Gringo Loco's body collapsed to the sand. His eyes spent the last five seconds of life staring at the crowd of Haitians—as they watched him die.

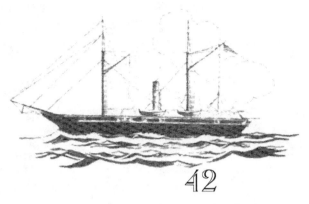

42

Rocks and Shoals

September 1869

The windowless room was a hot and humid small space in the middle of the second floor of Building Number Fourteen, United States Navy Yard, Washington, D.C. Wake had been told to meet his counsel there at two in the afternoon to prepare his court-martial defense. They were allowed the use of the room for one hour. He arrived five minutes early, sweating profusely from the heat of a late summer, and left the door half-closed. There were three chairs at the small chart table in the middle of the room and Wake sat down and pulled out of his valise a stack of witness statements.

Unable to concentrate on the content of the statements, he thought instead about Linda. In response to his letters about the court-martial, she had come by train all the way from Pensacola to be with him. Leaving the children in Pensacola with the Curtis family, she had arrived the day before, surprising him with her presence. He was overjoyed at her arrival, but not happy with her attitude, which had turned into loathing for the navy for what they had done to him. And to make matters worse, she made no attempt to conceal it, from anyone.

Wake was confined to the Naval Yard premises and living in the transit officer's section of Quarters B, where women were prohibited. Thus, he could not visit her lodgings at a cheap hotel, a block away on Ninth Street, and she could not visit his at the Navy Yard. They could, and did, walk hand in hand along the river and embrace under the oak and willow trees, but that was the extent of the affection allowed by the circumstances, which did not improve Wake's outlook at all.

In fact, he suggested to Linda that she surreptitiously join him in his room, invoking memories of their liaisons in Key West during the war to entice her. Her calmer head prevailed, however, and she explained that though she needed and wanted that also, his current legal situation was such that the consequences of that transgression of naval law would not be worth it. She added that she hated "the damn navy" for that too. The fact that he could not enjoy the affections of his wife due to bureaucratic legal idiosyncrasies made Wake angry at the navy himself.

Hearing the tread of someone approaching down the passageway and the door creak open, Wake looked up from the papers in his hand to the men who would be responsible for presenting his defense, and possibly saving his life. The two of them were completely different from each other in appearance and demeanor, but Wake desperately hoped they would be a cohesive, and persuasive, team.

Commander Andrew Stockton was a tall, thin, dark-haired man in his late thirties, his gaunt facial features giving him a predatory aspect, which was heightened by coal black eyes that displayed no emotion. Commander Stockton—graduate of the Naval Academy, class of 1856—commanded small gunboats during the war and had been the post-war executive officer of a steam frigate in the Mediterranean Squadron during Farragut's victory tour of Europe. He was now assigned to a year at the Hydrographic Survey Office in Washington before his next sea duty, which would probably be a command billet.

Known as an "intellectual warrior," he was widely read and as close to a lawyer as a serving naval officer was likely to get. Wake had never met the man, but requested him as senior counsel due to his reputation. He was the best on the list of potential line officers that had been put on court-martial standby duty. A civilian counsel was allowed by regulations, but Wake had no money for a real lawyer.

Stockton dropped a stack of books and pamphlets onto the scarred top of the government-issue wood table and sat in the chair across from Wake, pulling out documents from a pouch and opening books. He was obviously not enthusiastic with his assignment.

The man who immediately followed Stockton into the meeting room was Lieutenant Charles Hostetler. He was a jovial giant of a man with a ready grin, and it was obvious by his girth that he liked food and beer, but Wake knew something else about him. The man was intensely loyal to anyone he called a friend and absolutely fearless in the midst of danger. Wake had called him a friend since 1865, when Hostetler served as his executive officer aboard the armed tug *Hunt*, Wake's last independent command.

They had occasionally seen each other since leaving *Hunt* in '66, their last meeting being in a pub in Charleston a year earlier, where Hostetler had regaled Wake with stories of being gunnery officer of the *Contoocock*, a frigate with a reputation in the navy as a bad sea boat. Since she was decommissioned eight months earlier and turned into a quarantine vessel in New York, he had been on half-pay and living with his sister in Pennsylvania, but now, as an officer serving on court-martial duty he would get full pay for the duration of the trial. By contrast with Stockton, he looked very enthusiastic as he bounded into the room and grabbed Wake's hand.

"Peter, it's good to see you again, my friend. Over the last week or so Commander Stockton and I have discussed this little predicament and I've got no doubt we're gonna prevail."

Before Wake could reply, Stockton spoke for the first time.

"Lieutenant Wake, I am Commander Andrew Stockton, the senior counselor you requested for the court-martial. Lieutenant Hostetler, the assistant counsel, has filled me in on your character and I have read your record, which appears to be very good, with the exception of some irregularities in eighteen sixty-four regarding a certain U.S. Army colonel with whom you had a . . . disagreement while stationed in Florida. Other than that episode, which thankfully is mostly undocumented, I see nothing glaring in your records that shows that you are mentally unstable, insane, or have violent tendencies toward your superiors. Therefore, I believe that we may have a chance, but first we all three need to understand the nature of the charges, the difficulties we will face, and the consequences of failure. Are you ready to begin?"

The uneasiness in Wake's stomach had turned into gnawing turmoil at hearing the distant, and borderline insulting, tone of Stockton's voice.

"Commander, it's obvious that you don't want to be my counsel. Therefore I'll discharge you and take my second choice on the list."

"You're going to discharge me for my not wanting this case, Lieutenant Wake?" Stockton replied, his brow furrowed in wonderment. "Do you actually think that any career naval officer with half a mind *wants* to defend you? Especially on *these* charges? And in Washington of all places, with a board made up such as this? Tell me you're not that naïve, Lieutenant."

Wake was stunned. As he looked at Hostetler's obvious embarrassment he realized that Stockton was right. No one would want to tie their name with his case, or his fate. "Ah, yes, Commander. I guess you have a point there," Wake admitted.

"Good. I'm very glad that you are bright enough to see it. Now, can we begin? We have a lot to discuss."

Wake quietly assented, and Stockton began asking him about his most recent activities after he had received orders to present himself at Navy Department headquarters. Wake explained that after the *Canton* had destroyed Symons' vessel and gang in Haiti, he had steamed to Key West Naval Depot. As per the orders of the secretary of the navy he had then turned the ship over to the next senior, Lieutenant Connery, and made arrangements for his transportation to Washington.

Upon arrival in Washington three weeks ago, he had presented himself at the Navy Department, was asked for his sword by the chief of the Bureau of Navigation, placed officially under open arrest and confined to the limits of the Naval Yard, and told his initial charge was mutiny. He was given quarters in the transit officers' building and a week later received a preliminary charging document. At that point he was informed that the final charging document would be presented in three weeks.

Wake pointed to his papers and said they were the statements of his witnesses, which included the officers and petty officers of the *Canton*, officers of the Spanish warship *Sirena* and British warship *Plover*, and the statements of a Venezuelan diplomat and American businessman in Panama.

Wake concluded by saying he was innocent and would help his counsels in any way they needed.

"Very good, Mr. Wake," said Stockton. "Then the first thing is to understand the allegations against you. Here is the official charging document."

The legal form was put on the table and turned so Wake could read it. As his eyes passed down the page Wake felt his blood run cold when he got to the important part.

Charges and Specifications:
   That Lieutenant Peter Wake, United States Navy, on the 20th day of June, 1869, while aboard the United States Ship Canton, in the Caribbean Sea, did violate the following Articles of War contained within the Regulations of the United States Navy in the below specified manner:
   Charge One—Violation of Article XIII:
   Specifically that he,

>—*Treated his superior officer, Captain P. Terrington, U.S.N., with contempt by word and deed.*
>
>—*Uttered mutinous and seditious words to his superior officer, Captain P. Terrington.*
>
>—*Made a mutinous assembly against his superior officer, Captain P. Terrington.*
>
>*Charge Two—Violation of Article XIX:*
>
>*Specifically that he,*
>
>—*Disobeyed the lawful order of his superior officer, Captain P. Terrington.*
>
>—*Struck or offered to strike his superior officer, Captain P. Terrington.*
>
>*Charge Three—Violation of Article XX:*
>
>*Specifically that he,*
>
>—*Negligently performed the duties assigned to him by his superior officer, Captain P. Terrington*

Wake found it hard to breathe, for the room had suddenly gotten hotter, and he unbuttoned his coat.

"You *will* stay in uniform, Lieutenant Wake," commanded Stockton, his eyes leveled into Wake's. "The fact that the charges make you uncomfortable does not give you permission to violate the regulations of the service. Or do you habitually ignore regulations when you are uncomfortable?"

Good God above, he's arrogant but right, thought Wake. If I can't act calm and professional in here with my own counsel, how will I act in the trial in front of the men who will decide my fate? He buttoned up his collar.

"You're correct, Commander. I'd better get used to hearing those accusations, though they make me upset because of their speciousness."

"All right, Mr. Wake. Now that you know what they're saying about you, here's what can happen if the board believes those accusations that you believe are specious."

Wake already knew, but Stockton said the words anyway.

"You shall suffer death."

For what seemed like a long time no one said anything. Then Stockton spoke again.

"If you are lucky, Mr. Wake, the sentence will be twenty years to life at Portsmouth, if you are extremely lucky, it will be dishonorable discharge and public disgrace for the rest of your life."

Wake thought of Symons' dishonorable discharge document he had first read in the dark alleyway in the hellhole of Cartagena and cringed when he thought he might be termed in the same category. He glanced at Hostetler, but the man's eyes were on the floor, the door, anywhere but his friend. Wake felt drained of courage and wanted to stop all this and run away. He found it hard even to look at Stockton as the man went on relentlessly.

"And here, Mr. Wake is how—as I see it after reviewing the documents furnished to me—they are going to show that you are guilty.

"First, they will prove that you never brought Captain Terrington's deficiencies to the attention of the Navy Department prior to taking your action, though you touched at several ports from which you could have sent such a report. Plus, the surgeons' mate will testify that you never sought his opinion until after your decision was made. A *fait accompli*, as it were.

"Second, they will prove that you did treat him with contempt and uttered mutinous words, since you admit all that in your own statement of the facts where you describe confronting Captain Terrington.

"Third, they will prove, again through your own statement, that you did strike Captain Terrington by the manner of forcibly touching him within the store room and in his own cabin.

"And fourth, Mr. Wake, they will prove that you were negligent in your duties to assist your captain, which they will say is manifestly true because you deposed the man from his lawful command."

Wake wished there was a window he could see out, the room seemed to be closing in on him. It all was so unreal. He couldn't ever remember feeling this hopeless. "I don't know what to say, or do, sir."

Stockton showed no pity as he leaned closer and glared at Wake. "Well, you'd better figure out something to say, and how to make it sound convincing, pretty damned soon, Lieutenant Wake. Seventeen men have been executed by the United States Navy since seventeen ninety-nine—seven of them for mutiny. And being an officer is no protection. One of those seven was Midshipman Philip Spencer on the *Somers* in eighteen forty-two. You are fighting for your life, Mr. Wake, and nothing less."

"What do we do, Commander?"

"I believe that we've accomplished our first task, Lieutenant, which is to assess the situation from the standpoint of the enemy—which is how I view the prosecution in this case. And make no mistake, the prosecution will be done very well. The court has already been made up and notified. Commander James Wayne will be the judge advocate, or prosecutor. I know him to be a very thorough and articulate officer."

"And the board of the court?" asked Wake.

"I presume that you know that in a general court-martial the board may consist of between five to thirteen officers, at least half of which must be senior to the accused. I realize that you started your career during the war as a volunteer officer and were thus prohibited from serving on a board. But since you received your regular commission, have you ever served on a board in a court-martial, Lieutenant?"

"Three minor courts of inquiry at Pensacola, also one summary court-martial with a petty officer, but nothing involving a commissioned officer. I was a witness on a petty officer's mutiny case during the war, but they changed it to murder so as not to alarm the public," Wake said.

"Yes, I think I saw that it your records. Interesting. And what was that sentence?"

"Death," uttered Wake. He could still remember seeing them slowly swinging from the yardarm. "They hanged the three ringleaders."

"I see," said Stockton as he nodded gravely, then dispassionately continued. "Well, I've had the experience of serving on several, both during the war and afterward. They are solemn affairs, Mr. Wake, with Marine guards and the special court-martial flag flying aloft. Your sword will be placed amidship on the board's table, neither point nor hilt pointing toward you, until the end. On the board for this court-martial we will have as president a rear admiral they are bringing out of retirement especially for this case, Franklin Munroe. Good reputation as a seaman and commander.

"The other members are a commodore just back from command of a foreign squadron, three captains and two commanders, for a total of seven in all. Every one of them is a combat veteran and all have been ship captains. None served in the East Gulf Blockading Squadron, which I understand was your squadron during the war."

Stockton went down the list of names, none of which Wake knew. He was desperate for some positive information, or some constructive task to do, rather than endure this despondent litany.

Hostetler glanced at Stockton and finally spoke. "Peter, this all won't be easy, but we can win. You're the one who told me years ago that an opponent's strength can also be used as one of his weaknesses. These men have a lot of experience and have served under all kinds of commanders, including ones like Parker Terrington. They will understand what you went through, and why you did what you did. Because of their professional experience, they also know the 'rocks and shoals' better than most."

In his nervous exhaustion, Wake laughed at Hostetler's referral to the slang used by naval officers for naval regulations. "Yes, Charles, and I suppose they've been afoul of the 'rocks and shoals' a few times themselves." Turning to Stockton, then nodding at the stack of books, he said, "Have you found anything in regulations that assists me, Commander?"

"These?" he gestured to the stack, then pointed out each as he described them. "This book contains the one hundred ninety-four articles of the naval regulations of eighteen-fifteen, commonly known as the Black Book. Now this one here is better known as the Blue Book of eighteen-eighteen, this is the Red Book of eighteen thirty-two, and this little tome," he picked up a massive book, "contains the eight hundred articles of naval regulations from eighteen forty-one, compiled by Secretary of the Navy Spaulding. And finally, here are the eighteen sixty-two regulations from Secretary Welles, which we operate under today, with certain amendments from last year. For the last week I have studied every single one of the articles of regulations in each of these for some sort of a justification or protection of your actions, Mr. Wake, either current or even historical."

Wake took a deep breath. "And?"

"I have not found one."

Wake used all of his self-discipline not to scream in desperation. Instead, he looked at Stockton and asked calmly, "All right, Commander, do you see any strengths on my side of this?"

Stockton relaxed back in his chair and paused pensively, his eyes never leaving Wake. Then he answered. "Yes. Five things. First, of course, the alleged victim is dead and unable to testify. Second, you did manage to eventually find this maniac Symons and kill him. Third, you have several very credible witnesses as to your character. Fourth, the navy no longer has a judge advocate general since John Bolles of Massachusetts, who did good work by the way, has stepped down. Those duties have been taken over by the Justice Department—an independent group not under naval control—so that an appeal would have a bit of a chance. . . ."

"And the fifth, Commander?"

"And fifth, Mr. Wake, . . . by God, you have *me.*"

Wake looked at him carefully. "But do you believe in my innocence, Commander?"

"Mr. Wake, if I didn't believe in your innocence, I would not be in this stifling hot room talking to you and risking my career. I'm not in the habit of wasting my time, Lieutenant. I took this case because I know we can win it."

Wake saw the determined look on Stockton's face and it gave

him some courage. "Thank you for that, Commander Stockton. How exactly do you see our plan of attack, as it were, unfolding?"

"At this moment I don't know, Peter. But I'm pretty sure I'll think of something," replied Stockton, a mischievous grin forming on his face. "You see, I know the 'rocks and shoals' as well as any man in the U.S. Navy. And it will give me *great* pleasure to use them to make the incompetent bastards who put Parker Terrington in command of a warship regret that stupid decision, and also the malicious one to prosecute you."

Wake let out a sigh. Hostetler suddenly pounded the table and said in his booming voice, "By God, Peter, I think we've got 'em right where we want 'em, now!"

43

The Prosecution's Attack

October 1869

She wanted to go in the room and sit beside him, to hold his hand and help defend him against this persecution, if only with the look in her eyes. But Linda knew she wasn't allowed inside. The court-martial was not open to the public, and upon her protest her husband had reminded Linda that the United States Navy was not a democracy. He also told her that he had total confidence in not only his innocence, but his counsel as well. During the previous weeks he, Stockton, and Hostetler had gone over every statement, every event, and every avenue of questioning they could think of. He was ready, Wake told his wife. It was time to get it done.

The Marine corporal at the door stood to attention as Wake and his counsel entered, then closed it without emotion as Linda stood there, seething inside and fighting back the tears at the sad sight of her husband going in to face the court-martial without her alongside to support him.

She found it ironic that the proceedings were restricted to

keep out the non-participants, but not technically secret, so that periodically Hostetler would come out and update her on what was happening, trying to describe it in positive terms. She would ask questions, which Hostetler answered candidly, knowing the lady would see through a white lie.

She waited by herself in the middle of a row of chairs outside the doors of the court-martial room, as serious-faced officers with gold braid on their sleeves—much more braid than her husband had—marched past her apparently on important business. Petty officers and ratings would come along and say hello, far more friendly and somehow encouraging in their comportment. After a while, she noticed that the officers were barely looking at her, as if they could be tainted by association, but the enlisted men always made a point to greet her.

Throughout the day prosecution witnesses would arrive and sit in the chairs beside her, then be called in by the Marine sentry. The witnesses would not even look at her. She felt a mixture of fear and anger at them, and wondered what they were saying about her husband. Except for the last two witnesses. They were officers and smiled at her, with more embarrassment than anything else, as if they were attempting to excuse their appearance and encourage her. It was all so confusing and infuriating for Linda.

And inside the room, it was anything but encouraging for Wake.

The board was presided over by Rear Admiral Franklin Munroe, retired from fifty years of service, man and boy, in the United States Navy and called out for this specific assignment, which he described to the court as "an odorous and grim duty." Each member of the board was glumly silent as they made their oaths of office and sat down at the long table, covered with a dark blue cloth bordered in gold roping.

Lying on the table in front of the admiral's place was Wake's sword. The table crossed one end of the room and along either wall were the defense table and the judge advocate's table, where a yeoman clerk also sat and recorded the proceedings. A chair for witnesses was placed within the area bounded by the tables, so that a person testifying was being scrutinized on three sides. Four windows were open at the end of the room behind the board's table, but did little to relieve the oppressive heat inside.

Once the members were sworn in, Admiral Munroe gruffly explained that he would run a fair and thorough court-martial and that this matter would be concluded efficiently, with no "lollygagging or grandstanding" by the participants.

Then Commander Wayne, the prosecuting judge advocate, laid out the charges against Wake. Speaking with ominously deliberate precision, he announced each charge and concluded by saying the case was the most serious faced by the navy since the end of the war and that the outcome would be studied and utilized by naval officers for years to come.

Commander Stockton then stood erect, faced the court, and gave his opening statement. "Mr. President and Members of the Court, I agree with Commander Wayne's assessment of the seriousness of this case, but would further state that it is the most important case *ever* in the history of the American Navy. Our navy has always had a different *esprit*, one born of our native initiative and honor, and we have always been victorious because of that. Our navy is not composed of martinets, but of martial men—men who think and act. During the course of this proceeding, you will hear of one of the best examples of that tradition, Lieutenant Peter Wake. And when this proceeding has concluded, and his decisive courage has been made known, each of you will be proud to shake his hand for what he has done for our navy, and our country."

As Stockton returned to his seat, Munroe audibly harrumphed and ordered Wayne to proceed and "get on with his evidence and testimony." The judge advocate pleasantly acknowledged the order, then called Surgeon's Mate Mortimer Pullwood.

With a carefully coached style, Pullwood described Terrington as a man in pain due to the "debilitations of service in the navy," including "aches and pains in his joints," which the surgeon's mate diagnosed as probably arthritis due to extended tours of duty in damp men-o-war during the war. Pullwood further described Terrington as being in good mental condition, not melancholy, and very polite to officers and men. He thought Terrington the very best commanding officer he had ever served under and lamented the man's demise. To the direct question of whether Terrington was addicted to laudanum and rum, Pullwood said that in his opinion he probably was not, though he took it every day. He also testified that Wake had never asked his opinion of the captain's medical condition before removing Terrington from command.

Throughout his testimony, Pullwood would not look at Wake, only at Admiral Munroe. Commander Wayne complimented Pullwood for his articulate responses and smoothly asked the court to excuse the witness, as if no further questions were expected.

Before Wake's counsel could even request cross-examination, Munroe, who was not one to be swayed by the suave verbiage of the judge advocate, *ordered* Commander Stockton to question the witness. Stockton addressed Pullwood. "Is laudanum addictive?"

"It can be, sir."

"After how long?"

"Depends on the man and the pain, sir."

"After how long usually do you stop giving a man laudanum?"

"Six to eight weeks for bad cases."

"This pain of Captain Terrington's, did you document the source of it as a justification for your dispensing laudanum?"

"Oh, no, sir. He was the captain."

"Is that a violation of regulations?"

"Well, I suppose so, in a way. . . ."

"And your dispensing of the laudanum was in the usual manner for that type of pain?"

"Yes, sir."

"By your own statement earlier you said you gave him two to three doses a day, a tablespoon each dose. What is the standard you would give to a man each day who had, say, a gunshot wound to the leg? Remember, Pullwood, I have a copy of the surgeon's manual on my desk there. I am asking to see if you know."

"Well, that would depend . . . on the man, and the wound . . . and other . . . things, and . . ." Pullwood was totally confused, delaying until he could understand where the questioning was heading.

"Yes, it does. So let's establish the parameters. Please tell me how many doses *minimum* to that man? And for how long? A week? Two weeks?" insisted Stockton.

Pullwood knew exactly where the questions were going now, but he also knew they could check his answers. "Probably two a day, sir. For two to four weeks."

"And the maximum dosage for, say, a severe leg wound and pain?"

"Probably five a day, sir, for eight to ten weeks."

"If a man requested such a maximum dose for *twenty-five* weeks to handle the pain of a wound, would you certify that he could still go on deck and work at the same time?"

"Ah . . . well, no, I don't think I would, sir."

"Would it be cruel to make him work with that much pain?"

"Yes, I suppose it would, sir. But Captain Terrington didn't have no gunshot."

"But Pullwood, according to your testimony here Captain Terrington—the man you held in such dear estimation—was actually in the same amount of pain as a man who had sustained a severe gunshot wound and was taking laudanum dispensed by you for more than two times longer than the maximum—"

"I beg the court to object," interrupted Wayne. "Defense counsel is making a statement, not asking a question."

"Concur," rumbled Munroe. "Ask something, don't preach, Commander Stockton."

"Yes, sir. Pullwood, with all of this supposed pain the captain

329

was in, why did you not have the kindness or courtesy to your patient to make that condition known to the executive officer so that Captain Terrington could seek relief?"

"'Twarn't his business, sir," said Pullwood, exasperated. "'Twas between the patient and me."

"So you allowed a man with debilitating pain to continue to try to exert himself, and use the laudanum?"

Pullwood's eyes reflected his fear. "Ah, sir, that's what Captain Terrington wanted."

"And he wanted it five times a day, every day, correct?" asked Stockton with raised eyebrow.

Pullwood sagged in the witness chair. "He was the captain, sir. How do you say no to the captain?"

"Pullwood, are you under charges right now for dispensing laudanum improperly?"

"Yes, sir."

"Did you state in your statement that you and Steward Morely and Quartermaster Castle relaxed with Captain Terrington in his cabin over rum drinks and laudanum?"

"Yes, sir. We did that only sometimes, sir. The captain invited us, sir."

"Mr. President of the Court, I have no further questions of this witness."

Steward Morely was the next witness called by Commander Wayne. Under direct questioning he testified that Captain Terrington exhibited no signs of insanity or addiction and that it was clear that Lieutenant Wake did not like the captain and held a grudge because the captain had had sharp words to him once.

Stockton asked what those sharp words were about, to which Morely answered, "Dangerous seamanship in hazarding the ship at Haiti in May, where she was almost lost." The board members sat up, one asking for more details, which Morely was unable to give, since he was below for most of the event. But he did say that he heard Terrington chastise Wake for failing to notify him of a dangerous maneuver close to shore that had almost sunk the *Canton*.

It was obvious that Commander Wayne had no prior knowledge of the episode, but wanted to capitalize on its negative effect. When Stockton announced he had no further questions—to Wake's shock Commander Wayne requested to be able to re-examine the witness.

"How do you know the ship was in danger of being lost?"

"I heard the ship's officers talk about it, sir. And also the captain himself, when he came back below. He called Mr. Wake a 'damned upstart' he did, sir. Said he almost killed them all on the rocks of Haiti."

Wayne smiled and ended his questioning. Then Stockton rose and requested a question for clarification of a point raised by Commander Wayne. Munroe muttered yes and leaned forward, intensely interested.

"And was that event that you speak of the time, on May fifteenth, when *Canton* was able to save the entire ship and crew of the Spanish warship *Sirena*, which was about to founder upon the rocks of Haiti?"

"Ah, yes, sir. That was the name of that Dago ship."

"If it pleases the court, I have a sworn statement given by the captain of that vessel, Fernando Toledo, testifying to the professional skill and courage of Lieutenant Wake in effecting that rescue. Unfortunately, Captain Toledo was killed in action against the pirates, but his statement, written in anticipation of Lieutenant Wake's court-martial, will be entered into the record during the defense presentation. I have no further questions of this man."

Quartermaster Johnny Castle was called by Commander Wayne next. The grizzled man barely concealed his hatred of Wake as he entered. Keeping his answers directed to the admiral, Castle sneered at Wake as he listened to the questions. He testified as to Terrington's seamanship and his sobriety, saying that Terrington was "a real sailorman's captain" and that Castle considered him the best he had ever seen in twenty years of service, which he stressed included combat during the war. Castle then admitted that he was under charges involving laudanum, but countered that they were as trumped up as the ones against poor dead Captain Terrington, who was not even able to defend himself against the scurrilous slander.

Stockton only had one question for the quartermaster.

"Did you ever partake of laudanum with Parker Terrington, in the same cabin? And before you answer, please remember that you are under oath."

Castle's head tilted to one side, face grimaced, and muttered, "That is a *damned lie* . . . sir."

The final witnesses for the prosecution were the other two lieutenants of the *Canton*. Connery testified first, then Custen. Stockton had prepared Wake for this, explaining they were there by order, not desire. Still, it was unsettling for Wake to see each of them enter the room as witnesses for the prosecution. During their individual testimonies, Lieutenants Connery and Custen were sternly admonished by Commander Wayne to strictly answer either yes or no to his questions.

Each was asked if they had ever specifically seen Captain Terrington partake of laudanum, to which each answered no. Then the officers were asked if he had ever appeared falling down drunk or besotted by a drug while in their presence on the *main deck*. Each had hesitated, then reluctantly answered no again. The final question for each was if they had ever seen the captain hazard their ship in a like manner as Lieutenant Wake did on the shore of Haiti in May of 1869, to which each also said no.

Stockton's cross-examination inquired of them how often they had even seen Terrington on the main deck after April of that year. Connery said perhaps seven or eight times. Custen answered that it might have been nine or ten. Stockton asked them who, since April, had been making the command decisions aboard the *Canton*. Each replied decisively that it had been Lieutenant Wake.

The last witness for the prosecution was young ensign Noble. He was asked if Terrington had died as a result of enemy action, to which Noble responded yes, that the pirate had shot Terrington in the face when he had looked out the stern windows. Agreeing reluctantly with Wake's request, Stockton elected not to cross-examine and besmirch the final moment of Terrington's life. Stockton's reasoning was more practical—he didn't want to elicit sympathy for Terrington by attacking him post-mortem.

The last presentation by the prosecutor was the introduction of Wake's own statements, which Wayne characterized as a confession. Each member of the board was given a copy, and the board recessed while the officers read through the report Wake had sent the secretary of the navy from Panama in June, and the report he sent upon his return to Key West in August.

Two hours later, as a rainstorm beat against the panes of glass, the board reentered the room and sat at the table, each man looking at Wake. Feeling their scrutiny, he tried to not to show the fear inside him.

Finally, as the shadows were lengthening at the end of an agonizingly long day, Commander Wayne declared his presentation of the prosecutorial evidence of this shocking lack of the discipline necessary aboard a man-o-war was complete, and Admiral Munroe announced the proceedings adjourned until the following morning.

After everyone else had departed the room, Wake remained for a moment, then rose slowly from his chair. Shaken by the hard looks from the board after they read his statements, he steeled himself to face Linda. When he walked out into the corridor and saw her waiting there, however, he almost lost his composure. She was his life. As she had been during those darkest days of the war, Linda was his anchor.

They held each other for a long time before the two of them walked hand in hand out of the building. Without a word between them they sauntered down the pebble walkway to the front gate of the Naval Yard. The rain had stopped and the air turned cooler, as if the rain had washed away the pain of the day.

The Marine sentry at the gate turned and faced another direction to give them privacy, for the word had gone out about the young lieutenant's trial—a lieutenant who cared more about the lives of his men and the mission of the ship than he did about his career. Around the naval yard enlisted men, both sailor and Marine, were following the case, their hopes on his side. Linda took advantage of the relative seclusion and kissed her husband as they held each other again.

Wake straightened and smiled, whispering the first words he'd uttered since leaving the room, "Tomorrow is the day I get to tell them what *really* happened."

Then, so she couldn't sense his mounting anxiety, he turned and walked quickly away, back to his desolate quarters. Linda walked down the block to her hotel, made her way past the noise of naval officers and their wives in the bar, and up to her room on the third floor. She lay on the bed, trying to think of a way to get her husband to resign from this ruthless organization, in the remote chance that they found him not guilty.

She was tired of it all, of the years of tension and heartache, and wanted him *out* of the navy and as far away from these horrid people as possible.

44

Mindless Slavery

The day of the defense presentation dawned sunny, with the first cool crispness of autumn nipping the air. It was Linda's first experience of northern climes and she thought it wonderful, hoping it was a good omen. They met, as they had every day for the last month, with a kiss at the front gate, she trying to hide her anger and he trying to hide his fear. Commander Stockton and Lieutenant Hostetler arrived a few minutes later and the four of them walked to the building by the river.

"You'll get to meet some very interesting people today, Linda," said Hostetler as they passed under a massive oak tree.

"Oh, Charles—you were actually able to get them here?" she exclaimed. She had been privy to every aspect of the plan, but there had been some doubt whether certain parts would come to fruition. Hostetler was in charge of the crucial task of getting their witnesses to the court-martial, which was no easy task when some had to come all the way from the Caribbean.

"Why, Peter Wake," quipped Hostetler, "I do believe I heard some doubt in your lady's voice about my abilities. You need to get her morale under control, son."

"Charles, my friend, I promise you that when this thing is successfully concluded, that will be absolutely the *second* thing of Linda's that I'll get under control." Wake winked at Linda, prompting a jab in the ribs by her.

"Charles, I can't wait until you and Barbara get married," Linda added, speaking of Hostetler's fiancée. "I want to see how you'll control that lady!"

"Aye to that, Mrs. Wake. I think that Lieutenant Hostetler has met his match with that particular lady," said Stockton as they approached the building. "But seriously, Lieutenant Hostetler has done a very good job of assembling these witnesses. The court will be impressed by their variety and credibility."

And then they were there. Hostetler departed to arrange the witnesses' arrival as Wake kissed Linda one last time and disappeared with Commander Stockton behind the heavy paneled door with the stone-faced Marine guard in front. Then she took her chair and waited, but soon she was no longer alone.

Hostetler appeared shortly afterward with several men, including Sean Rork, whom Linda ran up to and hugged. She was introduced to the others, officers and petty officers from the *Canton*, including the two she had seen the day before. Hostetler explained that none of them could discuss the case or their testimony with her or each other, but that normal conversation would certainly be in order. She enjoyed seeing faces to put with the names she had learned from her husband's letters and the planning sessions for his defense. She told them that they all were as she had expected and that she greatly appreciated their helping her husband.

Then she sat down with Rork and they talked. Mainly about her children, but also about the old days in Key West and how Sean's family was getting along in Ireland. She asked if he was closer to finding a girl of his own to make a home, to which he smiled and said his home was the navy and that on a bosun's pay a wife would be destitute.

As they talked she felt her courage being lifted by the men

around her, and she understood even better her husband's devotion to them that was reflected in his letters. These men were the navy that Peter loved so much, not the petty career tyrants who put politics before honor.

Connery was the first called to the court room. As he entered he saw that the members of the court were leaning forward in their chairs in anticipation of hearing the defense's case.

"Lieutenant Connery, as acting executive officer from January to April of eighteen sixty-nine, did you ever see Captain Terrington under the effects of laudanum aboard the *Canton*? If yes, when and where?"

"Yes, sir, I did. Especially from April, when we were here in Washington, he seemed to stay below a lot. When I met with him in his cabin, his speech was slurred and he appeared groggy. I saw the blue bottle on his desk once and guessed then the origin of his behavior. He slept a lot of the time."

"Did you ever see him under the effects of rum?"

"Yes, sir. I could smell it on him. Mostly in his cabin. After April it got to the point where it was common."

"From April, you say? What exactly happened here in Washington in April?"

"The only thing I know that happened is that we got orders to go down into the Caribbean after the renegade American who had turned pirate, sir."

Connery had discussed his testimony with Stockton and knew not to describe or allude in any way to Terrington's relationship with Symons. The members of the board had read of all that in Wake's reports, but Stockton wanted to keep it out of all testimony. It was part of his plan.

"You testified yesterday that you saw Captain Terrington on the main deck of the *Canton* only nine or ten times from early April to mid June of eighteen sixty-nine, or approximately four months. Were these appearances becoming more frequent or less frequent during those four months?"

"Far less frequent, sir. In the last month we saw him only once."

Stockton ended his questioning and looked at Commander Wayne, who hesitated, then shook his head. But Commodore Baldwin of the board had a question.

"Was Captain Terrington a competent ship commander?"

"While I was aboard, he never demonstrated by personal action any competence in leadership or seamanship, sir," Connery answered.

Custen was called and asked the same questions, with equivalent answers. Wayne elected not to cross-examine, but Admiral Munroe himself asked a question, pointing a finger at the witness.

"Did you *like* Captain Terrington, Lieutenant?"

"Sir, it isn't my place to like or dislike a captain."

"And do you like Lieutenant Wake? He's not a captain."

"He is not a personal friend, but I respect his professional abilities, sir. Greatly."

Chief Engineer Winter was called and asked the same questions by Stockton, but there were no other inquiries by the prosecution or court. Then came Rork's turn. After Stockton's questions were answered, then Munroe again pointed his finger and gruffly asked, "Do you like Lieutenant Wake?"

"Aye, that I do, sir."

"Oh? Really? Did you like the other officers, including Captain Terrington?"

"I don't really know them others, sir. But I do know Lieutenant Peter Wake. We served together in gunboats during the war. I got ta know him well then."

"And why exactly do you like him, Bosun?"

"Because he is what I call a *believer*, sir. He believes in honor an' in the U.S. Navy an' doin' the right thing for the right reasons. Even when it ain't easy, or might bring him ta harm. I wish to Saint Patrick there were more like him, sir."

"So you consider him a pal, do you? Would you help him out?"

Rork sensed the course of the question. "Admiral, sir, I'd not do even a wee thing that'd bring dishonor ta Peter Wake, nor would that man even ask for such a thing as that. An' that, sir, is why I like him."

Munroe nodded his head thoughtfully and called for the next witness.

Other petty officers were called as confirmation of what had already been said, with little serious cross-examination. After the midday break, Stockton began to call in his special witnesses, the likes of which no officer serving on the board had ever seen testify in a court-martial. Stockton knew that these men would give information, both pertinent and credible, and that none was afraid of speaking the truth to senior naval officers.

The first was John Kramer. He testified that he thought Terrington was a timid incompetent fool and that he had no hopes that a naval effort against the pirates would be successful until Wake finally took over. When Wayne tried to mitigate his testimony by asking his *naval* credentials, Kramer bluntly said he had none, and if Terrington was representative of the U.S. Navy, then he'd be embarrassed to have any. Kramer ended by saying that if the Navy didn't want a man like Wake, then the American Transit Company certainly would—they needed men of action.

The next was a tall, distinguished black man, who was introduced as Ebeneezer Don Charles Basset, the United States Minister to Haiti since 1864, when Abraham Lincoln recognized the country officially. Basset testified as to the very good will and impression in that region that Wake had made, increasing the respect for the American flag there by his action against the pirates that had not resulted in any Haitian deaths, though the battle took place right among the people. The American naval victory there had also already dampened some of the maritime thievery and thus encouraged foreign investment in the island.

Stockton subsequently called Blaine Wilson, United States Consul General to Her Majesty's Crown Colony of Jamaica. He testified that the British government on the island was very impressed by Wake's actions and was inquiring as to whether he would be rewarded officially in some way, as they wanted to participate in that ceremony to show their appreciation.

Then came Eduardo Cervantes de Alba, the Chargé d'Affaires from the Nicaraguan Embassy in Washington. He expressed his country's appreciation for the United States Navy's obliteration of the pirate scourge on the Moskito coast.

He was followed by Don Pablo Monteblanco, who had come up from Venezuela to testify for his friend. Monteblanco explained the opinion of the United States in the region prior to the *Canton's* arrival and the remarkable change in that opinion since Wake's actions in Colombia, Nicaragua, and Haiti. Now the United States was seen as a power and ally that could be relied upon.

The final witness for the defense was Captain Rodney Russell of the Royal Navy. Russell gave his opinion of Wake's seamanship as superb and his operational planning ability as outstanding. Lieutenant Wake, he said, was an excellent representative of the American Navy. The Briton did not mince words regarding Terrington.

"The plan and leadership was Lieutenant Wake's from the start. By observing Captain Terrington's behavior in the few meetings he attended, I was apprehensive of going into action with that man trying to make decisions. I was greatly encouraged when notified that Wake had relieved him due to illness. It was obvious to the officers of the Royal Navy who met him that Lieutenant Wake was not the type of chap that would sacrifice the success of his mission for the mindless slavery of subordination."

The board was clearly impressed by the parade of witnesses. Afterward, Stockton submitted the statements of all of them into evidence, adding Captain Toledo's as well.

The afternoon light was waning when Munroe called for the court to adjourn for the evening. The next day, he said, would be the last for both sides, then the board would go into its deliberations, which would be secret. He looked at the members of the board and added that those deliberations would also be swift and that the sooner they got this disagreeable duty done, the better.

45

Repercussions of Perceptions

Secretary Robeson, how very kind of you to come over, especially at this unfortunately late hour," greeted Secretary of State Hamilton Fish as one of his aides escorted the secretary of the navy into the grand corner office whose windows overlooked the bustling streets of Washington four floors below. It was already getting dark and the gas lamplight reflected warmly off the paneled walls.

Robeson settled into the large upholstered chair in front of Fish's massive cherry wood desk. He had things to do and did not want to be there—but this damned Seward was forever meddling with the navy.

"Thank you so much for the invitation, Hamilton. My man said you wanted to talk about the situation with that renegade American pirate down in the Caribbean."

"Quite right, George. Since it's late, I'll get right to the point. There is a trial going on for the officer who took control of the navy ship and went after the pirates, I believe?"

"Yes, there is. It's a serious one involving naval discipline. The charge is mutiny. It'll be wrapped up tomorrow."

"Mutiny? Really? How very distressing that an American naval officer should do such a thing."

"I agree, Hamilton. It is embarrassing. We simply can't allow our ships' officers to depose their captains—even when they are not the best kind of captains, which this one wasn't."

Fish nodded pensively, then said, "My friend, have you heard of the reaction to this officer's actions in the Caribbean?"

Robeson's interest perked up. This must be why he was asked to come. Everyone knew that Fish was very interested in the Caribbean and had many contacts there, and also that he wanted to obtain more American territory in the region. Robeson was not against that at all, the navy could use some more coaling depots.

"Well, there were some witnesses from that area testifying today in the trial," replied Robeson. "I'm told they appreciated the navy's success against the pirates."

"Ah . . . I think it was a bit more that that," said Fish. "My sources, who are very well informed, advise me that the governments of the area are *exceedingly* grateful for what your lieutenant did—and impressed by the U.S. actions. In fact, I heard that they originally thought this man's decisive achievement was a result of a direct order by President Grant himself."

Fish paused to accentuate his point, which annoyed Robeson.

"Because of that," Fish continued, "they have diminished their appeals to the European powers for maritime protection and are coming back to the table, so to speak, to talk with us about various issues—issues that are of some importance to our hemispheric national interests, and to the President personally, and politically."

Robeson didn't understand where the secretary of state was going with his monologue, but it sounded dangerous. Fish always had some Machiavellian scheme going, but the navy secretary couldn't decipher this one.

"All right, but that's all good for us then. What exactly is your point, Hamilton? I've got an important gathering tonight, a delegation of railroad men from Trenton are meeting me at the Willard at eight-thirty."

Fish shook his head. "My point, Mr. Secretary, is that this trial is changing certain viewpoints, and that is not good. The Caribbean nations, including those who have the potential for a canal across the isthmus, have heard of this trial. They now are starting to believe that their original understanding was wrong— that the decisive naval success was *in spite of* the navy, and not of the government's wishes."

Fish regarded Robeson with a cunning smile. "They are even hearing the ridiculous notion that the navy actually sent a man who was a close relative of the pirate to make only a show out of getting him. Rumor has it that it was his brother, but of course, I find that quite hard to believe."

Robeson moaned inwardly. "You have my attention, Mr. Secretary. Please continue."

"Yes, well, I thought all of this might be of interest to you. That's why I asked for you to stop by so late. The result of all this attention to this trial is that those governments may not take us seriously, may even doubt our resolve."

Fish's tone lowered. "They are losing respect for our ability to project *force* in the Caribbean, in our own backyard. And respect of a country's force, sir, is the lubricant of international relations."

Robeson warily gestured agreement as Fish pressed on.

"However, if this internal litigation is concluded in a manner that could salve the disciplinary needs of the navy, and also show certain foreign leaders that we intended to do what we did, it would be a good thing, don't you think? By the way, was it really his brother that you sent down there?"

The secretary of the navy looked up at the intricately molded ceiling. Fish had him. "We didn't know that when we made the assignment. We didn't know the identity of the damn pirate until the *Canton* got down there. And, for your information, we sent the ship down there to get the job done, not to merely make a show of it. Unfortunately, we had the wrong man in command.

So you and the president want this all to go away so that you can get on with your political business down there?"

Fish shrugged and smiled. "Of course. Wouldn't that be the best for everyone?"

The morning chill felt invigorating to Wake as the four of them made their daily trek to the building. Stockton told them he sensed that his plan was coming to fruition, that their defense against the enemy's prosecutorial attacks had worked and their own flanking attacks were making progress. He also explained that Wake would not testify—that was too dangerous with a man like Wayne as prosecutor. Today would be the final arguments and then the board would sit in secret deliberation. Usually that took at least a day.

One hour later Commander Wayne gave his summation to the court.

"Mr. President and members of the Board of the Court-Martial. For the last several days we have been presented with evidence of several things. First, that Lieutenant Peter Wake did treat his superior with contempt, failing to notify him of serious decisions and intentionally failing to advise him of planning sessions with other ship captains. In fact, Lieutenant Wake acted with outside officers as if he were the captain of the *Canton*.

"Second, we have it from Mr. Wake's own report that he uttered mutinous words to his superior and held a mutinous assembly with officers and petty officers. This assembly having had the result of confining their captain and failing to render him aid.

"Third, we have heard of Captain Terrington's pain and legitimate need for medicine, as a result of arduous service during the war, something to which each of us here can relate.

"Fourth, again by Mr. Wake's own report, we have found that he physically assaulted his superior through attacking him in a storeroom and subsequently restraining him down into his berth.

"And finally, we have discovered, from his own report and from the testimony of others, that Lieutenant Wake negligently performed the duty assigned to him, that being to assist his captain in the command of the ship. In fact, gentlemen, this man," said Wayne, pointing at Wake, "did everything he could to undermine Captain Terrington's ability to command and the crew's respect for their commander.

"If he had supported his captain, if he had demonstrated that age-old custom of personal assistance between an executive officer and a captain, we would not be here today, and the honor and discipline of the United States Navy would not be called into question. If he had only tried to *help* Parker Terrington, Lieutenant Wake would still being serving aboard the *Canton*, probably the recipient of a letter of commendation from his captain.

"What was the true extent of Lieutenant Wake's actions against Captain Terrington? We will never know, because that naval officer is dead, killed in gallant action. What we do know is that Lieutenant Wake's behavior toward his captain was not that required by regulations or expected by decency, and his opportunism glaringly stands out by the evidence presented.

"Every ship captain, which includes every member of this court, knows he must have complete trust in his executive officer. That was denied Captain Parker Terrington and we are here to seek justice for that offense."

A short recess was held, for which Wake was relieved. The prosecution's summation made him alternately angry and confused. Then it was Stockton's turn.

"Mr. President and members of the Board of the Court-Martial, I shall be brief. Gentlemen, my esteemed colleague Commander Wayne did not have much to work with to support these charges. Not much at all. In fact, he has had to rely upon his rendition of the facts to craft an eloquent summation, one that if a person had not been in the court for the last several days to hear and read the evidence, would sound plausible and overwhelming. Through his articulate and passionate words—and not through the evidence—the ancient and ominous fear of mutiny has been raised.

"But in reality the contrary is true. You *have* been here. You intimately know the evidence. And each of you knows that there was no mutiny, real or imagined. Captain Parker Terrington was a man in pain, be it actual or imagined, who had been taken down a path of no return by the surgeon's mate. And that path led to a complete inability to function and command due to his drug addiction.

"Was Lieutenant Peter Wake in any way responsible for his captain's addiction? No, of course not. He didn't even understand what exactly it was until the infirmity had completely conquered the man. Was it his fault that he did not know? No, of course not. Through his loyalty he kept supporting the captain, and his ignorance of the true nature of the problem was due to the surgeon's mate maintaining the secret of the malady.

"Then what *did* Lieutenant Wake do? As we have seen and heard, he supported his captain to the point of running the ship while the commander lay in his cabin for days or weeks at a time. Then, when combat appeared imminent and command decisions would have to be made instantaneously, Lieutenant Wake did what every executive officer has done in this navy's history when faced with a similar situation. Realizing that his captain's sickness made him obviously unable to function in combat, Lieutenant Peter Wake took command, just as he would have had it been typhoid or yellow fever or dysentery.

"And when he took command, what happened? The mission was accomplished. A long, difficult, and dangerous mission against a determined foe was accomplished and the foe vanquished. This result is described by not only the other officers aboard the *Canton*, but by men of status and credibility, independent of the U.S. Navy, who were there and who saw the work of Lieutenant Wake.

"Commander Wayne has said that every ship captain must

have trust in his executive officer. How very true and how very appropriate to this case. Gentlemen, I think there is no doubt that every veteran ship commander would be honored to have a man like Lieutenant Wake serve as his executive officer. What better type of man to serve in that capacity than the kind of officer who has made this navy, and this country, what it is today. The finest in the world."

Admiral Munroe was blunt to the members of the board once the door closed and they were alone, all others having left.

"All right, gentlemen, I want to hear each of your opinions, and I don't care what rank you are." Munroe faced the junior member of the board. "You will start, Commander Higgins."

After each man had submitted his appraisal of the situation, with the two senior captains in favor of conviction, the three junior officers in favor of acquittal, and the commodore undecided, Munroe spoke again.

"Thank you gentlemen. I will give you my opinion tomorrow, and until then we will adjourn. I expect each of you to ponder this case, and the ramifications of your decision, throughout the night. I fear it will be a sleepless one for you. And at nine o'clock in the morning we will sit together again and render our decision."

Rear Admiral Franklin Munroe had an unexpected visitor that evening. He and the secretary of the navy, an old friend from New Jersey who had personally asked for him to come out of retirement and handle the court-martial, stayed up late in Munroe's quarters, discussing everything from the recent deaths of contemporaries to the future of the navy. And along the conversation's journey, the two old men also discussed the case involving young Lieutenant Wake and what had really happened aboard the USS *Canton* in the tropical waters of the Caribbean.

When Secretary Robeson left the front gate of the Naval Yard at midnight he smiled to himself. He and old Frankie had been able to salvage the mess, but it was a close run thing. And Fish most definitely owed him one after this.

The chief of the Bureau of Navigation, in charge of officer assignments among other things, was awakened at two in the morning at his home and given a strange message by the duty yeoman. Shaking his head in wonderment and uttering some oaths learned at sea forty years earlier, he dressed and went down to his office to handle Secretary Robeson's unusual request. Once there, he met with his senior yeoman, who had also been awakened, and had the orders written and copied out for the record.

As per the secretary's request, they would be delivered to the recipients at nine-fifteen in the morning.

This was the coldest morning in Linda's life. Raised in tropical Key West, she had never been north of Pensacola. The early winter air that had come down from Canada in middle October had everyone at her hotel speculating what was to come in November.

Wake held his wife close as they walked in silence to the court-martial building. She could feel the tension in his body belying the brave smile he displayed for her. At nine o'clock the Marine announced that the court was reconvening and for all authorized parties to enter to hear the decision. Wake embraced his wife, then entered the court-martial room with his counsel.

As Linda waited, witnesses for the defense started to gather in the hallway. Rork gave her a big hug, but she could see his eyes were filled with emotion. None of them spoke of the trial, instead making small talk in an attempt to alleviate Linda's anxiety. She loved them all for their efforts, but it was for naught—inside her anger was displaced by terror of what would happen.

Wake had only one thing in mind as he entered the room— the position of his sword on the table. If the hilt was toward the door he was acquitted, but if the blade's point was aimed at the door he was convicted. The officers entering ahead of him prevented Wake from seeing the sword, frustrating him. His legs felt weak as he made his way to the defense table and finally saw his sword on the table in front of Admiral Munroe.

Neither end was toward the door. The sword lay along the table as it had for several days.

His heart pumping with trepidation, Wake stood along with the others as Admiral Munroe entered. Then everyone sat as Munroe, showing a grim mien, whispered something to the commodore, who winced, then called the court-martial to order. The admiral beckoned Commander Wayne and handed him the written verdict, which he perused without reaction. The judge advocate in turn handed it to the yeoman, who then announced the decision as Wake and his counsel stood.

"After hearing all of the facts of this matter, it is the opinion of this court that the charges specified against Lieutenant Peter Wake, United States Navy, through no fault of the judge advocate, have been deficient in developing substantial enough supporting evidence to enable a prosecution of this case. It is therefore the order of this court that the proceedings held heretofore be redesignated as a special court of inquiry, and that the evidence assembled therein be remanded as confidential information to the custody of the board of the court of inquiry.

"It is further decided by the court that the special court of inquiry finds no supportable cause of action against Lieutenant Peter Wake.

"It is finally decided by this court that the matter is ended and that it will thus adjourn *sine die*. So ordered and published this nineteenth day of October, in the year of our Lord, eighteen sixty-nine, by direction of Rear Admiral Franklin Munroe, United States Navy, President of the Court. May God bless the United States of America."

Wake's hands were shaking and he felt close to a nervous breakdown when Munroe stood and held out the sword in both hands. "Lieutenant Wake, you may retrieve your sword."

Wake advanced to the front of the room, accepted the sword and was about to say thank you, when the admiral bellowed, "This court is now and forever adjourned!" and walked out, followed solemnly by the other members of the board and Commander Wayne.

Wake stood there for a moment by himself, then turned to see Hostetler chuckling and Stockton with a wry grin. "Commander Stockton, I don't understand at all. What does all this mean?"

"Peter, it means the whole thing never happened. There were no charges and this wasn't a general court-martial, only a court of inquiry. And the information gained is confidential to be held by the court—that means Munroe personally. You are free with absolutely no record. This is even better than an acquittal."

"My God!" shouted Wake, letting go of his self-discipline. "You did it!"

Stockton held up a hand. "No, I didn't do anything, Peter—you did. Your actions spoke loudly for themselves. We just let the age-old law of Washington politics take over."

Hostetler and Wake gave him a quizzical look, so he added. "The repercussions of perceptions, Peter. In the Caribbean you're perceived to be a hero. Can you imagine the repercussions to a politician in Washington who would punish a hero?"

Wake shook his head in disbelief at it all, then went out to tell Linda, but she already knew from the Marine who had heard it from the grinning yeoman. Through the petty officer grapevine, within minutes the whole navy yard knew.

He held her tightly, tears running down their faces, surrounded by men who had put their careers on the line to tell the truth about a man they respected. When he finally let her go and turned to the men, Wake couldn't get anything out. There was so much he wanted to say to them, but was choked by sentiment.

He took a breath and squeezed Linda's hand, then managed to speak. "Thank you, all. I know what it took to do what you did. And I will never forget it." Wake glanced at Linda and smiled. "For both of us, and our children, thank you. . . ."

The officers and petty officers in the hallway broke into applause, their hugs and backslapping and laughter echoing around the building. Behind Wake, a messenger made his way through the crowded hallway and stood in front of Stockton. "Commander Stockton, sir? Urgent messages for you, and Lieutenant Wake, from Admiral Frazier at the Bureau of Navigation, sir. I was told no reply is necessary at this time, only confirmation you received the messages." He then handed the surprised officer two envelopes and disappeared after Stockton acknowledged him.

The gathering grew quiet as Stockton silently read the message, then handed Wake his identical envelope.

"Repercussions of perceptions, Peter. It works both ways. We have embarrassed the department," said Stockton quietly. "So they can't just let us off that easy, can they? I am ordered to join the Tierra del Fuego Survey Expedition—the day after tomorrow in Philadelphia. I'll be the exec of *Choctaw*. We depart immediately to take advantage of summer in the Southern Hemisphere."

Linda looked at Stockton and asked, "Where is Tierra del Fuego?"

Stockton answered, "I am being sent, literally, to the bottom of the world, Linda. Tierra del Fuego is the land around Cape Horn, and we're to do a hydrographic survey in the area. It will take two years."

Wake tore open his own envelope and read his orders, the

blood draining from his face. He was ordered to join Commander Selfridge's Panama Survey Expedition assembling at the Brooklyn Navy Yard in two days. The expedition's mission was to determine a canal route across the Isthmus and they would be departing at the beginning of the year. The steamer *Nipsic* would be the flagship. Wake was assigned to the actual survey party and would be going through the jungle and mountains of that deadly place. He was speechless.

"What about you?" Linda asked, worried at the expression on his face. "Where are you going?"

"Back to the jungle, in Panama. A survey mission across the Isthmus. They're apparently getting us out of sight for a while, I guess. It says here I probably won't be back until the fall of 1871. I report in two days to Brooklyn," said Wake.

"Oh Lord, Peter. All this was on purpose," said Linda, the anger returning and welling up. "These damned politicians are punishing you for doing what was right! What's wrong with them? I hate this damn place!"

"Linda, please don't make it worse than it is."

"Worse! You're going into a place where hundreds die from fever every year! You know exactly what those fevers can do. They are sending you there to die, Peter. To get rid of you. Don't you *see* that?"

The hallway got silent, the men embarrassed for Wake and angry at the orders. When Hostetler broke the silence with his booming voice and suggested that all hands go to a watering hole he knew over on M Street, they started to disperse, wishing Wake and Stockton luck. Rork shook his friend's hand, leaned over and whispered something, then walked down the hall. Durling nodded, his concerned eyes saying it all. Stockton stayed behind when the crowd left, still reading his orders. Finally Stockton spoke up.

"Linda, the navy already had these missions planned and implemented. Naval officers would be assigned—if not Peter and me, then some other two. It's our profession. It's what we do." The commander strode away out of the building, following the others to the bar, leaving the couple alone in the deserted hall.

"He's right, Linda. At least I'll have a mission. A lot of officers don't have a billet and they go on half-pay. Plus, I do know a bit more about Panama than many officers, so I'm a good fit."

Through her tears, Linda said, "I just want you out of all this, Peter. Away from this kind of thing. I'm sick of it." She gestured around the building. "Just sick of all this."

"It's my *life*, Linda. You knew that years ago. It hasn't changed. I don't want to leave the navy, and I don't want you distraught. Can't we work this out?"

Linda shook her head and said, "God help me, Peter, but for some reason I do understand that." She took his hand. "Let's just get out of here now and be a husband and wife for these two days."

They left the building and turned right along the riverfront, thanking several passersby for their well wishes on his verdict. Linda was determined not to let anything spoil their last two days together, to savor every moment, so when she saw Admiral Munroe standing along the path she tried to alter their course to avoid him, but the older man gestured for Wake to join him.

Wake asked Linda to wait for a moment, then met the admiral, saluting as he approached. Munroe had been waiting along the path for Wake since the court had adjourned, and he got right to the point.

"I don't want to waste your precious time with Mrs. Wake, Lieutenant, but I did want to tell you, informally, two things. Things I want you to remember."

"Yes, sir?"

"First, do your duty well on this new assignment. People will be watching you. This is not a punishment—it is a test to see if you really are the kind of man we want to command the ships in the navy that will come in the future. I have every faith that you, and Commander Stockton, will pass these tests. So do some other people in this town. Important people."

"Yes, sir . . ."

"And the second thing I want to say is that every naval organization is bound to have some bad characters—even our beloved United States Navy. But it is crucial that we find those men and get them out, for our reputation is everything, absolutely everything. It can deter an enemy from attacking us, and it can weaken his resolve if he does. We cannot allow a dishonorable few to destroy what others of us have worked so damned hard to build for the last seventy years."

The admiral waited a moment, then put out his hand. "Son, it was your bizarre misfortune to meet up with two of those dishonorable few. I want to personally thank you for your actions."

They shook hands in silence. Wake watched the admiral walk away and then returned to Linda. She asked what the admiral had said.

He thought for a second, then smiled as he took in her beautiful green eyes. "That it's going to be all right. I've still got a future with the navy." He scrutinized her eyes. "Do I still have one with you?"

Linda's face softened, anger gone. "Lord help me, Peter Wake, but yes, you surely do and always will."

Author's Note

This is the fourth book in the Honor series of naval fiction and, as usual, I have blended my characters into an accurate description of the world they inhabit.

As a basis for this novel I have used the historical fact that after the American Civil War thousands of unemployed former warriors made their way to Mexico, the Caribbean, and South America, where they continued to ply their deadly trade as mercenaries. Some of their descendants are still there.

The portrayal of the tumultuous political conditions and players in the lower Caribbean, the leadership in Washington, and the sad decline of our navy from neglect are also accurate. The Clayton-Bulwer treaty is historical and has been much discussed ever since. The ships *Plover, Sirena,* and *22 Decembre* were actual vessels in the navies of Great Britain, Spain, and Haiti, respectively. Some of the realities of 1869 are just as valid in the twenty-first century—the Haitian coast is still hazy from smoke, pirates still ply the waters of Colombia (I know from personal experience), and the Cuna Indians still try to live their idyllic life away from interlopers.

The USS *Canton* is fictional, as are the characters (other than national figures) and their actions. They are products of my imagination and are not based upon any person, living or dead. This is a novel. It never happened.

But it could have.

Bob Macomber
At sea off the coast of Colombia
2 June 2004

Acknowledgments

Researching and writing this novel was one hell of an adventure—overcoming four hurricanes, personal crises, Colombian pirates, a Force Nine storm at sea, Cartagena cutthroats, Chilean naval intelligence, and computers that really ticked me off. Here are some of the folks who helped along the way:

Heartfelt thanks go to Captain Ullrich Nuber, a veteran of over forty years at sea, and all of my outstanding shipmates on the German freighter M/V *Hamburgo*. We steamed from Florida to Colombia and Panama, then down along the Pacific coast of South America, where I did research for a coming novel. During the five-week, ten-thousand-mile voyage I came to greatly appreciate the professionalism exhibited by this multinational band of men and learned quite a bit about human nature as well as about the perils, afloat and ashore, in that part of the world. Danke, spahseebah, salamat—thank you all, gentlemen.

Thank you to Juan Garcia, of Cartagena, Colombia, whose local knowledge, good humor, and resolute bearing proved very helpful in that dangerous place.

For Chief Mate Sergiy Yudyentsev, thanks for demonstrating that Russians and Americans have a lot in common and make great friends. Jens Graf, 2nd Officer, gets a smile and thanks for getting us out of the place he got us into at Cartagena. Thanks to 3rd Officer Eljohn Cervantes for navigational and celestial assistance, and several philosophical discussions on the bridge wing at 0400 in the South Pacific. For Cook Edmundo Medenilla, thanks for good food during the voyage and hilarious dancing at the Balboa anchorage.

Captain Marco Toledo of Guayaquil, Ecuador, a true sailor-gentleman of the old school, is acknowledged for providing very useful background maritime information and local knowledge.

The wonderful Cuna Indian people of the beautiful San Blas Islands along the remote eastern Caribbean coast of Panama have my great gratitude for showing me their islands and way of life—

truly an Eden. And, of course, thank you to Craig Myers, who got me through the Panamanian jungle to the ancient settlement of Porto Bello and the Church of the Black Jesus.

The lovely Nancy Glickman, kindred soul, astronomer, and patient teacher, has my profound appreciation for sharing her celestial knowledge and imagination.

Sincere thanks go to Lt. Richard Schnieders (CID/LCSO), the very best forensic cyber investigator I've ever known, for his brilliant work at recovering manuscript data that was lost while I was on the far side of the world. And while I'm on the subject of computers, kudos to Di Wehrle, who figured out how to get the mojo past the voodoo and into a workable state—and also for years of support and friendship.

For the incomparable Mary Alice Pickett, historian, teacher, and dearest of friends, who became the morale officer of the project and buoyed my spirits when I thought all was lost, a great big hug and atta-girl. Thanks also go to Sheba, assistant morale officer, who made me laugh when I really needed it.

To the legendary novelist, adventurer, and fellow islander Randy Wayne White, thank you for the support and rum, brother. To the novelist Roothee Gabay, thank you for years of help and friendship.

June Cussen, executive editor, is quite simply the very best in the business—an unsung hero. I am very lucky to have her on my projects.

And for all my readers around the world—thank you so very much. Peter Wake would be honored to have each of you in his crew. *You* are the engine that keeps me moving.

Onward and upward!
Bob Macomber

Robert N. Macomber's Honor Series:

At the Edge of Honor. This nationally acclaimed naval Civil War novel, the first in the Honor series of naval fiction, takes the reader into the steamy world of Key West and the Caribbean in 1863 and introduces Peter Wake, the reluctant New England volunteer officer who finds himself battling the enemy on the coasts of Florida, sinister intrigue in Spanish Havana and the British Bahamas, and social taboos in Key West when he falls in love with the daughter of a Confederate zealot. (hb, pb)

Point of Honor. Winner of the Florida Historical Society's 2003 Patrick Smith Award for Best Florida Fiction. In this second book in the Honor series, it is 1864 and Lt. Peter Wake, United States Navy, assisted by his indomitable Irish bosun, Sean Rork, commands the naval schooner *St. James.* He searches for army deserters in the Dry Tortugas, finds an old nemesis during a standoff with the French Navy on the coast of Mexico, starts a drunken tavern riot in Key West, and confronts incompetent Federal army officers during an invasion of upper Florida. (hb, pb)

Honorable Mention. This third book in the Honor series of naval fiction covers the tumultuous end of the Civil War in Florida and the Caribbean. Lt. Peter Wake is now in command of the steamer USS *Hunt,* and quickly plunges into action, chasing a strange vessel during a tropical storm off Cuba, confronting death to liberate an escaping slave ship, and coming face to face with the enemy's most powerful ocean warship in Havana's harbor. Finally, when he tracks down a colony of former Confederates in Puerto Rico, Wake becomes involved in a deadly twist of irony. (hb)

A Dishonorable Few. Fourth in the Honor series. It is 1869 and the United States is painfully recovering from the Civil War. Lt. Peter Wake heads to turbulent Central America to deal with a former American naval officer turned renegade mercenary. As the action unfolds in Colombia and Panama, Wake realizes that his most dangerous adversary may be a man on his own ship, forcing Wake to make a decision that will lead to his court-martial in Washington when the mission has finally ended. (hb)

An Affair of Honor. Fifth in the Honor series. It's December 1873 and Lt. Peter Wake is the executive officer of the USS *Omaha* on patrol in the West Indies, eager to return home. Fate, however, has other plans. He runs afoul of the Royal Navy in Antigua and then is sent off to Europe, where he finds himself embroiled in a

Spanish civil war. But his real test comes when he and Sean Rork are sent on a mission in northern Africa. (hb)

A Different Kind of Honor. In this sixth novel in the Honor series, it's 1879 and Lt. Cmdr. Peter Wake, U.S.N., is on assignment as the American naval observer to the War of the Pacific along the west coast of South America. During this mission Wake will witness history's first battle between ocean-going ironclads, ride the world's first deep-diving submarine, face his first machine guns in combat, and run for his life in the Catacombs of the Dead in Lima. (hb)

The Honored Dead. Seventh in the series. On what at first appears to be a simple mission for the U.S. president in French Indochina in 1883, naval intelligence officer Lt. Cmdr. Peter Wake encounters opium warlords, Chinese-Malay pirates, and French gangsters. (hb)

The Darkest Shade of Honor. Eighth in the series. It's 1886 and Wake, now of the U.S. Navy's Office of Naval Intelligence, meets rising politico Theodore Roosevelt in New York City. Wake is assigned to uncover Cuban revolutionary activities between Florida and Cuba. He meets José Martí, finds himself engulfed in the most catastrophic event in Key West history, and must make a decision involving the very darkest shade of honor. (hb)

Honor Bound. Ninth in the series. In June 1888 Cmdr. Peter Wake, U.S. naval intelligence agent, is in Florida at the end of an espionage mission to learn Spain's naval readiness in Cuba. A woman from his past shows up, begging him to find her missing son, and Wake sets out across Florida, through the Bahamas, and deep into the jungles of Haiti. Overcoming storms, mutiny, and shipwreck, Wake discovers the hidden lair of an anarchist group planning to wreak havoc around the world—unless he stops it.

For a complete catalog, visit our website at www.pineapplepress.com. Or write to Pineapple Press, P.O. Box 3889, Sarasota, Florida 34230-3889, or call (800) 746-3275.

CPSIA information can be obtained
at www.ICGtesting.com
Printed in the USA
BVHW07s2144170718
521861BV00001B/2/P